Cleavage

Also by Cleo Watson

Whips

Cleo Watson

Cleavage

corsair

CORSAIR

First published in the United Kingdom in 2024 by Corsair

1 3 5 7 9 10 8 6 4 2

Copyright © Cleo Watson 2024

The moral right of the author has been asserted.

A CIP catalogue record for this book
is available from the British Library.

HB ISBN: 978-1-4721-5730-0
TPB ISBN: 978-1-4721-5731-7

Typeset in Garamond by M Rules
Printed and bound in Great Britain by
Clays Ltd, Elcograf S.p.A.

Papers used by Corsair are from well-managed forests
and other responsible sources.

Corsair
An imprint of
Little, Brown Book Group
Carmelite House
50 Victoria Embankment
London EC4Y 0DZ

An Hachette UK Company
www.hachette.co.uk

www.littlebrown.co.uk

Cleavage (noun)

1. the space between a woman's breasts.
2. a social or cultural line dividing a society into groups with opposing political ideas.
3. the division of cells, especially in the early development of a fertilised egg.

Cast of Characters

Claybourne Terrace residents and family

Jess Adler – journalist at the *Sentinel*

Eva Cross – Special Adviser to the chief whip; daughter of Percy and Jenny Cross

Jenny Cross – author and features writer; mother to Eva; ex-wife of Percy

Rt Hon Lord (Percy) Cross – former UK Prime Minister turned author and after-dinner speaker. Eva Cross's father

Holly Mayhew – Percy's young American girlfriend

Cooper Mayhew III – Holly's wealthy father

Bobby Cliveden – Parliamentary Adviser to Moira Herbert MP

Mr Cliveden – Bobby's father

Mrs Cliveden – Bobby's mother

Jake Albury – Director of the Downing Street policy unit; Bobby's boyfriend

Jamie Whitmore – Eva's boyfriend

Mabel – a basset hound

The Labour camp

Rt Hon John Ramsey MP – Leader of the Opposition and Leader of the Labour Party

Christian Eckles – Director of Communications for John Ramsey and the Labour Party

Rt Hon Vicky Tennyson MP – Shadow Chancellor

Tanya Haines – Ramsey's Head of Strategy

Paul Marsh – Ramsey's Chief of Staff, a former civil servant

Joshua Udoka – Labour parliamentary candidate

The Conservative camp

Rt Hon Eric Courtenay MP – UK Prime Minister and Leader of the Conservative Party

Clarissa Courtenay – the PM's wife

Anthony Spiteri – Downing Street Chief of Staff

Nick O'Hara – Downing Street Director of Communications and Campaign Director at CCHQ

Rt Hon Natasha Weaver MP – Deputy Prime Minister and Chairman of the Conservative Party

Rt Hon Nigel Jackson MP – Chief Whip

Rt Hon Madeleine Ford MP – former UK Prime Minister

Michael Ford – Madeleine's husband

Rt Hon Victor Daniels MP – Chancellor of the Duchy of Lancaster

David Coker MP – Conservative MP

Moira Herbert MP – MP for Tipperton

Lord (Simon) Daly – former MP for Tipperton, now podcaster and 'thought leader'

Susie Coleman – Simon's ex-wife and most connected woman in Tipperton

CCHQ (Conservative Campaign Headquarters) Campaigners

Callum Gallagher – political strategist and former adviser to Percy Cross

Prof Don Fontaine – American political science academic

Beau Parker – American physicist

Dr Miguel Fernandes – American data scientist

Nate Mason – American mathematician

Journalists

Lord Finlayson – Chairman and founder of StoryCorps and proprietor of the *Sentinel* newspaper

Philip McKay – Editor of the *Sentinel*

Ed Cooper – Political Editor of the *Sentinel*

George and **Mike** – political reporters at the *Sentinel*

Teddy Hammer – journalistic legend, now freelance and able to write about whatever he pleases

HM Armed Forces Personnel

Captain Laura Lloyd – Royal Navy; the prime minister's Military Attaché

Major Jack Deacon – Commanding Officer of the SAS

General Sir Humphrey Cave – Director Special Forces (DSF)

Prologue

In the mirror of a deserted hotel basement gym, a woman gazes at her reflection as she completes a set of bicep curls. She smiles. Her body is perfect. Very tall, with large, toned muscles in her arms and shoulders that have been years in the making. She loves feeling powerful and slightly intimidating. Turning her back to the mirror, she moves her arms above her head in a body builder's pose and peeks over her shoulder to study her rippling back beneath her tiny sports bra. Pivoting on the spot, she brings her arms down to her groin and pops her pecs and six pack. She gleams with sweat, her heavy makeup wilting a little.

Next, she turns her attention to her thighs, squatting seventy kilos with ease. She groans and admires the veins appearing on her face and neck, but, before she can finish her set, she is disturbed by a man entering the gym. He is shorter than her and very slight, dressed in tracksuit bottoms, a T-shirt and thick glasses.

'Sorry,' he says nervously, holding up a large white bag. 'I didn't think anyone would be down here at this time of night. I've come to restock the towels.'

The woman arches her back, then struts over like a panther

until she stands impressively before him. She takes a towel from him and carefully dabs at her chest.

'Thanks,' she murmurs. 'I know it's late, but I needed some release. Nothing gets me off like lifting.'

The man bites his lip. He isn't just small compared to this spectacular Amazon, he's puny. Even his hands and head seem almost childlike compared to hers.

'Do you think you can lift me?' he asks in a reedy voice.

Smirking, the woman bends down and in one smooth motion pulls him onto one of her shoulders and parades him around in a circle like one might carry a winning goalscorer at a football match, his mousy hair nearly brushing the ceiling.

'That's not so hard,' the man says. 'I thought you would be stronger than that.'

'I'll show you strong, you little bitch.'

The woman carries him over to the weights area, lies down and begins to bench-press him. As she lifts him up into the air, grunting, her hand creeps between his thighs and cups his crotch. The powerless man continues his journey up and down, like he's on a fairground ride, his eyes widening in understanding and excitement.

When she has finished her set, the woman places the man down and undresses him matter-of-factly, like a doll. Next to her shining mahogany skin and juicy muscles, he looks ghostly pale, twig-like — except for his penis, which is like a huge, smooth pepper grinder.

The woman lifts him so that he's horizontal and holds him before the mirror, doing small pulses, one hand firmly running up and down his enormous cock. The man begins to whimper with pleasure, his arms crossed over his chest and his glasses steaming. After a couple of minutes, she squats with him, craning her neck at the bottom of the movements to suck for a few seconds. The man continues to lie helplessly in her arms, groaning.

Eventually, the woman places him on the bench, rips a hole in the crotch of her leggings and sits down – hard – on his face. She leans forward and continues to play with the tumescent member before her while rocking herself back and forth on the man's head, now completely enveloped by her massive thighs. She begins to grunt as though back doing her squats in the mirror.

Finally, she slides forward and straddles him, reverse-cowgirl, pushing down onto his cock with all her might.

'Who's strong now, bitch?' She's panting, riding him mercilessly, seeming to want to break his pelvis.

All the small man can do is breathlessly wail. 'You are ... you are!'

The woman groans deeply, then swings off the bench ready to take the man's c—

The door knob to the study rattles. The prime minister quickly snaps his laptop shut, hoping nobody heard the sound coming from the Blue Balls and Bazookas website.

Part One

1st April

CON 28% LAB 38%

MASS SHOOTING IN IOWA/

WARMEST WINTER ON RECORD

Houses of Parliament

At the entrance to Portcullis House in Westminster, a large queue of visitors has formed to go through security. It's like any other Wednesday morning for an MP when the House of Commons is sitting: meetings with businesses and charities; cosy coffees with journalists; Alka-Seltzer and a sizeable motion for those who hit the bottle a little too hard waiting for votes the previous evening. Assorted members of the public from constituencies, ranging from gaggles of schoolchildren to town mayors and high sheriffs, cluster round each other, waiting to be gathered up by harassed-looking researchers and given tours of the estate. And, of course, the draw of watching Prime Minister's Questions live from the gallery – a ticketed event, if you can believe it.

After blinking round at the atrium of Portcullis House, the

groups descend a small escalator to a large stone corridor. From here, they cross New Palace Yard to the more familiar old buildings of Parliament, beginning with a trip to Westminster Hall. Cavernous and echoing, familiar as the place where monarchs lie in state ahead of their funerals and where notables from Nelson Mandela to Barack Obama have addressed parliamentarians. There are a couple of interested nods at the mention of the small Chapel of St Mary Undercroft down to the left, where some MPs have chosen to get married, then they head up the heavy stone steps – 'And you're *sure* they didn't film *Harry Potter* here?' – and turn into St Stephen's Hall, lined with marble statues of previous Commons All-Stars, Pitt and Fox among them.

Finally, they're in Central Lobby, which can only be described as stunning. Everything is intricately designed and diligently cared for, from the marble tiling on the floor to the golden vaulted ceiling. The lighting is soft and the hushed tones people use add to the monastic sense of the place. To the right is the House of Lords and to the left, the Commons. If one could walk straight ahead, and move through walls like a ghost, you would be swimming in the Thames in a matter of metres. There are a handful of recognisable journalists around, and it's so exciting when the tour group's MP strolls towards them after exchanging a couple of serious-looking words with one of the hacks. Apart from ardent followers, most people think their MP is fine(ish). But in this environment, one really gets the point of them. There's something sacred about where they're standing.

While they pose for photographs, one couple ask curiously about the discreet doors that lead off the Chamber. 'Oh, they're handy little shortcuts for people with passes to get to different offices and dining rooms and things. Now, there's time for a quick cup of tea on the Terrace before PMQs ...' However, an interesting, distinctly un-touristy group has just walked through one of these little doors and is beginning a lengthy descent, along corridors and down staircases, to the deep underbelly of the parliamentary estate. There is no marble or gold here.

The chief whip, Nigel Jackson, and his special adviser, Eva Cross, are accompanied by the head of the Parliament Restoration and Renewal team and an engineer as they examine recent flood damage to the building. Eva, who has never been down to this part of the building, is amazed at the stuffy labyrinth of winding corridors, littered with rodent droppings. She wonders what else she's missed out on, when her boss nudges her and points at a used condom, carelessly tossed into a corner.

She grimaces. 'And they say romance is dead.' Then she touches one of the large bunches of electrical cables above her head. 'Where do those go?'

The group stops moving and the R&R head and engineer shrug at each other.

'Truthfully? We have no idea. And that's not an April Fool. This is the whole point. We can't even tell what's going on down here. She's a magnificent building but she's old and in desperate need of proper restoration. You've seen our reports – it will need to be at least a decade's worth of work and, frankly, in the billions of pounds. We patch her up as best we can, but . . .' The R&R head spreads his hands helplessly.

The chief whip, invigorated after a PMQs prep meeting, where he thought of some witty zingers for the prime minister to use at midday, can't help but remain upbeat. 'Her? Oh, come on, this isn't the bloody *Titanic*.' He bangs on the wall and puts on a plummy voice. '"She can stay afloat with the first four compartments breached, but not five. Not five!"'

'Flooding isn't really our problem, sir.' The engineer sucks his teeth. 'It's fire from the electric. Wires everywhere, plus the rats and mice, mean we're in serious danger of a spark pretty well all the time. We've got a twenty-four-hour fire marshal as it is, but we have little electrical flare-ups most weeks. And we've got bits of stonework dropping off the ceilings, concrete crumbling to dust ... she's a ticking time bomb.'

'But people have been banging on about Parliament catching fire or getting swept away by the Thames for ages. It – sorry, *she* – withstood the Blitz, for Christ's sake. I think she can manage a few mice and the odd kettle fusing. Just, I don't know ... find a couple of cats and some electrical tape.'

'A cat wouldn't stand a chance. There are legions of rats. Fearless and huge. We'd need all the residents of Battersea to overcome them,' the engineer snaps back hotly.

'Chief, this isn't intended to be a conversation about the need for repairs,' says the R&R man calmly, stepping in front of the engineer. 'That's already been established by experts. What we want to discuss with you is plans for how Parliament can sit while this essential work takes place. You're aware of some of the plans, of course.' He brandishes some bound reports.

'Yes.' The chief nods glumly. He's seen the options: the Commons sits in the Lords, who go to the QEII Centre across the road until the work is complete; Parliament sits on a new floating chamber on the Thames; the whole lot of them are transported to somewhere more central on the map of the UK – York has been suggested – and a virtue is made of taking decision-making out of Westminster until the work is complete, which is likely to be in twenty years or so.

'Well, we need your help in getting MPs to agree to the move. They're, uh, somewhat reluctant to change.'

The chief knows why. He feels the same way himself. He fought tooth and nail to get into the Commons, to sit where Churchill and Attlee and Thatcher sat. He likes the sound of hundreds of shoes on stone corridors and drinks on the Terrace and the gilt and leather and masonry. Why should the current lot have to give all this up and sit in some sad, modern pine-and-glass monstrosity for the rest of their careers so that some snotty-nosed kids get to come back to his old stomping ground in twenty years' time without the risk of a few minor burns?

Eva recognises the pugnacious expression that has spread across her boss's face and takes over.

'I'm afraid you're right – they are quite dug in. The trouble is that with an election looming, few MPs are really focused on whether Parliament is standing, if they aren't going to be in it. Listen.' Eva takes the reports and smiles reassuringly. 'We'll go back to the drawing board with all this and think carefully about next steps. Perhaps we can make sure the PM and other party leaders come down and see the damage for themselves too. In the meantime, thank you for all your hard work in keeping the place going.'

Eva and the chief shake hands with the men and turn to leave. Just as they get to the end of the corridor the engineer pipes up.

'This is urgent, you know. She could go up at any time.'

Without turning or slowing, the chief lifts his hand above his head and gives a thumbs-up.

2nd April

The King kicks himself free from the tangled limbs of big-bushed stable girls and rises from his canopied bed.

'I'm up,' he bellows. Countless men of the Privy bustle in to retrieve his nightshirt and secure his codpiece and test his breakfast swan for poison.

'Your Majesty, the business for today.' The Lord Chamberlain clears his throat and pulls out a scroll. 'The Spanish ambassador will be along later to discuss the war, then we are beheading the Countess of Cardiff—'

'Isobel? Why?' The King gasps, straining over the chamber pot.

'Witchcraft, Majesty.'

'Ah, yes, of course.' The King ruminates on the exceptional spell she had him under only days ago. He spent ages writing that poem for her about a 'whizzy' green-eyed woman – he left out his thoughts on her breasts – to bring her round to the idea of letting him give her one. Then the 'one' in question got back to the Queen. They always did. 'Can't we just . . . I don't know . . . put her in a scold's bridle or something?'

'I think not, Majesty. The Queen is quite insistent.'

The King pictures his wife's rageful, pinched face, free of the public mask of greasy paint and drawn-on eyebrows. Her mood is hardly helped by her latest regime to maintain her figure and youth: a diet of raw quail eggs and regular ice baths. Whizzy Izzy, a veritable peach of a woman, couldn't contrast with the Queen more strongly. He supposes he could intervene to spare the woman's life but it's never worth the hassle, not when his marriage brings such generous lands and patronages from the Continent. Last time this happened, the Queen arranged a sermon in church that had the King sweating throughout. Very embarrassing.

'Ah, right-o. The Queen is particular in these things. Tell me, have we got to the bottom of who has been writing those parchments about her?' The King ponders, still straining rabbit-sized offerings into the pot, ready for his doctors to study.

'Not yet, Your Majesty. Although of course we are destroying each one we find.' The Lord Chamberlain struggles to keep his mouth in a firm line. The amusing illustrations accompanying the stories about the Queen's spending habits and public vanity projects are getting increasingly rude. He has often wondered, though, why the King seems so content that the parchments are circulating as freely as syphilis. In the Lord Chamberlain's view, though it certainly helps that the Queen takes the bulk of public anger for high taxes, poor food, brutal wars and various diseases, it doesn't become a ruler ordained by God to let a narrative take hold that his wife is really the one wearing the tights.

'Not my copies, I hope?' The King lets a young fellow – the son of an earl, most likely – take the now full chamber pot away for inspection. Proximity is like this. You have exceptional access to the King, learn every secret desire in his heart and hear every word to come from his mouth. But you also have to deal with what comes out of his arse.

'Regrettably, sire, a plague has broken out in Parliament again. Caused by vermin, you see.'

'The rats or the members?' The King chortles. The rats concern him little. They can at least be exterminated. The real vermin, *however, are a constant thorn in his side, curtailing his plans and cutting his spending.*

Just then, the heavy door cranks open and the King swivels round. He lives in a constant state of paranoia that one day that sound, of heavy riding boots on stone floor, will mean his death. Today, however, it is Sir Henry Dauntsey – his face forever bubbled with pox scars – and a cluster of his men, all in their customary black. These men – or Royalist fanatics, as they truly are – make up the network of spies that track down, monitor and snatch those who work against the Crown. They know of the sexual proclivities and financial states and secret worship of each bishop and nobleman and courtier, and they feed this intelligence to Sir Henry, who decides how to punish possible misdemeanours and probable threats to the King's reign.

Sir Henry, who is now speaking seriously to those present about the recent worrying behaviour of the King's cousin that suggests he has designs on the throne, is key to the whole royal operation. His sleepless nights of strategising mean the King and the Court sleep easy, even if they are distinctly uneasy in Sir Henry's presence while awake. It isn't just his image, although that is in all respects revolting. It is the rumours that the King and the Court hear about Sir Henry's actions when he deems someone to have done something suitably egregious. The beheadings are quite straightforward and the King has perfected the expression of regretful wistfulness on those public occasions. But it sounds like the various tortures and punishments in advance are growing increasingly experimental. It began with fingernails being pulled out but, if the whispers are right, things appear to have ramped up to live skinnings, crushings and force-feedings until human paté is produced, which Sir Henry eats on water biscuits with a little fig relish. All right, some allegations defy belief. But the little sack on a string round Sir Henry's neck, rumoured to be made from the scrotum of his proudest scalp, doesn't exactly help quell the whispers.

14

Sir Henry finishes speaking and those assembled murmur agreement. The King, trying to deep-breathe away the flicker of paranoid panic that these little chats with Sir Henry generally bring on while his shoes are fastened, nods at the expectant faces and listens to the rest of the day's affairs. Presently he's away with his men on an early morning hunt around St James's Park to fight off the strain he is starting to feel against the buttons and stitches of his clothes. The body of the King is of immense importance and maintaining this particular temple occupies a great deal of thought for those around him.

But he's distracted and stops regularly to stare into space.

'Your Majesty, are you quite all right?' asks Cuthbert the Loyal, pulling up alongside his master.

'All I can think about is the Countess of Cardiff's daughter.' The King sighs. 'Does she have green eyes too?'

'Felicity? She does indeed. It is most gracious of Your Majesty to have her in your prayers.'

'Of course. Just in my prayers, you know. As a subject.' Felicity. Fizzy. Whizzy . . . The King wonders whether it would be smooth to make a pass at her at her mother's beheading. It is an awfully good poem to go to waste.

'You know she is to enter God's service tomorrow? She to a nunnery; her brother to a monastery . . . '

Fuck that, the King thinks. I'd sooner abolish them.

Percy, Lord Cross of Molton and Georgetown, and former British Prime Minister, closes the book and stares out over the packed theatre, letting the applause wash over him.

'Lord Cross,' his waspy American interviewer shouts over the din. 'Thank you so much for being with us here in Los Angeles. And thank you for that fabulous reading of your first novel, *The Loin King*. That accent, right, folks?' The audience whoops.

Percy dips his chin in bashful acknowledgement.

'So, this book is of course set in Tudor times, but we

understand it is in fact drawn from your experiences of being prime minister. Why?'

'For two reasons. One, I found being in Downing Street very much like a Tudor court in atmosphere. Paranoia about betrayal – although of course being sold out to the French or burned as a witch set the Tudor stakes rather higher than leaking our childhood obesity strategy to the *Telegraph*. That same need my team felt for proximity and access, constantly fighting to get into meetings or pop into my office or get a desk right outside the door. The pomp and ceremony … the constant fluffing from eager officials and sycophantic ministers keen for promotion. Running round the park with my security detail in the morning and the fussing from diary managers about what I was eating and whether I had a cold coming on.'

There is a little ripple of laughter.

'And the second reason?' the host prompts.

'Lawyers, my dear. By shoving everyone into corsets and ruffs, I've distorted the characters of anyone who might sue me for libel.' Percy pauses for more laughter.

'Have you got any future projects up your sleeve?'

'Oh, yes.' Percy slaps his hands on his knees and turns to face the audience. 'I'm writing my first play! It's all about the nuclear bunker in Downing Street. Miserable place. Not been tarted up since Thatcher's time. The play's about an emergency with all the big cheeses crammed inside and how they wish they were outside, taking their chances with the nukes.'

'Oh, you mean like our Situation Room?'

'I suppose I do, but ours is nothing like what you see in the movies. Very stuffy. After all, a fart from the national security adviser is still a fart.'

'Now we have some questions submitted by the audience.' The host swivels in her seat, keen to change gears.

'Fire away.'

The host picks up an iPad and begins to read out the first question.

'"It's in the public domain that there is a bidding war underway to secure the movie rights for this book."'

She pauses for an, 'Ooooh,' from the audience. It is something Percy has had to get used to over the course of his American tour.

'"You've written a lot of X-rated sex scenes in the story. Do you think these will be included in any film or TV adaptations?" Oh, that's fun.'

'I certainly hope so. Indeed, you probably think it is a bidding war for money on the pitchers' side. It is in fact a scramble from me to see who can get closest to full penetration on screen. A race to the bottom, as it were.'

The joke doesn't quite land.

'Uh ... Okay, so someone has focused on the portrayal of the Queen. They ask – quote – "Do you think this is a fair representation of a woman who has no official voice of her own, as was the case with your wife at the time of your premiership? Even if you are hiding behind the context of the fifteen hundreds, don't you think this is a very sexist characterisation of someone who should have real agency?" – end quote. Gosh, that's a tough one!' The host leans forward, clearly pleased to see the old goat under a bit of pressure.

'No, it isn't,' Percy says simply. 'It is my view that, regardless of the century, women accorded a certain status have always had power. Whether that was Anne Boleyn carefully placing members of her family at Court or my own wife's media contacts.' There is a little tutting and muttering from the audience. 'Oh, some of you don't agree? Just ask Mrs Courtenay.'

Percy holds up an iPad of his own. The screen shows a recent front page of the *Sun*, the front page screaming the words *PM's wife caught calling the shots* accompanied by a photo of

Clarissa Courtenay wrapped in a Cruella de Vil-style fur coat, her phone clamped to her ear. The audience laughs again. The story is about, at first glance, a very average Tory backbencher called David Coker. The trouble is, it isn't an average story. He is a member of the All-Party Parliamentary Group on Drugs Reform and joined a fact-finding trip to Amsterdam to learn about marijuana policy there. By all accounts he did himself very well during his three-day trip in the city, but his mistake came when he expensed the taxpayer for his entry to various sex shows and hostelries in the red-light district. Eagle-eyed journalists spotted the entry and, after a few calls to other members of the APPG, who were unaware of Mr Coker's activities in Amsterdam, the demands for his resignation from the Commons began.

But Coker didn't go and nobody could understand why. That was until it was revealed that Coker was being protected by none other than Clarissa Courtenay, the prime minister's wife. The pair have known each other for years, right back to their schooldays in a small town in Cheshire, where they dreamt of busting out to the Big Smoke, and Clarissa has given her old friend assurances that 'he will not be sacrificed on the altar of a moral panic'. Coker, idiot that he is, confidently divulged all this to an assortment of MPs in the Commons tea room and the lobby had it within minutes. Coupled with the usual suspicion of MPs about the influence of the prime minister's spouse – beware of pillow talk! – there has been a feeding frenzy.

To try to rally her position, Clarissa has been putting members of the government under pressure to say supportive things about her in the media. But, unfortunately, a number of these texts have leaked. The fallout has been bad, with countless opinion pieces from ancient rivals dating back to her time as a journalist, implying Clarissa has personally ended careers in politics and journalism, prompting questions from the ecstatic leader of the opposition about her influence on government policy, staffing and strategy. Much to everyone's surprise, Clarissa hasn't turned her back on Coker.

'Well, I'm going to ask a follow-up question of my own, if I may.' The host doesn't wait for a response. She interviewed a Pulitzer Prize winner last week. Time to have some fun. 'I see that your ex-wife's diaries, which of course sit in non-fiction unlike yours, also came out last week and have currently out-sold you in the *Sunday Times* bestseller list.'

'So?' Percy frowns, though his ears turn pink. Jenny, his ex-wife and Eva's mother, is on something of a high just now. It's true that her book is doing fantastically well, but she also has a new, in her words, 'beau' – a world-famous ageing rocker. As far as Cool Britannia goes, Percy's feeling just a little outdone.

'So how do you feel about that? There are some choice stories in there about you ...'

The host hears her producer in her ear. 'Which you must not get into, okay? We agreed to just focus on his book.'

Percy, knowing this agreement, grins. 'Oh, I'm thrilled for her. And to come out in the same week is ... splendid. I'm trying to encourage a two-for-one deal on Amazon.' He looks earnestly at the host, wondering if he can try a different tack to win her over. 'But, listen – I'm not pretending that this book is *Ulysses*. Jenny is a far more talented writer than me, and, doubtless because it is a diary, her book is far more meaningful to her. It's only right that she's outselling me!'

The host is taken aback. She doesn't often have displays of self-deprecation on her stage. 'Well, that's ... very good of you to say so. Okay, we've got a question about an issue a little closer to home. "It's well known that you're currently dating one of America's most eligible bachelorettes."'

'We call them spinsters,' Percy interjects. 'Although that doesn't quite fit Holly, does it?'

'For sure. Great job getting her to cross the Atlantic!'

'Well, I am very charming . . . and dynamite in the sack, of course.'

'Right.' The host longs to roll her eyes but judging from the loud laughter, the audience has been captured. "We understand her father, Cooper Mayhew, is mulling a presidential bid. What advice would you give him?"'

'Do it. Political girls are the wildest by far . . .'

An hour later, Percy makes his way to the bar in his hotel. It's at the stage of the evening where straps have slid off shoulders and hands are resting on knees. The kind of time and place he would have revelled in not long ago. Now he generally avoids this scene altogether, but Holly is travelling to join him from Hawaii where she's been on holiday with her parents and Percy has some time to kill before her arrival, so he'll have one drink while he waits. And perhaps just a little flirting, if anyone spots who he is. He needs to keep his ego nice and bloated on trips like these, as he bounces between cheerful events surrounded by admirers and reading nasty book reviews alone in his hotel room.

He orders a dirty martini and is biting into an olive when he hears a deadpan voice, betrayed by its Northern Irish accent. Percy would know it anywhere.

'Wotcha, Perce.'

'Cal!'

Callum Gallagher, a tricky but brilliant strategist from Belfast and Percy's first proper adviser. Under Callum's ruthless, focused stewardship as a parliamentary researcher, Percy rocketed from lowly backbench MP to the cabinet. Unfortunately, he had to ditch his maverick lieutenant at that point as the then-PM, who dubbed Callum 'a real Mic(k) – Mad Irish Cunt', knew him to be too extreme in his views and too effective for his own good (the good being the PM's). Cal was accused of leaking negative stories about the administration, so he promptly planted a few policy booby traps and moved to California. He and Percy have occasionally spoken over the years but, despite everyone's prediction that they would reunite for Percy's premiership, Cal stayed in San Francisco, doing something obscure with digital marketing and hanging out with tech bros and hedge-fund billionaires.

'It's okay, I know this chap,' Percy says to the plain-clothes police officers, who have to go everywhere with him and have appeared seemingly out of nowhere. 'Don't mind my personal gendarmes, Cal. They're a bit bored, as in the old days I'd be absolutely dripping with Russian honeytraps. But what are you doing here?' Percy thumps Cal several times on the back.

'I'm in town for some meetings and thought I'd come and listen to your reading.' Cal orders a Negroni.

'What did you think?'

'Shite.' Cal takes a long sip. 'Shite book, shite interview. And I assume Jenny has gone ballistic.'

Percy's ex-wife, though busy with her trendy new jet set, is not above logging on to Twitter to air her views on her former husband.

'She's on a transmitting hiatus, thank Christ. Got a new boyfriend and he's all into yoga and veganism and ditching tech. Plus he's working on another album – apparently the old fart might play Glastonbury – so Jenny's got to keep her trap shut for a bit. She says that any connection with me is bad for their brand . . .'

'Glasto, eh?' Cal grins. 'And you're stuck doing this. I hope you're at least getting paid a feckin' fortune.'

'Oh.' Percy tries to look uninterested. 'Well, the money isn't bad . . .'

'Good to see you haven't changed, Perce.'

21

'Well, I have changed a bit. You may have noticed, for example, that I am currently sitting here speaking to an ugly Northern Irishman instead of a bosomy blonde. And I'm well out of politics. Couldn't be happier. Especially as Courtenay's screwed. Election in under a year and he hasn't got a hope.'

'Is that so?' Cal says, unmoved.

'Surely! The polls are terrible. They've got no coherent plan or policies. Pretty much every newspaper has had enough of them. Looks like everyone but the *Sentinel* is turning, and those guys look loony for sticking with him so firmly. I can't see Eric turning this around . . .'

Cal almost whispers, 'It can be done.'

'No!'

'If Courtenay has got balls. I've been paying a bit of attention to UK stuff. If he is willing to agree to a plan and aggressively, unwaveringly execute it, it *can* be done. Big difference between governing and campaigning, after all.'

Percy indicates to the barman for another round. 'Are you saying I should get back in the game?'

Cal sighs. 'Not everything's about you, Perce . . .'

'All right, all right. Still, maybe I should remain open-minded. You know I'm still the top-ranked politician among members? Strikes me they could do with a bit of popularity . . . and remember my daughter, Eva? She's working for the chief whip now.'

His seat in the Lords keeps Percy tantalisingly close to power but just out of reach. Perhaps a clean break would have been better. Or perhaps he's perfectly positioned to re-enter the fray. He's been listening out for the call to return to power but Courtenay's first year has been such a flop that Percy cracked on with *The Loin King* and has all but tuned out of SW1.

'Good for her. Anyway, nobody gives a feck about what the membership thinks so shove your ranking where you like. Got to think nationally now. And super strategically.'

'Yes, I suppose. Anyway, it isn't just the members who like me. Lots of people do.' Percy folds his arms. He forgot how brutally honest Cal could be. He decides to change the subject. 'So, how do you find living in California?'

'Yeah, good. A lot of very bright people around. I've made a bit of dosh and wondered about coming back to the UK but I'm shacked up with an American girl so I'm not sure. Same as you, I hear.'

'That's right! Holly Mayhew.'

'I hear her old man is thinking of a presidential run.'

'Possibly. Not sure he should, though. Not exactly what you'd call cerebral ...'

'Don't think that matters here. Or back at home, at that. Just got to have the right team and the right plan. A chimp could run in the modern game. Just look at Courtenay – he looks the part and that's enough for a lot of people.'

'That's true ...' Percy wishes he could read minds. He has always found Cal a mystery and is reluctant to come out and ask the burning question, 'Are you saying I should get back on the pitch?' in case he is met with a sneer. But why else would he pop up like this? Percy's always hated asking Cal questions about politics, often left feeling like he's asking a grumpy chess grandmaster what the little horse pieces on the board are called.

'Anyway,' Cal checks his phone, 'I'd better run. Good seeing you, Perce.'

Cal nearly snorts at Percy's misty expression. Of course his old boss thinks it's all about him. Percy's so addicted to the thought of power and glory that his pupils dilated at the very mention of an electoral win. It couldn't have been easier to get his greedy cogs turning. All the commentary over the years about Percy being a 'different breed of politician', but his desires – to be adored, to be recognised and to be at the top – are the same as the rest of them.

'Right, yes.' Percy jumps up and, after pausing to give the barman his room number for the drinks, trails Callum to the lobby, feeling like a needy puppy. 'Cal ... All right if I give you a call at some point?'

Cal, busy texting on his phone, doesn't look up but raises a bored eyebrow. 'Sure.'

'Good.'

Percy pats him gingerly on the shoulder and plods thoughtfully to the lifts. Maybe he should ease up a bit on Clarissa Courtenay for the rest of the tour.

New Broadcasting House, London

Back on GMT, the team at *Politics Tonight*, the BBC's flagship weekly politics show, are preparing the final hours before they go live. The editor and producer are excited because they have an exclusive interview with John Ramsey, the leader of the opposition and likely future prime minister, and they've put together a large panel of 'experts' to predict when, between now and January, the general election will be held. They've also got a segment with a range of councillors up for election at the forthcoming locals in May, with the Tories due a mauling, the Lib Dems – who always do well at these contests – likely to make gains and Labour, who are sanguine, aiming for the big win. It's the first electoral test for Courtenay and Ramsey.

So a busy and exciting show. But there's just one problem: the guest from the government, Conservative Party Chairman and Deputy Prime Minister Natasha Weaver, has vanished.

Weaver has been outside for a steadying fag but she's still jittery. She always gets like this ahead of a big sit-down interview. What if she fucks it up and everyone hates her? Might her career end at any moment? Where has her confidence gone? In her mid-fifties, she's reliant on Spanx for a smooth outline beneath her pencil dresses but the result is undeniably good. There isn't much she can do about her flyaway, frizzy blonde hair but she balances it out nicely with sexy stilettos and a decent coating of lipstick. Not exactly universally adored among MPs, party members rate her highly. The women, because she fiercely says what she thinks, and the men, because they want to give her one.

She's heading back to the studio, drumming her hands anxiously against her thighs, when one of the junior Central Office bods sent to nanny her appears round the corner, frantically searching for her. Bingo. The man must be about twenty-five years old and his visible relief at finding her is sweetly endearing. But what the fuck's he called? Craig. Or maybe Creg. Chris?

Weaver stops walking, leans her hip against the wall and beckons him with a finger. He almost jogs down the corridor, flattening his hair with one hand.

'Hi,' she whispers, radiating her finest smile.

'Uh ... Hi, Minister,' he murmurs back. *He smells nice*, she thinks. *Clean.*

Weaver opens a door behind her and peeks inside. It's a small room with a few cardboard boxes stacked in a corner and a wheeled office chair on its side. Without looking behind her, she reaches an arm out, grabs the young man's lapel and pulls him inside.

'Want to relax with me for a minute or two?' Weaver says quietly, placing a box in front of the door and inclining her head at the chair. 'I get so nervous at these things.'

'Yeah ... yeah. Uh, definitely,' he stutters, dropping his binder of briefing notes he's been carrying around for her and lunging forward to right the chair. She walks towards him and, with tantalising slowness, takes hold of his tie and pulls him down as she takes a seat.

'Okay,' she murmurs into his ear. 'Do your best, then.'

He looks confused for a moment, as though debating whether he should say soothing affirmations or encourage deep breaths.

Then Weaver starts running her long nails up his arms and over his chest. She can't help grinning to herself as she notices him grip the armrests of the chair. It's a great thing, having these young men around the place. They're ready and eager for action, and very discreet. Crucially, they're quick to satisfy and she needs to get back to the studio. The young aide creeps his fingers up beneath Weaver's skirt and between her legs.

'Oh, M-M-Mrs Weaver,' he mumbles through her Spanx, as her sharp nails clamp down on his head and push him down. 'This is awesome. This ... I ... f-f-fuck, I can't believe this is happening. The party chairman! What a f-f-fantasy ...'

Weaver's torn between asking him not to call her Mrs Weaver – with their age difference it makes her feel like a secondary school teacher with her pupil – while dying to thank him. This is new. They're normally as quiet as mice, as though anxious not to break the spell, and she's taken aback by his – Chris's? – flattery.

He gets to work, his young tongue massaging her eagerly.

'Fuuuuuck,' he groans. 'You're the fucking boss. You're the best ... at all of it. Should be PM ...'

She sits up. 'Really?'

'The greatest prime minister we've never had ... yet.'

Weaver leans back again, pleasure coursing through her. As his hands dig into her thighs, his mouth too busy to speak any more, she moves her hands to her chest and pinches her nipples through her push-up bra. Within seconds, Weaver shudders with surprise and satisfaction.

'Ministerrrrrr.' He sighs, rocking back on his haunches and wiping his mouth.

Weaver pulls out a compact mirror and checks the damage to her make-up. She hopes the face she had on from the lunch-time show she joined as a panellist will still be okay, but the heavy foundation has effectively cracked under the strain of the last few minutes. She'll just have to get the make-up artist to start again.

'Well.' She rises and looks at the young man, who is standing in the corner, shy and subservient again, clutching his binder. 'That was fun. I'll, uh, see you around. Maybe wait a minute before you come out.'

Weaver knows she doesn't need to tell him to keep his mouth shut. He's too hopeful that it might happen again. And besides, would his little friends even believe him if he told them? He nods and she leaves, her ego restored. She could do with another cigarette, though.

3rd April

Downing Street

Percy's daughter, Eva Cross, is at her desk in the chief whip's office first thing in the morning when her phone vibrates. A message from her boyfriend, Jamie.

All OK for tonight? Looking forward to it x

Eva feels a now familiar stab of guilt. She's not really looking forward to it at all. Jamie is a nice guy and she knows she should count herself lucky, but she feels suffocated by him these days. Mainly, she just isn't attracted to him any more. Sex with Jamie no longer excites her. The last few times, she's only orgasmed when she's closed her eyes and pictured herself with someone else. She'll think of some excuse to put him off, but there's an immediate follow-up.

The trouble is, she hardly ever thinks of him now. Her plan this evening is to blow Jamie off, run a bath and fire up her vibrator with some well-chosen videos of alleged stranger-on-stranger action on Pornhub. Ignoring both messages, Eva returns to the *Crash* website, a Westminster gossip blog, which has another article about her father's bombastic tour of America – this time a late-night talk-show interview. In the past, this is the exact kind of thing that would have horrified her, but she's learnt to bump along with her father's eccentric behaviour and has even started to enjoy it.

> Favourite book: *The Loin King*, of course! You can get it at every reputable bookshop. And a few disreputable ones too.
>
> Strangest thing about America: Hm ... I think the Girl Scout cookie phenomenon is very odd. In the UK, children are taught not to accept sweets from strangers. Here, the kids wear these cute little strippergram outfits and are the ones to bring the sweets right to your door. Is it just a very elaborate front for the FBI's paedo tracker team?

'Well, at least he's showing some personality,' Eva's boss, who is hovering silently behind her, says with a sigh. The chief whip, Nigel Jackson, is ageing horribly. He's been in post less than a year but the strain of passing legislation through the Commons and keeping Conservative MPs in line is taking its toll. He hasn't lost a single vote but he has lost a good deal of hair and has the look of someone who was halfway through being embalmed before the undertaker realised he still had a pulse.

Eva nods in agreement. 'Yes, that's never been his problem. It seems to have made a lot of people over there quite cross though. The White House had to issue a statement saying there is no specific "FBI paedo tracker team". Then they had to admit that maybe there should be one ... '

'Honestly, I would kill for a nice row about hunting down nonces. At least we'd be tough on crime! As things stand, we're fighting a general election this year and most of the country can't even recognise a photo of the PM. And the ones who can think he's a knob. Except, of course, the very small percentage known only to the security services, who regularly write to him saying they love him so much that they'd like to kill him, stuff him and keep him as some sort of sex mannequin. And most of those people aren't eligible to vote ... '

The chief flops into a chair.

'Well, maybe you should have a chat with Dad,' Eva says, closing the *Crash* tab and thinking about this morning's well-timed text from her father.

Perhaps we should invite your boss over for dinner when I get back.

'He's an expert in starting completely pointless fights. Look at his last few columns ... '

The chief examines his fingernails, lost in thought, while his team of whips file into the room for their morning meeting. It's true. Percy is the king of manufacturing headlines out of nowhere through his *Sentinel* column and occasional media appearances. Whole petitions have been launched from his rants about separate recycling bins and bringing the BBC's ten o'clock news back to 9 p.m. And he's popular. Amazingly so, when you consider that he had to resign in disgrace.

'Boss ... ?' The deputy chief whip asks hesitantly.

'Sorry, let's crack on.' The chief sits up straight. 'Okay, who'd like to start?'

Someone raises a hand.

'Yeah. You may have heard that one of my lot – David Nicholls – went completely bananas on a WhatsApp group last night. Same old after the Coker stuff. Got himself pickled then picked a fight about MPs who he thinks are being promoted over folks like him.'

It's a common story. The role of chief whip, after winning votes, is to maintain discipline among Tory MPs. This past year has won prizes for scandal: secret taxpayer-funded second homes; secret taxpayer-funded second families; a particularly raucous trip to Brazil for a group of MPs on a trade delegation, complete with photos of bejewelled G-strings and feathered bras – worn by the MPs. Coupled with hesitation from the centre to do any really bold policies, the party's image is shot and the polls almost laughably bad. The David Coker–Clarissa Courtenay story has been the cherry on top of the nightmare trifle – and it has made MPs turn against Number Ten and the PM. After all, is there anything worse than an 'unelected prime minister' who really runs the show?

'All right, I'll take him aside and explain that the reason he hasn't got a job isn't because anyone else has been given preferential treatment – it's because he's shit. And pulls stuff like mouthing off on WhatsApp after he's had a few drinks. Chippy fucker.'

'Come on, he's just shirty because he thinks his seat is gone at the next election.'

'Well, if he carries on this way, he thinks right.'

'All right, try this.' Another whip raises a hand. 'We've got a real problem with this hotmp.com website. Nobody's getting anything done because they're constantly logging in to see what their rating is and voting for themselves.'

'Yeah, I notice you're doing pretty well on there, mate . . .'

The meeting continues, whips throwing troublesome names about and discussing the business for the day – the different votes that the government needs to win. Eva notes down the people the chief whip will need to speak to personally or any that the PM should make contact with. It strikes her that lots of those on the list aren't the usual troublemakers.

It is common that, about a year out from a general election, MPs fall into line and sheepishly do whatever the leader of their party says so that, as a group, they appear coherent and competent when they ask the public to vote for them again. But something different is happening this time round. Accepting each body blow of a poll after the next as fact, and therefore assuming they are going to lose their seats regardless, the Conservative MPs have made the decision to go rogue, reasoning that 1) they can't rely on the national party and leader to save them, so looking strident and independent locally is their best bet for holding their seats and 2) if they are about to need new jobs, having name recognition will help with bookings for *Dancing on Ice* or with an executive position at Centrica.

Winning votes in the Commons is one thing, but holding a fractured and unhappy parliamentary party together is quite another. The chief half hoped, at the start of the Coker debacle, that the prime minister's refusal to demand a resignation would bolster MPs' support, seeing him being loyal to one of their own. But the moment Clarissa was dragged into it, that hope was doomed. It became about special treatment and influence, and from an aloof, snobby character that few Tory MPs have even met. No wonder the chief is losing hair by the fistful.

Once the meeting is over, Eva accompanies the chief one door along the pavement to Ten Downing Street, where they have been summoned to join the PM's morning meeting. Normally the chief goes alone so Eva's invitation surprises and concerns her. Is it so she can be bollocked about her father's press tour? She reflexively folds her arms at the thought. She's not his keeper. Eva isn't invited to Downing Street for official meetings, but she is here a lot under cover of darkness, sneaked up to the flat every couple of weeks to meet secretly with Clarissa Courtenay, the prime minister's wife.

Since Eric Courtenay took office, Clarissa has taken Eva under her wing. They may even be friends. Eva is cautious, assuming it is just a smart woman keeping tabs on the nerve centre of gossip, the whips' office. Or perhaps she is trying to stay friendly towards Eva, who knows the full extent of Clarissa's skulduggery during last summer's leadership contest, when Clarissa was willing to throw anyone – including Eva herself – under the bus.

The truth is that it took Clarissa a matter of weeks to realise her husband taking high office was not her ticket to the unmarked VIP lounge. In fact, as many have found before her, her unclear status as the PM's spouse (the UK doesn't have an official First Lady) seems to repel most interesting people – not helped, of course, by this recent incident with David Coker. Clarissa's bored, and somehow more and less visible than she'd hoped. As a result, Clarissa sees Eva – talented, ambitious and capable – as a sort of project.

Eva deposits her Apple watch and phone in one of the cubbies near the front door (as she doesn't hold a Downing Street pass any more, she mustn't carry electronic communication devices with her around the building – an anti-snooping measure) and jogs down the corridor to catch up with the chief. They join the small chattering group outside the PM's office, pouring themselves cups of coffee and trading gossip. Jake Albury, the director of the Downing Street policy unit, beckons her over. She sees a lot of Jake these days, as he is dating one of her best friends and housemates, Bobby Cliveden, who works in Parliament.

'Tell me, would you ever be an MP?' Jake asks.

'Bit heavy for eight thirty, isn't it?' Eva laughs, struck as usual by how Jake manages to look simultaneously exhausted and handsome, and admires his shabby but beautifully cut suit.

'Come on, you must have thought about it.' Another man who Eva hardly recognises inches over to join the conversation.

'Hello, Nick.' Eva clinks coffee cups with Nick O'Hara, the holder of a huge job – Director of Communications for the prime minister's office, as well as the campaign director at CCHQ. He carries the weight of the world on his shoulders, with everyone expecting him to take the fall for what will surely be a disastrous general election result for the Conservatives. Nick, a former journalist, has had to learn about campaigning later on in life, but what he now doesn't know about fieldwork – knocking on the right doors, staying within election rules, where to allocate money to spend on campaigns across the electoral map – isn't worth bothering with. He has always been bright and cheerful but he's aged worse than the chief, looking simultaneously gaunt and bloated and far away from his usually gym-honed, well-coiffed self.

'Anyway, answer my question,' Jake presses. 'Have you thought about being an MP?'

'Nope.' Eva is ready with her stock answer. 'I'm not interested. Seen how the sausage is made this past year and, you know . . . Dad. How about you?'

'Not me.' Jake frowns. 'But Nick was just telling me that he wants to tap up Bobby as a candidate. I hope she bites. She'd be really good.'

'Bobby? She'd be brilliant! I don't know why I haven't thought of it before.' Eva grins but feels a surprising nudge of jealousy. Why isn't anyone approaching her?

Still, Eva isn't at all surprised that Bobby's been zeroed in on. Her campaign for mental health units last year simultaneously closed off Madeleine Ford's premiership with a neat bow and opened Eric Courtenay's with a stinking turd, as he got on the wrong side of public opinion and argued hard to sell them off. In normal times Bobby might be *persona non grata*, but

Jake's popularity in the administration and her efforts to win the Tipperton by-election for Moira Herbert after Simon Daly stood down in disgrace has made her one to watch.

Eva's thoughts are interrupted when she notices Jake looking over her shoulder and straightening up. The prime minister has arrived.

'Hello, hello,' Eric Courtenay, the tall, silver-haired and broad-shouldered Prime Minister of the United Kingdom of Great Britain and Northern Ireland, parrots the many 'Good morning, Prime Minister's, as he sweeps through the crowded corridor and into his inner sanctum.

'What's up with Nick?' Eva whispers to Jake, as they follow the group into the room.

'Anto's been up his arse for months,' Jake mutters back. 'He's read a couple of campaigning books and thinks he's David Plouffe now. On to Nick day and night, demanding all kinds of mad stuff that is sidetracking him from properly preparing for the local elections – let alone his day job. The guy's exhausted and his confidence is wrecked. Not there, that's for the adults.' He grabs Eva's elbow and steers her away from the polished circular table, which the PM, chief and a handful of other middle-aged men sit at.

'PM, as we have local elections in a few weeks and a general election by January, we want to talk about our overall electoral strategy and latest polling. I'll be taking the lead, if that's okay,' says Anthony Spiteri, Downing Street chief of staff.

Anto, as he insists on being called, is widely agreed as a surprising choice for senior adviser. Formerly a partner at a Magic Circle law firm, he was pushed into Number Ten by an old friend of Courtenay's – who insisted the PM must have a 'grown-up' in charge – and has struggled to find purchase in the building. Handling senior business people and fighting with the Treasury over the government's various economic statements is a doddle for Anto, as is reading the various submissions that go into the PM's box. But Anto knows nothing whatsoever about politics or people and seems unable to learn on the job. He rubs everyone up the wrong way and has created a tense, frustrated culture in the building, often culminating in him screaming at somebody junior. Having none of the answers himself, he hates the PM's reliance on advice from Jake, whom Anto finds bookish and aloof, and Nick, whom he deems nothing short of an oik.

Eva glances at Nick, who has presumably put the work together, and is staring glumly at the table. The PM nods wearily, accepts a cup of coffee from his diary manager, and the session begins.

Anto distributes then reads aloud the latest polling, just to be absolutely sure nobody escapes the grim picture: the Conservatives are behind Labour on every policy issue (crime, economy, health, and so on) and value (trustworthy, competent, compassionate, et cetera); the PM, when discussed in focus groups, is either seen as fairly neutral (i.e. nobody seems to know who he is) or as out of touch and uninteresting; the party is on track to lose as many as half of their seats in the general election – and their power.

'Excuse me.' Eva raises her hand after flicking through the sheets. Anto, who is sitting at the table, has to swivel in his seat to look at her. 'This is probably a stupid question but on the number of seats we lose – does that take into account the boundary changes?'

'The what?' Anto asks, mystified.

'The boundary changes. You know, the lines between constituencies are being redrawn so that the vote share will likely change in our existing seats. Some new seats are being created and some are disappearing altogether. Your assessment here of seat losses.' Eva holds up the sheet. 'Is this based on the current electoral map or with the boundary changes in mind?'

Anto reddens. 'Uh, I didn't know about that.'

The chief mouths, 'What the fuck?' gleefully at Eva.

Nick raises his hand. 'Sorry, just to, uh, add to what Anto has said ... This is with the boundary changes, I'm afraid. But I think it's important to note that this is the very worst-case scenario and—'

'Thanks for clarifying, Nick,' Anto snaps.

Nick visibly shrinks into his seat.

'Right, so this is the state of play,' the PM says, rubbing his eyes. 'What's the plan to turn it around? We have until the end of the year, and locals in May ...'

'Yes, so ...' Anto recovers his oily tone. 'What really pops out of the polling and focus groups to me is a need for grip and order. It's obvious that has fallen by the wayside since Madeleine Ford left office. We must appear to have a handle on things. And we must *deliver*,' Anto emphasises the word, 'on crime, transport and health in particular.'

There is a long pause. While the PM frowns at the words 'Madeleine Ford', the rest of the group skip ahead.

'Sorry, but, Nick,' the chief says, turning to the comms director. 'Is that your assessment?'

'Well, I-I—' Nick stammers.

'No, it's mine,' Anto says, expanding defensively like a puffer fish.

'Right, and we deliver all this by the end of the year ... how? With purdah that's about six months—'

'Purdah?' Anto looks blank.

The chief smiles at him pityingly. 'In the run-up to elections, the civil service has to stop all but the essential running of government. You know, Border Force and job centres and keeping the lights on. They can't churn out government policy ideas at that point as it gives the party in charge an unfair advantage. So we only have up to that point to get anything done, which looks like less than six months. I would *love*,' the chief's voice drips with sarcasm, 'to know what fantastical new policy ideas we are going to grip and deliver on trifling matters like crime and transport and health in that time.'

The chief glances at Jake, who Eva could swear responds with a wink.

There is a long silence, then Anto gestures at Nick. 'Well?'

'Well, this is rather thinking on my feet.' Nick clears his throat and turns to the PM. 'Anto is half right about the need for delivery. But we've got to remind people of what we've achieved in the past and essentially say, "Look, this is where ten years has got you. Give us a few more to finish the job." That also means addressing the grubby image the party has gained this year. We need to clean up – and fast – to look competent and capable. We've had three by-elections since you became prime minister, all of them lost to Labour and the Lib Dems on sleaze. And for the local elections, which are of course just weeks away, it is just about expectation management for the losses we're expecting.'

Anto snorts.

Determined to support Nick when he's been put on the spot, Eva and Jake nod in agreement. Encouraged, Nick continues.

'So, beyond the locals, we mustn't discount what we've learnt about public perceptions of you personally, Prime Minister.'

'What, you think they can learn to love me?' The PM squints.

'Not exactly.' Nick grimaces apologetically. 'But look at what they're really saying. Words like "distant" and "unremarkable" are much better than a firm negative view. The leader of the opposition is about the same, although his words are more positive: hard-working, unshowy, safe. He does also have negative terms like "smug".'

'So?' the PM says, looking faintly encouraged for the first time since the meeting began.

John Ramsey, the leader of the Labour Party, leaves Courtenay feeling like the sole characteristic they have in common each Wednesday after PMQs is the need to convert oxygen into carbon dioxide. The one thing the PM has a surplus of is about three inches in height. And that's only because Ramsey is stooped from all his years carrying books for his doctorate in human rights law. And his time pitching tents in Syrian Red Cross camps. The bastard.

'I'm a bore and he's Professor Bore?' There is a little wave of sycophantic laughter from a handful of people in the room, led by Anto's loud guffaws.

'What I'm trying to say is this is where I think we have an edge.' Nick flattens his palms on the table. 'We try to make people feel better about us and what we've done. We quietly clean up the party's image and loudly make the contest about personality. And we use the next six months to help the country get to know yours. Remind them of your service record and so on.'

The PM thinks about Ramsey's time in the Red Cross camps in the desert again. Do Courtenay's almost identical sandy photos from his army days, with the addition of the rifle he's holding, have the edge? The present-day visual certainly doesn't hurt. Tall, upright and coolly handsome, Courtenay is acknowledged, even by his detractors, as 'at least seeming prime ministerial' at meetings with other heads of government and at various state occasions. Ramsey just can't seem to get the presentation right. He's always wearing a suit and tie, but he has the habit of doing up his jacket buttons, like he's wearing his secondary-school blazer for the first time. It bunches up over his midriff if he gestures with his arms. Courtenay supposes it works with Ramsey's 'I'm not like the rest of the political class' schtick, but still – there's losing an election, then there's losing an election to a man in square-toed slip-ons.

'It's all about me?' the PM asks, doubtfully. He hates doing hand-grabbing and baby-kissing at the best of times, but his confidence is at an all-time low just now. Clarissa, lashing out like a wounded animal, seems to spend all day stewing in the flat, thinking of the meanest things she can say to him the moment he's through the door to cheer herself up. Maybe countless days on the campaign trail with stays overnight wouldn't be the worst thing after all.

'And how do you propose we do this miraculous party clean-up?' Anto asks. 'I'd be interested to get Nigel's view, seeing as it's within his purview.'

'Not just about MPs, mate,' the chief replies nastily. 'Hardly helps that you're snapped in corporate boxes at football and cricket matches the whole time.'

'Nick.' The PM cuts in quickly before Anto can respond in kind. 'Any thoughts?'

'Well ...' Nick looks uneasy. 'I suppose, again, it is really about perception. We could revive your zero-tolerance language from the leadership campaign. And actually have a zero-tolerance approach this time ...?'

Nick glances uncertainly at the chief, who shrugs as if to say 'may as well try'.

'And.' Nick sucks in a breath. 'We really need to get a handle on this stuff going on with your ... with Mrs Courtenay. Get some clear blue water between you and her on personalities and ... and how much you're seen together.'

There is another long pause, during which Nick wipes sweat from his eyebrows and everyone watches the PM, wondering how he'll respond.

The PM considers Nick's words. Clarissa won't like it, that's for sure. She's already picked her outfits for the G7 and the Buckingham Palace banquet for the incoming state visit from Japan, anticipating many photo opportunities. On the other hand, Nick's plan presumably means time away from her. There'll be hell to pay when he explains it to her. Perhaps the chief can do it?

The PM frowns and Anto (mis)reads the expression.

'Nick, can I speak with you, please?' Anto stands and gestures to the door. 'Privately?'

Nick, appearing to crumple further into himself, rises dejectedly and leaves the room. Eva tries to smile at him encouragingly – his plan is the only workable thing they have, after all – but Nick keeps his eyes lowered, a strange expression on his face. Once the door closes, it occurs to Eva that his hands were balled into fists.

Eventually the door bursts open and Anto glides back into the room, wiping his coffee-soaked face with a tissue and sporting a surprisingly triumphant look.

'Where's Nick?' the PM asks.

'Gone, I'm afraid. He's resigned from his post with immediate effect. We can't have someone attacking your wife like that. Totally disrespectful.'

'What the fuck?' the chief says with a gasp, turning from Anto to the PM. 'Nobody loves Clarissa more than me, but we all know what he said is right. And now we've bulleted the one person with a workable plan, that isn't based on "grip"?' It is a word hated by countless chief whips. Every Number Ten is hit with the accusation from the back benches of a lack of 'grip' at one point or another and it normally means a tedious cycle of staffing changes and pointless briefings from the political team to MPs to make them feel important and involved. 'The man was doing about ten different jobs!'

'And.' Anto ploughs on. 'We need a better attitude to the upcoming local elections. We can't just roll over and accept defeat. We can do better than Nick as campaign director.' He examines the stain on his Hermès tie.

'Oh, is Paris Hilton available?' The chief glares back.

'Now, Chief.' The PM raises his hands between the two men like a boxing referee. He's praying Anto has a good suggestion. 'Let's hear him out. Anto, who do you have in mind?'

41

There is a pause while Anto smooths his hair. 'Me.'

'You . . . for what?'

As the PM asks this, he's aware of the chief whispering under his breath, 'Christ on a bike.'

'As campaign director. Instead of Nick.'

The PM wonders what to say. He doesn't want to undermine his chief of staff, but Nick is key to his organisation and beloved by everyone. But he doesn't want to seem disloyal to Clarissa. How has he lost control of what was meant to be a straightforward meeting? Then he wakes up to the number of people in the room. If this leaks, it'll be a nightmare. He stands up.

'Can everyone leave, please. Except the chief whip and Anto.'

Eva follows Jake to the outer office where, once the door is closed, the PM's principal private secretary – the most senior civil servant in Number Ten – ushers Jake into a nearby room.

'Jesus,' the PM's diary manager says, seemingly to herself, biting down on a biscuit. 'I'm meant to be starting a diet today, but the stress levels around here are pushing me over the edge.'

Before Eva replies, Jake returns.

'What a morning.' Jake chuckles. 'Sounds like Anto laid into Nick for showing him up in there, then accused him of attacking Clarissa. Baited him pretty badly and Nick just lost it. The PPS had to grab him round the middle to stop him smacking Anto in the face after the coffee toss. God, I wish . . .'

'So he's really gone?' Eva asks, wondering whether she can get a standing invitation to these morning meetings. There isn't a TV drama anywhere close to it.

'Yup,' Jake mutters. 'And I bet you the PM agrees to let Anto have a crack at being the campaign manager. He's hopeless when it comes to this sort of thing. Just can't say no, even if it means his own neck on the chopping block.'

'You need to get rid of Anto. He's awful. Not just at his job. I mean, really *awful*. He's the only man I've ever met who walks into a room knob first.' She thrusts her hips forward in perfect imitation of Anto's laddish posture.

'Trust me,' Jake nods at an open copy of the *Sentinel* featuring a small diary story about Anto accepting a day of golf with a FTSE executive on a work day, 'we're doing our best. And remember – Nick is on the outside now, where he can do Anto a lot more damage.'

The PM's office door opens and the chief stalks out.

'Come on, young lady. We're out of here.'

Eva waves at Jake and the chief shakes his head darkly, then they march down the corridor to the famous black front door. Eva pulls her phone from the cubbyhole and spots another needy text from Jamie, but looks up at the sound of running footsteps approaching.

'Nige – you haven't quit too, have you?' Jake is panting after chasing them down.

'Are you mad? Things are just getting interesting . . .'

Central London

Jess Adler stumbles out of a side exit of the fetish club and into an alley, peels back her latex sleeve and checks her watch. Shit. If she doesn't get a move on, she'll be late. Jess tugs off the rubber snorkel obscuring her face, hoping the telltale suction marks on her pale face go quickly, stuffs it into her bag and pulls a cream cashmere jumper over her body suit. She swaps her buckled stiletto boots for trainers and, checking her reflection in her motorbike wing mirror, congratulates herself on her night-to-day transformation. She hops on the bike and screeches to St James's Park.

Jess zips so speedily through the traffic that she arrives with enough time to find a table in the busy, tourist-filled café and

43

jot down a few ideas in her notebook. After moving to London from Glasgow to join the *Sentinel* last year, she has become one of the busiest journalists in Westminster. She now has a column in the *Sentinel* on top of her standard news gathering, plus a podcast about investigative journalism, where she interviews the people who've broken some of the biggest stories in living memory. If she isn't at home with Eva and Bobby, in their slightly bizarre living arrangement with Percy and his young American girlfriend, Holly, then she's either out chasing a story or chasing something else at this fetish club, which comes complete with a sadomasochism 'dungeon'. In short, apart from her wholesome home nights, she's generally torturing unwilling politicians by day and rather more willing PVC and leather wearers by night. She suspects some overlap between the two but the masks keep everyone's dignity intact.

So, a quiet moment like this to think about anything beyond the next five minutes is a luxury. She's interrupted though. Ed Cooper, the political editor at the *Sentinel* and her boss, won't stop bothering her. It wasn't long ago that a text from Ed made Jess's heart leap. The trouble is, her interest in seducing him has evaporated, not helped by looking at his middle-aged dick pics in the cold, sober light of day. Once Jess felt she had some control over Ed she didn't have a challenge any more (and meeting his wife at the office Christmas party didn't help), while Ed has swung in the other direction, aware that Jess is starting to slip away, so clinging on for dear life.

She knows she should be careful, though. Jess doesn't want anybody to learn of the odd relationship she's had with Ed for the last year or so. The explanation that, because they've never actually had sex or oral or any direct touching, they haven't had an inappropriate relationship, doesn't exactly hold water. Do sex toys in lieu of them physically touching count? Maybe it's weirder than just a straightforward bonk, despite what she tells herself.

In the meantime, Ed's messages now bore her rather than turn her on.

I thought about you in the shower this morning.

So what.

Jess puts her phone down on the table and turns back to her notebook. But she can't stop her mind wandering to the person she's waiting for: Christian Eckles, the new director of communications for John Ramsey and the Labour Party. Jess has only met Christian once before and didn't pay him much attention because she was on the hunt, trying to nail down a story. He was cute but just a very tall and quiet guy, an unknown Labour speechwriter and strategist, drinking in the pub while journalists and party people chattered around him. But the little coup he has just staged to get the top job has intrigued her. It takes guts, cunning and patience to pull off what he's just done. Unless Jess charms him fast, she will have very little access to the next Number Ten administration – if the polls are anything to go by.

Thinking all of this for the twentieth time, Jess aimlessly doodles a picture of Snoopy under a neatly drawn heading: *Ideas*.

'I see the *Sentinel* has a new cartoonist,' a slightly breathless voice says. 'Sorry I'm late.'

Jess snaps the book shut and stands up. Christian is so tall that she has to tip her head back to look up into his face, which is almost translucently pale apart from a few freckles and a pair of amber eyes. He has amazing Nordic bone structure, reddish hair and a soft, low voice, like some sort of metropolitan Viking.

'Nice to meet you.' She offers her hand.

'We've met once before, actually,' Christian says, sitting down opposite her and running his hands through his silky, mink hair. 'In the Two Chairmen?'

Jess registers pleasant surprise at him having remembered. 'Of course. Well … good to see you again. And congratulations.'

'Thanks.'

'Well, thanks for meeting with me,' Jess says.

'Sure. Seems every journalist under the sun has been in touch to introduce themselves in the last couple of days; even though I've been around for a while. I feel like the Ugly Duckling, just after he's become a swan.'

Jess wonders why she didn't pay him a bit more attention before, just for sexual appeal alone. Now she needs to think about how to separate herself from the pack. 'That's what happens when you take people by surprise.'

'True,' Christian reflects. After a pause, he smiles.

Wow, she thinks. His whole face transforms. She wishes she didn't have the latex suit underneath her sweater. She's feeling uncomfortably hot.

'I'd just like to discuss terms of engagement,' Jess says, deciding that being professional and to the point is her best bet. 'I'm sure you're speaking to my editor at the *Sentinel* about the paper's business with your team more generally, but I'm keen to know how you like to work with hacks.'

'You know, you take a very different tack to your colleague, Cooper. With him it was a big lunch and "mate" this and "I've always admired you from a distance" that. A distance! He only followed me on Twitter when I got appointed. The tact of a bull.'

Jess raises her eyebrows.

'So.' Christian pauses for a moment, drumming his long fingers thoughtfully on the table. 'I guess that means I'll be dealing with you.'

Jess registers an unmistakable squirm between her thighs. *No*, she tells herself, *get a grip. You aren't out of your current scrape yet.*

'Great. I'm looking forward to it.'

46

Christian fixes her with his orange, fox-like eyes and murmurs, 'Me too.'

They chat some more about Ramsey's appearance on *Politics Tonight* but once Christian has left, Jess stares into space for a long time.

This is not what she expected. Jess was after a rapport with him, not a crush. *Oh, this is not ideal,* she thinks. *You need to get back to the dungeon this weekend, strap on your mask and spank someone senseless to get your head straight.*

Her thoughts are interrupted by her phone buzzing again. Ed:

Did my shower message make you touch yourself?

That's enough. She'll just have to keep Christian at arm's length and follow her own advice about professionalism for now. But she can knock another problem on the head in the meantime.

She replies to Ed's message.

We need to talk.

Burma Road, Houses of Parliament

'Y-you're breaking up with me?' Ed stammers, after Jess has closed the door of their shared Westminster office.

'What do you mean breaking up? We're not going out,' Jess hisses, waving at Ed to sit down. 'You're married!'

'You know what I mean.' Ed's voice rises. 'What we've done together is hardly the normal behaviour of colleagues.'

Jess shushes him.

'Don't you shush me! Do you *know* what I've done for you?'

'Piss off, Ed.' Jess folds her arms. 'You've not given me a leg up. *I* break my stories, *I* built up a relationship with Finlayson, *I* earned my column and—'

'I don't mean that. I mean the risks I've taken. My marriage, my kids ... the sneaking around? And,' he lowers his voice, leaning in meaningfully, 'to say nothing of how sore my arse was after you insisted on trying pegging with that enormous ... thing. I was fidgeting about so much, the whole office thought I had haemorrhoids.' The boys in their team – George and Mike – still gleefully bring in bunches of grapes to the office and leave them on Ed's desk with *Get well soon* notes and he's afraid to correct them.

'Listen,' Jess says. 'What did you think was going to happen, Ed? You're *married*. And a father. You have a reputation and a public profile ... Surely you realise this was never going anywhere?'

Ed looks wistfully at the floor.

'Is there someone else? Finlayson?'

'Urgh, as if!' Jess retorts. But she smarts at his perceptiveness. Not just about the possibility of someone else, but that someone being Finlayson. Nothing has ever happened but there's no question that his lordship has left the metaphorical door open at a couple of their private dinners recently. Jess has certainly thought about it and she's been with older men before. But when she really, truly gets down to the nitty gritty, could she stomach seeing the ancient proprietor naked? Plus there's the heart-attack risk.

'I thought you valued your career more,' Ed says with a sigh, a little smile creasing the corners of his mouth.

'What's my career got to do with this?' Jess's hands move to her hips.

'Oh, everything,' he says lazily. 'If you break things off, I'll get you fired. It's that easy. I just put a call in at the top ...'

'But—'

'I've done it before,' Ed says. And Jess believes him.

'Ed, this is blackmail. You're going to blackmail me for sexual favours? I . . . I'd rather quit!' Jess spits.

'Quit if you want, but I'm not asking for anything as distasteful as that. I'm just saying that any hint I get that you may not be co-operating with me professionally, or that you're cooling off from me, means you're fired from the *Sentinel*. And I'll do everything in my power to put "Jess Adler – Journalism Superstar" in the dustbin.' Ed grins sadistically at her. 'Just . . . humour me.'

Ed is no fool. He isn't overplaying his hand and demanding sex. That would send Jess into the stratosphere. He's just asking her to play along as before. Jess thinks hard. She's worked her arse off – and his – to get this far. Perhaps she can tolerate this situation a bit longer while she works out a more elegant solution. After all, Jess was smart enough to never send Ed suggestive photos. Texts, sure. But he sent all sorts of snaps of himself – and it's definitely him, you can clearly see his face – doing anything from being naked or wanking or half choking himself on his wife's pink fluffy dressing-gown cord. Ed must know what Jess has and therefore needs her out of the picture if she isn't going to play ball. But if her own career is at stake, she's willing to do anything.

'What if I send your wife our messages?' Jess tries one last-ditch effort.

Ed sighs. 'You'd hardly be the first. Obviously I would prefer that you didn't, but I can live with it. The question is, can you live with your messages out in the public domain – and being jobless?'

Jess looks into his inscrutable face. Is he bluffing? She can't risk that he is. Ed grins.

'Right, so we'll just continue as if this little chat never happened, shall we?'

Very slowly, trying to keep the look of revulsion off her face, Jess nods.

Central London

Christian Eckles trudges onto the Jubilee line train at Westminster station after a long day in the leader of the opposition's parliamentary office. It's late enough that he easily gets a seat. He swings his backpack off his shoulder, stifles a yawn and pulls out a book on left-wing economics.

He can't concentrate on the page, though. Just in his line of vision, the young man next to him is watching porn on his phone, completely oblivious to his neighbour's cocked head. Christian can't hear the sound – the guy's at least had the sense to put his headphones on – but the video is nonetheless compelling.

The camera is being held at what would be head height for the male partner, so it looks like the young woman in the video is performing the sex acts on the viewer, as the man is entirely out of shot, except for his enormous cock. Christian raises an eyebrow as she moves from blowjob to handjob.

It isn't just the surprise of seeing porn in public that keeps Christian staring. It's that the star of the video reminds him so vividly of Jess Adler. Pale skin, dark hair, intense and teasing eyes. As she flips around and the couple begin doggystyle, the man taking a handful of the actress's hair, Christian has to move his economics book over his crotch.

When he gets home, after a slightly stiff-legged walk from the Tube, Christian slams the door shut and hops onto the sofa, imagining himself slipping off Jess's rubber leggings and running his hands through her hair from behind too.

5th April

Con 27% Lab 41%

School attendance down 9%/

Wildfires in California

Houses of Parliament

'Sorry, can I just squeeze past?' Bobby Cliveden's hands are cupped to her mouth but the entrance to the ladies' bathroom is blocked by a young woman in a tabard.

'I'm afraid you can't go in there.' The woman puts her arms in front of the doorway. 'Maintenance problem.'

'There's going to be a maintenance problem out here if I don't get to some kind of toilet or bin in the next five seconds,' Bobby says. Her mouth is filling up with saliva. The woman hesitates for a moment then lets Bobby through the door.

She makes it to the cubicle just in time. Her breakfast heaves out of her, making her eyes water. After a while she flushes and pulls the lid down to sit and recover, her chin cupped in her hands. She decides she'll take a break from the Portcullis House cafeteria for a while, although in the year she's worked in Parliament she's never been ill from food there before. More likely to be Jess's exotic fish tacos last night. She shivers thinking about them.

She needs to leave and get to the Terrace, where she is meeting the former Downing Street communications director, Nick O'Hara. But as soon as she starts to stand up, she feels another wave of nausea and sits back down, gulping. Suddenly she's smacked by another gag and turns, kneels and lifts the lid just in time. She closes her eyes and takes careful, shuddering breaths, then realises that her knees are wet.

She looks around and sees the floor is covered in water. Bloody pipes again.

After a few minutes of steady breathing, Bobby wipes her mouth with a tissue, dabs at her watering eyes, flushes again and opens her cubicle door.

She washes her hands but the hand-dryer won't work – electricity must be out because of the flooding – so she shakes her hands as she exits.

A few minutes later Bobby and Nick are on the Terrace, watching sunlight dance on the murky water of the Thames.

'So.' Nick sips his coffee. 'What a pleasure to meet you. Obviously, Jake has talked about you a fair amount but your mental health unit campaign last year speaks for itself.'

'Oh, thank you. A pleasure to meet you too ... Are you all right after everything at Number Ten?'

'Fine.' Nick has come into Westminster today, his head held high after his fiery exit from Downing Street, on a mission. He'll meet with members of the lobby to brief a flattering version of his departure. And as a special favour to Natasha Weaver, the party chairman, he's tidying up a couple of threads from his campaign director role – which includes candidates. The pair of them, who have fought their way up the SW1 ladder with street smarts and determination, are sick of the entitled, private-schooled Oxbridge types that are everywhere. No better are the newer breed of microphone-grabbing 'voice of the people' local MPs, who are meant to represent Weaver and Nick's communities. They want to track down effective, smart and hard-working people like Bobby and rebuild the party in their own image.

'But let's cut to the chase. You're working for Moira Herbert, is that right?'

'Yes.' Initially hired by Simon Daly MP, now Lord Daly, Bobby became Moira's main staffer in her parliamentary office after helping her with the by-election to replace the disgraced Daly in Tipperton. She loves the work – part social worker, part press officer.

'I'm told you're doing an excellent job. What next?' Nick fixes Bobby with his brilliant blue eyes. Bobby hesitates for a moment.

'Well ... I'm enjoying my role with Moira. It allows me to see my parents regularly and I think I'm getting the hang of things ...'

'Listen.' Nick clears his throat. 'Until recently, I oversaw the candidates team at CCHQ so presumably you have a clue about what I want to ask you. So let's get on with it. Would you like to stand as an MP?'

'Yes,' Bobby says loudly and clearly, taking herself a little by surprise.

'Good. And let's be specific. How would you like to be the MP for Tipperton?'

'What?' Bobby says, aghast. 'Squeeze out Moira? Absolutely not!'

'Are you mad? Moira's going nowhere. But you know about the boundary review, of course.'

Bobby nods uncertainly. 'I think we're getting carved up a bit.'

'Correct. Split in half, in fact. Or near enough. So,' Nick says quickly, seeing Bobby's eyes widen, 'although the stronger majority will be in the new seat of West Tipperton, which I've no doubt Moira will be encouraged to take, the second one – very marginal – will be Tipperton proper. We need a native,' Nick counts off on his fingers, 'someone enthusiastic, experienced, a natural campaigner and ... I may as well say it, with a fantastic local story.'

He looks at Bobby expectantly.

'Well, are you going to do it?' There is a pause. 'Do you think all the men who are putting their names on the list are being coy?'

It's all Bobby needs to hear.

'Yes. Yes, count me in. What do I need to do?'

Nick grins. 'Right ... '

They're off, Nick explaining to Bobby the steps she has to complete: pass a Parliamentary Assessment Board (PAB); apply for a seat, in this case Tipperton; get on their shortlist of candidates and perform well enough at the Tipperton association selection meeting to become their prospective parliamentary candidate. Then there's just the small matter of fighting a general election to become an MP. It is a time-consuming and expensive endeavour, littered with disappointment and bad luck. Some brilliant people try for years and never succeed. Some absolute twits do it the first time round.

'So I'll go over to CCHQ and get you to a PAB as soon as possible. Do some practice beforehand, because there are a few questions you need to be pretty clear on. You know, define a woman ... ' Nick raises an eyebrow at Bobby.

'Oh, um ... well, someone with a cervix. Or ... or not?' Bobby flushes.

'We'll work on it.' Nick stands. 'Now, you'd better go and talk to Moira about all this. She should be delighted with the possibility of having you as a neighbour. But it mucks up her staffing arrangements, I'm sure.'

Bobby watches Nick leave the Terrace and looks out at the Thames again. After a minute or two she stands to leave too. The salty, oily smell sighing off the tidal water, or perhaps her excitement, is making her feel nauseous again.

Downing Street

Clarissa Courtenay stares moodily out of the window, watching the Downing Street groundskeeping team struggle to shepherd some ducklings from the Number Ten garden pond into a cardboard box, ready to be carried to St James's Park. Someone had told her this pantomime happens most springs, as a clever duck will spot the sheltered little pond, safe from foxes, and lay their eggs. When they hatch, the safest place is with the foxes, away from the Downing Street cat. The pond has existed since 1991, and only since then because of a misfired IRA mortar that was meant to hit a cabinet meeting and landed a few feet to the right. Clarissa looks at the flowers and greenery and wonders whether she can patch over the gaping, ugly hole in her reputation half as well. She expects that this Sunday's papers, for the second week in a row, will not be kind.

'What about this one?' Her husband enters the room holding a green tie with tiny daisies on it. 'Seems about right for an Easter service, don't you think?'

Clarissa sighs.

'I don't care, Eric. So long as it doesn't have something actively bad on it, like swastikas ... or my face, I hardly think it matters.'

She's getting sick of him trying to check in with her all the time, bringing her little things like advice on clothes or social media photos, like an eager puppy. It just irritates Clarissa

55

and makes her kick him harder. She glances at the untouched hatbox near the door, then turns back to the ducklings.

'Listen, I'm sorry you can't come to Westminster Abbey today.' The PM approaches cautiously and touches her shoulder. 'I know you were looking forward to it. But with everything a bit ... hot just now, the team think it's best for you to keep a low profile.'

Clarissa shakes his hand off – she can't stomach being touched by him at the moment; they've not had sex for weeks – and heads for the door. What has she done wrong? Shown a bit of loyalty to a friend, put in a good word where she can ... It hurts her, but she knows the team is right to keep her out of the public eye just now. She realises that if you're the queen in chess, darting around to protect the stupid king all the time, sacrificing pawns and bishops, eventually you might be knocked firmly out of the game yourself.

Still, Clarissa's having a drink with Nick O'Hara later, whose departure she roundly bollocked her husband for. A man of ideas and street smarts, perhaps he'll have some thoughts on what Clarissa does next.

'Oh, yes, I was so looking forward to a live performance of you butchering a Bible reading. Now, if you'll excuse me, I'm off for a bath and a wank.'

Going via the kitchen for a bottle of wine and a glass, she heads upstairs.

The PM looks dolefully at the tie, then threads it round his neck and heads downstairs, wondering if his wife will ever look at him with love or lust ever again. His time in office has been miserable so far. He can't seem to get anything right and the 'perks' of being prime minister just make him feel worse. He was humiliated at Davos, the famous ski-resort gathering of the wealthy and influential, when he got his speaking notes muddled up. He can hardly fit in his armour-plated Jaguar, having to fold himself up like a deck chair to get his long legs in. And he just wants to cry at the weekly audiences at Buckingham Palace, the only time he feels he isn't being judged.

When he gets downstairs, Anto, Jake and his PPS are waiting for him.

'PM, before you head to the Abbey we need you to meet the shortlist of candidates to be your new military attaché,' Anto says, handing over a sheet of paper containing brief biographies of a handful of armed forces personnel.

'They've been through rigorous interviews to get this far and these final three are all very well qualified,' the PM's PPS says, 'so this is really just a chemistry test. You know, to see how you gel with them personally. After all, this person will accompany and brief you on all defence-related visits, meetings and issues.'

'All right.' The PM shrugs and trudges into his office. His three advisers give each other curious glances then follow him. They've been holding back these interviews as something of a treat, to imbibe the tired PM with the energy he normally gets from talking to military folk, soldier to soldier. He's impossible to cheer up at the moment.

At least the interviews have given the women in the building some enjoyment. The candidates are in full dress uniform and, while they sit in the waiting room and wonder if this strange place will be their new posting, special advisers and private secretaries traipse past in goggling, giggling groups.

The initial reception in the PM's study isn't markedly different.

'I always forget how wonderfully understated the Royal Marines' kit is,' the PM says, shaking hands with his first interviewee and immediately cheering up in the presence of the plain navy suit, white belt and white peaked cap. 'I can't do up the top button of my old mess jacket any more without turning purple . . .'

They have a useful conversation, the young man clearly well briefed and respectful towards the prime minister as both the holder of the office and as an ex-military man. There aren't many politicians with Courtenay's service record.

The second candidate, a Light Dragoon, also impresses with his grasp of detail and presentability.

'How can I possibly choose between these two chaps?' the PM cries, when the door closes on the second pair of broad shoulders. 'They're both perfect.'

'Well, Prime Minister, you still have a third interviewee,' the PPS says.

'Ha. Well, he's got tough competition.'

'She, sir,' Jake says quietly, pointing to a bio on the sheet of paper on the desk.

There is a pause while the prime minister attempts to close his gaping mouth. 'Now this is interesting,' he says, a flinty look creeping across his face. 'Let me guess. Is this the comms team trying out a new angle? Think a woman in uniform in my Armistice Day pictures will give me an edge?' The prime minister folds his arms and smirks. 'I wasn't born yesterday, you know.'

'Yeah, we all thought it would be so cool if we could brief out that the person advising you on pressing the nuclear button is a woman,' Jake says tersely. 'You know, victory for the girls, blame any botched decisions on her period . . . '

'Okay, okay.' The PM raises his hands like he has a gun pointed at him. 'I'm so used to being told about optics . . . '

'This is not about comms or optics or unconscious-bias training, PM,' Anto says greasily. 'You need the right ma . . . *person* for the job.'

'All right.' The PM smiles and nods at his PPS. 'Fire when ready.'

The woman who enters wears the smart, double-breasted

and brass-buttoned skirt suit of the Royal Navy. Teamed with low heels and thin black tights, the whole look would be demurely sexy if it weren't topped off with a curly-brimmed little white hat, which with her smiling face gives her the look of a Matey bubble-bath bottle. What the PM notices first, though, is her amazing height and breadth. She's like the *Xena: Warrior Princess* of his deepest digital fantasies.

She is introduced by the PPS as Captain Laura Lloyd.

'Prime Minister,' Laura says in a gentle Welsh lilt, smiling warmly.

'Hello, Captain.' The PM shakes her hand, which feels like a slab of steak. 'Now, tell me about yourself . . .'

They talk for nearly an hour in an uninterrupted flow. Jake, Anto and the PPS are merely spectators, as Laura and the PM discuss everything from the UK's NATO membership and armed forces gossip to Laura's interest in mental health support for serving military personnel and training schemes for veterans. Laura's face is so open and kind, her eyes clear and cheerful, that the PM finds the conversation is like a warm bath after the weeks – or years, really – of frosty put-downs from Clarissa. He's not sure if it's her defence knowledge or just her gentle manner, but Laura makes him feel reassured. He would love her to take him in her strong arms and squeeze the anxiety out of him.

He's so absorbed in the conversation that the PM only just makes it to the Abbey ahead of the royal family for the Easter service. After the first hymn is over – 'All Things Bright and Beautiful', which the PM sings at the top of his voice – he leans in on his way to the lectern for his reading and whispers into his PPS's ear.

'Contestant number three, please, Gerald.'

The PPS nods, his mouth creasing into a little Mona Lisa smile.

6th April

Con 26% Lab 41%

Royals united at the Abbey/

Freak snow in Spain

Burma Road, Houses of Parliament

Now that Jess has so many extra professional commitments at StoryCorps, her colleagues, Mike and George, have had to pick up some slack. They're making no secret of how much this annoys them. After all, Jess is younger than them and less experienced, but she's able to turn down assignments if she has a column or podcast episode that the higher-ups consider a greater priority.

'Just because we aren't Finlayson's darlings, going out for cosy dinners with him,' Mike grumbles.

'Oh, don't worry, boys. Jess can't stay in his lordship's good books for ever . . . ' Ed smirks. There is something menacing in the way he says it that puts Jess's teeth on edge.

Things have crescendoed since Jess and Ed met a few days ago. Ed, perhaps shoring up support, is being especially charming towards Mike and George, inviting Mike to lunches with ministers and even sharing his by-line with George on an interview with the shadow home secretary. In fact, he's on a mission to suck up to every man he works with, posting oleaginous Tweets about the *Sentinel* editor, Philip McKay, and loudly agreeing with the points raised by men in meetings. Still, he can only extend his sweetness so far. The women at HQ are reporting a return to his behaviour from before Jess joined the *Sentinel*.

'He's doing his same horrible shit, trashing us in editorial meetings and asking every woman who confronts him if they're just going through menopause. How did you stop him before?'

Jess is sensible enough not to say, 'Because I had a pseudosexual relationship with him that I can't seem to leave.' But she's getting a phone call most days from disgusted *Sentinel* female staff. When she talks to George and Mike, they seem completely unconcerned, even pleased at her impotent outrage.

'It's just Ed's way,' says George, plopping an aspirin into an Irn-Bru after another heavy night. 'He's more comfortable with men.'

'Exactly,' Mike grunts, filling out his monthly expenses form with his parliamentary dinners. 'You can't just bleat about women in the workplace the whole time. Maybe if you pulled your weight around here you wouldn't feel like he's giving you such a hard time ...'

Ed, meanwhile, continues to drop nasty hints about her future. He's also sending her progressively more revolting messages. It's all Jess can do to reply with an acknowledging thumbs-up emoji. Knowing she is unlikely to get much support, Jess still attempts to tackle the subject with the *Sentinel* editor. She can't tell Philip any specifics about her position with Ed, but she wonders why he won't step in on behalf of the women of StoryCorps.

'Ed's a great guy, but ...' Philip rubs the bridge of his nose, lost for words. 'You seemed to get the hang of him before – can't you help?'

'I've tried. Frankly, I don't understand why you haven't got him on a last warning. How do you let him get away with this stuff?'

'Well ...' Philip looks uneasy. 'Ed's a special case. A real talent we can't afford to lose.'

'You bloody can! Philip, he's being a bastard to everyone. Why don't you speak to Finlayson about him?'

'Not everyone. I find him a pleasure, frankly. And George and Mike couldn't speak more highly of him! Anyway,' Philip looks shifty, 'Finlayson has his hands tied ...'

And this is the exact problem. How can Lord Finlayson, one of the wealthiest and most powerful people in the country, be in any way beholden to Ed Cooper?

Jess decides to ask Teddy Hammer about what he knows over lunch at a quiet terraced restaurant. Teddy is a lobby legend, having broken some of the biggest stories in journalism over the past three decades. He now writes freelance about pretty much anything he wants. As a result, he is a regular guest on Jess's podcast and they have become firm friends after he took her under his wing at the start of her lobby career.

'Ah, I wondered when you were going to start thinking about this.' Teddy nods his grizzled grey head approvingly over his glass of wine. 'I wasn't going to help you at all, but I'm thinking of retiring from journalism soon so feel more inclined ... You're right to take an interest. I hear that Ed is cooler on you now that you have your own thing going on and it's only a matter of time before he starts whispering in Finlayson's ear.'

Jess clenches her fists. Ed threatened exactly this when she said she'd go to his wife and he's needled her about it since. Is it possible he'll make a pre-emptive strike and get her out of the way regardless? She needs to get to the bottom of this. Urgently. Her career and her sanity are on the line.

'So you know something's going on there?' She can't resist leaning forward in her seat.

'I have a theory – which I won't share with you!' Teddy laughs as Jess opens then instantly closes her mouth. 'You have to work this out for yourself. But let's think a little, shall we? What possible reasons could Finlayson have for protecting Ed like this?'

Jess thinks.

'Ed knows something about Finlayson that nobody else does.' Isn't that what she's doing with Ed right now? She thinks of what she has on her phone. 'And he has evidence.'

'I agree.' Teddy lights a cigarette and continues to gaze at her.

Jess thinks on. But Ed has worked at StoryCorps for ages. When might he have got this information? Wait – it's obvious.

'I need to get his employment record and pinpoint the exact timing that he got promotion and favour.' She's really speaking to herself now. 'I wonder if I can get someone from HR to help me ...'

'Very good.' Teddy grins. He flicks some ash. 'You may also wish to consult his archive of articles and see what he was working on around the time he got bumped up.'

'Brilliant.' Jess jumps up. 'Um ... do you mind if I run? Sounds like I have a career to safeguard.'

'Godspeed!' Teddy waves her off with his wine glass.

7th April

Con 26% Lab 42%

Rumours of interest rate rise/
Arctic ice loss worsens

Downing Street

It is Tuesday morning and members of the cabinet assemble at
Ten Downing Street as usual. The chief whip finds these to be
tedious meetings – everyone crammed around the green baize
table, running through a pointless agenda cooked up to keep
them busy. His colleagues who speak, mostly unnecessarily,
do so for two reasons: firstly, to sycophantically try to trade
up into a more prestigious job by appearing energised and
full of ideas, and, secondly, to appear in the official cabinet
minutes for posterity. He wishes he could show the impatient
young MPs in his party why their eagerness to reach a seat in
this room is misplaced. Like the Ghost of Cabinet Present,
he would raise a cloaked arm to the game of hangman taking
place between the Wales and Scotland secretaries, wedged at
the bottom of the table, or the almost visible thought bubble

above the cabinet secretary's head: *I wonder if the other lot will keep me when they come in . . .*

The chief glances around the table and looks at the glum faces, several of which he personally tried to bury during last year's leadership contest. The truth is that they're all just animals, who have clawed and gnashed at each other until one of them, currently Eric, is at the top of the pecking order. Those assembled round the table now are the same old beasts but now they're stuck together in Cabinet Collective Responsibility. They bare their yellow teeth, ready to draw blood if the PM loses the general election. Loyalty is fleeting.

The chief retreats into his head and watches a video he saw that morning.

Scene: The Chamber of the House of Lords.

Time: A late sitting the previous night.

Peers have congregated to vote on a piece of legislation about planning, many of them in black tie from the dinners they've had to quickly dash away from to vote. Winding up the debate are the young Lord Foulkes for the government (Madeleine Ford's ex-political secretary and Eva's old boss, who has been an instant hit in the Lords and was quickly made Minister for Housing and Communities) and the grey Lord Grubley for the opposition, a fusty old accountant with a knack for numbers.

Lord Foulkes waits to respond and close the debate while Lord Grubley drones on, the green benches fidgeting and sleepy, some holding their heads in their hands.

'And so, my noble lords, I would ask you to turn your attention to clause three of the Bill—'

'BOR-RING!' A deep, petulant voice trumpets from the government side.

Percy Cross, back from his book tour and lounging just behind Lord Foulkes, has his hands gleefully cupped round his mouth. The ministers on the front bench, including Lord

Foulkes, struggle to keep their faces straight. Even the opposition benches are desperately stifling giggles. The video has already become a TikTok sensation, with kids all over the country daring each other to shout 'BOR-RING!' during this morning's school assemblies.

The chief's mouth twitches. Natasha Weaver, sitting opposite him, misreads his smile and thinks it's directed at her. She winks. The chief stares past her shoulder, doing his best to ignore the glittering pendant dipping into her plunging neckline. It is vital that Weaver doesn't think he's making a pass at her. She can be incredibly persistent with even a smidgeon of encouragement.

When the meeting is finally over, the chief slips into the PM's office. Anto follows him.

'Bad news,' the chief says once the door has closed.

'Oh, goodie . . . ' The PM groans. He was looking forward to his first meeting with Laura Lloyd, the new MA, who's wearing a sleeveless dress today. Her toned arms are bigger than his.

'Vic's going to stand down.'

'Vic? As in the chancellor of the duchy of Lancaster? CDL? Resigning?' Anto gasps.

'Well summarised, Anto,' the chief sneers. 'Yes, Vic. No, not resigning but stepping down at the general election. As in, he won't be standing again for his seat and will not be sitting here with us next year.'

'Fuck a duck.' The prime minister winces.

The chancellor of the duchy of Lancaster sounds like a pantomime dame, but is a significant job in government, generally held by a trusted MP. They are the highest-ranking minister in the Cabinet Office, the government department that oversees everything from constitutional reform to national security.

'And, as a popular older member of the parliamentary party, this will send a bunch of our MPs into a tailspin. It doesn't exactly scream a vote of confidence in our electoral chances.'

'When will it be public?' the PM asks weakly.

'He's about to come in and tell you, so I should imagine some time today.' The chief looks from the PM to Anto, disgusted at their crumpled attitudes. 'But I have an idea . . .'

Both of them goggle at him expectantly. God, he misses having Clarissa around to add a few political brain cells to the assembled group's average from time to time.

'We fire him.'

'What?'

'Oh, come on, we may as well try to look strong in this. Whether you like it or not, he is absolutely screwing us. If one of our most competent ministers is standing down at the next election, what confidence do you think that shows in your leadership? And he's not even that good! Just sits in the middle ground, wittering. Anyway,' the chief says matter-of-factly, 'I've got some stuff on the old fucker we can use.'

'Like what?'

'Let's just say his government car is doing a hell of a lot of unnecessary mileage. His wife's dry-cleaning, his grandchildren's nursery pick-up . . .'

'Sounds a bit thin.' Anto guffaws.

'I strongly advise you to stay out of this one, mate. Wouldn't want you to get your nice suit grubby.' The chief smiles unpleasantly and turns to the prime minister. 'And his special advisers have been using it to go clubbing in Soho and Shoreditch until the early hours.'

The chief resists the urge to stick his tongue out at Anto. The PM says nothing.

'Look, it's not ideal but you can't always be gifted hookers or cocaine. It's how you spin it. He's still broken the Ministerial Code. And we really need to think about our MPs just now. You will always do better with them by showing strength rather than looking weak. And Vic stepping down is weak. Leave it with me?'

The PM stares at his desk and then gives an imperceptible nod.

'Well, who should we replace him with?' Anto rubs his hands together. He's not been part of a reshuffle yet and is rather looking forward to it.

'I have an idea for that too, actually,' the chief says, glad to get to the real point and pulling his phone out of his pocket.

The chief plays the video of Percy Cross from the night before, Anto tutting over the PM's shoulder.

'Are you mad?' Anto smirks, glad to score such an obvious point at last. 'You think we need *him* in government? Even without the fact that he has just written what he himself refers to as "a chub-a-chapter", the man sucks all available oxygen out of every room he walks into. And you talk about a sleaze-free run at a general election campaign? Hell-o? Have you forgotten why he had to resign as PM?'

'That is true, Nige,' the PM concedes, turning in his chair.

'Do you know how many hits that video has had so far today? Right now, the guy is popular and interesting – and with *young* people, amazingly – which is a hell of a lot more than can be said for any of the people we've just had to share an hour of our lives with next door. We need personality, remember? Listen.' He sits on a chair and cups his chin in his hands. 'The minute he attracts just a bit too much attention, we torch him, okay? And at this stage, what do we have to lose?'

'Isn't CDL quite an important role?' the PM asks vaguely. 'And a bit weird to give a key cabinet job to a peer, no?'

'Nah, plenty of precedent for lords having government jobs. We just get a minister to do stuff from the Commons when questions come up. And sure, CDL *can* be important. But we'll just strip out all the major stuff to other ministers. Someone energetic can take on national security, the budget, the Union and so on. Percy can swan about the TV studios and help us win the bloody election.'

'Why would he take it then?' Anto asks.

The chief has to acknowledge the reasonableness of this question. 'He may not. But it's campaigns he likes doing and if it's the election we point him at and the public we have him engaging with' – he leaves out the words 'in lieu of the PM having a personality' – 'then I reckon he'll be in.'

'We give him responsibility for the election campaign?' Anto asks quickly, anxious about sharing his new 'campaign director' title.

As predicted by Jake, the PM agreed that Anto could have a trial run at the local elections, which decide a chunk of the UK's councils, next month. Oblivious to much of the serious political discourse, partly because so many pundits overlook the importance of local elections, Anto hasn't understood what a hospital pass he has signed himself up for – and it hasn't occurred to anybody to set him straight.

Of the Tory MPs who have council seats up for election, most are expecting losses. Aside from bin collections and potholes and all the things most people actually notice in their daily lives, losing councillors also means losing people to knock on doors at the general election. Running a council is a paid job. So, if someone loses their seat – and therefore their job – in May, they're unlikely to feel particularly motivated to go out and help save someone else's seat – and job – later in the year.

'Are you fucking mad? Obviously not. Percy doesn't have your administrative skills, Anto.' The chief knows when to lay it on thick. 'So we get him out and about doing any stuff the PM can't or doesn't want to do. He'll do a better job than Nat on the CCHQ side of things. The members love him and he is good at communicating. And he knows his flaws. He'll bring in the right people to make him do a good job.'

There's another long pause, while the PM wonders if he can palm the TV debates off on Percy.

'Don't make me regret this.' The PM sighs and waves the chief away.

'Yes, Prime Minister. Anto, make sure Vic doesn't speak to the PM before I say so.'

'He's waiting outside, isn't he?' Anto says.

'He'll barge in if you try to tell him to come back later, so ...' The chief cracks open the door between the PM's office and the Cabinet Room. 'Look, nobody's in here. PM, you slip through the door at the end and into the garden. You can scoot up to the flat or round to the café for a cuppa. Then Vic will find the nest empty.'

The chief does a little bow and leaves. Before the door has closed, the chief is pulling his phone out of his pocket, ready to start a fire.

Ed Cooper answers on the first ring.

'Chief. To what do I owe this pleasure?'

'What are you working on just now?' the chief says, nodding to the custodian, who opens the front door for him to leave.

'This and that ... Why, got something good?'

'Depends if you want another scalp. A cabinet one. So' – the chief doesn't wait for a response. As if Ed Cooper, or any journalist, is going to hesitate to break a story that will take out a major player – 'I strongly recommend you start asking the Cabinet Office some questions about CDL's GCS car usage. See how you get on and let's speak again before this afternoon's lobby briefing.'

Claybourne Terrace

Percy leans back in his chair, breathing in the wonderful smell of home. Books and leather and the new scents that have arrived

70

over the past year to breathe life into the place: the binding florals of Holly's expensive perfume and Bobby's efforts in the little back garden; the trendy candles favoured by Eva and Jess's experiments in the kitchen. He's missed this while he's been away.

'Explain it to me again, Chief,' Percy says.

He can practically feel his pupils dilate as the chief whip explains once more the job the prime minister would like to offer him. Percy's conversation with Callum Gallagher in that Californian hotel bar was extraordinarily well timed, as he wouldn't have considered this a couple of weeks ago.

'CDL's a good one. And you really don't want me delivering anything on the government front?'

'Nah, not really. Maybe the odd speech or photo op, but we've got other people to do the heavy lifting on policy. It's more of a front-of-house-type job. We need a campaigner, mate.'

'Do I have to do a load of boring party stuff?'

'Nope. As chairman, and as a pin-up for the nutcase wing of the membership, Nat Weaver will do all that. You're our public person to help gear things up for the election. The new face of the operation. Well, the old new face.'

'And, uh, what about financial interests? It's delicate, of course, but I've only just got back in the black. Dual citizenship really screws me, you know. Double tax. I wonder sometimes about just giving the US one up ... Anyway, tell me the quid pro quo. What pro do I get for my quids? Or,' he smiles ruefully, 'my lack of them.'

'I can check with someone at the Cabinet Office about proprietary stuff, but I'm sure we can work something out.'

'Isn't Eric all uptight about sleaze again?' Percy thinks of the lines that have been coming out of Number Ten in recent days, courtesy of Nick O'Hara's advice at his final meeting in the PM's study. 'Won't he be a bit uptight about it all?'

'Well,' the chief says thoughtfully. 'What I would advise the prime minister is that earning outside money through book sales and so on isn't a problem, so long as you don't try to hide it. You know, sterilise with sunshine. What's wrong with you making legit money now? When you were PM, the issue with money was that you didn't have enough! In my experience – and I've made a hobby of political character studies – the MPs who are wealthy or are happy not being wealthy are kosher. It's the ones who aren't rich but wish to be who are corruptible and that's what leads to sleaze ...'

Percy looks at the chief carefully. 'You're a strange sort of man, aren't you.'

'Who wants to be normal?' The chief shrugs.

'Touché.'

'So, listen.' The chief checks his watch. 'Are you going to do this or what?'

Percy wants to bite his hand off, but he feels the need to call Cal and ask his advice first. Percy knows Cal, the almost prophetic Cal, will tell him if he is inadvertently walking into a trap.

'I could do with a bit of time to decide. When do you need to know by?'

'I've got something cooking which will break ...' The chief feels his phone buzz. Ed Cooper has published the story about CDL's government car usage: *It is understood that the prime minister is minded to ask for Victor Daniels to resign from his post while an investigation gets underway.* 'Right now. So we would like to announce it asap.'

Percy texts Cal.

Can you talk?

It reminds him of the texts he used to send his mistresses when Jenny checked his phone. Innocuous enough but, in their own way, needy. Those were the days.

Now there's a new fire in his belly. Since he left office, Percy has spent roughly one evening a month lying in the bath with a decanter of whisky, 'Nimrod' playing on his Alexa and his laptop sitting on the loo seat, set to a YouTube video of Winston Churchill's funeral. Tears stream down his face as he watches the cranes on the Thames lower in a strange mechanical bow of respect at the coffin, as it sails past on a barge. Percy once thought he might get the same kind of adulation at his own death, but his premiership knocked that on the head. Perhaps this is a second wind – a chance to go down in the history books as a great statesman after all.

Cal fires back immediately.

Yes.

'You're a busy man. Can you give me thirty minutes? You'll have an answer from me by the time you're back at Downing Street.'

The chief slaps his thighs and stands. 'Fair enough.'

As the chief walks to the front door, he glances into the kitchen where his eye catches a laundry rack decked out with dozens of pairs of bras and knickers in every imaginable colour and material. He pretends to be fastening his coat and spots a delicate mesh peach set, a black silk teddy, a Calvin Klein cotton thong and a scarlet lace suspender belt.

As he heads down the street, the chief whip tries to concentrate on what he needs to do next about this CDL situation, but despite his best efforts his mind keeps wandering back to the laundry rack and the question of what possibly belongs to Eva.

Blackheath

Ed Cooper can't sleep. He's had a decent amount to drink, which doesn't help, and he's been tossing and turning for over an hour.

Fresh off a huge scoop – it's not every day you get to break the news that a senior and very well-respected member of the cabinet has been fired for gross misconduct; the details about the special advisers using the government car to go clubbing, vomit-covered seats and all, has triggered a whole new wave of opinion pieces and podcast episodes about the murky role of SpAds – he has an inescapable bundle of pent-up, nervous energy. He texts Jess.

Are you awake?

He may as well sneak downstairs and enjoy a sexy back-and-forth. But her WhatsApp status shows she was last online at 11.30 p.m. and it's now past 1 a.m. She must be asleep.

Maybe it's just as well. Jess has scooped him on Victor Daniels's replacement, Percy Cross, and just thinking about her makes him feel irritable. Ed still can't really believe she tried to break things off, or that she threatened to reveal all to his wife. He can see the photos he's sent to Jess and would sooner die than have his family see them too. He'll squash Jess like a fly if he has to.

Ed rolls over, his face scrunched up, and spots his wife's bare shoulder.

'Are you awake?' he whispers, but she doesn't answer.

He suggestively rubs her back but she doesn't stir, completely out for the count.

He lies on his back, wondering how cross she will be if he wakes her up. After a while he slides his hands under the covers and starts thinking about what he'd like to do to Jess. After all, she can't stop him thinking what he wants. He smirks, picturing how indignant she would be if she knew what he was doing to her in his imagination. As he gets more excited, his thoughts grow increasingly more violent and degrading. Jess's insolent face makes him want to pin her down, choke her and feel her fight against him. He'd fucking teach her a lesson.

Mrs Cooper continues to lie perfectly still, her eyes wide open, listening to the rhythmic rustling from her husband's side of the duvet. She hears him finish and realises that she'll have to change the sheets tomorrow, but it's a small price to pay.

9th April

Westminster

At 9 a.m., Percy steps proudly into his Cabinet Office car and heads to Whitehall. When he arrives, the crush of photographers relents to give him a small amount of space to walk into the building. He can't resist turning to smile and wave when he reaches the top step. His protection officers are back in their suits.

From the moment he finished his call with Cal ('Go for it, Perce – but try not to fuck it up this time'), Percy has been bouncing on the balls of his feet. Last night he was bundled in to meet the prime minister in private, then the announcement was made, at Percy's insistence, to Jess at the *Sentinel*, then Chris Mason at the BBC. Every newspaper has carried his return to government on the front page, with headlines ranging from *The Curse of Perce is lifted!* in the *Express* to *PM has heavy Cross to bear* in the *Mirror*.

MPs are largely divided by the new appointment. Plenty are angry – Vic Daniels has done his best to assert that he's been stitched up after he intended to announce he was standing down and his friends are furiously trying to get journalists interested in the story; a plum cabinet job has gone to a member of the House of Lords instead of a talented MP and the young thrusters on the green benches feel put out; everyone has been parroting lines on standards in public life for days and Percy Cross, aka Prime Sinister, has been brought back into the fold to confuse the message.

Still, shock and some elation overrides all of this with each and every one of them wondering – including the PM's enemies – if this new appointment, in its sheer weirdness, might just be a stroke of genius. This sense increases that evening when Percy, after a busy first day of inventing nicknames for each of the civil servants in his private office and arranging lunches with every conceivable newspaper editor, speaks at the 1922 Committee meeting of Conservative MPs.

'Let's face facts, I'm no good to you on policies or governing ...' He shrugs self-deprecatingly. 'You chaps – and chapesses – have all that in spadefuls. And you're no doubt wondering why one of you isn't doing this job with that in mind. But,' Percy raises his voice at the mutterings of agreement, 'my job isn't to do any of that. I'm here, quite simply, to keep you fine folks in your seats for another five years – at least. I'm here to win you the next general election.'

'My lord,' someone Percy doesn't recognise shouts from the back, putting emphasis on the word 'lord'. 'This hardly sounds like a government role that benefits the country. Surely campaigning is a job you could be doing in your spare time anyway? The public simply won't swallow this.'

'Ah, that's where you're wrong.' Percy puts his hands on his hips and stands with his feet apart. He feels like he's back at the Oxford Union. 'You see, it's my belief that keeping this party in government for as long as possible is what benefits the country.' A few murmurs of agreement. 'While my cabinet colleagues are doing a phenomenal job, they need more time and space to complete their missions set by our fine prime minister. I therefore see my job as buying them time, long term. And in the short term, I will buy them space. I'll shelter them from the blows of the hurly-burly news cycle. I'll be doing the media rounds and on the road doing the nonsensical visits that clog up their diaries. I'll ... I'll come and speak in each and every one of your seats, raffling off bottles of whisky and locks of my own hair if necessary.'

The rumble of approval that has been building up explodes in peals of laughter.

'So, listen.' Percy waves his hands for quiet. 'Let me do this. Let me serve you. Let me win. Let *you* win, more importantly.' More shouts of approval. He raises his voice and holds his right hand, fist clenched, with his left. 'You think the public won't swallow this? They won't get a chance to chew.'

The room fills with the deafening sound of hands slamming on desks. It doesn't occur to anyone present that, as a peer in the House of Lords, Percy isn't even eligible to vote at the general election.

Claybourne Terrace

'Dad, do you really think the mic drop was necessary?' Eva asks, when the residents of Claybourne Terrace sit down for dinner that night.

'A mic drop, Percy? What year do you think it is?' Jess shakes her head over her meatballs.

'Girls, girls.' Percy laughs. 'MPs love that sort of thing,

okay? I'm actually quite impressed so many of them got it. You normally need pop-culture references to be as dated as *Yes, Minister* and as offensive as *Little Britain.*'

'Well, Moira said the atmosphere was great,' Bobby says quietly. 'Sounds like you really turned the room around.'

'Well done, babe.' Holly plops a helping of goji-berry salad onto Percy's plate.

'Yeah, well done, Dad. Of course. But,' Eva shifts uncomfortably in her seat, 'why are you doing this? Your book's doing okay and you're enjoying the Lords . . . I thought you were done with politics?'

'Oh, pork chop.' Percy looks pityingly at his daughter, then sighs and spreads his hands. 'We all say we're done with politics but nobody ever really means it. Life is one huge rat race. And politics? Well, that's some pretty fun rats.'

'Have you thought about who your SpAds will be?' Jess asks. 'I assume you're entitled to two. One for media, one for policy,' she says to Holly's questioning look.

'Not really.' Percy yawns. But in truth, he has given this a good deal of thought. He just doesn't feel ready to talk about it, not least with a journalist at the table. He trusts Jess completely but the adviser he has in mind would undoubtedly smash the firewall she has created between work and home. It is just an adviser, singular. There's nobody he can think of in the wonk world that he hasn't burnt all his bridges with. Percy's idea for his media SpAd is someone strategic and, to their core, political – and they're in the market for something new and interesting.

'Hey, are you feeling okay?' Holly's voice cuts into his thoughts, but she's directing her question at Bobby, who looks slightly grey.

'She's been dicey for a few days,' Eva says, while Bobby sips on a Diet Coke. 'A bunch of bugs around so guess it's one of those gastric flu things. And she has her PAB soon . . . '

Again, Eva feels that familiar pinch of envy. The question of why nobody has asked her to stand for a seat preoccupies her more every day. Not that she even wants one. But it's nice to be asked.

'It's so annoying,' Bobby says. 'Just comes in waves. Fine one minute and rotten the next.'

'You poor thing.' Holly rubs her shoulder. 'I've got some great herbal teas. Ginger is good if you feel nauseous. Let me make you some to take to bed.'

'Thanks,' Bobby says. 'I think it's just the stress of this MP stuff, you know? It's really exciting but there's just so much to prepare. And all that on top of the day job . . .'

'Get used to it, Bobcat,' Percy says. 'Once you're an MP you'll find there's a load of stuff – unpaid stuff – you do in addition to the day job. Stomach ulcers become the norm.'

'Don't scare her, Dad.' Eva wags her finger. 'Besides, that's rich coming from you. You've just talked yourself into a day non-job!'

Percy roars with laughter. 'That reminds me. I've got to slip out for a bit. Meeting this chap Anto Spiteri for a drink at his private members' club. PM's chief of staff. Do you know him?'

'I've met him,' Eva replies coolly.

'Thoughts?'

Eva wrinkles her nose. 'I don't want to prejudice you.'

'Aha.' Percy rises from the table, rubbing his hands. 'He's volunteered to give me tips on how to handle Nat Weaver, who I'm going to try to woo over breakfast tomorrow.'

'Breakfast? Babe, that's a bit unfriendly, isn't it?' Holly says over her shoulder, pouring hot water into a mug.

'Darling, old Natski is handsy at the best of times, so I don't want her any more lubricated than she is over black coffee and orange juice.'

'It's true.' Eva nods. She turns to her father. 'I don't know where you're taking her but it can't be the Wolseley. She's banned.'

'For breakfast?'

'Allegedly it's her in *Crash*. You know, the unidentified lady member spotted giving a donor a handjob under the table.'

'Well then.' Percy straightens his tie. 'Anto has a high bar to reach.'

After dinner, Jess heads to her room and lies on her bed. She's too tired to go to her fetish club. In fact, now that she finds Ed's messages so off-putting, getting her kicks from subversion has, for the time being, lost its appeal. She needs something, though, to keep her entertained.

She pulls out her phone and looks around at the different apps. No, Tinder or Bumble or Hinge won't work. Jess can't risk being clocked by – or worse, match with – someone connected to SW1. And she doesn't have time to go bar-hopping – to say nothing of the fact that she wouldn't want to bring a total stranger to Claybourne Terrace. Imagine the awkward questions if they bump into Percy? And going to a complete stranger's home isn't without risk.

Jess has just about given up when an advert pops up: *Fawn – the dating app for those who are shy in the streets and demons in the sheets. And always discreet.* She clicks on the link. The app could be tailored for her. It's a hookup app – strictly hookups – for people who need that instant fix with guaranteed discretion. You even sign an NDA to join.

She thinks carefully, trying to see any pitfalls, then signs up with her middle name, Amy. Users are recommended to use a photo on their profile that gives a sense of who they are and what they look like, while distorting recognisable features. Jess decides to go for her best feature, simply pulling down her jeans and photographing her lace-G-stringed arse.

Within seconds Jess is pulled into a whole new world and it isn't long before she's exchanging flirty messages with a fun guy just a couple of miles away . . .

10th April

Con 25% Lab 43%

Odds Shorten on Summer Election/

Wildfires in Australia

Pimlico

Bobby looks around the GP waiting room, her hands twitching nervously in her lap. She's glad her appointment is first thing in the morning; the surgery is already filling up. A harried woman in her fifties is speaking to the receptionist, gesturing to a man in his eighties, who Bobby takes to be the woman's father, coughing into a John le Carré. There is a play area where a crying, snotty toddler is smashing a plastic telephone into the bookshelf, colourful children's stories flying everywhere. The little boy's mother looks exhausted.

Bobby tries to concentrate on her notebook – she is making herself another to-do list of everything Moira's office needs to sort out – but the combination of nausea and toy-smashing and guilt makes it hard to focus. Especially the guilt. There are unwell children and old people in need of care and here she is, taking up a valuable appointment just because she feels a bit sick.

She is staring into space, wondering whether she should have persevered with Holly's herbal remedies a bit longer, when a middle-aged man pops his head out from behind a door and calls her name. She puts her notebook back into her bag and walks a little unsteadily over to him.

'Hi, Roberta,' the doctor says, closing the door to the waiting room and sitting down.

'Hi, Doctor. Thanks for seeing me. Although I actually go by Bobby, if that's okay.'

'Fine. So, Bobby, what seems to be the problem?'

'Well, I keep having these bouts of nausea. Been happening for about a week now. I feel absolutely fine and then dreadful. I thought it would go away but it hasn't. And I feel really tired all the time.'

'I see.'

'Look, I don't want to waste your time, but I've not been feeling great and this tiredness just doesn't feel right. Maybe it's a weird bug? I've been quite stressed out lately, so I wonder if it's that.'

'Could be.' The doctor slips his glasses up his nose. 'First things first, let's do the easy stuff and see what we can rule out, starting with a urine sample. Infections can make you feel very poorly and tired so it could be a UTI or something.'

Bobby takes a plastic cup to the loo and returns a couple of minutes later, her sleeve pulled down to shield the residents of the waiting room from its contents. She notices the toddler is still wailing, no mean feat with the leg of a mucky soft toy jammed in his mouth.

'Okey-dokey,' the doctor says. 'Pop that there and make yourself comfortable.'

Bobby's so tired that she lies down on the bed, wondering

for the dozenth time whether she's making a fuss. The doctor begins to lower different strips of paper into the cup.

'Hm, I wonder . . . I'm just going to try something . . . '

Bobby looks at the ceiling. She was hoping the GP would have an easy and obvious answer right away. If she could just have something to stop feeling sick, she'd be happy.

'Bobby, can I ask . . . Are you aware that you're pregnant?'

'What?' Bobby sits up. 'Are you sure?'

'Very.' The doctor gives her a thin smile.

'Fuck . . . ' Bobby whispers.

The doctor doesn't say anything.

Bobby thinks hard. Did she have a period this month? She can't remember. She wants to cry at her stupidity, panic rising in her chest. Twenty-five years old and it doesn't occur to her to write her periods down, so that when she feels sick and has missed one, there is an obvious answer that doesn't require her embarrassing herself in front of a man her father's age. And wasting everybody's time.

'I'm sure this is a lot to take in,' the doctor says kindly, sitting on his chair and leaning forward so his elbows are on his knees.

'Do you know how . . . how far along I am?' Bobby hears herself ask, looking at her feet, which are dangling pointlessly off the bed. They work out the date of her last period.

'So about four weeks. Now . . . ' The doctor studies her face. 'You have lots of options.'

'Uh-huh. Well, thank you, Doctor.' Bobby slides off the bed and pulls on her coat. She has no idea what she should be doing. 'I, um, what happens next? Do I need to scan it or . . . ?'

'Take a breath. Just think about what you want to happen next.'

'Yes. Great. You're right. I think I need to speak to . . . somebody.'

'All right. Take care of yourself, Bobby.' He hands her a few pamphlets. 'Call the surgery whenever you need.'

Bobby steps out into the waiting room, where the toddler is now screaming at the sock he has pulled off his own foot. His mother has tried to placate him with a banana, which he has mashed to a pulp in his free hand. Bobby exits the building as fast as she can, the exact frequency at which the toddler's cries are pitched seeming to run through her like electric shocks.

She stumbles into the street and pulls her phone out of her pocket, weighing up what to do. Should she call Jake first? Or her mum? Or the girls? What does she even want to happen? It's hardly a convenient time to have a baby. She's twenty-five. She's only been with Jake for a year. She's just decided to become an MP. And yet, she wonders, what if . . .

She stands in the street, paralysed, when her mind is made up for her by a message popping up on the WhatsApp group she shares with Jess and Eva.

Jess: *How was the doc, Bob?*

Eva: *We're both still at home if you want some brekkie.*

Bobby looks at the time. Just gone 9 a.m. The GP surgery is only a couple of streets over from Claybourne Terrace. Her tummy rumbles. Now she understands that her nausea isn't from food poisoning or a bug, she feels ready to eat. She definitely wants some breakfast.

Bobby: *See you in a minute.*

Claybourne Terrace

'So, how did it go?' Jess asks, plopping some boiled eggs into egg cups. Bobby and Eva help themselves and start slicing their buttered toast into soldiers.

'Well.' Bobby thwacks the top off her egg. 'I'm pregnant.'

86

'*What?*' Eva gasps, tea spurting from her mouth.

'How?' Jess sits down, dazed. 'I mean … don't you use protection?'

'I, uh …' Bobby has to fight back the urge to laugh. What she's about to say sounds ridiculous. 'No.'

'WHAT?' Eva's hands slap to her cheeks. 'What have you been doing?'

'I …' Bobby does laugh now. She can't help it. 'I just haven't got round to sorting it out. So we … we pull out.'

'Pull out …' Eva whispers. 'Bob, you're one of the most organised and responsible people I know. What the fuck, dude?'

Bobby is still laughing. 'I know … it's so stupid when I hear myself say it out loud.'

'Okay, well, let's not dwell on the how.' Jess puts her hand on Eva's arm. Bobby's hysterical laughter is not what she was expecting and she's concerned that if Eva pushes her too far, she'll blow up. 'Let's think of the what. Specifically, what does Jake think?'

'I haven't told him yet,' Bobby says, her laughter suddenly killed.

'Hm.' Jess frowns. 'How many weeks?'

'Four.'

'Phew. Okay, well, you've got a lot of options. You can do the pills at home at this stage. Or go to a clinic. Or go to a hospital. The main thing is,' Jess holds Bobby's hand and Eva takes the other one, 'we're here for you, okay? It's going to be fine.'

Bobby looks from Jess to Eva, wishing she had told Jake before her friends. Abortion hasn't even occurred to her. It's something she never thought she'd have to consider. But Jess is there straightaway. Bobby's reminded of how she felt a year ago, like she is considerably younger and less experienced than her two friends.

'But I'm not sure I want to go down that road …'

'Wow, okay.' Jess raises an eyebrow. Without thinking, her thoughts pour out of her. 'Are you sure you don't even want to consider it? I mean ... you have this MP stuff coming up and being pregnant, having a baby ... it'll make things much harder careerwise.'

Bobby frowns.

'But I don't think about everything careerwise first, Jess. I know lots of people in politics and journalism have some blind ambition' – she leaves out 'like you' – 'but I come at things the other way. I'm just interested in representing my local area. If they don't want me for any reason, that's fine. But I don't see why it would put me off having a child.'

'But you're only twenty-five!' Jess replies, trying to sound as gentle as possible. She feels this curious responsibility to stop Bobby from making a terrible mistake. 'Whichever way you look at it, this will have a huge impact on your life. I mean, do you think Jake is going to be putting his prospects on the back burner?'

'Oh, shut up, Jess,' Bobby snaps. 'You don't know what you're talking about. You've never even had a boyfriend, so what would you know about what Jake would do? Jesus, I wish I hadn't said anything to you about this. I should have known you'd try to smother me with faux-feminist, girl-boss nonsense. Not everyone thinks their career is the most important thing, you know.'

Jess stares at Bobby as though she's slapped her. Bobby isn't wrong – Jess hasn't ever had a boyfriend. But she's never had it thrown in her face like this. Anyway, she was only trying to help, especially with her own career under threat.

'Listen.' Eva coughs, keen to head this off before Bobby and Jess have a proper fight. The pair of them turn to face her, as though they've forgotten she's there. 'I think we're all just in shock, aren't we. And ... and we all have different priorities.

Maybe you should give Jake a call, Bob. Obviously we're going to support you whatever, all right?'

Jess blinks. 'Yeah. Yeah, of course we are,' she murmurs.

'Thanks.' Bobby breathes heavily, avoiding Jess's eye. 'You're right. I'm going to give Jake a ring. See if he can meet me.'

'Okay. Good luck, babe.'

As she walks up the stairs, Bobby can hear Jess hiss in hushed whispers to Eva. She catches 'been on the pill since I was sixteen' and 'didn't have Jake down as one of those "I just hate condoms" guys' as she closes the door to her room. She texts Jake an SOS and, while she waits for a reply, hears chairs scraping on the kitchen floor and the front door open. Bobby's alone, for now.

Conservative Campaign Headquarters

'Okay, chaps, we have just over three weeks to go and Labour are nearly twenty points ahead of us,' Percy says to the group assembled around the table. 'Blow me away.'

He is at CCHQ with Anto, Natasha Weaver and the assorted members of the campaign team to hear a presentation on the May local elections, hoping to be reassured that it won't be a complete washout. Last night's drink with Anto and this morning's breakfast with Weaver were identical for Percy in a few regards: the long-windedness of the conversations, the obsequious, clumsy effort to flatter him and the conclusion that neither Anto nor Weaver really have a clue what they're doing. Running a proper campaign is just fundamentally different from anything either of them have ever done before.

Anto kept talking about the businesspeople and celebrities he could probably get to do endorsements – 'you know, like Oprah advocating Obama' – until Percy got tired and pointed out that the residents of Stoke-on-Trent Central are hardly going to care about whether their bin collection is run by a council championed by the runner-up from *I'm a Celebrity*. Weaver, meanwhile, wanted to get Percy on board for a 'Chairman's Champs' group, which would involve Weaver handpicking a selection of donors for monthly piss-ups at a private members' club in Mayfair, the proceeds of which would be split between the party coffers and what is clearly Weaver's own private war chest for another leadership bid when Eric Courtenay is surely booted out after losing the general election.

Percy glances from Anto to Weaver now. *By all means be contemptible. But be useful, too.*

'Okay.' A young man in glasses clears his throat. 'Perhaps I could take you through our polling first, to give you a sense of where we are?'

'Sure.' Percy folds his hands on the table. 'Opposition stuff? Dirty dossiers and so on?'

'No, just polling and focus groups. My colleague,' the young man points to an even younger man next to him, who nods at Percy, 'does all the attack stuff with the press team.'

Percy nods back. 'Take it away . . . '

They run over the same data the prime minister saw a few days before. Percy has already heard it, having been briefed by the chief when he took on the CDL job, but he wants to hear it from the team. Without Nick to guide them, he wonders how the young group will fare.

The first young man presents the data well. What makes Percy really sit up is how he analyses it, seeing an opportunity to attack John Ramsey's 'safe pair of hands – not the same old pair of hands' image as undynamic and maybe even damaging. The second young man follows up with a series of Ramsey's past views, which fly in the face of much of what he says now.

Percy smells a flip-flopper, and a dull one at that. His favourite kind of opponent.

Next, Percy asks to hear about the overall campaign strategy and messaging for the locals. Anto steps in.

'Well, I think I'm best to tell you about that, but I'm not quite ready for the big reveal.'

'When will you be ready?' Percy asks. 'Surely people are casting postal votes in a couple of weeks.'

'I only need a few more days, just to put some finishing touches to it.' Anto smiles greasily.

Weaver pipes up. 'Well, Anto, we really need to crack open the bonnet, get into the weeds and see what's really going on here ...'

It's a classic Weaverism, used in meetings to seem like she's contributing without really saying anything.

'Uh-huh,' Percy murmurs. No help is better than this. 'Okay, let's talk some more about the attack lines. This is great stuff ...'

Half an hour later, Percy stomps out of CCHQ feeling irritable. They're young and they're good, but they aren't being managed. They need a proper campaign director at the helm. What can Percy do? As he wondered after breakfast with Weaver, her pudgy little hand on his knee the whole time, eating her kedgeree one-handed, are Number Ten expecting him to work miracles this close to D-Day? He might just put in a few calls to the papers to firmly distance himself from this imminent disaster.

Soho

Eva ducks into the small Italian restaurant and immediately spots Jamie.

'Well, this is romantic,' he says with a grin. 'We've not had a last-minute lunch for ages. And not far from yours – I've cleared my afternoon for some top-level shagging . . .'

'Ah, that sounds fun but I'm afraid I can't stay for long. I just wanted to run something by you.'

'Gosh, okay. Why the urgency?'

Eva has been fizzing all morning, hit strangely by Bobby's pregnancy news. On the one hand, it means nothing. But on the other, her competitive streak – egged on by her father's renewed interest in politics – has been firmly woken up. She's got her wits about her enough to use birth control, for Christ's sake, so why isn't she being approached to become an MP too? So, crying off her meetings with the whips and feeling the need for the sharpest possible advice, Eva headed straight over to the Number Ten flat for a chat with Clarissa Courtenay.

'Finally.' Clarissa sighed. 'I wondered when you'd get to this. Of course you should stand. I mean, honestly – if Eric can be prime minister, then the sky's the limit. Now, let's line up our ducks. You aren't married, are you, so tell me about this boyfriend.'

'What about him?'

'What does he do . . . will he support you . . . are we likely to hear wedding bells anytime soon? If he's an asset, you should use him. It's very handy to have someone to help charm the old biddies from the associations, which is crucial to getting selected. What's his name?'

'Jamie Whitmore. He works in finance. I . . . I don't think marriage is on the cards.' Eva knew as she spoke that it definitely never would be. She loved Jamie, but increasingly in the way that she loved buttery baked potatoes on a cold day. Comfort food, not something enticing that got her mouth watering. Her heart sank at the idea of the real work being to charm old biddies. Was that really what it came down to? 'And as for being supportive, he has been great so far but he might be taken aback by this. I've never given him the impression I'd like to be an MP before.'

'Well, if he's up for it, he sounds like a definite plus point.' Clarissa scrolled through Jamie's LinkedIn page. 'Works for Jeremy Spears, that wealthy party donor, so money won't be a problem. Good-looking and presentable. I'd sound him out asap. You need him fully on board – or out of the picture altogether.'

Clarissa had lost interest in political scheming – perhaps finally learning her lesson. Her long chat with Nick O'Hara had got her thinking about a whole new rebrand. Something admirable and international. She'd got feelers out with the likes of Hillary Clinton and Angelina Jolie. Some serious humanitarian awareness-raising could be just the ticket, either to pull her back as an asset to Eric, or to launch Clarissa herself as a proper name in her own right. She was only bothering to advise Eva because everyone else had gone out of their way to give Clarissa a wide berth post-David Coker, while Eva had remained kind. Plus it couldn't hurt to have one future star of the party in her debt should Clarissa need a favour in a few years' time.

'Eva?' Jamie takes her hand and snaps her back into the restaurant.

'Sorry. So ...' Eva takes a deep breath. 'I wondered how you'd feel about me becoming an MP?'

Jamie's grip slackens.

'But, Eva, you've always said you'd hate to be an MP ...'

'Well, perhaps I've changed my mind. And I want to know what you think. Are you up for it?'

'What do you mean "up for it"?' *Maybe it runs in the family,* Jamie thinks as he sits back in his chair. 'Am I up for the scrutiny and harassment and even less of your time? You know

I've always supported your career but I never thought it would come to this.'

'What did you think it would come to?' Eva can tell Jamie isn't on board – and senses a perfect opportunity to end things altogether. She's been searching for quite some time for a way to break up with him where she doesn't come off as the villain to their circle of West London friends. To be unsupportive of her career in the 2020s? She knows she can win that PR war if it comes to it.

'Honestly, I suppose I thought you'd keep mucking about in Parliament until the election and then, if the Tories win you'll keep at it for a while and, if they lose,' Jamie decides to leave out *which seems more likely*, 'then you'd get a more reliable job in the private sector somewhere. You're very employable.'

'Oh, *am* I?' Eva folds her arms. 'Despite just mucking about in Parliament?'

'That's not what I'm saying. I just thought our future to-gether would see you a bit more settled, particularly if we have children. Maybe moving out of London. A commute to Parliament will be tough then. I'll earn enough so you won't have to work ...'

Eva stares at him. Has Jamie simply been counting on poli-tics to keep her busy for the time being, an interesting hostess at dinner parties with his City friends? She has always said she would support him when the going got tough in his career, but it has never occurred to her that Jamie wouldn't settle for win-ning Best Supporting Actor for the biopic about her life: *Eva*. She feels righteous about what she's about to do.

'Do you even know what you're saying?' She fights to keep her voice steady. 'You sound straight from the 1950s. You don't think my career matters and you've only supported me with a view to having me being a good little wifey one day.'

94

Eva jumps up from the table and marches to the door of the restaurant, a little dramatic flair suddenly coming to her.

'I never want to see you again!' she shouts, bounding out into the street, feeling free.

Claybourne Terrace

Jake and Bobby gaze at each other for a long time.

'Are you sure?' Bobby asks again. 'You aren't just saying it?'

'I'm completely sure,' Jake says, beaming. 'I mean, we aren't *that* young. I'm thirty. And my parents had me at about your age.'

'Mine too.' Bobby's allowing herself to get excited. They've been talking all day, first in her bedroom and then walking aimlessly around the neighbourhood. Over lunch and countless cups of tea (which Bobby changed to decaf halfway through) they've reached a decision.

Now, back in Bobby's room, they are lying down on the bed and talking quietly about their excitement and joy and surprise. Then Bobby's phone rings.

'Hello?'

'Hi, it's Jackie from the candidates department at CCHQ. Listen, I know you weren't due until next week but we have had a slot open up for a PAB tomorrow. I'm ringing to see if you can take it.'

'Oh, w-well ...' Bobby stammers. The Parliamentary Assessment Board – the first step she must complete to become an MP.

'I'll level with you – I'm not sure how many more we'll have before the May elections. And if you really are interested in Tipperton, the selection will go ahead as soon as the boundaries are passed. Sorry if you have plans, dear, but I'd go ahead and cancel them.'

'Right. Okay. Just a moment.' Bobby presses the phone to her chest and whispers to Jake about what is happening.

'Why not?' Jake whispers. 'It's only the PAB. Not a life sentence.'

Bobby nods. It's true – and she probably won't even pass. She may as well see where this takes her.

'Yes, please, Jackie. I'll be there. Thanks very much for giving me the opportunity.'

Once she's hung up, Bobby looks at Jake and instinctively puts a hand over her tummy.

'Do you think I should tell anyone about this?'

Jake looks at her steadily. 'Honestly? No. For starters, you're only at four weeks. Don't a lot of people wait a while in case something happens ...?' He frowns. 'And then, like I said, this is only the PAB. You're just exploring your options. You don't have to tell anyone anything. You don't even have to run if you don't want to later down the line.'

Bobby nods slowly. What Jess said is right, though. If she does get to the seat selection stage, is it likely a Conservative Association is going to pick a pregnant, unmarried twenty-five year old as their prospective candidate? She looks a step further. Will the constituency elect her? Polling day has to happen by January. She'll either already have the baby or be on the cusp of giving birth by then.

'What are you counting?' Jake asks, looking at her tapping her fingers.

'Weeks. I'm due just before Christmas. So if I get selected, and if the general election is this winter, it won't exactly be a secret that I'm pregnant.'

'One step at a time, okay? Who knows when the election will be ... A Christmas baby, though. Pretty cool ...' Jake hugs her and Bobby nestles into him. 'It'll be all right.'

They hear the front door open and Eva and Jess chatting animatedly.

'Helloooo?' Eva calls up the stairs.

'Shall we?' Jake turns to the door and offers Bobby his hand.

Feeling suddenly nervous, Bobby grips him tightly.

They join Eva and Jess, who are sitting at the kitchen table with a bottle of wine, in deep discussion about Eva's break-up with Jamie.

'When it really comes down to it, I wasn't even looking forward to seeing him any more. He's a lovely guy but ... urgh, you should have heard how he was talking!' Eva clinks glasses with Jess.

Jake coughs and the girls look up.

'Well ... ' Bobby looks from one to the other. 'We've decided to become parents.'

There's a second or two of silent astonishment, then Eva jumps up and pulls Jake and Bobby in for a hug. Jess rather reluctantly joins them.

'Fuck me,' Jess says, struggling to sound enthusiastic. 'This is ... great!'

When they've pulled away and are sitting down, Eva shakes her head in disbelief.

'You know, I really thought we had a few more years in the tank before we went from "Oh my *God*! You're *pregnant?*",' she gives a look of faux horror, 'to "Oh my God! You're pregnaaant!"' She presses her hands over her heart.

'Yeah, it's pretty crazy,' Bobby concedes.

Jess can feel Bobby's eyes on her as she tries to act as positive as possible. If only she'd kept her trap shut instead of starting that stupid fight earlier. Even if there was someone she wanted a family with, Jess has always been certain that her career comes first (assuming Ed Cooper hasn't burned hers to the ground). Then relationships. Then babies – maybe. It's the obvious order of things. Bobby clearly disagrees. So where does this leave them?

'Have you told your mum yet? What did she say?' Eva asks, picturing the expression on her own mother's face if she told her she was expecting a baby. She reckons her dad probably wouldn't bat an eyelid.

'We haven't told her yet.' Bobby feels a little flutter of panic. 'Or Jake's parents. We only found out today, after all. But we'll do it later. Actually ... I kind of need you guys to keep this under your hats for a while. A lot can go wrong in the first trimester so this might come to nothing.'

'Yeah. We could really do with a bit of time to work out stuff before it's out there, anyway.' Jake says. 'Starting with Bobby's PAB tomorrow.'

'Shit! That's tomorrow?' Eva cries. Everything is moving so fast. Bobby has a PAB and a baby on the way. Eva's single and seatless.

'Yeah, I have a last-minute slot. Do you think I should mention ... this?' Bobby points at herself.

'Fuck, no,' Jess says quickly. Then, seeing the others looking surprised, she tries to soften her voice. 'I mean, there's no need. Not yet.'

'Yeah,' Eva agrees, trying to sound upbeat. 'I don't want to panic you, Bob, but I've heard some bad stories about women applying for seats and being turned over because they're even considering kids at some point, or are "childbearing age", let alone actually pregnant. We should keep this under wraps for as long as possible.'

'Isn't that dishonest?' Bobby asks, a little balloon of panic inflating in her chest.

'This is politics, babe.' Eva grins. 'You won't be accused of lying for what you aren't saying ...'

At 6 p.m., the residents of Claybourne Terrace gather in the living room with Jake to drill Bobby with PAB questions.

Percy, though in many ways the most qualified, is the least helpful. He keeps insisting that 'gags' are what really matter over policy or ideology and treats the whole session as a joke. Leaving his ministerial red box unopened, he eventually turns on *The West Wing* and screams with laughter at the earnest politicking, occasionally bellowing things like 'Oh, you silly sod! It's all very well saying that now, but you have no idea what a tit you'll look when there's an inquiry about this!'

Eva and Jess aren't a whole lot better, getting into scraps about how Bobby should deliver a particular line to take. They're both ratty, Eva feeling jealous about Bobby's big day of life progress and Jess stewing with regret about what she said to Bobby this morning.

Worry means nobody sleeps well – Bobby with nerves for her PAB; Eva with her sense of immense urgency about where her life is going; Jess with her complete disbelief that one of her best friends will be a mother by the end of the year, and the annoying buzz of messages from Ed, who still dangles her future at StoryCorps before her; Percy with his concern that his rehabilitated image might be crushed within weeks, and Holly with her horrified shock that Percy hasn't initiated sex and, still worse, wearily declines her offer for the first time since she's met him.

11th April

CON 24% LAB 43%

AVERAGE AMBULANCE WAIT 50 MINS/

STORMS HIT NEW YORK

Claybourne Terrace

The following evening, Bobby, Eva and Percy sit down to a wonderful dinner in the kitchen prepared by Jess and Holly. Everyone seems determined to be cheerful. Holly has laid the table with the best dinnerware she could find and Jess, buoyed up by a rendezvous she has planned via the Fawn app later, has bought most of Waitrose, including canapés to keep everyone going while she finishes making her lamb tagine and moussaka. She's hoping to make amends with Bobby before she heads out. Eva has cheered herself up by buying a selection of self-help books and aspirational autobiographies, and Holly, wearing a full set of lacy pink underwear under her charcoal wool Celine dress, is looking forward to rousing Percy back into action at bedtime.

Percy has spent a good deal of the day scheming with the

chief whip about the future and can feel some semblance of a plan coming together. Plus he's got his pick for media SpAd agreed by the Cabinet Office.

He sips on his vodka and tonic, which Bobby has prepared so Percy and Holly don't notice she just has tonic, and regales the kitchen with a recent sighting of Lord Daly, formerly Simon Daly MP, Bobby's disgraced ex-boss.

'Apparently he was mooching around Annabel's at midnight, trying to get any surrounding young women to join him by buying magnums of champagne. Guess that podcast thing is paying quite well . . .'

The girls groan. In a surprising and deeply irritating development, Simon Daly is now one half of a new hit podcast about politics, where he styles himself as a centrist man with big ideas. He and his ex-Labour counterpart rattle off their critiques of current politics – without a word on their own failings, of course – in front of huge live audiences, who have bought into the supposed 'frenemy' relationship.

'Alas, if only he were still an MP. Truly a great talent taken from us too soon . . .' Eva makes a gagging motion.

'Just goes to show,' Jess says with a snort. 'You can literally be outed as a sex pest but, far from a prison cell, if you've got the right mates in the right places, you're golden . . . How can everyone's collective memory be this short?'

Bobby talks through how her day has gone at the Parliamentary Assessment Board, starting with a psychometric test – 'What a good idea. Might have rooted out some nutters in my day,' Percy interjects – and followed by a series of exercises and challenges, some in groups, designed to work out who has the makings of a quality MP. Following Eva's advice to hit the right sort of mature Thatcherite tone, Bobby wore a navy-blue midi dress, the kind of low heels favoured by BA cabin crew, Eva's pearl earrings and, of course, the obligatory flesh-coloured tights. Although she didn't have many years of dedicated service to the party, her backstory was so strong – running a local then national campaign on mental health, parents with public sector backgrounds and a Cambridge University degree – that the assessors seemed impressed.

'Dad, is it true you've picked a media SpAd? Seen some chat about it on *Crash* today,' Eva asks, keen to talk about something else.

Percy draws himself up. 'As a matter of fact, I have. Tell me, have you girls heard of Teddy Hammer?'

'You're joking!' Jess cries.

'Am not. Don't you think it's a master stroke?'

'It's brilliant,' Jess says. 'I just can't believe it. I never thought he'd ... well, go to the dark side.' She wonders whether this means Teddy will tell her more about his theory on why Ed holds such influence over Lord Finlayson. And does this mean she'll now have him as an adversary, protecting the government when she comes knocking with a story?

'Wants to try something new.' Percy decides to leave out their gentleman's agreement that he's allowing Teddy full access for the book he wants to write, chronicling the next year or so.

'When is it public? I mean ... how do you feel about me scooping it?' Jess asks slyly.

'Yes, go for it. I know Teddy likes you and he's already told his freelance people, so fire away.' Percy stretches his hands behind his head, looking smug. Jess blows a kiss and immediately pulls out her phone. 'I can't wait, you know. We had a lot of fun, back in the day. Lots of business together.'

'Well, I smell trouble,' says Eva, thinking about what Anto has coming for him.

South London

Jess has done her usual routine of heading up to bed with everyone else. But instead of donning pyjamas and night cream after her shower, she brushes her teeth, puts on clean underwear and pulls her jeans and sweater back on. No need for fancy outfits or seduction techniques. Her Fawn subscription is just to satisfy her immediate needs: in and out, so to speak. Home in time for a decent kip.

On her way downstairs, she slips a note under Bobby's bedroom door, apologising for their row, explaining how she meant well with what she said and reiterating her full support – including future babysitting duties.

She slips out of Claybourne Terrace, being careful to check the front door alarm before she goes, and messages J, the letter her liaison on Fawn identifies himself by, to let him know she's on her way. Jess considers texting Eva and Bobby to let them know where she's gone, but the app has a feature where users confirm they have safely arrived at their destination and returned home. This is bound to be one of the least risky shags Jess has ever had.

Her motorbike storms over the river and in record time she's ringing J's doorbell, feeling just a small tremor of trepidation. What if he's a toad in the flesh?

But the guy who answers is actually quite cute.

'Hi, Amy,' he says with a grin. 'My name's J—'

'I don't need to know your real name,' Jess says quickly. She doesn't want to get into telling him hers in return, or the inevitable small talk that follows.

'Fair enough. Want to come in?' J stands back and Jess walks up the stairs, pulling her sweater over her head as she goes, tossing it back for him to catch. She's not wearing anything underneath.

'So have you done this before?' he calls after her.

Jess turns to look at him, her head cocked on one side.

'I mean,' he's panting a little from the stairs, 'the app. It's my first time.'

'Me too,' Jess says. 'Worth a try though, isn't it?'

'Yeah . . .' J says. 'Funny to get straight into it without any preamble, isn't it?'

'Leave that to me.'

Jess lets her bike helmet fall to the floor with a clunk and walks forward. She drops to her knees in front of him and unzips his jeans. Her urgent, flicking tongue gets to work on him so quickly that it's a minute or two before J realises that he's still clutching Jess's sweater. He's never been with someone so assertive, generally being the one to make the first move himself.

Worried he'll finish before they've really started, J throws Jess's sweater onto a nearby chair and pulls her up until she's on his kitchen counter. He's determined to show he can match her.

J pulls Jess's jeans down, tugs her underwear to one side and buries his face into her, his hands creeping up her ribcage to play with her hard rosebud nipples. It is intensely gratifying when she begins to moan softly and wriggle about on the coun-tertop. Her fingers comb at his head, pressing him into her.

All in all, this is better than I could have hoped for, Jess thinks, as she pushes J's face away, kicks off her jeans and shoves him towards the chair with her jumper on it. He sits down and, while he pulls his boxers down, Jess rolls a condom onto him.

Keeping her thong on, she shimmies onto J's lap and slides him inside her. He cups his hands under her bum, feeling her jiggle rhythmically against him. Jess arches her back and J dips his head forward and sucks urgently at her tits.

Without breaking stride, Jess moves one hand around until she is fondling J from underneath, alternating between his balls and his perineum. Her other hand reaches forward and tugs at her underwear, so the fabric tightens against her clitoris. Within seconds they're both crying out.

'Well, thanks for that,' Jess says, after she's pulled her clothes back on. Hopefully this keeps her fantasies about Christian at bay for a while.

'No problem.' J grins. 'Maybe we can get a drink some time?'

'No,' Jess says firmly. 'Sorry, but I didn't get on this app for dates and stuff.'

'Do you want to do it again some time?' J asks. Is he being rejected? This hasn't happened before.

'Not really.' Jess stretches, enjoying being able to torture someone again. 'You're a nice guy but ... this is all a bit pedestrian for me.'

After Jess has left, J lies on his sofa for a long time. Well, that was a first.

5th May

Con 24% Lab 44%
Knife crime up 13% this year/
Famine in Sudan

Claybourne Terrace

'Hello, and welcome to the BBC's coverage of the local council election results.'

Just over three weeks later, the residents of Claybourne Terrace have settled themselves in the living room. One way or another they have been working on these elections for weeks. Jess has been trying to think of a fresh angle to the media-agreed line of the electoral doom of the Conservative Party, settling instead on the Labour machine and its adoption of Lib Dem campaigning tactics. Percy has been keeping a hawkish eye on Anto's campaign management, planning an immediate strike when the inevitable dismal results come in, and making cheerful visits in a few target areas. From the whips' office, Eva has been trying to calm feverish MPs, who fear losing all of their councillors. And Bobby has been spending a lot of time in Tipperton with Moira, ostensibly to help save their local councillors, but really to get a sense of what the Tipperton seat will be like when it splits in two.

Now she's back on track with Jess (she still reads Jess's note from time to time), Bobby feels truly hopeful about the future. She has told her parents about her pregnancy, who took it far better than she could have hoped – delighted, if surprised. A grandchild is a grandchild and they both have something momentous to look forward to. What they can't understand is her desire to become an MP – and a Conservative one at that.

There are two big points that have won them over: all the wonderful things she could do for the area and the realisation that, should she win the seat, she will live part-time in Tipperton and they would therefore see their future grandchild every weekend. They had taken a long walk with Jake around the constituency for the purposes of future campaigning, getting more excited with every step. Now she has passed her PAB, Bobby needs to focus on the next step. Luckily Susie Coleman, the ex-wife of Simon Daly, is committed to getting Bobby selected. Susie is an influential member of the community, working part time at the Tipperton Mental Health Unit while studying for her PhD, and the daughter of the local association chairman so she's able to call every Conservative Party donor in the area. She is almost unrecognisable from the cowed, quiet woman of a year ago. Her divorce from Daly is now through – 'we got him nicely over a barrel' – and she's finally truly living again.

'We are expecting a tough set of results for Prime Minister Eric Courtenay and the Conservatives . . . '

'No shit!' Percy shouts at the TV.

'Do stick with us as we bring you the results through the night.'

Jess has had a couple of glasses of wine and is dying to message Christian, the Labour comms chief, about how things are going at his end, but suspects every journalist is doing the same. They speak most days now, conspicuously professional in their conversations. But the odd lingering pause leaves her wondering if he's thinking the same thing as her. The gradual pictures they are managing to build about each other – they're both single, it turns out – and the leap Jess feels when his name pops up on her screen are making her nighttime fantasies increasingly intense. Her Fawn liaison with J feels a long time ago, and really rather bland.

Jess is also increasingly preoccupied with the knowledge that Lord Finlayson can be manipulated. She has yet to learn his secret and get Ed off his back, but, if she ever does, what would it mean to the old proprietor if she could save his bacon? The possible gains are worth putting up with Ed while she chews over Finlayson's predicament and escapes from under the guillotine Ed is building for her career.

'Couldn't we work out some arrangement where we sleep in shifts?' Bobby asks, breaking into Jess's thoughts. It's only just gone 10 p.m., but these days Bobby has usually been in bed for at least an hour by now.

'The Tipperton results come in quite soon, Bob, so you should be tucked up in good time.' Eva is consulting a document on her work laptop and monitoring the different MP WhatsApp groups she's part of.

'I'm definitely not staying up late, seeing as I'll probably be required to go out on the telly tomorrow and say the results are,' Percy coughs, '"disappointing but above expectations … *let me be clear*, we've listened to what people have said and are determined to show our working by the general election …"' he chunters.

Downing Street

A mile away, Clarissa is perched on a tartan armchair in the room that used to be Margaret Thatcher's study, a cup of Darjeeling cradled in her hands. A soft smile plays around her lips as she watches the Number Ten political team struggle. Her husband has been in an annoyingly good mood recently, although Clarissa doesn't realise that this is because of the arrival of Laura Lloyd, and Clarissa's enjoying watching him deflate as the results come in. The night has hardly started and the Conservatives have already lost eight hundred councillors and, for once, there's no way any blame can be levelled at Clarissa. Here are the results of the geniuses left in charge.

Anto, suddenly waking up to his hand being on the tiller for this colossal shitshow, is trying to stay calm and buoyant.

'The incumbent always comes in for a bashing at locals, don't they?' he says soothingly to the PM, whose head is in his hands.

The chief and Jake talk quietly in a corner, throwing the odd disgusted look at Anto and kicking the toes of their shoes against the wainscoting. As the evening drags on, they take it in turns to slip out of the room and call every journalist they can think of to shoulder all responsibility onto Anto. The calls to reinstate Nick have already started.

Downstairs, despite the late hour, the usual business of government continues. The prime minister's PPS reads the notes the boss has scribbled on that day's box submissions, anything from plans for a new house-building policy to his G7 itinerary, suppressing a shake of the head at the sheer vapidness of some of his responses. The duty clerk processes these notes, reconfirms the next day's diary (Anto has optimistically put time aside for a celebratory lap of any council gains) and keeps an ear out for the various phones at their desk. This is the time when the calls, if they come, can be serious and scary because they are well out of normal office hours. The time for news of terrorist attacks, military strikes or royal deaths. An assortment of diligent officials and special advisers wade through policy documents and emails, yawning over the wine they've surreptitiously poured into chipped mugs.

Laura Lloyd is at her desk, thinking about the prime minister. The MA/PM relationship is really not as she expected. There are some strange vibes. She thought it would be strictly formal, seeing as she is likely the final person the PM will turn to for advice before drastic measures like launching airstrikes or ordering fleet movements. But it isn't like that at all. Their talk is easy and flowing. He is surprisingly keen to confide in her. It has got her wondering why he got into politics to begin with. He clearly prefers taking orders rather than giving them. He *looks* the part but seems incredibly uncomfortable with his office. He looks hunted, for want of a better word. Why's he doing this job?

North London

The leader of the opposition, John Ramsey, is watching the results in his Islington home with his wife and core team: Christian Eckles, who is preparing media lines, Paul Marsh, his policy lead and chief of staff, Tanya Haines, his head of strategy and Vicky Tennyson, the shadow chancellor.

'Get in!' Ramsey punches the air ecstatically as a fresh batch of results comes in, showing the PM has managed to lose councillors in his own constituency, Chatterham. The group clusters around him to high-five and clink glasses, except Christian, who is pounding away at his laptop. He doesn't see much point in getting too excited, and worries that all the talk of Labour 'definitely' being in Downing Street by January is unhelpful. Sure, these results settle Labour MPs and give a sense of momentum. True, it consolidates Christian's own position – he's already being talked up online as an electoral genius. And, yes, it will make the conversations that he wants Ramsey to have with centre-right media editors, proprietors and thought leaders much easier. But, otherwise, he knows this is essentially a protest vote, an opportunity for the public to rail against the ruling party that can be easily reversed with the right campaign at the general election.

At his core, Christian has doubts about Ramsey and the rest of the team. Christian is a good campaigner and deft political mover, but he considers these as simply tools to bring about long-term, deep-rooted systemic change in how the UK works. He's sick of nobody dealing with the hard stuff – the NHS backlog or care homes – and he's tired of politics being about party loyalty and media performances, rather than competence. He's increasingly of the view that his colleagues and political master want his campaigning smarts but aren't at all interested in his plans for government. In fact, for all his talk about being 'different', Ramsey's appetite for urgent, systemic change and tough decisions is tiny. Still, Christian can't dwell on that now. Got to win the election before he can start the real battle – to stop the Labour Party sounding different but essentially being the same old Tories once in power.

Christian's thoughts are interrupted by his phone buzzing. He immediately checks it, hoping it might be a call or message from Jess Adler. She must be the only journalist in the lobby who hasn't been in touch to figuratively kiss his arse. But it's just a greasy congratulations text from the shadow health secretary. The shadow cabinet, most of whom were furious about his coup, have been more persistently grovelling than Ed Cooper this evening, who won't stop calling him 'mate'.

On the other side of the room, Ramsey can't help glancing warily at Vicky Tennyson to see how she's taking the results. The shadow chancellor is a beautiful woman, her mother Vietnamese and her father a former Derbyshire coal miner. When the mines closed, Vicky's mother became the family's economic powerhouse, providing a mobile nail service, which became a salon and eventually a small chain. The Tennysons pushed their only daughter to succeed, resulting in a place at Oxford to study economics, and neither of them let her forget how they strived for her success. Vicky is clever, both academically and through instinct, and hungry. She was a dangerous final contender for the leadership last year and it's no secret that she had every union behind her. Added to that, though Ramsey was told it was the right decision to make her Shadow Chancellor, if Labour gets into power she will hold the purse strings for the administration. With a powerful part of the party machine, plus the prime ministerial cheque book in her power – and the Rolodex she is building of top UK businesses, who are banging on the door to meet her – she makes him nervous. Vicky is smiling while the results flood in, but Ramsey never really knows what she's thinking.

What she's thinking is, in a word, *patience*. Vicky is smart enough to know that Ramsey is an acceptable face of the modern Labour Party. He's got nice, touchy-feely values backed up by his career in the charity sector. He's presentable and a good communicator. He is a man, which, whatever she has said in countless interviews to the contrary, does actually seem to matter when it comes to the Labour Party choosing a leader. Ramsey can wear all the 'This is a Feminist' T-shirts he wants but the fact is that Labour are yet to elect a woman, even if they've had women 'acting' while a man is picked for

112

the full-time position. Why? Vicky has pondered the question so many times without getting tired. Not even tired of the countless think pieces last summer trying to explain her loss to Ramsey: *Daring to say the unsayable – is the public ready for an Asian woman Labour leader, and prime minister?* She feels Ramsey's eyes on her and she glances up to grin at him, the smile not quite reaching her eyes. She needs to ride this particular wave and get her timing right.

Bermondsey

In a blacked-out townhouse, Conservative Party Chairman and Deputy Prime Minister Natasha Weaver MP has her hands full. To be strictly accurate, she has pretty much everything full – the club she attends with her husband, Greg, who is busy in another room, has its standard night well underway and Weaver is leaning over a leather sofa (wipe clean, she supposes) with a cock in both hands, and one juddering her from behind. She keeps her mouth free to bark instructions to her companions. It's a personal record, she realises, and she's looking forward to telling Greg about it later. They absolutely love comparing notes at the end of these evenings or trading fantasies. The timing of this particular event couldn't be better. She'll have lovely glowing skin for her media round later, when she goes out to bat for the PM. Not that he deserves it, the brute, bringing in Percy Cross to undermine her. Weaver instinctively squeezes her hands into fists at the thought and the gentlemen to either side of her cry out in pain.

'Sorry, boys.' She mustn't let her mind wander. This requires the same concentration as rubbing your tummy and patting your head at the same time – while being rear-ended by a monster truck.

113

Weaver glances across the room and spots one of the other long-time attendees, a member of the Labour front bench, struggling to adjust his gimp mask, which has gone askew during his exertions. Those folks have gone nuts tonight, voting fever proving a powerful aphrodisiac. In fact, now she thinks about it, parliamentarians always get excited around elections and leadership debates and big votes. People get blinded by the opportunity for power, translated to lust, and mistakes are made. She increases her wrist action to the two tasks, starting to work up quite a sweat.

Weaver often wonders whether one of the many parliamentarians who regularly come to these events will expose her. Certainly she has thought of exposing them. But they each know the mutual destruction that comes with uttering a peep about belonging to this community. It would be one of the few pluses of being in the opposition, she reasons. Or losing her seat altogether. Who cares how Weaver gets her rocks off then? Might as well go the whole hog and start an OnlyFans account. Beats writing her memoirs. Anyway, she concedes, there has already been a fair amount of blood-letting on that front, thanks to the leaked photos of her up to no good in her parliamentary office during last year's leadership contest. She was incredibly heartened by the letters and messages she got from people all over the country, celebrating her lifestyle and honesty. Turns out some people don't mind if their politicians are shaggers, so long as they aren't hypocritical about it.

All that being said, she has to live on something and her MP salary of £86,000 plus her ministerial one of £65,000 keeps her nicely afloat. Which serious private sector company is going to employ her? And she doesn't much like giving speeches. Maybe she can get a column in the *Sentinel* and a bit of TV work. Finlayson has always appeared to be very open minded ... No. She mustn't think like that. She has to stay on after the general election. She's actually good at this! Maybe another leadership bid beckons.

Her thoughts of waving to the cameras with Greg outside the famous Downing Street front door are interrupted by her phone ringing. She squints at the screen. The Downing Street press office.

She releases one of her companions, puts in her AirPods, and resumes her busy wrist action.

'Hello, Minister. How're you doing? Managed to get some rest?'

Weaver thinks for a second, thighs still rhythmically slapping against the sofa, her wrists starting to cramp up.

'Not really, but I feel all right. I'm just, uh ... at the gym.'

'At three a.m.?'

'One of those twenty-four-hour ones. I find it's the quietest time to come. You know me,' she says, breathing hard between thrusts. 'I don't need much sleep.'

'Yeah ... Well, anyway. We think you should head into Millbank in the next hour or so, so you can see some more results coming in and to comment in real time. It's not going to be the usual "disappointing set of results" stuff. We're preparing to announce some interesting things.'

Weaver pauses to lick spunk off one of her hands. 'Go on.'

'We can't tell you yet – I don't know myself – but we've been told we can promise you that you'll know before it's public,' the voice says, sounding excited.

Weaver hangs up and shouts back to the man at her rear.

'All right, I've got to get going. Give me your best big finish.'

6th May

Con 24% Lab 44%

Election Terror for Tories/

Typhoon hits India

Downing Street

The chief whip's energy is so at odds with the rest of his team's on their conference call – everyone is in their constituency, fielding gloomy incoming calls and messages from MPs about how many councillors they've lost – that one of them messages Eva to ask:

Is Nigel having a breakdown?

He says to just keep an eye on the news today

Eva replies, wondering what on earth is going on, before stuffing her phone into a Downing Street cubbyhole. She and the chief have been invited in for another meeting, presumably to ask about the mood among MPs. If so, it'll be a brief discussion: not good.

As expected, pretty well every right/centre-right newspaper is carrying source quotes admitting 'a disappointing set of results' and vibes of despair at Anto's campaign strategy and management, frequently carried with a photo of Anto in a box on a freebie at Wembley or the Royal Albert Hall. 'We've got to get a proper team and a proper plan of attack together or we may as well just hand over the reins now,' are the politest words the papers can print. The left-wing outlets, though cautioned by Christian not to predict certain victory at the general election, had an enjoyable time in their editorial meetings, mocking up photos of Courtenay looking hangdog and Ramsey looking cheerful. The general line is that this 'stunning set of results' shows the total collapse of the Tory Party and its grip on the nation. The Conservative MPs and the weak prime minister are chiefly to blame for this. It doesn't trouble anyone that Labour haven't really done anything to win this new support – they just aren't 'the other guys'.

'For crying out loud,' Percy says, leaning back in his chair. 'Labour can carry on doing nothing and let our voters drift over to them. It's the easiest campaign in the world! Which is what brings us all here now . . .'

He looks around at the prime minister and his team.

'People aren't wrong to ditch us. The party's been in charge for ten years and we're completely out of ideas. Luckily, Labour don't have any new ones either. Which is what gives us a chance at winning another term. But not like this. It's time for a nuclear option.'

'What . . . how?' the PM says, his expression desperate and lost.

'No, no. Wrong question. You mean . . . *who*.' Percy turns to Teddy Hammer, who is currently serving, rather precariously, as Percy's media SpAd and the Downing Street communications director until a suitable replacement can be found for

Nick O'Hara. He's already getting great material for his book. 'Bring him in.'

'Bring who? What the fuck is going on?' Anto, deranged by tiredness and humiliation, has placed an arm over the prime minister's chest as though to protect him from a bullet.

'Get off me.' The PM shrugs him off petulantly, craning his neck round at the door.

There is a collective intake of breath as Callum Gallagher saunters in with Teddy.

'Hullo, Cal.' Percy stands up to hug him. 'Now, who don't you know?'

Callum waves to Eva, and shakes hands with the rest of the group. The chief almost vibrates with excitement, while Weaver actually titters. Anto looks deeply unhappy, his usually pale face matching his salmon-pink shirt.

'So, sounds like you're all a bit fucked,' Cal mutters, when they've settled back down in their seats. Everyone nods, except Anto, who folds his arms across his chest and takes in Cal's scruffy T-shirt and stubble.

'Can you help?' the PM asks, unable to resist leaning forward a little.

Jesus, Cal thinks. *What a poker face.*

'Possibly. Question is, can you help yourself? You can win, for sure. But it requires agreeing to a proper plan and then ruthless execution. Ignore the wailing from the MPs and the chattering from the hacks.'

'What sort of thing do you have in mind?' Anto asks.

'We need the right people in place and, eventually, the right research and messaging. Reshuffle, reallocate political power with a big reshape at CCHQ – starting with bringing Nick O'Hara back.' As far as Cal is concerned, Nick's return is non-negotiable. They've been speaking constantly over the past forty-eight hours and Nick has told Cal everything he can to

118

prepare him. 'Stop letting MPs think they have any say in how an election will be won, or it'll all be about the Union and trade deals and culture wars ... In fact, stop talking about MPs and the Conservative Party at all.'

'Are you mad?' Anto huffs a fake laugh. 'The Conservative Party brand is the most important asset we have.'

'Nope. It's done.' Cal shakes his head in disbelief at the chief, who winks back at him. 'I didn't pay much attention to the local elections yesterday, but I'd have to be blind, deaf and dumb not to clock that "we hate the fucking Tories. Anyone but the Tories. Literally anyone" was the most salient message with the public. Labour don't even need to offer an alternative. People just think, correctly in some cases,' Cal glares at Anto, 'that you're a bunch of useless wankers and they may as well give the other wankers a stab at it.'

'Well.' Anto puffs out his chest defiantly, while an ecstatic chief whip looks on. 'What about our excellent track record of delivery? We've made a lot of progress with school curriculums, net zero and, uh, building regulations ...'

'You understand fuck all about delivery. People have to feel it. They need to see the cranes building their hospitals and schools, the diggers creating their houses – which they need to be able to afford to buy. Campaigning is an emotive issue and if you run on a list of technical achievements, you're fucked.'

'Why?' Anto, along with much of the rest of the group, looks surprised.

'Because the contrary argument is far too strong. The list of what you've promised but haven't achieved is too long. Labour can simply ask people this question: do you feel better off since the Tories took power ten years ago? The objective answer for most people is no. How hard-up people feel will trump delivery of, what was it, building regs? Jesus.'

Cal shakes his head again. He's tired of explaining that how you connect with people and make them feel is key.

'So . . . what do we do?' the PM finally ventures.

'I'll work that out soon enough. But you have to talk about the future, not just what you've already done. Track records don't count for much and nobody ever votes because they feel grateful. Look at Churchill in 1945. He literally defeated Hitler – but that didn't mean the public voted him back in, did it? Because he didn't talk about the future. And that was the bloody Nazis! It must be heart-over-head stuff. Not heart-over-head-over-arse, which seems to be where we are now.'

'Great. So . . . when can you start?' The PM folds his hands comfortably in his lap.

Cal grins.

'Well, hang on a second. I'm not just doing this for my health. I've got a few conditions if we win. First,' he counts off on his fingers, 'we need proper funding for science and R and D. We need to think properly about skills, and let's start with committing to more technical colleges and apprenticeships. And, of course, a complete rethink of our defence, security and civil services.'

The PM had been nodding happily along until Gallagher's final sentence. This is one of the few things Courtenay feels really strongly about. He knows they could be better, but he has an instinctive faith in those institutions. Each time they drop in, he feels sure the various deep-state services are run by good chaps making the right decisions. And it'll cause quite a row to rejig anything to do with the civil service. Anto, who is gripping the table with white knuckles, clearly feels the same way.

'That's a bit extreme, isn't it?' Anto stutters.

'Not really. They're crying out for a proper overhaul. And besides, it may never happen, if I don't win you the election.' Cal clasps his hands behind his head.

The PM tries to think of a response but knows he's snookered. He shrugs. Maybe something will come to him later. Perhaps Clarissa will turn her mind to it, assuming she hasn't finally pinned down Amal Clooney for lunch.

'All right, well, what do you need?' The PM cracks his knuckles.

'Firstly, I need you to sign this.' Cal brandishes a sheet of paper with his list of policy demands.

'What do you mean "sign it"?' the PM says.

'I mean, I would feel more comfortable if you signed. So we all know what's been agreed here. Otherwise . . . I'm out.'

Cal's tone of voice is calm and pleasant, but he doesn't blink. The PM stares back at him, then glances around at the rest of the group, as if hoping someone will come to his rescue. Anto harrumphs a bit but can't think of anything. They all know the PM's willing to sign a blank cheque at this point.

Once the sheet is dutifully signed in Courtenay's loopy hand, Cal explains what he needs as campaign director to turn the Tories' electoral prospects around.

'I want to bring over a team of quants from America. Data scientists and physicists and a trusted professor to make our models. They will be doing all our data analysis from now on and need to be plugged into the CCHQ campaign machine, so we are putting resources into the right places. Their research will help inform the reshuffle, too. We need the most competent – if there are any – and trusted people in strategic roles. It doesn't hurt to have some who don't dribble down the camera lens in TV interviews, too. And I want to move some people around. Nick back today, obviously. And, while it makes sense for Eva to stay in the whips' office as we land this changing of the guard with MPs, she should move to CCHQ and help the quants settle in until the election is called.'

Cal cocks his head at Eva, who smiles back. Suddenly

becoming an MP has lost its glamour. The chance to learn campaigning from the Svengali of strategy doesn't happen very often.

'What else?' The PM nods to Anto to start writing everything Gallagher says down. It is several hours before the group disperses, most of them far happier – and all of them far more focused – than they had been at the start of the meeting.

8th May

Con 23% Lab 44%

GP appointment backlog critical/
Bees in crisis

Chequers

After managing to muzzle Natasha Weaver with the promise of a big profile interview in next weekend's *Daily Mail*, Teddy lands the news of Callum Gallagher's return about as well as he can in Sunday's papers. Jess's special piece for Sunday's *Sentinel* carries a detailed retelling of Friday's meeting, and draws up the respective campaigning machines preparing to do battle for the Conservatives and Labour later in the year.

The chief whip, Eva and a chosen coterie of advisers spend Saturday calling key MPs to land the news with them – 'Crikey, we might actually win the damn thing with that mad bastard back!' one greybeard cried – while Percy tours the Sunday political shows, finishing with a star turn on *Sunday with Laura Kuenssberg*. There is palpable excitement in SW1, cut only with panicky speculation about cabinet and shadow cabinet reshuffles, with MPs ready to square up to each other and send needy, begging missives to their respective chief whips.

After months of despondency that both her and her husband's reputations are slowly but surely sliding down the bog, Clarissa feels a familiar, hopeful rush of endorphins start to course through her as she scrolls through the Sunday papers on her iPad. It doesn't hurt that she has a meeting next week with the American ambassador to discuss the First Lady's interest in a new spousal programme to raise awareness for something-or-other to do with women or children. Vogue *cover, here I come,* Clarissa thinks. This afternoon she needs to sit down and do her research. Until then, the PM is out running around the Chequers grounds. He really deserves a treat on his return. And he'll be nice and limber. Perfect.

Fifteen minutes later, the prime minister carefully pushes the door open in case Clarissa screams at him for waking her up. But the bed is empty. He shrugs, kicks off his shoes, flicks off his socks and pulls his T-shirt over his head before tossing it onto the floor. His shorts and boxers follow, tangled in a sweaty mess at the foot of the bed. Courtenay doesn't get as many perks as he'd like as PM but proper cleaners mean he and Clarissa have become slobs, leaving dirty clothes and cups wherever they please.

The PM pulls on a towelling dressing gown and, rubbing his eyes, wanders into the bathroom where he stops in his tracks. His wife is lying in the bath, an intent look on her face that he's not seen in months.

Wordlessly, she rises from the water and, without reaching for a towel, walks slowly towards him, water dripping off her bath-oiled curves. She raises a finger and pushes him very gently and slowly back into the bedroom. All he can do is obey, his mouth dry.

Clarissa pushes softly at his shoulders and he sits down in

an armchair, still mesmerised. With agonising care, she lowers herself down until she's kneeling before him and slides her fingers up his thigh until she can feel his cock, which seems to have a pulse of its own in her palm. Not taking her eyes off him, she lowers her head.

'W-wait,' the PM stammers. 'I've not showered. I'm all sweaty ...'

'I don't care.' Clarissa smiles at him for the first time in ages.

As her dark hair heads downwards, the PM doesn't protest. After months of sexual starvation, which his furtive porn habit and bathroom wanks haven't satisfied, it is the most magnificent feeling. The change from the chilly run outside to his wife's warm mouth is both comfort and desire. Her slightly rough tongue massages his tip and her fingers playfully stroke every pleasure point. Within seconds he is sighing in ecstasy. For Clarissa's part, she's taken back to the sex they had during last year's leadership contest, when they were winners. Eric would return from a run or the gym and she'd have to have him right there on the kitchen table or on the hallway floor. It's the taste. Sweat, but also a hint of something muskier, animal-like.

Before he is close, Clarissa stands and pulls her husband by the dressing-gown lapels onto the bed. He has missed having her dominate him like this.

'Let's go together,' she whispers, kneeling either side of his head and lowering herself down so she can continue where she left off. He's missed this so much. He feels almost ravenous for her, ecstatic at how she's responding to his tongue and lips and nose. His hands grip her thighs as she intensifies her sucking. They're both on the cusp of orgasm when there's a knock at the door.

'Good morning, Prime Minister, Mrs Courtenay ... We just wondered if you have any special orders for breakfast? And there are a few calls that need to be returned.'

Clarissa sits bolt upright, smothering the PM.

'Just piss off, will you? We'll be down in a minute.'

They return to each other. An hour later they stumble downstairs, almost hand in hand.

9th May

Con 22% Lab 45%

Madeleine Ford ffs!/

Mudslide in Pakistan kills hundreds

Westminster

The big news from the reshuffle is that the former prime minister, Madeleine Ford, is back in the cabinet as foreign secretary. She was hard to persuade – the Courtenay team had, after all, petrol-bombed her premiership – but a private meeting with the PM, Percy and Cal eventually brought her round. Ford is committed to seeing through her China trade deal, seeing as she put in everything she had to get it over the line, then has her sights set on the climate-change agenda. Al Gore, John Kerry and Arnold Schwarzenegger have already Tweeted their delight at her joining the cause and are jockeying to meet with her first. The press are obsessed, as she joins a tiny list of ex-prime ministers who have returned to serve after their time at the top. Now, with Percy, there are two of them in one cabinet. Political commentators and biographers are pulled from studio to studio, trying to make sense of such an extraordinary move. A blogger doorsteps Ford's husband on his way home from work, shouting, 'Do you think your wife has another big job in her?'

Michael smiles shyly at the camera, deciding to comment for once. 'She has about five.'

In the meantime, the Americans arrive at CCHQ and Eva heads over to join their first meeting. Cal introduces her to each in turn: Dr Miguel Fernandes, a soulful Hispanic data scientist who sold the IP on his PhD thesis to a hedge fund for a million dollars because he thought it was 'only okay'; Beau Parker, a walking-Ralph-Lauren-advert physicist who realised as a college student that through 'pretty straightforward modelling' he was predicting the outcomes of elections better than every national poll in the US, so thought he may as well make a living from it; Nate Mason, a tattooed metal-head mathematician with a special interest in how human emotions and behaviours can affect numbers and how they are measured, and Professor Don Fontaine, a Dumbledore-ish political science academic, who has written countless papers on political persuasion and mobilisation and taught Cal as a student. All of Don's team – who can't be a day older than thirty – are dressed in a combination of long- and short-sleeved T-shirts with bold logos on them, while the seventy-five-year-old Don wears chinos, thick glasses and a kindly expression.

Because the general election hasn't been called yet, the official period for campaign spending hasn't started, so a generous donor sent an enormous cheque to CCHQ to cover the air fares and accommodation for this motley crew. When the time comes, every penny spent will be scrupulously scrutinised. But until then, the party can spend the money as they wish, so long as they record their donations correctly.

Cal begins by explaining the rules that govern campaigns in the UK. The young Americans stare in disbelief. Finally, Beau slaps his hands onto his head.

'Goddamnit! What kind of rinky-dink campaigns can you even do here? You can only spend pocket money ... can't buy up ad space on TV or radio ... can't even say libellous shit about your opponents! *Man*, I will never say anything bad about Super PACs again.'

'And your TV debates don't mean nothin'', Nate muses, flicking through some polls from the last election. 'They don't shift the dial at all.'

'And everyone's ditching their landlines,' Miguel adds. 'Gonna be tricky to do polls.'

'You Negative Nellies.' Don chuckles. 'Listen, Cal. Can we take over this room for a few days? We're gonna need as much data as possible about the last few elections, plus anything recent like by-elections. We'll need access to how you view the electoral map—'

'We use Vote Source,' Eva chips in.

'Okay, great. What else ... And,' Don taps the table thoughtfully, 'enough energy drinks to sink a ship. That all, fellas?'

But there's no response. Miguel, Beau and Nate are crammed around a laptop, deep in conversation. Cal puts his finger on his lips and signals to Eva to leave as quietly as possible, as if to avoid waking a sleeping baby.

'Bit intense, aren't they?' Eva says, when they've closed the door.

'You wait. I've got an idea I want them to test out. If it works, it will be ... interesting. Now, Eva.' Cal pulls his eyes away from the glass door, where the data team are now writing algebra on a whiteboard. 'I need you to look after them. You heard them in there. If they think our spending rules are bad, just wait until they make contact with our MPs. You have to protect them from all outside interference. In fact, I don't want anybody to know who they are. Okay?'

'Okay,' Eva says, feeling like her heart is pumping properly for the first time in ages.

16th May

Con 25% Lab 45%

PM attacks Labour record in Wales/
Earthquake in Turkey

Labour Campaign Headquarters

A week later, after a minor reshuffle on the Labour side – the key people like Vicky Tennyson have kept their roles – Christian is looking through the latest polls. The Callum Gallagher news has spooked him more than he'd like to admit. Secretly, Cal's book on political campaigning is one of Christian's favourites. He even used it as a handbook for his coup just a couple of months ago. And now the guy's had a few years to learn a bunch of American techniques. Christian flips through some suggested attack ads on the PM from his team. Dog shit.

His main concern is that in just one week, the Conservatives have gained an average of three points in every national poll. Well within the margin of error, of course, but what if they keep this up? Christian can't see what their core message is yet – they seem to be playing with a few ideas, pressing random

Labour pressure points – but what happens when Cal works out what resonates? Christian pulls up a calendar. It's mid-May now. By law, the general election has to be held by January. That's a long time if the Tories are going to start creeping up the polls by this much each week. He bargained that his arrival and sudden change of tack on the Labour side was about as last minute as could be, and would kneecap CCHQ's campaign machine. Not any more. He realises that the best way to slow Conservative gains down would be to shorten the time they have to catch up. Christian needs to find a way to bring polling day forward. But how?

He thinks about Cal's book.

Obviously one of the key trump cards the governing party holds is the ability to choose the timing of a general election or referendum. However, if you can convince the public a vote is needed NOW, you'd be surprised what cowards MPs can be about agreeing to an earlier polling date. Chicken suits outside events and firm exchanges across the Chamber are stunts. You need to make voters feel like the country is at a standstill until they can vote. Time for Change is a powerful mantra . . .

The word *standstill* has got his brain whirring. Christian scratches his chin and fires up the BBC website. A small story in the sidebar reads: *Talks break down between Government and Unions on pay deal.* The unions behind refuse workers and baggage handlers are all on the cusp of strike action, coordinating across different local councils and regional airports in solidarity. The Tories might have the bosses, but Labour have the workers. If industrial action goes ahead, holidays would grind to a halt and a month of missed bin collections in the heat will drive people mad. The unions are by no means straightforward to deal with, and will be very wary of having their members politicised in any way, but it is interesting to think about. Will Christian be able to persuade Ramsey that a summer of discontent is what's needed?

He spends the rest of the afternoon commissioning new polls on public attitudes to strikes, the messages that he thinks could persuade people to support such action and who the key union officials are behind each group.

Leader of the Opposition's Office, Houses of Parliament

At 6 p.m. that evening, unable to keep the idea to himself any longer, Christian calls a meeting with Ramsey, Paul Marsh, Tanya Haines and Vicky Tennyson. He explains the problem.

'We've all seen the polls this week. Cons are three points up across the board.'

'They're a blip,' Paul Marsh says with a yawn. An ex-senior civil servant from the Cabinet Office, he was brought in to steady the ship when Christian launched his putsch in order to signal the new set-up as entirely respectable. Paul's very organised and his time in the Foreign Office will prove useful in government, but his campaigning experience is zero and his political instincts are rooted in the 'small p' politics of civil service jostling and parliamentary handling.

'Let's hope so. But if they aren't and the Tories make consistent gains like this then this is bad.'

'What do you suggest?' asks Tanya, raising her over-plucked eyebrows. In a crowded field, she's easily the most hostile to Christian in the team, after being kept on when the previous chief of staff and director of communications were axed. Christian suspects Tanya is primed to damage him in any way

133

she can, not least because the ex-director of communications is her husband. They disagree on pretty much everything. Despite her Cheltenham Ladies' College and Oxford University education, and her comfortable family trust fund (her mother is 'the Hon' somebody or other), Tanya is evangelically of the Left and, frankly, considers Christian dangerous. Christian thinks Tanya is the epitome of champagne socialism, a hopeless hanger-on and hypocrite.

'We need to pressure the government into speeding up their timetable for the election.'

Ramsey rubs his eyes. 'How?'

'We convince the public that an election needs to be called as soon as possible.'

The group looks back at him, perplexed. Tanya looks positively gleeful.

'Oh, well.' She claps her hands sarcastically. 'Let's just do that then.'

Christian ignores her. 'We create the conditions so that they're fed up with how the country is run and how out of touch Parliament looks.'

'Wake up, Christian. People already think that.' Tanya rolls her eyes.

Tennyson, though, is seeing beyond what the others see. 'It makes sense. But how?'

'Strikes,' Christian says. 'You all know that talks have broken down between the government and the refuse and baggage-handling unions. Well, we let them get on with it. These are services that will drive people mad this summer if they aren't running.'

'Fucking hell. People are hardly going to thank us for sending everyone on strike all summer! I thought you were a strategist.' Tanya smirks. Ramsey and Paul also don't look convinced.

'Obviously *we're* nowhere near this. But, let's say the strikes go ahead – there's no reason we can't capitalise on them.' Christian folds his arms. 'Look, after the momentum from the locals, we have a lot more media outlets looking to be sympathetic towards us. We just need to help nudge this all in the right direction . . .'

'I get it.' Tennyson leans back in her chair, impressed. 'Holidays screwed up, streets stinking. Tory MPs pictured on exotic beaches or safely in massive houses. Parliament in disarray when it returns in September. A strong "this can't go on" speech from John . . . What do you think, Paul?'

Paul is nodding, slowly and deliberately. Everyone knows he worked in the Cabinet Office on industrial action a few years ago. He'll be able to predict the exact weaknesses in the government's response to strikes. Coupled with Tennyson's union connections, everyone in the room is waking up to how this could work.

'But won't everybody hate us for it?' Ramsey asks.

'I can't emphasise this enough: *we are nowhere near these strikes kicking off.* We do nothing and see if they happen. It's only if they go ahead that we work out how to support them and attack the government. It can't just be about pay, for example. I've put some polls out into the field and will focus-group the lines I think could work. I just want to put this to you first, to see what you all think and to explain how this can speed up an election being called – which is our key objective. The only thing I'm sure of is that the more time we give CCHQ to get their ducks in a row up to polling day, the more trouble we're in.'

'It's not ideal, but I don't see another way round it.' Tennyson turns to Tanya. 'Anyone else got a better idea?'

Tanya sniffs and says nothing. Tennyson turns to Ramsey, her eyebrows raised.

'All right,' Ramsey says uncertainly. 'In principle, we will go with this plan. But I want us to reconvene the minute the poll is back and you've got your messages focus-grouped.'

The meeting breaks up, Tennyson doing her best to stifle a smile. This Christian character's pretty good.

Islington

In his study at the top of the house, John Ramsey puts down his pen and tucks the last of his papers into a folder. In the hours since the meeting in his House of Commons office, he has been to two different receptions to give speeches and dropped into a transport-policy dinner. Despite his effort to be engaging for these appointments, worry has been eating away at him all evening. In the months since he became the leader of the Labour Party, he's been able to just sit tight and let the Tories implode. Now Labour are finally coming onto the pitch. But Ramsey is riddled with doubt. Part of him hopes that Christian's focus groups will come back against the strike idea. Then he can just carry on doing nothing.

He wonders about going to bed but he knows he'll toss and turn and disturb his wife in this state. He gets up from his chair, opens the study door and creeps out onto the landing, listening. Satisfied that his family are all soundly asleep, he silently closes the door and returns to his desk. Opening an incognito browser tab, he scours a couple of Asian Babes websites until he finds an actress resembling Vicky Tennyson and unzips his trousers.

17th May

Con 25% Lab 44%

Electoral Commission hacked/

Blackouts in Beijing

CCHQ

At 4 a.m., Callum Gallagher gets a text from Don. The team is ready to update him on where they've got to. At 9 a.m., Cal gathers the Americans, Eva and Nick O'Hara in a meeting room.

'What we're about to learn must not leave this room, okay?' Cal glares around at the group. 'I mean it. I'm not even going to tell the prime minister. He won't understand it anyway.'

The politicos in the room nod in acknowledgement and turn to face Don, who is standing in front of a whiteboard, bobbing on the balls of his feet.

'So, based on Cal's theories, we've come up with something that we're pretty excited about,' Don says. 'First though, there are two things we need: to learn more about what the public think and how we find people beyond our base who might vote for us.' He writes down *1. Polling public* and *2. Target new voters* on the whiteboard. 'But there's a big blocker on how we do it.'

'What's the problem?' Nick asks, tearing his eyes off Miguel, who he's been side-eyeing since they shook hands at the start of the meeting. Privately, Nick is grateful to have had the last couple of weeks of unemployment to throw himself into the gym and sauna. He pulls off his jumper in the hope that Miguel notices his arms under his T-shirt.

'GDPR,' Don replies. 'It used to be that, via Google and Facebook and so on, we could use cookies to track people across the internet *and* learn a huge amount about them. If you can build up a profile on somebody, you can work out what ads will likely work on them and people like them. These big companies would sell that data to people like us. GDPR rules mean we can't do that any more, so we are limited, on those platforms, to advertising to those people we know are already committed Conservatives, because they've "liked" certain content – or to everyone. Now, we never want to advertise to everyone, as we'll just turn some people even further off us by appealing to them.'

'Don't tell me you guys have found a way around this,' Cal says, leaning his elbows forward on the table.

'We think so.' Don grins and sits down. 'Nate?'

Nate stands and removes his baseball cap, so his shaved, tattooed head is fully visible.

'Okay. Just hear me out, because this is going to sound crazy.' Nate huffs out a deep breath. 'I've been digging back through some stuff and found a paper suggesting porn preferences are indicative of personality type – and even policy preferences. Yes, porn,' he says to the bemused faces around the table. 'Through their search terms, people are explicitly telling us about their fears and desires, far more deeply than any focus-group discussion can do.'

138

'Fears? Surely just desires?' Eva asks, trying not to look guilty.

'You would think that.' Nate nods. 'But fear or interest in exploring your own personal taboos is a huge motivator in porn searches. For example, in the US you may be surprised to learn that one of the most popular categories in the conservative, religious South is "trans". Like I said – desires and fears. And a fairly safe space to explore them. But what does this mean? Interpretation is the key step. Perhaps it means a curiosity about or even envy of trans people if you feel like you live somewhere where you repress your true self. Or maybe, if fear is the dominant reason for this search, the South is a smart place for any presidential hopefuls to kick off a culture war . . . '

'It makes sense.' Nick chuckles, now looking anywhere but Miguel. 'Porn speaks to your deepest taboos and curiosities. Genuine honesty. It's like a poll or focus group that you can't lie to.'

'Exactly. Anyway,' Nate continues, 'I've looked into it and a lot of these sites are a bit freer about their users' data than, say, Facebook. It seems that the only real scrutiny they're under by the government is how easily kids can access their services, not cookie usage or GDPR. Nobody is thinking about their possibilities with data and users are allowing tons of their personal information to be collected by these sites. For example, users can be tracked by location using device ID. So we can see where they are. And with their porn preferences, according to this paper, we can build up a pretty reliable psychological profile of them.'

Cal is clutching his sides with glee. 'So you're telling me that we can track people across the country and build a profile of the most honest versions of them? Then, what, make a kind of heat map of the most-searched terms in an area? If we're talking about fears and desires, we can work out what people in a certain place want, then how they'll vote . . . '

'Sure. It's like what we used to be able to do before the rules changed. It's the same as being targeted by any product, really. And we can actually do you one better.' Nate nods to Beau.

'Yeah, so I've been getting my head around Vote Source and the electoral register here.' Beau stands now and sweeps his floppy blond fringe out of his eyes. 'I reckon we layer this porn map of preferences over the standard map of constituencies. The register tells us basic stuff like age. I think that we can form a more accurate view of voters when we combine porn preferences with location and age than any of the models we've used in the past, like education level or ethnicity.'

Cal and Nick exchange delighted grins.

Don stands again, removing his glasses and cleaning them thoughtfully with a tissue. 'We just have to work out what these preferences mean. If you are, let me see . . . from the West Midlands and you're a fifty-five-year-old woman, you reliably vote Labour and your search term is "fisting", what does that tell us about you? How can we persuade you to vote Tory?'

Eva, who has been concentrating hard to fully understand the discussion so far, hides a smirk.

'Why not double down on the porn aspect?' Cal is slightly manic now, excited by an idea and tickled by the absurdity and simplicity of their plan. 'You already know that we don't have enough landlines for decent polling in the UK any more. We target people on gaming apps and Xbox and stuff already. Why not do ads for paid surveys on porn sites? Learn what these correlations mean from the people themselves.'

'Brilliant!' Nick crows. 'You said it yourself, Cal, that voting is emotive. We just need to translate all of this into the right messages to the right people in the right places. It's the best way to get to the bottom of what, uh, fisting means for voting preference . . .'

'The only thing is . . .' Cal rubs his eyes and looks at what's

140

written on the whiteboard. 'We need to keep this very hush-hush. Miles away from the media and all our MPs. Not that they'd understand any of it, but they do know what porn is ... Nick, we'll need to think of something to keep them busy during the campaign. A giant dead cat.'

Eva speaks up.

'Cal,' she says quietly, not wanting to burst any bubbles but feeling duty-bound to ask the question. 'Is this strictly legal?'

All heads swivel in a vaguely accusatory way towards her.

'Sure it is.' Cal stretches nonchalantly. 'It isn't our responsibility to verify a website's GDPR practices. It's their responsibility.'

'But ... we are the government.' Eva bites the inside of her cheek.

'*We* aren't.' Cal waves his hand around the room. 'Anyway, you heard Nate – the only regulation the government is interested in is making sure little kiddies aren't seeing weird sex stuff before they're good and ready.'

Eva presses on. 'If that's the case, why don't you want to share this with the PM? Sounds pretty straightforward to me.'

Cal looks at her pityingly. The PM might like to know about the porn map, but there's no way he will understand the beauty of what Cal's doing.

'We all know that great swathes of the public look at porn all the time and that it is a billion-pound industry. But it's just too mental. Even by my standards. We can't risk anyone finding out about it or there'll be a giant uproar and the loophole will be closed. You work with Tory MPs. Can you imagine what they would say if we unveiled this plan? They hardly need encouragement to start door-knocking in nothing but a blue rosette. No, the PM can hardly wrap his head around the idea of profiles like "Scarborough Man" or "Aldi Woman". He'll lose his tiny mind at "Billericay Gang Bang".'

Leader of the Opposition's Office, House of Commons

'All right, so we have the focus-group data back,' Christian announces to Ramsey, Tennyson, Tanya and Paul. He can't quite hide a smile. 'In summary, the public hate strikes. Something we've always known,' he says quickly, when Tanya opens her mouth. 'But, there's a message that really works: working conditions. People are sympathetic to refuse collectors dealing with leaking shit and rabid animals and the assumed exposure to disease. Same for baggage handlers, worrying they'll get blown up by bombs in suitcases or fucking their backs up in the pissing rain. Both jobs are far more demanding and skilled than people realise. The crucial thing is that – one – we don't talk about money, so this is less about a pay dispute and more about a protest at conditions. Two. We make sure the strikes are the fault of the government, who are in charge of the talks and have therefore "let" them happen. And three. We don't talk about the unions – ever. We focus on organic, gut-wrenching individual stories about conditions that we're simply listening to, so it feels like the underdogs taking on the evil Tories.' Christian smacks his fist into his palm. 'Which they are.'

'Sounds straightforward enough.' Tanya nods and gives the smallest hint of a smile, the first time she's responded positively to something Christian has suggested since he joined. 'I assume it's pretty easy to convince people that the government is to blame for all this. It's not like everything else is going so well – ten years of the Tories in power and pretty well every living cost is up.'

Everyone murmurs agreement except Tennyson, whose brain is working overtime. How should she play this? She's already seen as in the pocket of the unions. The *Daily Mail* have dubbed her 'the Scarlet Woman', implying she is a dangerous communist (Chinese-ish, she supposes), while using some of the most suggestive possible photos of her in the editorials. Publicly encouraging industrial action won't play well for her, not least with her new business connections. And in case Christian's plan doesn't work in persuading the public to demand an election immediately, or it comes back to bite them further down the line, maintaining her distance could be smart. The best play is surely for her to stay quiet and watchful.

'So should I be out on the picket lines? And should the rest of the front bench?' Ramsey asks, seemingly reading Tennyson's mind.

'I don't love the picket-line visual,' Tanya interjects. Paul nods fervently, wondering what his former colleagues in the civil service would make of all this.

'No, definitely not. We should arrange for you to meet with a bunch of the strikers in working men's clubs and in their homes and stuff. You know, you hear directly from them what their lives are like. And then you can do interviews, calling for the government to respond. Remember, people don't want to feel like we're pulling the strings.'

Tennyson spots her chance.

'Presumably you'd like this nowhere near me.' She tries to make her smile look tinged with regret. 'Far too close to the unions. And CCHQ can dig out all those pictures of me at student protests ...'

Christian raises an eyebrow at her. It's not the first time she's seen further down the line of possible outcomes than Ramsey.

'Yes, that would be a very good idea. John is with the strikers, while you reassure business leaders behind closed doors that we aren't a bunch of nutters.'

Ramsey almost chuckles. Now it's *his* chance to fight for working people, not Tennyson's. He's been lapping up everything Christian has been saying about meaningful, caring interviews and speaking directly with the strikers. The main criticism of Ramsey within his own party is that he can seem aloof and that his career as a charity worker, academic and human rights campaigner is unrelatable to working people. One of his problems is that he is struggling to differentiate himself from Eric Courtenay, particularly as far as the left of his party are concerned. They're both well spoken and grew up in comfortable, middle-class homes. They had interesting careers (i.e. not in banking) internationally before coming to Parliament, which they've entered with little difficulty and adjusted to with ease. They're both scrapping over the same bit of centre-ground, speaking to working families about music lessons and grammar schools and the cost of a university education. And they're both out of fresh ideas.

Ramsey rubs his hands. 'June's around the corner. Sounds like these strikes can't come soon enough.'

Part Two

5th August

CON 20% LAB 45%

THIS *STINKS*!/

HOTTEST JULY EVER RECORDED

Chequers

After pushing through the remaining weeks of term after the torturous May elections and taking Clarissa away on a miserable 'holiday' to North Wales in July, the prime minister has decided to have a weekly meeting with his political team at his grace-and-favour home during the summer recess to prepare for the autumn. There has to be a general election in the next five months and there is party conference season to consider. The PM, dressed in chinos and a cashmere jumper, is moodily eating his breakfast – a plain egg-white omelette and black coffee – while reading the newspaper front pages at the ornate table in the cavernous Chequers dining room. Yet again, the bin strike dominates. A particularly gruesome photo on the front of the *Guardian* shows a young mother pushing a pram past a wall of refuse bags, an enormous rat inches from her foot, just waiting to scurry up the pram leg and gnaw at the baby inside. It puts the PM off his omelette, so he can only imagine what this is doing to parents – a key voting demographic – across the country today.

Christian Eckles's plan has worked beautifully. For weeks now, in addition to the bins, the disruption for holidaymakers and foreign visitors at airports has led the news agenda, the baggage handlers' action proving inescapable. A few right-wing newspapers have continued to bleat feebly about wage inflation and Britain being in danger of going back to the 1970s if John Ramsey continues to show sympathy for the strikers and gets the keys for Number Ten, but on the whole the press and public have swallowed Christian's lines in one gulp. Downing Street has not even been able to rely on the usual dirty profiles of strike leaders – the hypocrisy of a union spokesperson privately educating their children or a leader being on an expensive holiday while their fellow members picket – to deter support. Astonishingly, fairly glowing profiles of some of the union leaders, who sound, well, normal on the radio compared to politicians, have also carried in many of the Sunday supplements.

Twitter, Instagram and TikTok are teeming with sob stories of ruined holidays and stranded elderly parents and the news broadcasters and papers have had one of the easiest recess periods in history reporting on the chaos. Mercifully, television and radio aren't yet able to transmit the stench of rubbish rotting in the summer heat, but hardly anyone has been able to escape it in real life. Apart, of course, from the handful of Tory MPs – and a few Lib Dems – wealthy enough to holiday abroad (baggage isn't a problem when you have a mate with a private jet) or who live in a romantic rustic setting where bins are stored far from the homestead, and where they've got packs of dogs to kill rats.

Christian's attack team have kept journalists busy pointing

out these honourable members, and the pieces that have appeared showing the juxtaposition between them and struggling members of the public have driven people wild with fury for the political class. Christian has been able to sit Ramsey perfectly against this, forbidding Labour MPs to do anything that looks vaguely enjoyable and sending Ramsey on a family holiday to Butlin's and a tour of tragic photo opportunities like helping to move stinking bin bags away from pensioners' homes. He is looking thoughtful and warm and thoroughly down in the trenches with the public.

Tanya Haines was also correct: the public is having no difficulty believing that the government is responsible for their misery. The general inconvenience of trying to leave their homes without a dandyesque perfumed handkerchief pressed to their noses has made people feverishly irritated. Even the government's suggestion for people to travel to a holiday within the UK, thinking this will avoid baggage problems and boost British tourism, has caused road-traffic chaos and rage in rural and seaside communities, which are now overrun with up to twenty times their normal populations. What doesn't help is the complexity of how the strikes have come about, involving numerous different councils vis-à-vis bin collections, and multiple airlines and airports in regards to baggage handlers. The government is struggling to explain who's to blame or what the hold-up is. Leaking nappies and stranded holidaymakers, meanwhile, say it all.

Rage and the sense of feeling trapped by the smell and record-breaking heat over July has even seen little ripples of civil unrest. Skirmishes have broken out in a handful of nightclubs in major cities. Neighbours have increasingly aggressive confrontations about whose bin bags are in whose driveway, some resulting in police charges. Teenagers have started a TikTok video dare of jumping off walls – the higher the better – into

149

piles of rubbish. The nation's mood is close to breaking point and the PM feels like a spoilt, out-of-touch king. He is sitting in the stunning surroundings of Chequers, demanding higher taxes, suggesting that his peasants give brioche a try.

Presently, he's informed that his team have arrived and are preparing for their meeting with him upstairs. The PM wipes his mouth and nods to Clarissa, who ignores him. The last few weeks have meant another period of distance. In part, this is due to all the negative press – the *Mirror* got a brilliant photo of Clarissa walking past some bin bags to a waiting car, plastic carrier bags protecting her suede Manolo Blahniks – and the inevitable sense that Clarissa is saddled with a loser again. It also doesn't help that Clarissa is now focused on her soon-to-be life after Downing Street. September will be big for her: Balmoral with the royal family to push her charitable credentials and the annual United Nations summit in New York (known as UNGA) to meet with Michelle Obama to talk about world hunger and children's health.

The PM, meanwhile, has used every possible opportunity to meet with Captain Laura Lloyd, his newly appointed military attaché, whose warm strength envelops him in sharp contrast to Clarissa's coldness. He's simply drawn to her. She brings a degree of assurance and kindness to his life that he hasn't experienced before and he has to fight the urge to reach out to touch her all the time. Laura has encouraged him to spend more time with Madeleine Ford, the foreign secretary, and he has found genuine respect and admiration for her. After all, there aren't many people that he can discuss the specific burdens and cares of being prime minister with. The PM is frequently hit with roiling waves of shame that he brought down her premiership the year before and wishes he could explain that he hadn't really wanted to damage her, but knows it sounds pathetic to say it was all engineered by his wife. The irony is that, while domestic problems persist, Ford's performance as foreign secretary has seen her rocket up in public-approval ratings. And her stock is rising internationally – every foreign minister wants to meet with a former world leader.

The PM enters the Long Gallery and heads to the middle of the large mahogany table. Among the oil paintings and Persian rugs, his team, dressed in casual clothes as though they are attending a strange weekend house party, look out of place. The Americans have even taken off their baseball caps. Only Percy, who looks at home anywhere, and Anto, who is clad in his customary salmon-pink shirt and navy gilet, look comfortable.

'Well, Prime Minister,' Cal says from the end of the table, raising his chin in greeting at Clarissa, who has slipped into a seat next to Eva, her curiosity roused. 'We're ready.'

Cal is ready to present his plan. Or at least, the version of his plan that is palatable for political civilians. He glares out of the window at the beautifully manicured lawns and flower beds, the huge trees in full summer greenery. Miles away from a putrid bin bag.

The PM waves the *Guardian* front page in the air. 'Will it help with this?'

Cal grins. Typical MP to bring up the newspapers first. It's not like these strikes have come out of nowhere. The government has been sitting on one side of the negotiating table, able to see the rage of the unions about pay and working conditions. What nobody could have banked on, Cal supposes, is how these strikes would resonate with the public. Since when did they support strikers? Still, the PM's 'woe is me' attitude is tiresome. After all, he's the one that backed removing the cap on bankers' bonuses in the first week of the strikes. Talk about misreading the public mood ...

'I think so. What is happening now is pretty obvious. I've literally written a book on the subject. Campaigning is war, okay? This is about one side getting the other side on the right ground to fight on, like any military commander does with high ground or swamps. Labour want a quick war. Home for Christmas and all that. So they need to shorten the timetable to an election, making it hard for us to catch up with such an insurmountable lead – which they currently have. *On paper.*'

Nobody speaks, so Cal continues.

'What I'm saying is that the polls – averaging forty-five per cent Lab, twenty per cent Con, right? – are soft. They're bloated up by this strike stuff and can be popped with a pin, if we have the right kind of pin. Labour think they are being clever, riling up the country to force an election, but I don't think it matters now.'

'Labour?' Anto says, playing with his gold cufflinks. 'If this is them pulling the strings with the strikes, shouldn't we go on the attack about it?'

Cal rolls his eyes.

'They haven't kicked off the strikes. At least, if they have, they are being far too smart to be caught out. But they're making the most of the situation, putting themselves on the right side and fuelling the public rage. You can try to blame Labour if you like, but it'll backfire. For the first time in living memory, this industrial action is actually popular with people! Talking about conditions over pay has reached hearts, and even the hearts that remain cold are sick and tired of dumb politics, like your support for bankers' bonuses. The demands for an election have already started . . . Can someone grab that board?'

Eva immediately jumps up from her chair and pulls a large whiteboard on wheels into the centre of the room. Clarissa bristles with annoyance. All right, Eva is easily the most junior person present, but has it occurred to her that she's the only one who moved from her seat, and the only woman at the table?

Well, the only one not married to the prime minister. Eva needs to be taken aside afterwards and told that she will only get the treatment she deserves in powerful rooms if she expects it, and is not just grateful to be there. Clarissa wonders, too, how Eva's journey to become an MP is progressing. She's not heard from her in weeks about it, and been too busy with her own projects to check in.

The truth is that Eva hasn't given life as an MP a moment's thought now she's got her new job. The last few weeks have been the most interesting of her career so far. Cal and the Americans invite her to all their meetings and she's understanding that campaigns go far beyond rosettes and leaflets. Cal reckons she has a real flair for it. It's politics as she's never known it before.

Cal gets up and stands by the board, which has a map of the UK on it with dominant red, blue and yellow patches, plus a few splotches of purple, green and orange.

'Here's our current electoral map, divided up by which party has which constituency. This,' he flips a clear sheet over the map with areas shaded in different colours, 'is the map if we win the seats we think we can, including the new target seats we have assigned based on the research we've been doing. You can see some of our loyal places haven't changed colour, while some unexpected places are now heavy targets. Cities are of fresh interest to us, particularly those in the North and Midlands. And we have specific messages for each area.'

'A decent majority!' Percy exclaims, gazing at the large patches of blue. 'How do we do it?'

The chief and the PM thump the table in approval.

Cal gestures to Don, who joins him at the board.

'Message specificity, basically. We've been learning a lot about the British public these past few weeks,' Don says, flipping another sheet onto the map, this time showing a more intricate, zebra-like pattern across the UK in different bright colours. He and his team have painstakingly layered the most popular porn search terms in different regions over the existing electoral map, and have found enough places where specific arguments can move whole constituencies towards the Conservatives. 'For example, look at the magenta areas. These are where strong messaging on immigration will resonate best. And the lime green shows where economic anxiety is most pertinent and therefore where reassurance on the economy would be strongest. There are a few other colours in there too, all representing tailored issues and messages that our most persuadable voters in these places are interested in hearing about.'

Don, of course, doesn't explain how these messages and issues have been cracked. They've put the theory of the academic paper on pornography preferences, which surmised that for many people, porn searches echo the particular fears, taboos or fantasies they have, in practice. Focus-grouping porn site users about their preferences has helped Don's team learn what these desires translate to, and therefore what messages touch on these people's deepest anxieties and hopes – and what promises would make them vote for a party.

For example, in some areas the search for videos of a small, vulnerable-looking woman being dominated in a gang bang by a bunch of large men translated, when probed in focus groups, to anger around weak crime and justice policies. The search for videos of porn actors role-playing employees doing seemingly degrading acts for money (a secretary being creampied by her boss in exchange for a raise, for example), exposed the fears of those feeling financially vulnerable and in need of reassurance. Interestingly, when they worked backwards, the Americans found little difference between what traditional Labour and Tory voters search for. This surprised and then delighted them. What is clear is that these voters, who might usually commit themselves on party lines, can be persuaded to

154

vote differently if the message and idea are strong enough – so the Conservatives may even be able to chip away at the Labour base vote. As Cal observed on learning this: 'Cut us and we all bleed the same blood, even if we think it will be blue or red. It follows that we're the same old filthy pigs underneath it all and we can't help that either.'

'Jake and his team,' Cal nods to Jake, 'are already drawing up policies that will resonate with these voters. And Nick and I are on the case with the right messages. We'll target ads online and in our leaflets, and flood local radio.'

'But what about the national campaign?' Percy chips in. 'This is all clever, but I assume it's down to individual Facebook ads and local posters. But what are we meant to say and do overall?'

Cal grins again and gestures to Don. 'Yup, we're coming on to that.'

Don pushes his glasses up the bridge of his nose, choosing his words carefully. The key theme that came out of the research was dominance and power. For example, some of the most popular searches are for the role play of step-parents with stepchildren and teachers with students. For a while, the team were stumped by what this could all mean. Then Beau realised that he could track the frequency of website logins and the times of day that people log in. In summary, Britons are watching a lot of porn. Weekday mornings are especially popular and, after crudely assuming this must be home workers or unemployed people, the team realised workers are watching porn on their phones at work. But why? Focus groups had the answer: stress, boredom and a sense that they've lost control of lives they feel stuck in. Once they'd put the dominance searches and the frequency of logins together, the team discovered a desire for clear leader-ship. People want a proverbial 'strong man' at the helm to feel secure – and a clear, strong strategy for the campaign was born.

'Well . . .' Don hesitates for a moment. 'The same theme kept recurring when gauging the public mood. People are stressed, bored and despondent about the future. People are also fed up with politicians parroting back what they think the public thinks. They'd actually prefer someone who they disagree with on plenty of issues, so long as they give a sense of confidence and vision. Maybe even, uh, dominance. In essence, they want strength and leadership – someone who makes them feel hopeful about the future.'

Percy is nodding. 'I see. A sort of Thatcher figure. You know, you may not have agreed with her, but you at least understood what she stood for?'

'Bingo,' Cal says, wondering what Maggie would have made of how he put together this particular strategy. He turns his attention to the PM. 'You already know my views on the party. Our research compounds that. We need to make this a presidential-style campaign, where you are the strong, decisive figurehead. Any question you're asked, you have a clear answer with no prevaricating. No gaffes, no efforts to look "relatable" or "authentic". You're the fucking Terminator now.'

The PM thinks, hard. Despite his appearance, he's not adept at modern politics, where mobile phones catch you eating or walking or clapping weirdly. He enjoys things like COBRA meetings and security briefings from MI5, and finds it hard to suddenly switch hats and be jovial at a children's charity tea party in the Downing Street garden. He finds thinking on his feet hard in front of a microphone and TV camera, unable to tread a tightrope on a hot topic. But he can take orders and be undeviating once he understands what's asked of him. This is the campaign he was born, bred and moulded to do.

A smile spreads over his face and he glances at Clarissa, who gives him an almost imperceptible nod. She's made the same calculation as him.

'I like it. I bloody like it!'

The politicos around the table erupt into excited discussions while Don and Cal wordlessly sit down.

'As Cal mentioned, we're working on a tight manifesto,' Jake says, when the room has quietened down. He's already been given his list: immigration, tougher sentencing, economic boosters, and is told there is more to come. 'But when do you need it for? What timetable are we working to?'

Jake isn't just interested for work reasons. Bobby has been duly shortlisted for the Tipperton seat and the candidate selection will take place next week. She's also nearly twenty-weeks pregnant and hitting the stage of needing floaty tops as she transitions from looking like she's had a big lunch to carrying a distinctive bump. Her due date is 22nd December, so the timing of the election is crucial. Will she make it to polling day without popping? Or will she be door-knocking in the January chill with their baby strapped to her chest?

'Good question.' Cal stands up again and flips the board with the map on it around, so it shows a calendar charting August to January. 'The first thing is, we should pay absolutely no attention to the strikes and the calls for a general election immediately. It's just noise and bowing to that kind of bleating breaks our "strong man" campaign before we've even started. And as I said, the polls are as liable to collapse as soufflés. So, Prime Minister.' Cal points at the copy of the *Guardian* on the table. 'Don't spend any more time reading that stuff.'

The PM tosses the paper onto the floor. 'Done.'

The group laughs, except Jake, who is watching Gallagher closely.

'Anyway,' Cal turns back to the calendar, 'we want timing that works for us. We should rule January out. We don't want people voting who are feeling the pinch of their credit card bills and wading through a month of sobriety. We'll stick to this year, so everyone's looking forward to Christmas. So, we need some time to get you looking strong and to finesse some of our messages and modelling. Chuck in a couple of weeks on top of purdah, I think you announce at conference that you're calling for an election on . . .' Cal runs his pen down the Thursdays in December. 'The second.'

Jake lets out a held breath. 2nd December gives Bobby three clear weeks before her due date. She'll be visibly pregnant throughout the campaign but hopefully her local background and community story will inch her over the line.

'Why announce it at conference?' Anto asks. 'Everyone knows it has to be at some point this winter. Why the secrecy?'

'It gives me something to actually say at conference . . . forty minutes of waffle otherwise,' the PM says.

Cal grins and nods at him. Anto looks like he's swallowed a wasp.

The group breaks for lunch, the PM practically skipping down the stairs with Clarissa back on his arm, but Cal lingers behind, looking thoughtfully at the calendar. He's taking quite a gamble in suggesting this election timetable. A lot can go wrong in eight weeks, and that's not including the next six weeks or so until conference, which is plenty of time for gaffes. His major concern is the media getting a whiff of how their model has been built, although he supposes it is telling that nobody in that room pushed him and Don on exactly how they came up with it. His other worry is that the opposition parties run tight, disciplined campaigns that focus on the real issues. What Cal needs is a nice row that everyone will get thoroughly distracted by. Christian might be trying to cut time, but Cal is seeing a way to create it. As he heads down the stairs, he spots Nick and Miguel slip into a bedroom and close the door.

*

After several more hours of discussion, Eva is getting into Percy's ministerial car for a lift back to London when Clarissa calls her back into the house. She leads the way into a sitting room, which Eva remembers watching TV in while her parents were entertaining during Percy's prime-ministerial days. Nick is waiting for them.

'I'll cut to the chase,' Nick says. 'Now we've got a confirmed date for the election, we need to sort out candidates for our final few seats. I've just had word from the chief that David Dalgleish is going to have to step down in Battersea. Health stuff.'

Eva raises an eyebrow.

'No, I actually mean it. Some kind of horrible cancer, poor man.'

Eva murmurs an apology. She's too used to her time in the whips' office, concocting euphemistic terms like 'health' or 'family' when an MP is leaving public life, when more accurate descriptions might be 'cottaging' or 'ketamine'.

'Yes, well, we must plough on.' Clarissa turns to Eva. 'We think you should go for it. It's only over the river from your home. And we can guarantee you a pretty easy selection run. You're Percy Cross's daughter, after all.'

Eva frowns. 'But . . . but is that fair? And anyway, what about my work for Cal?'

Still, she can't pretend she isn't flattered. It was only a couple of months ago that Eva resented Bobby for being approached to stand. And here she is, hand-picked for a plum seat.

'Fair schmair,' Clarissa says briskly. 'I thought this is what you wanted? And I'm sure Cal will be fine without you. Like I say – you'd only be across the river anyway.'

'And at this stage we rush everything through,' Nick says winningly, 'so the whole process will take no time at all. Anyway, all Cal's work is for nothing if we aren't getting decent MPs like you elected. Well, what do you think?'

Eva stares into a nearby cabinet, stuffed with a collection of silver cups and teapots. This is a hell of an opportunity. Will she get one like it again? Yet, she's more absorbed in her work than she's ever been before ... For his part, Nick likes Eva but this goes against every instinct he has for who becomes an MP and how they do it. But they've reached a critical stage of requiring bums on seats.

'We haven't got all day, Eva,' Clarissa says, sounding testy. 'I've got a Zoom call with some people at The Hague shortly.'

'All right,' Eva breathes. 'I'll do it.'

'Good,' Nick says, while Clarissa beams at her. 'I'll get the ball rolling.'

10th August

Claybourne Terrace

It's early in the morning and Jess is tetchy. Tomorrow, Bobby will be standing before the selection panel for Tipperton. She could be an MP in a matter of months, on top of becoming a parent. Eva, meanwhile, seems to be having the time of her life working with Callum Gallagher and just a matter of days ago she was hand-picked to stand as an MP too. Jess has never felt more remote from her friends, stalling in pretty much every area of her life. Until recently, she had been acknowledged in their group as the most successful. At least, so she thought. But now? Sure, her podcast is plodding along. As is her work for the *Sentinel*. But that means nothing if Ed can get her fired at any moment. Resentment towards Eva and Bobby, who have no idea of the tense situation Jess is in, is starting to grow.

What she could really do with is some sex. This is her driest patch ever, but she hasn't known where to turn. Ed's messages persist, but leave her cold. She hasn't got time for the fetish club and hasn't revisited the Fawn app since her encounter with 'J', which was months ago now. Fawn's confected thrill is as unnatural and insubstantial as a marshmallow. Jess hoped that Eva might use her new-found summertime singledom to go bar-hopping together, but she's either been hobnobbing in the office or hanging out in the Caribbean with her mother. The person Jess has really wanted to see is Christian. At the couple of lunches and coffees they've had – Jess doesn't trust herself to suggest dinner – the meeting has ended with a strange lingering moment, crying out to be filled with a kiss. She's placated herself by investing in some new toys and a serious stock of batteries, but the stiflingly hot nights in her small room and the visions of his cool, clever face are torture. She needs some release.

Still, Jess will be busy for the next twenty-four hours. This morning she's travelling to Herefordshire, to join a prime-ministerial visit to the SAS. Unusually for a defence-related visit, perhaps in return for the *Sentinel*'s refusal to drub Clarissa after the David Coker affair, Number Ten have invited the paper to send along a journalist to cover it. As the defence correspondent is due to go into labour any day now and Ed is in Padstow with his family, Jess has been chosen to go. As she packs a small day bag, starting with emergency tampons, a cordless phone charger and a Dictaphone, Eva and Bobby lie on her bed, talking about Bobby's imminent selection interview. Eva is paying close attention, now that she has been whipped through the early stage of passing the Parliamentary Assessment Board, as she will have a selection of her own to do soon.

'What are you going to say about living in the constituency?' Eva asks.

It is generally the case that constituents want their MP's main home to be in the constituency they represent. There have been dozens of stories about second homes and the related financial misconduct that comes with them over the years, but affording to run a London and constituency home is impossible for most people. Luckily MPs are given support for housing as, if your constituency is on the Shetland Islands, you can hardly commute every day.

'Right,' Bobby says brightly. 'I'm planning to live with Mum and Dad when I'm in Tipperton. I'll need help with the baby and hopefully I can save some money. Then I'll be with Jake when I'm down here.'

Jess, who has been bending over her backpack and squeezing her sunglasses into a side pocket, snaps upright. 'You're moving out?'

Bobby looks bashful. 'Well, of course. You don't want a baby around here, do you? It'll scare all the men away.'

'They aren't exactly bashing down the door, Bob.' Eva laughs sourly.

After breaking up with Jamie, Eva thought a summer of hot sex might be on the cards. But it's been dire. Even a trip to Mustique at the end of July to join her mother, Jenny, and her rocker boyfriend, was a washout. Despite rumours of film stars and musicians and Kennedy family members on the island, the only love bites Eva got were from mosquitos. Thank goodness all the work with Cal and the Americans has been so interesting – plus the prospect of a parliamentary seat. Autumn will most definitely not bring politics as usual.

'Sure, I just ... I just didn't really think about it. Of course you'd move out.'

Jess's chest suddenly tightens. This change unsettles her. Bobby is going and what if Eva moves out if she wins Battersea? Jess can't stay here with Percy and Holly like some weird

163

adopted child. She zips her bag closed, fixes a grin on her face and straightens up.

'Well, on that bombshell, I'd better get going.'

Jess hugs both girls and swings the bag over her shoulder, blinking hard. As she marches down the street to the Tube station, she gives herself a mental slap. The moment she's back from this visit, she'll pursue Ed's shadiness with fresh strength, she'll find a new place to live and she'll get laid.

Stirling Lines, Herefordshire

At Hereford station, a uniformed young man in an old Land Rover picks Jess up.

As they rattle along, the driver gives careful, guarded answers to Jess's questions (he's presumably been warned to be discreet) while the terrain outside grows increasingly wild. Eventually, they stop at a checkpoint where a large red sign reads: *Danger: Military Firing Range.* Jess has her identity checked by a cheerful squaddie. Throughout their exchange he throws her bashful glances. She can't help but notice how attractive he is in his beret and regrets not packing her make-up bag. And some deodorant.

When they pull up in front of a series of ugly breeze-block buildings, another uniformed man whips the passenger door open for her and Jess is shown into the main building to meet SAS Commanding Officer Jack Deacon, and Director of the Special Forces, General Sir Humphrey Cave. Jess isn't sure if it is their shared calm self-assuredness or the fact that Jack looks like Jason Statham, but she finds herself truly, pathetically flustered when speaking to them. They have a disconcerting habit of simply not reacting in any way to a lot of her observations, or giving each other a knowing glance in response to some of her prepared questions. She finds herself filling the awkward silences with any old nonsense that pops into her head. 'I really love your berets' is perhaps her lowest point. Her mouth actually waters when Jack casually rolls up his sleeves to reveal heavily tattooed forearms. What has come over her? Surrounded by all these men in uniform, she's acting like a dog in heat. So much for the fresh Herefordshire air clearing her head.

Before heading to the helicopter pad, where the PM is due to land shortly, Jess nips into the bathroom. 'You must get a grip of yourself,' she says aloud into the mirror, after she's splashed cold water on her face. *And,* she thinks, *get some cock when you're back in town.*

The sight of the prime minister arriving in a Chinook is, admittedly, spectacular. Once the huge rotors stop turning, the PM and his team – Captain Laura Lloyd among them – stride down the ramp. The PM looks in his element. The boots, chinos and fleece that can look curated and clumsy on many politicians simply look right on him. He strolls over to the group of servicemen and says hello to them all, chatting easily. Jess is surprised when he turns to her.

'Ah, Ms Adler. I know you by reputation of course. And no Ed? Well, well. Looks like old Finlayson's got a new favourite.' When Jess doesn't react, he continues. 'I should know about his favourites. My wife, Clarissa, is very tight with the old chap still. Dates all the way back to when she worked there as Ed's contemporary! Great how you journos keep these connections going ...'

They load into trucks, Jess thinking. She wondered why StoryCorps left the Clarissa–Coker stuff alone. It never oc-curred to her that Clarissa could be getting special treatment from Finlayson himself. She thought it was just because the execs didn't want to annoy the administration by attacking the PM's wife. In fact, Jess forgot that Clarissa is a StoryCorps alum. She's very tight with Finlayson, far beyond ex-employee status. The trucks jolt along and Jess wonders if she could perhaps triangulate Ed's work history with Clarissa's to see if they worked on anything specific together that explains the special treatment they both get . . . Silently thanking the prime minister for his moment of bouncy, exhilarated chattiness, Jess regrets that she can't get back to London right away.

Instead, the trucks drive around to a corrugated-iron building, where Jess watches firearms of various sizes and descriptions being fired at different targets. After thirty minutes or so, Jack, the dashing commanding officer, suggests Jess have a try. He hands her a heavy rifle and shows her how to tuck it against her shoulder, all the while warning her about where she aims the barrel. Up this close, Jess can smell him – fresh sweat, sandalwood and something made of pure, animalistic pheromones. Perhaps it's his smell or his gentle, murmuring voice that raises the hairs on her neck, or maybe it's the thrill and terror of holding a killing machine in her hands. The weight of it makes her left arm shake slightly as she raises it, takes aim and fires. If it weren't for Jack's huge palm against her back, she'd have been thrown off her feet by the kick. Jess grins up at him, her shoulder feeling like it's been shoved from its socket.

Next, she's handed a pistol to try. As she wraps her fingers around it, standing with her feet firmly apart, shoulders slightly rounded, she feels far more comfortable. She fires a few rounds.

'I think we've found your weapon, Ms Adler,' Jack says, the hint of a smile on his lips.

'I'm not so sure – I think I'll stick with a pen,' Jess says with a laugh.

The PM, meanwhile, has been winning cheers and rounds of applause for his abilities with a firearm. His height and his broad, muscular frame easily carry the camouflage jacket he's been given. The rifle, which would look awkward and hammy in any other politician's hands, looks entirely at home in his. Jess glances over at his target, which has dozens of holes blasted into it. The one next door, belonging to Laura Lloyd, hardly has any paper left. The soldiers standing around the rifle range are all nodding enthusiastically. Evidently Laura has won whatever little contest was going on between them. Jess watches with interest as the PM rubs Laura's shoulder as they clamber into the trucks once again and head to the main building for lunch. Very chummy.

When they enter the officers' mess, there is a crescendo of scraping as chairs are pushed back and the men stand in respectful silence for the prime minister and Gen Sir Humphrey. Jess feels dozens of pairs of curious eyes burning into her as she follows Jack to the head table and wonders how often they have a woman on base. Spotting a seat next to Laura, she darts into it. Jack sits opposite them.

'So how does it feel to be the first woman in your role?' Jess asks Laura, once they've introduced themselves and Jess promises that their conversation won't be printed. 'I suppose it must help that people know you can shoot a man at twenty paces.'

It occurs to Jess that it probably doesn't hurt that Laura looks strong enough to punch someone's lights out with a flick of the wrist.

'Blindfolded,' Laura jokes. 'Yes, I'm enjoying it. Obviously it is really exciting to work for a politician who understands defence matters. The briefings are very straightforward. And it is fantastic to have days like today, where you're seeing all the work that goes into keeping the country safe.'

Laura glances over at the PM and Jess sees he immediately returns her look. It's certainly quite a connection they have, surely well beyond the normal PM/MA relationship. She decides to press a little harder. She needs a story out of today, something different to other defence writers. 'The Mystery of the Pretty Military Attaché' has the potential to cause a bit of trouble . . .'

'Yes. And it must be hard because you know how these things work on the inside, yet you see your boss getting misunderstood by the public. I'm thinking, of course, of the blow-up last summer during the leadership contest over the PM's service record in Somalia and the accusation that he committed human rights violations.'

Jess exchanges a look with Jack. She finds his dispassionate gaze strangely unnerving. Her horniness, far from being cooled down, is in serious danger of boiling over entirely. She needs to concentrate.

'But that was all disproven,' Laura says quickly.

'Exactly,' Jess says. 'But that must be a real frustration. That people don't understand how this all works. It's possible to make almost anything innocent appear murky, if you know what I mean. And then the PM's political enemies can cause him problems . . .'

Laura looks a little confused about how to reply. Jess wonders if she's the first person to imply Laura's relationship with the prime minister is unusual, maybe even inappropriate. Is Laura spluttering for a response now because she's been rumbled, or because she really hasn't a clue what Jess is getting at?

'Of course,' Jack cuts in, coming to Laura's rescue. 'For example, in the SAS there are plenty of grey areas that we're compelled to operate in. Depending on how it's spun, the public can struggle to see it as heroic . . .'

'You guys all seem pretty heroic to me,' Jess says, staring into Jack's unblinking face until he looks back down at his plate.

'Now, ladies,' Gen Sir Humphrey calls along the table to Jess and Laura. 'I hope you haven't done yourselves too well at lunch. We've got a surprise for you this afternoon.'

Jess looks at Laura in panic, wishing she hadn't been so testy with her.

'Don't worry,' Laura says kindly. 'I've already been briefed. It'll be fun.'

Piling back into the trucks, they drive for a couple of miles, Jess realising too late that she should have taken the chance to run to the loo back at base instead of flitting around Jack. Why did she have so much water at lunch? Bloody Jack making her mouth dry with nervous tension. The trucks lurch over pot-holes, testing Jess's bladder to the limit.

When they finally stop, they are greeted by a couple of enormous Chinook helicopters and racks of strange, rubbery adult-size Babygros, which look like early underwater diving suits. They are told to put them on, which is easier said than done as they have no zips or buttons. Laura shows Jess how to climb in through the tight rubber neck-hole.

'These are dry suits,' Laura explains, while they struggle to squeeze themselves in, like toothpaste being inched back into the tube. 'They keep you completely dry. See how they're sealed at the cuff and neck?'

'But we aren't near water, are we? We're in the mountains.' Jess straps a helmet on. Knowing she's now trapped inside the suit, she's even more desperate for the bathroom. At a shout, the men and Laura start boarding the Chinooks but Jess re-mains on the ground.

'Come on!' shouts Jack.

'I ... I can't,' Jess cries back.

'You're not scared of flying, are you?'

'No, I ...' She hesitates. She simply can't face telling this gorgeous man that she has a basic bodily function to fulfil. Jack takes her hand and guides her under the rotors.

'Look out, lads,' he shouts, as they climb the ramp at the rear of the nearest helicopter. 'She's feeling a bit tender.'

Jess straps herself in and, over the thud of the rotors, quietly chants to herself to not wet her knickers. There's a worrying lurch in her stomach as the craft leaves the ground, then she's hit by a strong smell of fuel and hot metal.

After a few minutes, Jack speaks over the intercom.

'Okay, Prime Minister, lads – we're going to take a swan dive over the reservoir. We'll just do about twenty feet today. Pair up.'

'Here, you'll need this.' Jack hands Jess a life jacket.

As Jess puts it on, nonplussed, the rear ramp of the helicopter lowers and the men around her begin to organise themselves. Laura and the PM automatically stand next to each other, Laura clamping his arm tightly, which he doesn't seem to mind. Jess looks out of the window and sees the helicopter is hovering over water.

'What the hell is going on?' she yells. 'We're still in the air!'

'We're going to jump in the reservoir, okay?' Jack shouts back.

'NO!' screams Jess. 'Not okay!'

'I'll hang on to you. Watch these guys.' He gestures to the men, who are waiting in line for a signal from one of the Chinook crew members to exit. 'See how they run, rather than jump? We're going to sprint together. Then just let yourself drop.'

'Won't I land on the person in front of me?'

'No. The chopper's still moving.'

'What?' Jess yells in horror.

'Come on, let's go!'

'No, Jack. I . . . I need a wee!'

Jack grips the strap of her life jacket and they run forward together. Jess finds it hard to move her feet in the heavy, oversized sack and worries she'll fall out head first. She has a second's glimpse at the misty waves, whipped up by the powerful rotors, before she and Jack drop through the air, her scream catching in her throat, and plunge into the freezing water.

An hour later, Jess and Laura are towelling their hair dry in the bathroom, thanking scientists everywhere for waterproof mascara. The PM's team are leaving soon, but Jess has just had news that a tree has come down on the line outside Hereford and all trains are cancelled for the rest of the day. Gen Sir Humphrey has invited her to bunk at the barracks. Jess, who can't stop thinking about Jack's strong arms pulling her out of the reservoir, just wishes she hadn't told him about her desperation for the bathroom on the flight.

'So.' Jess catches Laura's eye in the mirror. 'You and the PM ... get on well, don't you?'

Jess thinks about what else happened in the reservoir. Laura and the PM, bobbing in the water together, laughing and splashing each other. Not exactly subtle.

Laura turns to face her, looking peeved. 'You're not the first person to notice that we get on. I'm not embarrassed about it. I'm sure it's easy to join certain dots, if you're willing to assume a few things.' She watches Jess, then sighs. 'I suppose I'd ask you to consider if you'd make the same judgement if I were a man.'

Jess starts brushing her hair with her fingers, frowning. Laura hands her a small hairbrush from a backpack. She's right, of course. Jess wouldn't think anything of the friendship at all if Laura were a man. Just a beautiful bromance.

'I'm sorry, Laura,' Jess says in a small voice. 'You're right. That's exactly what I thought and I can't apologise enough. Can I give you a bit of advice, though?'

'Shoot.'

'Be careful. You say I'm not the only one to make this stupid connection. Well, people in Westminster gossip. Don't let this get back to Clarissa Courtenay. She's dangerous – and I don't think the PM can help you if his wife turns on you.'

Laura's smile fades.

*

171

Once the PM's helicopter has taken off, Jess is invited to the officers' mess for pints of local cider. Jack, she notices, often addresses her, as though to include her. For once, though, Jess is content to be quiet and observe, thinking about what she needs to do when she returns to London. The dip in the freezing water and her exchange with Laura have cleared her mind. She needs to focus, get Ed off her back and get laid.

Jess isn't distracted for long, though. The group moves outside, where a small bonfire has been lit to ward off the evening chill. A soldier hands around hot sausage rolls and Jack, slipping another cider into Jess's hands, joins her on a bench to watch the flames. They look out across the stunning mountain range, the last of the evening light dipping away as the summer fields turn purple and blue. The first stars are coming out in the clear night sky.

'I could get used to this,' Jess says. 'Do you sleep outside often?'

'Pretty often but it isn't like this. No fires and hot food and cider, that's for sure. Less glamping, more freezing your bollocks off in a ditch.'

Jess is intensely aware of where she and Jack are touching through their thick clothing, along the thigh and hip and shoulder. He's as warm as the fire and she would like to cosy herself under his arm. The cold water wiped away her lust earlier, but now the fire and the stars and the cider, and the soft voice and musky smell of this real-life Action Man, are combining in an intoxicating rush. Jess longs to kiss him.

Jack explains more about how he and his team sleep outside on operations and exercises. At various points they have been required to get from one place to another over a couple of days without maps or compasses, while evading detection. He's hidden in freezing cold streams to avoid infrared and snatched sleep in the desert, surrounded by snakes and scorpions.

172

'How do you find where you're going?' Jess asks, wondering whether he's sensing her waves of lust and how he might react to an advance from her.

'There's stuff we learn about. And if all else fails.' Jack gestures up at the sky. 'Stars.'

'Can you teach me?' Jess asks slyly, spotting a chance to get him alone.

'Sure, but it's too bright around the fire.' The corner of his mouth twitches. 'We'll have to go into the darkness a bit.'

They slip away around the side of the concrete building, Jess hoping that Jack's reluctance to announce a stargazing lesson to the group means he is thinking along the same lines as her. As they take a path into the bracken, Jess feels Jack's fingers graze very softly, very deniably, against hers. Maybe it's because they're away from the fire, but she shivers deliciously. She reaches her fingers out to him and grips his hand in return.

Jess glances heavenwards and stops walking, taken aback by the vast scattered canopy above her. She's never seen stars this clear and bright, completely unblighted by light pollution.

Jack stops too.

'Pretty good, right?' he murmurs, taking a step towards Jess so that they're a mere inch from each other. They stand for a moment, watching the sky. It's so quiet that Jess can hear the gentle hammering of Jack's heartbeat through his huge chest.

'Better than good,' she whispers, reaching her hands up behind his head and kissing him.

The response is instantaneous, the coyness of the day burned out. Jack kisses Jess back, gently at first and then with increasing hunger, and lifts her easily from the ground so she can wrap her legs around his waist. Frantically now, they kiss each other's necks and ears, while Jack carries Jess a few steps to a crumbling stone wall so she is sitting eye to eye with him.

Jess fumbles with the buttons on his khakis, feeling the heat emanating from his body, desperate to be up against him. She wonders for a moment about asking him if he's married or has a girlfriend, but she doesn't want to know. She needs this for herself and isn't responsible for Jack's decisions. It's been a long time since she's allowed herself to give in to this palpable sense of urgency to be with someone, just for one night, to sate her.

Jack is murmuring in her ear and it's driving Jess wild. 'I've wanted to do this all day . . . the minute you held that gun . . . '

Jess has managed to wriggle her leggings down her thighs now, her coat just about protecting her bare skin from the cold, gritty stone wall. Jack's right hand shifts Jess's thong to one side and he begins to sweep his slightly rough thumb in circles against her, occasionally pausing to slip a finger inside. She sighs softly into his ear. He responds by pressing harder, moving faster, his free hand stroking the small of her back, then her ribcage, and then sneaking under her bra to gently pinch her nipple.

Jess wants to make this last as long as possible but she can't. She can feel heat build within her, ready to burst out of her throat.

'I'm going to come.' She manages to moan as quietly as possible, unsure how well sound can travel back to the campfire, before throwing her head back in a silent, eye-rolling cry.

As she recovers, lying back on the wall, Jack gently unzips her coat and kisses her stomach, his warm breath ticklish against the chilly night air. Jess strokes his hair for a moment, then pushes him back and hops off the wall, pulling her leggings back up. She can just make out Jack's face in the darkness, looking at her expectantly.

Jess pushes him back against the wall, creeping one hand down into his unzipped cargo pants, and kneels. Jack's commando – of course – and Jess nearly makes a joke, but she's too focused. Annoyed with herself for going for instant

174

gratification, she wants to tease out Jack's pleasure to the point of agony, so she is as gentle as she can be. But before long she can hear him grunting through gritted teeth and a hand very softly but insistently presses the back of her head closer to him. She supposes a long time on a base with no women must be taking its toll. Holding back a sigh, Jess takes more of him in her mouth and speeds up.

'Hey.' Jack hisses. 'Easy, tiger. Not just yet.'

He rummages in his pocket and pulls out a condom.

Jess looks at it for a moment. Well, it's a bit presumptuous. Who carries a condom around with them on a prime-ministerial visit? Has he done this before, taken random women out to study the stars?

'I told you I've wanted to do this all day,' Jack teases.

Then, Jess realises, she doesn't care about this either. She isn't going to see him again. Besides, she's wanted to do this all day too. Perhaps she is a little foolish for thinking she's been the seducer – looks like the strong-and-silent treatment works on her after all – but who cares? At least her instincts have been right once today.

Grinning, Jess takes the condom and rolls it onto him, being careful to put the wrapper in her coat pocket. She doubts he's the type, but she doesn't want Jack to have proof to brag to his men about laying the lady journalist.

Jess stands, kicks off her trainers and pulls her leggings off. Jack moves to lift her back onto the wall but she skims past him and braces her forearms against it, turning her head to smile at him. Jack's so tall that he has to put his feet well apart. As he carefully guides himself into her, he grunts with pleasure. His hands grip her hips as he finds his rhythm, then they creep up her sides to play with her breasts.

But Jess wants to orgasm again. And there's only one position she can truly count on.

175

'I want to be on top,' she says, gasping.

Jack stops and gingerly takes a step back. Jess turns and pushes him to the ground. She kneels down and is pleasantly surprised by how springy and comfortable the terrain is. She was braced for hard, stony, cold ground but they're on a bed of bouncing bracken.

Jess lowers herself down until she's straddling Jack, who is now in complete darkness apart from his eyes, which capture glimmers of the stars. His hands move back to her hips as she begins a rhythm of her own, then one of his hands inches forward to massage her clitoris as the other grips her arse.

Jess speeds up, rushing them both to climax. She's breathing hard now, while Jack is arching his back against the ground, trying to get even deeper into her.

'I'm close,' he mutters through gritted teeth. 'Do me a favour and . . . slip one in, will you?'

Jess sticks an index finger into her mouth then reaches her hand behind her, pausing until she herself is right on the cusp, before obligingly sliding it into Jack's arsehole.

He immediately gasps and convulses, hissing air between his teeth as quietly as possible.

Jess slides off him and they lie together in the bracken, panting. The air is so fantastically crisp and oxygenated that Jess feels almost high.

After a few minutes, she pulls her leggings and trainers back on while Jack rummages around in his pocket and pulls out a hip flask. Jess takes a sip. Whisky.

As they cling together for warmth under the stars, passing the hip flask back and forth, Jess thinks what a perfect encounter that was. If only it had been with Christian.

11th August

Con 19% Lab 46%

Record-sized rats in Luton/

Water table at record low

Tipperton

Bobby stares at her side profile in the bathroom mirror of the community hall. There's no getting away from it – despite her best efforts in sourcing a smock dress, she's very clearly either swallowed a cantaloupe or she's pregnant.

She's had a few sleepless nights, worrying about what to say to the Tipperton Conservative Association about her impending birth. Eva and Jess still insist she should keep her pregnancy a secret, but what will this mean for her relationship with her constituents going forward? It's touch and go now, so there's no chance she can hide her condition by polling day. Starting off with a lie hardly feels the way to go. Finally, she turned to Percy for advice.

'Well, this is a pickle you've got yourself into,' he said. 'I'm glad we've got one troublemaker in the house! Now, let's think.

Eva and Jess are right – the fear will be that you just shove off on maternity leave the moment you're elected. But,' he holds a hand up as Bobby opens her mouth, 'it's your job to convince them otherwise. You've got to take these people in hand. Tell them what's what. And if you hit a particularly sticky point, then just give them the old "my grandfather didn't fight the Nazi fascists just so we could hand the country over to a bunch of communists".'

'That works?'

'Like a charm.'

Bobby smooths her hair behind her ears. Though it's not exactly her style, Percy is right that she should be front-footed. Maybe the association members will accept what she has to say and maybe they won't. But at least she's talking on her terms.

Taking a deep inhalation, Bobby leaves the bathroom and sits with the three other candidates, waiting to be called through to the main hall. She glances down the row. They're also astonishingly young – the man next to her looks like he hasn't had to use a razor yet. These are the ambitious types looking for a 'no-hoper' seat to fight at this election, knowing they won't win, so they can later go on to fulfil their dreams of becoming cabinet ministers after paying their dues. Bobby wonders if any of them have even been to Tipperton before. Or the last time they left the interior of the M25.

One by one, her fellow candidates are called into the hall. Through the double doors she can hear smatterings of applause, murmurs and grumbles. Then, after what feels like an agonising wait, it's her turn. As she steps onto the stage, she notices Susie Coleman, the former MP's ex-wife, waving to her from the second row, next to Bobby's mother and father. Mr Cliveden, despite being on his longest ever streak outside the local mental health unit, looks anxious to be in such a crowded room, but he gives her a thumbs-up nonetheless.

Bobby makes a short speech, outlining her family's roots in the area and her commitment to her community. There is a quick round of applause when she mentions her campaign to save the Tipperton Mental Health Unit, which gives her a boost. She outlines her goals of expanding the local A&E department, keeping the local libraries open and extending and improving the rail line so that Tipperton residents don't have to depend on driving to the next nearest station twenty miles away. Remembering her own teenage frustration of relying on her parents to get around, Bobby talks about the need for more buses to connect the local towns, but she is careful not to attack the current government. She wants to show she's independent-minded, but also a team player.

Next is a series of questions covering all sorts of policy areas and some local 'gotcha' questions, testing how well Bobby actually knows Tipperton. She bats each away, starting to enjoy herself now, knowing the pinstriped suits next door won't have stood a chance at this point. A red-faced old man at the back of the room pipes up.

'Ms Cliveden, you seem an accomplished young lady, but I've read in the papers that some folk are suggesting we should have an age limit for MPs, so they can only stand when they're thirty. It seems like a good idea to me. What do you think?'

'Well.' Bobby smiles. She wonders how older generations can complain about the young being work-shy or lazy, yet be troubled by them showing political ambition. They can't have it both ways. 'Being only twenty-five, I don't want to talk myself out of a job, so perhaps this should only apply to Labour candidates.' There is a rumble of appreciative chuckles. 'Do you mind if I ask you a question in return, sir?'

The old man nods and people exchange curious glances with their neighbours.

'Do you think we should force MPs to stand down at the

standard retirement age? Obviously it would be a shame to lose so many of the current members of the Commons who do amazing work with a huge amount of experience. But if we're prescribing age limits, why not look at both ends of the spectrum?'

The old man gives her a chastened smile. There is a lot of murmuring and even some scattered applause. Feeling momentum behind her, Bobby meets Susie's eyes. Susie raises her hand with the question she and Bobby prepared in advance.

'Ms Cliveden, I think some here are perhaps being a little coy with the real question they wish to ask. You're a young woman, and in a relationship with the director of the Downing Street policy unit.' There is more murmuring, not all of it positive. Local associations can be very suspicious of a candidate they think has been thrust upon them by the centre. Bobby is also pleased that Susie didn't refer to Jake as a 'boyfriend'. She has been referring to him as a 'partner', hoping it sounds more serious and grown-up. 'What are we, your constituents, to do when your mind inevitably turns to children and maternity leave and a leave of absence from your duties?'

The room is silent, every face turned to Bobby.

'Well.' Bobby clasps her hands together to keep herself steady. 'I've been pondering this question a lot lately. That's because . . .' She glances around at the expectant faces. 'That's because I am in fact pregnant right now.'

There is a torrent of whispered mutterings.

'But I'd like to explain why I'm here anyway. I've of course been told that associations don't want pregnant women – or even women who may become pregnant at some point – as their MP. I was also told I could expect the worst kind of prejudice about being an unmarried mother, as though the Conservatives are still stuck in the 1950s. Some said to keep this a secret for as long as possible, to give me the best chance of being selected.' Bobby casts her eye across the room again, studying the faces carefully. 'But I refuse to be dishonest with you.'

'That's all very well, miss,' an elderly woman calls out. 'But what about us? When are you due? What are your plans?'

'Yes, of course. It can't be the case that I disappear the moment I'm elected and leave you to it.' The elderly woman folds her arms and nods. 'I'm due at Christmas. So yes – I'd be campaigning as your candidate while pregnant, so I'll level with the rest of the constituency too. Otherwise people will probably have a few questions when I knock on their doors during the election with a beach ball under my jumper.' There are a couple of laughs. 'I'm fortunate to have my parents living here, and who would want to live anywhere else? Meanwhile, my partner will be based in London, which is where I'll be during the week for votes and parliamentary business and so on. But I'll be in Tipperton for the majority of the week.'

'That all sounds fine, miss.' It's the old lady again, her hands now on her hips. 'But what about those first few weeks? That's a probation period for most people. It sounds to me like you'll just be checking out as soon as you get the job!'

Bobby nods again. 'Yes, I understand. I will need your patience for the first few weeks. But I'll be here in Tipperton, getting the hang of things, and I'll have a proxy vote in Parliament.' Bobby silently thanks Eva for explaining the proxy system, where the Speaker of the House can grant permission for an MP who has to be away from the Commons to essentially vote remotely through another.

Bobby steps forward and clasps her hands together. 'I think the most important point is this – I didn't go to a fancy school. I went to the local high school here and I worked my socks off to get into Cambridge, where I learnt a lot but was certainly not at home in the quads and at the formal dinners. I've worked

181

in Parliament for over a year now and I expected the calibre of MPs to be a selection of the brightest minds and most moral, principled people in the country. And they aren't. Frankly, I think I can do a damn sight better – even with a baby strapped to my chest.'

Bobby chances a smile at the rumble of approval and hopes the elderly woman is now satisfied. And indeed she is. As Bobby is getting into her mother's car, feeling like she could walk on air, the elderly woman accosts her in the car park. But only to show her that she has already started work on a knitted baby-sized cardigan. In royal blue, of course.

Claybourne Terrace

Everyone is home for dinner, although they're all a little distracted. Jess, after a long sleep to recover from her night in Hereford – she and Jack slept outside and woke at dawn, covered in dew, ready to go one more time against the breeze-blocked wall of the mess before sneaking to their beds – has been at her laptop all day. Remembering on the train home that she was actually sent there with an assignment, Jess thought about trudging out some text about the models of the different guns and vehicles used in their exercises, or the future of AI and drones in combat, but chose to do something else. Why pretend she remembers any of this stuff after having her brains banged out by the commanding officer?

Instead, Jess has focused on the PM's abilities as a marksman and natural soldier, being most at ease with a group of 'fellow' alphas and generally allowing her to see him in a completely new light, away from the awkward PMQs exchanges and clumsy interviews. Just about avoiding a puff piece, Jess's article will be coming out in tomorrow's *Sunday Sentinel*. She knows Lord Finlayson and the Downing Street team will be pleased, but Jess wonders whether Christian will say anything to her about it. Perhaps a spat with him will at least distract her from the temptation of the alternative. In the meantime, she has arranged to meet a mole from StoryCorps HR tomorrow, courtesy of Teddy Hammer, to work out where Clarissa and Ed's paths crossed.

Percy should be cheerful, because he has been told he can have a headline speaking slot at the Conservative Party conference in October, where he has been given full permission to tell whichever (PG) jokes he likes, so long as the overall message is a rallying call for the general election. But he's had a rather trying day otherwise. Asked to visit a seat in South Wales to help with local canvassing and fundraising, he was thrilled to learn that he'd be judging a beauty pageant as part of his itinerary. It came as a bit of a shock to realise, once the contestants came out on stage, that it was for children.

'I thought I was having a heart attack,' he says, knocking back a gulp of gin and tonic.

Holly's soothing words about child beauty pageants being common in America – 'I was Miss Supreme Little Darling Palm Beach, myself' – and a large bowl of crisps calm him down.

Eva has the thrill of being the ultimate Westminster insider: she knows something nobody else does, including her father and the prime minister. Plus there's the added frisson that it's to do with porn. It's just a shame that her lack of love life means she's in danger of skewing the main search term for Pimlico to wild one-night stands, her own preference. Still, there's her imminent Battersea selection interview to look forward to, which is only days away. Conservative Twitter is alive at the news that Percy Cross's daughter is on the shortlist and her phone won't stop buzzing with good luck messages from SpAds and existing MPs. Professionally at least, things couldn't be better.

Bobby is weary after her train back to London and nods off on the sofa in the drawing room well before dinner. She stirs just as it's time to sit down, but is so shattered that she takes a tray up to bed. Percy and Holly wolf their food and head up for an early night too, leaving Eva and Jess alone in the kitchen.

Jess washes up and Eva dries, but Jess keeps stopping and gazing out of the kitchen window.

'What's up?' Eva says, getting impatient.

'Nothing much. Just quite a bit on.' Jess resumes her scrubbing. She'd like to tell Eva about the meeting she is having tomorrow with the woman from StoryCorps HR. In fact, she'd like to tell her everything about Ed and how he could destroy her – holding it all in is horrible – but she knows better. Now that this business involves Clarissa, the line between private and professional is in danger of being crossed. Jess hasn't forgotten that Eva's been willing to pass on information to Clarissa in the past and they seem to have become friendlier recently.

'Hm, all right. I know we're both feeling sad about Bobby moving out. Well, I've been thinking.' Eva nudges Jess gently. 'If I win Battersea I really ought to live there. I bet Dad will help me buy a flat. The royalties for this latest book are insane! Well ... how about we live there together? Two single gals. Easy to pop to Brixton to see Bobby and the baby. Only across the river from here for Sunday lunches ...'

'Really?' Jess grins. 'Oh, Eva, I would love that! It has been on my mind, you know. I wondered whether I should find somewhere alone. But this is so much better ...'

'It's a deal then. Now.' Eva gropes around for something else to keep Jess talking. 'How was your trip to Hereford?'

'Well ...' Jess considers for a moment. Why not? Swearing Eva to secrecy, Jess tells her all about her night with Jack.

'Ooh, you're so lucky.' Eva looks glumly out of the window

at the overgrown garden. 'I'd kill for something fun and easy like that.'

'Well, it is time you had a bit of fun. It's been ages since you split with Jamie and you've had your head stuck in work. Time to meet someone and let your hair down. Why not join an app?'

Eva scoffs. 'You must be joking.' She's talked to Jess and Bobby enough times about her fear of apps. And something tells her that the last thing she needs for her run as an MP are embarrassing press stories about her love life, or lack of it.

'Why not? You haven't got time for bar-hopping or parties just now. Anyway.' Jess pulls off her rubber gloves and shows Eva her phone screen. 'I'm not talking about any old app.'

Eva stares. *Fawn – the dating app for those who are shy in the streets and demons in the sheets. And always discreet.* She splutters but keeps reading.

'You can tell it was created by a woman,' Jess breathes. 'They have a non-negotiable condom policy! What do you reckon?'

'I've always fantasised about this kind of liaison, but ... Have you used it?' Eva asks warily.

'Yup. Only once. It was pretty fun but a bit vanilla for me.' Jess's mind flicks back to her evening with J. 'Been too busy since.'

'All right. It's been four months since Jamie. Let's do it,' Eva says, wondering what she's letting herself in for.

12th August

Con 19% Lab 47%

Bin rats giving dogs suspected rabies/
Freak snow in LA

South London

Eva stares at her phone as the bus trundles over the Thames and wonders for the tenth time if this is a really stupid idea. The athletic young guy whose photo she's looking at is handsome enough, and was funny and clever in his messages to her on Fawn, but is this just an insane risk? Perhaps she's more like her father than she thought. Still, there's no denying that she's excited. Eva's always longed for an encounter like this, a no-strings one-night stand that she's only lived out in her digital fantasies, but been too afraid to approach a complete stranger. At parties with her university friends, she would never take someone home, fearing gossip and snide remarks. God, what a tedious existence.

Twenty minutes later, Eva presses the buzzer for the flat and waits, hoping her face hasn't gone too red in the heat. It's still

186

warm and light outside, which helped with her claim to Percy, Holly and Bobby that she was off to a barbecue in Clapham. After forensically shaving her legs, and then her bush, which she had abandoned like a wild garden over the summer, she chose a broderie anglaise minidress, which showed off the tan she's been working on in the Claybourne Terrace garden after her Caribbean holiday.

As she hears footsteps coming down the stairs, Eva considers simply running away. But, she reminds herself, the app gives her a layer of safety, both physically in case the guy's a psycho, and in terms of discretion. Before she can make up her mind, the door opens and a pair of laughing, chocolate-brown eyes smile out at her.

'Eva?' He has a warm voice with a slight London accent and a trendy faded haircut. Eva nods. 'I'm Joshua. Come in.'

Eva follows him up the stairs, her heart hammering, noticing how nice his bum is through his jeans. She really ought to say something, but she hasn't a clue how to start this off. Luckily Joshua, perhaps because he is hosting, is happy to lead.

'First time?' he asks. Eva nods again. 'Same. It's a bit odd, isn't it. Drink?'

'Please,' she manages to murmur, looking around his open-plan living/dining/kitchen area. It is neat and in the style of most young professionals who can bulk-buy from Loaf. Elephant grey and navy blue. There are books everywhere, lining each shelf, stacked under the coffee table and piled on side tables. 'On your own here?'

'Yeah.' Joshua hands Eva a glass of rosé, their fingers brushing. Eva blushes, avoids his gaze and focuses on the ice cubes bobbing about in the wine. 'I like it. But I might have to move soon. How about you?'

'No.' She hesitates. 'With friends.'

'Ah.' Joshua looks sideways at her. 'I guess that's why you

wanted to meet here. So.' He sits down on the sofa and gestures for Eva to join him. As she settles down, she notices that he smells delicious, vaguely minty. 'Why have you joined the app?'

'If you don't mind, I'd prefer we don't reveal too much about ourselves,' Eva says, trotting out the line she rehearsed with Jess. 'Seeing as this is a one-off.'

Joshua raises his eyebrows. It reminds him of what that wild dark-haired girl said a few months ago.

'All right.' Eva sighs. 'If you want the truth, I'm on here because I came out of a relationship a few months ago, I work a hard job – and I just want to have some great sex because I'm unbelievably horny.'

Eva takes a huge mouthful of wine, her eyes stinging a little as she swallows. They both know why they're here. Why does there need to be this small talk?

Joshua laughs softly. No, she's different from the dark-haired girl. Softer. Not as assertive.

'Now, don't you feel better getting all that off your chest?' He takes a large sip too, not taking his eyes off her. 'I'm in the same boat. Thought I'd give this app a try and . . . ' he looks at her sideways, biting his lip, 'I can't wait to get started.'

Eva smiles at him properly for the first time. Very gingerly, he leans in and kisses her. Eva kisses him back, tasting toothpaste and wine as his lips seem to thaw against hers.

Joshua's free hand, cold from the glass, moves to Eva's neck, sending a small shiver down her shoulder. She leans to the floor to put down her wine glass and kisses him back more urgently, both of her hands now wrapped around his neck. Joshua plonks his wine glass on the windowsill and reaches over to Eva, pulling her onto his lap.

Eva slides over, playfully sticking her tongue into Joshua's ear as his hands travel up her bare thighs and under her dress. He breathes longingly into her tits as she runs her fingernails

188

down his shirted back. His erection fights through his jeans against her pubic bone.

Joshua makes straight for Eva's clit through her underwear, feeling the fabric soaked through with lust already. Eva unbuttons his shirt and tugs it off over his shoulders, before running her fingers over his toned and, in a first for her, shaved chest. Thank goodness she's been so aggressive with the razor herself.

She bites his ear as he slips a finger inside her. Joshua grins and flips Eva around so that she's lying on her back on the sofa and he's kneeling on the floor before her. Wordlessly, he pulls her underwear down and begins kissing his way up her inner thigh, his finger still moving inside her. His head disappears beneath her skirt and, within seconds of his tongue rhythmically massaging her, Eva's moaning in ecstasy.

Just before she's about to succumb to orgasm, Eva pushes Joshua back and pulls off his jeans as he lies back on the floor and, laughing, looks at his watch.

'My, my. We met twenty minutes ago. Time flies, doesn't it?'

Grinning, Eva puts a hand over his mouth and climbs on top of him.

Fifteen minutes later, they lie on the floor, panting, surrounded by scattered books and cushions and with angry carpet burns on their knees and lower backs.

Eva drinks deeply from her wine glass and wonders about pulling her dress back on to hide her body. But then, she considers, she isn't going to see this guy again. Who cares what he thinks of her naked? It's so freeing to not give a toss, after years of self-conscious worrying.

'Want a tour of the rest of the flat?' Joshua says quietly. 'There's *so* much more to this place than from the fridge to the sofa in four steps . . . '

Leaving her clothes behind, Eva follows him into the bedroom.

'Very impressive.' She points at the rack of carefully ironed shirts along one wall.

'And here's the bathroom.' Joshua pushes open a side door to a room tiled in dark green. In the corner is a huge power shower. His eyes narrow at her. 'Fancy a wash?'

Eva knocks back the rest of her wine and, wrapping her arms around his neck, kisses him again. His cock digs into her immediately.

Moments later, they're under a cascade of warm water, Joshua pinning Eva's hands above her head as they slam against the wall.

14th August

Greenwich

Jess is at a café, waiting to meet the StoryCorps HR employee that Teddy Hammer has connected her to on the quiet. The woman turns up looking conspicuous for a sunny August afternoon, wearing dark glasses, a baseball cap pulled low over her nose and a hooded parka.

'Crikey, you look like Leonardo DiCaprio sneaking out of a nightclub.' Jess smiles, trying to make her feel at ease, having dealt with enough sources in her time to understand how jumpy people can be.

'I know it sounds mental but I nearly didn't come. Just got in a weird panic. Anyway, I'm boiling under here, so I hope this is worth it for you.'

Jess takes the large brown envelope from the woman, opens it and peers through the gap at the top sheet inside. The record of Clarissa's career movements within StoryCorps. This should do it. But, Jess frowns, is she being too trusting of this woman who, though evidently anxious, has willingly handed over company records on Ed Cooper and Clarissa Courtenay? Is this some kind of trap?

'Do you mind me asking why you're doing this?' Jess asks.

'I trust Teddy. And ...' The woman sighs. 'I've been around a lot longer than you. Ed Cooper has been the biggest problem for me in my entire career at StoryCorps. Have you any idea how many crying employees I've had in my office? Do you know what we've spent on legal bills and severance packages to squash the people with the guts to complain about him? It's not that I care about StoryCorps – it isn't the first huge, soul-sucking organisation that I've worked at and signed people off from for stress. But I do care about bullies. And Ed Cooper is a bully. And he's protected for some reason, even against the interests of a giant corporation. Something very fishy has to be going on for that to happen.'

'You're right.'

'Listen.' The woman leans in. 'You're the only person who has ever bothered to dig into the guy and figure out what his influence is – and how high up it goes. So that leads me to believe you're taking this seriously.'

'Deadly,' Jess says firmly, though she is unwilling to say anything further because, frankly, she still doesn't know if she's chasing her tail. She definitely doesn't want to give anybody the impression that she's closer to an answer than she is. False hope is no hope.

'Can I give you one bit of advice, then – with my, er, HR hat on?' The woman lowers her voice. 'This needs to be a proper job. You can't half-skewer someone. I've seen it enough times. I don't mean a public beheading. But it has to be total annihilation as far as his influence at StoryCorps is concerned, or the blowback for you will be appalling.'

Jess nods to show her understanding. This has occurred to her – she can't have Ed able to rally.

'I understand.' Jess stands to leave. 'Thanks again.'

'You're welcome. Remember,' the woman grips Jess's arm, 'you're not safe if the fucker's still intact. You've got to do a proper job.'

Do a proper job, Jess thinks when she gets home, looking again at the sheets of paper from the envelope on her bed. They are the StoryCorps employment records of Clarissa Courtenay and Ed Cooper, which show that they had remarkably similar career trajectories at the company. Although Clarissa acts as though she was born into the highest echelons of society, she is the daughter of a Cheshire postmaster and had to start at the bottom of journalism. She and Ed were both lowly reporters who managed to work their way to London via Finlayson-owned regional papers. Once in town, Ed was on the technology desk, duly trotting out stories on the future of flying cars and the launch of the iPod, while Clarissa helped put together a daily email newsletter for the City section of the *Sentinel*, part gossip and part business news round-up. Then things suddenly changed around the mid-2000s. Ed became a prominent reporter and commentator, with an astonishingly high salary to match, while Clarissa shot up the executive ladder, focusing her energies on Finlayson's foray into television. What happened to trigger this remarkable improvement in their fortunes?

Jess does at least have a window to work to – mid-2005 – as by the autumn of that year, both Ed and Clarissa have received their promotions and increased pay packets. The mystery is why. It doesn't even sound like they sat on the same floor. Might they have met as young, ambitious reporters? Were they lovers? Or is it just a coincidence?

There's a knock on the door and Jess hurriedly shoves the sheets under her duvet.

'I've made you a G and T.' Eva pushes the door open; Bobby follows with a bowl of crisps and a glass of orange squash. 'Where have you been? Everything okay?'

'All good.' Jess takes the fizzing, icy tumbler. 'Just running around on a story. How was Sunday evening?'

'Well.' Eva flops down on the bed, too excited to spill the beans to notice the paper crackling beneath her. 'Stubble rash in my nether regions aside, it was so fun. What a freeing experience. I feel sort of sad not to have done this kind of thing before.'

'Isn't it dangerous?' Bobby asks, when Eva explains the concept of the app and what happened on Sunday night. Bobby watched *Antiques Roadshow* with Eva's dad that evening.

'I know what you mean, but the app tracks you and makes sure you check in when you're home and stuff. And I sent my location pin to Jess's phone.'

Bobby feels a little stab of jealousy. Why wasn't she told where Eva was? But this is how it will be from now on. Eva and Jess living together, Bobby catching up with them when she can. Them out on the tiles, her wiping baby sick off the tiles. Completely different frames of reference.

'Anyway.' Eva nestles back into the cushions. 'It totally did the trick. Can't wait for my next one.'

'If it was so good, why don't you just see the same guy again? He sounds a good try,' Bobby asks, her mouth full of crisps.

Eva gives Bobby a pitying look.

'That's not the point of this app. Or why I'm on it, anyway. Or Joshua. I can't fall back into my usual pattern of clinging on to the next guy I meet.'

She's only half telling the truth though. Eva's wondered often over the past forty-eight hours about whether to message

Joshua on the app, which has an infuriating feature that shows her when the user she's looking up is online. He is online a lot, but silent. Now he's got his first time out of the way with her, he's presumably fixing up all sorts of other hookups, preparing to pour a stream of different women glasses of wine and go down on them in his living room. *Or*, an ugly voice says in the back of Eva's brain, *maybe he just didn't think you were worth a second visit.*

16th August

Battersea

Eva peers through a crack in a side door at the audience assembled for her selection, straightens up and walks onto the stage.

Quite unprepared, compared to Bobby in Tipperton, Eva is aware that many of the people in the room work in the City, that they don't want to pay any more income tax and that they like to think of themselves as socially liberal and modern. Deciding to keep the focus of her government experience on her time working for Madeleine Ford, who she suspects the attendees feel naturally more aligned with, Eva wonders if a single person present could accurately pinpoint Grimsby on a map.

There is an interested flutter of whispered conversation when she introduces herself and the association members listen to her opening statement in silence, apart from one woman of about

196

Eva's age, who shifts in her seat and tuts with apparent frustration. Unlike Bobby, who leant into her local connections and her commitment to be a voice for the community rather than a Westminster politician, Eva pushes heavily on her ambitions for high office (it's a risk, but Clarissa has advised her to bank on her association wanting a future cabinet minister) and her commitment to attack the current Labour mayor of London. Eva does well in the question section, even though the young fidgety woman regularly scoffs and even mutters a derisive 'ha!' from time to time. Happily for Eva, the young woman doesn't appear to be a particularly popular member of the association. She is shushed several times and more than one person rolls their eyes when she stands to ask her question.

'Miss Cross,' she begins. 'Surely if we select you then we're fulfilling all the accusations of gross nepotism levelled at this party for generations. Your father was prime minister, and is now a member of the House of Lords and a cabinet minister. You yourself were a government special adviser. Why should we be saddled with carrying on the Cross dynasty, when we should frankly bury it along with the Blairs and Benns?'

The young woman looks around smugly as if expecting roars of approval, but most members of the group look embarrassed.

'You're quite right, of course.' Eva smiles serenely. 'My father was prime minister. You're also correct that I have been given every chance in life, which is why it's high time for me to give something back. As for your accusation of nepotism . . . ' Eva pauses for dramatic effect. 'Many people might think that being Percy Cross's daughter has counted against me for most of my life.' There is a tinkle of laughter. 'But it's forced me to be better than the expectations people have of me, which, as you can see, can be quite low,'

Eva smiles again at the young woman, who stares stonily back.

'I won't apologise for being my father's daughter. Although I've been granted all sorts of privilege, laziness and an assumption of political success aren't among them.'

It occurs to everyone there that, with his daughter standing, there is a strong chance they will have Lord Cross coming to campaign in the constituency from time to time in the coming months. Everyone would love a selfie with him.

'All right,' the woman replies. 'Where will you live then? Carry on in Daddy's townhouse?'

There are a few dissenting groans and a lot of uncomfortable seat-shifting. *This woman really is doing God's work*, Eva thinks. Her questions are reasonable and could unstick Eva quite badly, as she really has benefited from Percy's help. But the way she asks them is so aggressive, and Eva is staying so calm, that the room is firmly behind one of them – and looking ready to oust the other.

'Well.' Eva keeps smiling. 'You're right again. Like around a third of other twenty-five-year-olds, I live in my family home. I'm keen to remedy that so I'll obviously move to Battersea if elected – and prioritise affordable housing in Parliament to be able to buy here. Hopefully you'll agree that's reasonable.'

The young woman sits down, looking sour. The questions continue, but it's clear that Eva has made the right impression. Even the local councillor candidate who, it transpires, is the boyfriend of her interrogator, couldn't get the room behind him in the same way.

As Eva makes her way home to celebrate her selection with her friends in 'Daddy's townhouse', she gets a message from Clarissa, currently in Zurich, forwarding a Tweet from an attendee:

> Eva had her father's ability to think on her feet, albeit with a dash more professionalism.

Claybourne Terrace

Percy and Holly are out when Eva gets home, but Jess and Bobby are waiting for her with a bottle of champagne and some party poppers.

They all have a wonderful time, tearing into the young woman from the selection and working out exactly how quickly they can get from Battersea to Brixton.

'It's good timing, your selection tonight,' Bobby says, knocking back the last of her orange squash. 'Moira says that there are a bunch of Labour selections too. I wonder how we can find out if that includes Tipperton and Battersea. Would be good to know who our rivals are!'

'W-what?' Eva stammers. 'I had no idea that was happening. Hang on – let me text Nick at CCHQ.'

The three of them sit quietly for a moment. Jess is getting tired of the constant MP chat, which seems to be the only thing Eva and Bobby want to talk about just now.

'Not Tipperton tonight, Bob,' Eva says, reading Nick's text. 'That's next Thursday. Ooh, but they've just announced Battersea. Some guy called Joshua Udoka. Let's look him up. J-o-s-h-u-a. U-d-o ... Oh. Oh, fuck.' Eva stares at her phone. '*Oh fuck oh fuck oh fuck.* It's *him.*'

'Who?' Bobby says, taking the phone from Eva. 'Who is he?'

'He's the guy from Fawn,' Eva says, a real note of panic in her voice. 'I ... I fucked the Labour candidate for Battersea!'

'Are you sure?' Jess takes the phone from Bobby. She stares open-mouthed. She has met Joshua Udoka – J – before. Well, *met* would be an understatement. What are the chances of both her and Eva sleeping with the same guy straight out of the gates on this app?

'Y-yes,' Eva moans. 'Look.' She takes the phone and shows her friends the Fawn profile. It is definitely the same man as the

Joshua Udoka wearing a red rosette on Twitter. Eva's going to have to share a platform with this guy all autumn, argue with him at hustings and debate with him on local media. And all the while he'll be able to taunt her with the knowledge that he's seen her naked. Tits out, vag out, the lot.

'Fucking hell.' Jess sucks her teeth. 'You don't think he knew, do you?'

'Well, now I do!' Eva is fighting back waves of horror. Could Joshua have known? The news of Eva's candidacy was out by the time they met. Surely he was keeping an eye on his possible rivals. Eva keeps having flashbacks of herself talking dirty, begging for more . . . on all fours . . . with Joshua's jizz all over her face and breasts in the shower. 'Oh God . . . ' Moaning, she curls into a ball.

'It's okay.' Bobby rubs her back. 'Even if he did know, which seems highly unlikely to me, he's in the exact same position as you. It takes two to tango, after all. You've seen him naked and doing embarrassing stuff. It's not like he'll want to out himself for being on this app. Or for . . . shagging a Tory.'

'Bobby's right,' Jess says soothingly, wondering whether to mention their common connection. 'There's no way this character is going to do anything. He's signed the app's NDA too, remember. And who knows? This could be a good thing.'

'How the fuck can it be good?' Eva mumbles, her face squashed into a pillow.

'Well, you know what they say about public speaking.' Jess can't resist. 'Picture your audience naked.'

Eva sits bolt upright, mascara leaking down her cheeks.

'That isn't fucking funny, Jess. If it wasn't for you, I wouldn't even be on that bloody app. What a stupid risk. Now my parliamentary career could be over before it's started!'

'Hey,' Jess says warningly. Now clearly is not the time to say she beat Eva to the punch. 'You can't complain to me, follow my advice and then blame me for how it turns out. Besides, I thought you said he was great in the sack?'

Eva starts crying again. 'I'm sor-ry,' she wails, throwing her arms around Jess's neck. 'You're r-right.'

Jess and Bobby glance at each other over Eva's heaving shoulders, waiting for her to cry herself calmer. After a while she sits back into the pillows and sniffs.

'Seriously though,' Eva says. 'All this time spent carefully avoiding men in Westminster, being a good little girl and,' she sniffs again, 'having the most boring sex imaginable with Jamie. And this happens?'

Bobby passes her a tissue, while Jess tips the rest of her drink into Eva's glass and hands it to her. Eva takes a reviving gulp and gives a watery smile.

'It's all very well picturing Joshua naked. A treat really. But,' she manages to steady herself, 'he's seen me naked. It's just awful. And the worst thing is . . . '

'Shh, what's the worst thing?' Jess asks gently.

'I'm so itchy down there. All that shaving . . . every time I need to scratch I'll remember what a terrible mistake I've made!'

'Barbara Castle never had to put up with this shit,' Jess sighs.

30th August

CON 18% LAB 48%

BELOVED SAFARI PARK LION POISONED/

SEA LEVELS AT RECORD HIGH

CCHQ

Two weeks later, Callum Gallagher is sitting in the dark, watching Vicky Tennyson being interviewed by Beth Rigby for Sky News. The two women are in the Tennysons' first nail salon and, as the shadow chancellor shapes, buffs and paints Beth's nails, she describes her early life.

It's a genuine human-interest story, the kind politicians would kill for. She describes how she used to sweep in the first salon after school, before working her way up to nail technician to help pay for university. Her parents made sure that she earned every penny she made. As the only child of Vietnamese heritage in her town, Tennyson also talks about her early experiences of racism and ignorance. 'It hardened me up, both to words hurting but also to trying to really understand people, not just saying, "Right, well, you're clearly just a bigot and should be ignored now." Politics is a doddle by comparison.'

They work through to the present day, where Tennyson is careful to praise John Ramsey as 'a fantastic Labour leader and obviously the right man for the job of prime minister', and to talk about her role as shadow chancellor. Beth brings up the refuse and baggage strikes, which are still raging.

'You are very closely associated with the trade union movement. Can't you use your influence to help end the strikes?'

'I have no doubt that union members would be downright offended at the idea that they have political masters who order them about. That's certainly not my relationship with them. These are hard-working people fighting for better conditions with a government who are deaf to concerns about physical and mental health. That being said,' Tennyson shifts in her seat, 'I think these incredibly brave people have made their point. The government clearly won't negotiate but we all know whose side the public are on. We have an election coming up – I think it's time to end the strikes and let the ballot box finish the job the strikers have started.'

This is in exact contrast with John Ramsey's words at lunchtime, when he served pints at a working men's club and insisted the strikers should continue until the government relent.

In the darkened room, Cal's face is passive, but his mind is busy. He mutes the TV and watches Tennyson's beautiful, even features stare out at him. This woman is very clever. A great communicator – God knows that talking about taxes and budgets usually sends people to sleep, but Tennyson sounds like a human being when she does it – and totally relatable. Forcing the interview out of London and into the salon was savvy. The manicure was a great touch. Tennyson's lot must be watchful of how she's received by women. Christ, he'd kill to have her on his bench. Why aren't Labour using her more?

203

Cal types Tennyson's name into Google and reads about last year's leadership contest. Sounds like she very nearly pipped Ramsey, who carried the bulk of the parliamentary party but had close to zero union support. It was neck and neck among members. Thankfully they picked the safe dud. Cal would put money on those couple of relaxed-sounding sentences from Tennyson putting an end to the strikes. And it'll make Ramsey – and any other front-bench politician – look weak.

Cal sends an email to Nick and Don, asking Nick to dig out the CCHQ attack file on Tennyson – standard fare for political parties, who gather together what they can on their different opponents to use on a rainy day, or in an election when things get desperate – and asks Don to focus-group her. Tennyson is the real danger now. But for who?

Labour HQ

'For fuck's sake!' Ramsey rages, his hands on his hips and his usually smooth hair flying in different directions. He is standing in front of a huge TV, watching the BBC News at Six, which carries the story that the refuse and baggage handling strikes are over. 'Look at that smug cow,' he hisses, pointing at Tennyson's face, as her comments on the strikes are carried in full.

'She said you were the right man for the job,' Tanya says, trying to soothe him.

'The sodding Beeb didn't carry that though, did they?' Ramsey growls, sinking into a seat.

He knows this is technically a win for Labour. They have seemingly done the job of the government by successfully calling for these strikes to end. But it's not been a win for him, John Ramsey, after his remarks at lunchtime. In fact, he looks a complete tit. The Tories have been quick to point out that Labour are being inconsistent with their message to the public, and Tennyson is either calling the shots – or just doing what she wants.

The rest of the country, meanwhile, is obsessed with the big new story. Terry, an adored lion at Longleat safari park, has been killed by poisoned meat fed to him by a visitor. The public are outraged and amateur sleuths are in their element. Who said what about ending strikes hardly registers.

'It's fucking annoying all right,' Christian says, 'but it gets these strikes over on more or less our terms. Today's the first day the news has led with a new story. Once you're knocked off the top spot by a dead lion, you know it's time to move on. Listen – you get on with your conference speech. I'm going to go and bollock Vicky.'

Tanya gives Christian a curious look – she's normally tasked with wrangling the shadow chancellor's team – then nods.

'Come on, boss,' she says. 'We've got work to do.'

Christian meets Vicky Tennyson at Gordon's Wine Bar, a popular Westminster haunt. Tennyson supposes this is deliberate, so that any eavesdropping politicos can report to the papers the telling-off that she's surely about to get. Not if she can help it.

'Christian.' She smiles as he plonks himself down at the table. He's not taken a summer break and could clearly do with one. There are deep shadows beneath his eyes, which are red. 'Drink?'

Christian accepts the large glass of white wine she pours and closes his eyes for a moment, preparing what to say.

'I suppose you've been sent to tell me off,' Tennyson says quietly. 'And I can understand why. Look, I wasn't trying to cause trouble but ...' She wonders for a moment about lying and saying something about being caught off guard or not realising her words would be taken seriously, but decides against it. Christian deserves more credit than that. 'These strikes couldn't go on for ever. You know that. I'm sorry John couldn't be the one to do it but, honestly, would the unions have listened to him? No. So he'd have been humiliated. And, well,' she shrugs apologetically, 'I saw my chance and I took it.'

Christian bobs his head up and down slowly. She's right. He has been thinking hard over the past few days for a way to elegantly bring the industrial action to a close. Seeing as he has no control over whether the government might have come up with a resolution, Tennyson has saved him a job.

'Well, thanks for your honesty. It is a fucking pain though, Vicky. Why couldn't you have warned me first?'

But he knows the answer to that. Should he have got a whiff of what she was planning, Ramsey would have gone berserk and cack-handedly tried to say the same thing himself to thin air.

'Do we have that kind of relationship?' Tennyson tips her head to one side. 'Your lot clearly distrust me.'

'I'm not in my lot.' Christian shakes his head. 'I just want us to win, okay?'

Tennyson looks at him carefully. She has to be very delicate with what she says next. If Ramsey gets even a hint that her loyalty might waver – even though everyone knows how this game really works – she could be finished before she's started.

'I do too. And I mean really win. Not just the election, but actually turn the country around and start changing things. Do you ...' She lets a fingertip skim the lip of her wine glass. 'Do you think John thinks like that?'

Christian becomes fully alert for the first time in the conversation. This is very dangerous territory for him. Could Tennyson be laying him a trap? After all, Tanya usually deals with her and Tanya would happily see Christian's head on a spike. Or is she being straight with him, with the same doubts as him about Ramsey's commitment to really do anything with the mandate Christian is fighting to get him?

'I think John's taking one step at a time,' he says finally, splashing more wine into their glasses.

'You're a tremendous asset to him, you know,' Tennyson murmurs, swilling the glass and holding it up to the light. 'And to the whole Labour movement. Just make sure your talents and ideas are appreciated.'

'Thank you, I will.' Christian feels the need to get away. This conversation has not gone the way he was expecting. He stands to leave. 'In the meantime, do me a favour and behave, will you? I've got enough on as it is without our side descending into chaos. Leave that to the Tories, yeah?'

Tennyson smiles and nods. 'I'll run everything by you in future. I promise.'

She watches him leave, sits back in her chair and finishes her wine in peace.

Later that evening, at various addresses across the UK, regional leaders of the different unions for refuse workers and baggage handlers answer their doors to bottles of champagne. There are no cards, sender details or a return address.

25th September

Claybourne Terrace

Jess dumps a load of clean laundry onto her bed and begins to fold it. She's leaving for the Labour Party conference in Liverpool this afternoon. It's a particularly pressurised time of the year for a lobby journalist, as after the first few frazzled weeks of the new Parliamentary term, they charge around the country from one conference to another, sniffing out stories and maxing out their expense accounts on breakfasts, coffees, lunches, dinners and drinks with one MP or adviser after another. Jess is just back from the Lib Dem conference in York where everybody kept forgetting the name of the party leader, there was an almighty row about legalising marijuana as part of the election campaign and a vigorous couple were caught shagging against the glass window of the fourth-floor level of the hotel stairwell. By all accounts it was a very quiet conference this year.

208

Jess just has time to stock up on fresh pants before her train leaves for Liverpool. The highlight, by a long way, will be dinner with Christian tomorrow evening, on the eve of John Ramsey's headline speech. She is forcing herself not to feel tempted into believing she might be on a date.

'I can't believe you're off again,' Eva says from the bed. She and Bobby always seem to congregate in Jess's room these days. 'I can hardly make it through one party conference! How do you do all of them?'

Jess crams a packet of cigarettes – always handy to have around the bars in the evenings at these things, like a prison snitch – into her bag. 'Berocca and hand sanitiser to ward off bugs. Caffeine to wake up. Alka-Seltzer for hangovers. And this,' she brandishes her Rampant Rabbit, 'to fall asleep.' It seems to her that the synthetic pleasures of toys are the only safe way to get her kicks for now. Learning about Eva and Joshua has creeped Jess out. She just hopes she'll never need to reveal the truth to Eva about their mutual Fawn fling. What a lot of drama for a perfectly ordinary orgasm.

Eva, meanwhile, can't stop thinking about Joshua. He has messaged her a couple of times to see if she wants to meet up again, but Eva has deleted the app without replying. Even if he didn't know who she was when they hooked up, he must know now. They're going to meet face to face soon enough. Hopefully in the cold light of day, when she isn't blinded by lust and excitement, Joshua will turn out to be a sexless loser.

Bobby's had the best summer of them all, sexually speaking. Once she hit her second trimester, her sex drive rose tenfold and there have been entire weekends at Jake's flat where they've only left the building to recharge themselves with food before falling back into bed. However, her bump has now caught up with her and she's started to get backaches, swollen feet and random bouts of acne on her back and chest. Sex has lost its allure. Besides, she and Jake have been so busy throughout September that they've hardly managed a meal together.

'I haven't been to a conference before. What's it like?' Bobby asks Eva. This is true – last year she was busy working on a by-election to get Moira elected as MP for Tipperton. Before that, she'd never even heard of party conferences.

Eva's been every year since she can remember, although this will be the first time that she's attending as a candidate with some buzz around her. As a teenager she spent most of her time being supervised by her mother or watching TV in her parents' hotel suite. As a SpAd, Eva ran around, frantically trying to print last-minute speech amendments or prodding snoozing elderly attendees in the main hall to check they weren't dead from boredom. This time she'll be there in her own right.

'It should be fun for us this year, being candidates. I've been invited to some good dinners,' Eva continues. 'And a bunch of parties. The *Spectator* bash, a ConHome dinner for future stars ...'

Jess cocks her head at Eva. Does she have an idea how obnoxious she sounds?

'Oh.' Bobby feels her face flush. 'No, I've not been invited to any of that. Although I'd have probably slept through it anyway ... Most of my diary is Tipperton stuff, which Moira and I will be able to do together. And I'm going to go to all the sessions on transport and health. And then, well ...' Bobby folds her hands.

'What?' Jess looks up from a pile of shoes.

'Well, there's this opportunity for new candidates to speak on the main stage this year.'

'Oh, yeah, I saw that,' Eva says. 'Didn't go for it though. Why waste a perfectly good speech on a near-empty room?'

'You're probably right. But I could do with the experience so

I submitted something anyway and . . . ' Bobby raises her chin. 'CCHQ were so pleased with it that I've been invited to introduce the PM for his big speech.'

Eva's mouth drops open. Here she's been wanging on about parties and dinners and Bobby's introducing the sodding prime minister on national television! Her stomach coils with jealousy.

'Hey, that's awesome.' Jess grins, patting Bobby's thigh.

'Thanks! I'm pretty nervous about it but it's a cool opportunity.'

Bobby can't help but feel a bit pleased about the look on Eva's face.

'Well.' Jess stands and swings her duffel bag over her shoulder. 'I'm off. I'll see you guys in Birmingham.'

Eva manages to unclench her teeth in time to call, 'Have fun!' and then turns to Bobby, determined to change course.

'Do you want to practise your speech? And have you thought about what to wear?'

As they head to Bobby's room, Eva puts her arm around her.

'Well done, Bob. This is so cool. Want me to get you on the *Speccie* guest list . . . ?'

26th September

CON 20% LAB 45%

TENNYSON CHARMS CITY/

STORM TINA HITS UK

Liverpool

Jess catches a glimpse of herself in the mirrored wall along one side of the restaurant. Has she overdone it? She's technically covered a lot of her skin, but the long, polo-necked black dress is skintight and captures every curve of her body. Perhaps the red lipstick is what tips it over the edge. She can't go back and change now, but Jess hopes she doesn't look like she's made too much of an effort – the worst thing one can do, in her view.

'Hi Jess.' Christian puts a hand on her shoulder and she half rises to give him a quick peck on the cheek, wishing she could bury her face into his neck.

'Oh, shit.' She notices a lipstick mark on his cheek and dabs at it with her napkin, laughing nervously.

'Hello, hello,' a familiar, droll voice says. 'This is all very cosy.'

212

It's Cooper, standing with his feet apart in his customary dorkish way.

'Hi, Ed.' Christian stands to shake his hand.

'I didn't realise you were coming along, boss,' Jess says, hoping the dim lighting hides her blushing cheeks. Ed is eyeing her dress with undisguised interest.

'Thought strength in numbers would be a good idea.' Ed signals to a waiter for another chair. 'Now, shall I take a look at the wine list?' The *Sentinel* expense account is allowed to be rinsed during conference season, and Ed considers the two-week period a waste if he doesn't sample the best wine he can each night.

Jess orders a dirty martini and prays she makes it through the dinner in one piece. Every time she and Christian ask each other a direct question, Ed, his napkin tucked into his collar, blunders in, determined not to be left out for a moment. There's no way she can risk even a bit of light flirting in case Ed punishes her later – or, worse, misreads it as directed at him.

Christian answers Ed's increasingly drunken questions about policy and shadow cabinet in-fighting in a tolerant but bored way. Clearly his feelings towards the man have not improved the more he's got to know him.

'Is it really true that one of your manifesto policies is outlawing cousin marriage?'

'Yup, a pretty minor one though,' Christian replies, wondering if this is a leak from Tanya. 'It may cost us any hope of winning Norfolk or the Forest of Dean, but I think it's worth it.'

'And what about this strapline "Time for Change" all over the conference? Bit samey, isn't it?' Ed chortles, perusing the wine list again.

'Maybe. But it works. We keep asking the same question: the Tories have been in charge for ten years – do you feel better off than you did before they came to power? And everyone says, "No. It's time for a change. Give someone else a go." It's as simple as listening to people.'

Ed grunts and gets up to use the bathroom. Christian and Jess finally have some time to talk alone.

'I must say.' Christian looks through his lashes at Jess. 'I was a little put out by your defence puff piece about the PM last month. Are we going to get similarly special treatment?'

Jess feels a little nudge of lust between her thighs.

'I don't give special treatment.' She dabs a finger in the sauce on her place and licks it clean. Christian watches hungrily. 'But if you want to invite me on a suitable visit, I'm sure I'll see a new side of you.'

Christian is about to reply, but before he can, Ed plonks himself back in his seat after what must have been the fastest piss in history.

'Anyway, where was I?' Ed opens his red-wine-stained mouth wide, searching for his next belligerent comment. 'Oh, yeah ... well, he was such an incompetent cunt that I came up with a new nickname for him. Incompe-cunt!'

Jess uses the opportunity of Ed roaring his head off to glance at Christian and meets his gaze. She quickly turns her head back to Ed, nodding in agreement at whatever he's saying. Does she dare do what she really wants? If it backfires, she can always say it was a mistake. Still, Christian's eyes bore into her and embolden her.

Jess leans forward and props her chin on one hand, as though absorbed in what Ed is saying. Very carefully, she stretches her fingers out under the tablecloth and inches them towards where Christian is sitting. She reaches out and runs her fingertips over Christian's knee.

She glances over at him and sees that he's now looking at Ed, a soft smile playing around his mouth. The thought suddenly occurs to her that he's smirking at her blunder. But just as she moves her attention back to Ed and withdraws her hand, Christian's hand has grasped hers. Jess can hear the blood rushing in her ears as the strong fingers lace and unlace with her own, softly stroking the inside of her palm. Short of being able to embrace properly, their hands clutch and writhe for them.

'And then I said, why the fuck should I care? And she ...' Ed drones on, refilling his wine glass again, slopping much of it on the white tablecloth.

Jess sips her wine with her free hand. Under the table she guides Christian's hand up her dress and onto her thigh. Still nodding along to Ed, she silently tips her knees apart.

'Anyway, she gave me some shit about journalistic ethics. And do you know what I said?' Ed slurs, looking at both of them in turn, his eyes in slightly different directions now.

Jess shakes her head, prompting Ed to answer his own question, while she cautiously slides Christian's hand up her inner thigh. He leans forward and when his fingers reach the top, gives a sharp intake of breath. She's not wearing underwear.

Jess releases his hand and leans back in her chair, tenting her fingers on the arms thoughtfully and leaning towards Ed, so she can shift her pelvis forward to the edge of her seat towards Christian. There they are, out in public and under Ed Cooper's nose. Soon she has to cover her mouth with her hands to stop herself from making a noise.

'Sorry, am I boring you?' Ed asks her, thinking that Jess is stifling a yawn.

'Not at all. Although.' Jess looks meaningfully at Christian. 'It is getting late. Shall we all call it a night?'

'Good idea.' Christian withdraws his hand from under the table and signals for the bill.

'You're both boring arseholes, aren't you?' Ed chunters. He takes a final slug of wine. 'I'm going to the main hotel bar. Find some fun people. Unless anyone else around here fancies being fun for once?' Ed grabs Jess's wrist.

'No, thanks.' She smiles, peeling his fingers off her. 'A lot to do tomorrow.'

'Suit yourself.' Ed stands. 'I'm off for a proper drink.'

Jess and Christian both stare as Ed marches out, then they stroll to the door and wait for their coats.

'Where are you staying?' Jess asks casually, doing up her buttons.

'In a hotel room, about three doors down from the leader of the opposition and a bunch of police officers.' Christian smiles regretfully. 'You?'

'An AirBnB around the corner. It's quite nice. A one-bed off the beaten track . . .'

They're outside the restaurant now. The wind is getting up and the night has turned chilly. The street is busy with conference-goers staggering back from restaurants and receptions to hotel rooms or late-night bars.

Jess holds out her hand for Christian to shake. Why hasn't he accepted her very obvious offer? Has she scared him off by being so brazen?

'Well, thanks for coming out with us. I found it incredibly useful. I just hope it wasn't a waste of your time.'

Christian clasps her hand. 'I can easily say that is the best conference dinner I've ever had.'

They smile at each other, then Jess turns and walks away.

Christian watches her for a moment then does the same. He pulls his phone out to check the dozens of messages that will have come in.

At the top is a text from Jess with the address to her AirBnB.

1st October

CON 21% LAB 45%

TORIES BEGIN CONFERENCE/

WINTER ENERGY BILL HIKE

Birmingham

A few days later, Jess is trying to concentrate but flashbacks of a few nights ago keep clouding her mind. Christian leaning against the door frame, grinning mischievously when she answers his knock. Being thrown around as easily as a rag doll. The bathroom taps jamming against her back as they fucked against the sink. The early morning light outlining Christian's creamy broad shoulders as he quietly dressed and slipped out.

He's texted her once since –

Last night was fun. See you soon. C

– but Jess hasn't known how to reply. Usually she'd send something like *Same*. Or, more likely, nothing at all. A clear signal that that was a one-off and shouldn't be acknowledged again.

But she doesn't just want a one-off. That text is so polite – the kind of thing he would likely have sent if the evening had ended with the restaurant bill. Are they now just going to pretend it never happened, that their relationship is entirely professional? For the first time in her life, Jess has no idea how to proceed.

She forces herself back into the room – the hotel room, to be specific – where she sits before the prime minister, who has granted Jess and Ed a crucial interview over coffee. Jess wouldn't normally like it, but she's relieved that Ed is here today, dominating the questions so Jess can take a backseat.

'Look, I know not everyone is going to warm to what I'm saying,' the PM says, trotting out the carefully curated lines that Nick and Cal have drilled into him. 'But at least I've got a clear view. On any issue. Which is more than can be said for John Ramsey. I think the public are looking for someone consistent, reliable and strong. A leader. And that's me.'

Ed is lapping it all up. This strong-man stuff is gold. Jess gives her head an imperceptible little shake, as though to clear it. Another strong man has floated into her mind. One who refused to let her dominate him. For the first time in her sexual experience, Jess allowed – and loved – a man taking control of her.

'And any scoops for your speech tomorrow? Anything you'd like to tell us?' Ed asks winningly, slapping his hand on his thigh.

'Because it's you, Ed.' The PM grins. 'Keep your ears primed for a bit on sex and the age of consent. I think it makes more sense to stagger it. Right now, a sixteen-year-old can have sex with a forty-year-old, so long as they aren't their teacher. Creepy, right? But if you're sixteen you can't date someone who is fifteen. Why not make the half your age plus seven rule official? Now.' He stands to shake hands with them both. 'If you don't mind, I'd better go and listen to the foreign secretary's speech.'

Jess and Ed walk down the corridor together.

'Thanks for just shutting up for once and letting me get on with it,' Ed says quietly. As usual, he has a vicious hangover from last night's champagne receptions. He told her before the interview how his evening ended when a particularly blotto MP shat himself in a karaoke bar and Ed had to help him back to his hotel.

'Hey, no problem. I got to do the SAS trip, didn't I?' Jess returns brightly.

'Are you coming to watch Madeleine Ford? Will be interesting to see her back on the main stage but as Foreign Sec.'

'Nah, I promised I would go to Percy Cross's event. He's doing an in-conversation with Michael Dobbs about political fiction. Something tells me that *The Loin King* isn't going to stand up very well against *House of Cards* though ...'

A few doors down from where Ed and Jess interviewed the prime minister, Eva Cross and Clarissa Courtenay sit on a sofa with their knees tucked beneath them, sharing a bottle of champagne.

Clarissa doesn't want to venture out into the main conference venue before she sits in the audience for her husband's speech tomorrow, so has sequestered herself in the prime-ministerial suite in a beautiful Elizabeth Taylor-style house coat. She's living off room service and has commandeered Eva to be her companion.

Eva is finding this conference less fun than she anticipated. Doing it as a candidate is exhausting. What can it be like as an MP? As a break from glad-handing Battersea association members or skittering around different parties and dinners, Eva is only too happy to replenish her blood alcohol levels with Clarissa.

For about the fifth time in the last two days, the two women are obsessing over Joshua Udoka and whether he knew who Eva was when they connected on Fawn.

'You honestly couldn't make it up!' Clarissa says once again, topping up their glasses from the bucket beside her. 'But let's face it – if he's tuned into Westminster politics, how could he not have known who you were?'

'Exactly.'

Eva is creeping about on Joshua's Twitter and Instagram pages several times a day now. Partly just to see what he's up to – he's already been far more visible than Eva in Battersea, which she must remedy when she returns from Birmingham – but mainly to look at his pictures and glean more about him. He's very active in his community, helping at various charities and doing pro bono work for young offenders when he isn't working at his solicitors' firm in the City. She's ashamed by the pang of jealousy she feels whenever a woman is photographed with him. Are any of them his girlfriend? The constant guessing and obsessing is worming away at her.

'The only really good thing about it,' Clarissa says musingly, 'is that he's directly involved too. Had you bedded his friend, I suspect this would already be out there. But because it's him and he's got to be a squeaky clean good boy, he will want this kept just as quiet as you.'

Eva shrugs.

'Personally I'm not so down about it as you. It should put real fire in your belly. I mean, you really *must* beat him now.'

'Oh, I know.' Eva sighs. 'It's just been a weird couple of days.'

She tells Clarissa about Bobby being picked to introduce the PM tomorrow on the main stage. It's particularly awkward because Clarissa briefed against Bobby last year, incorrectly suggesting to Ed Cooper that Bobby was the lover of Simon Daly and was pregnant with his child – based on a dud tip given to her by an unwitting Eva.

220

'Oh, don't bother about that,' Clarissa says airily. 'Her speech won't be carried by the broadcasters, just Eric's. And even then, conference speeches are hardly blockbuster. We all pay attention of course, but nobody in the real world gives a toss. And that's the prime minister! Now.' Clarissa stumbles to her feet. 'Shall we take a look at my outfit choices for tomorrow?'

2nd October

Birmingham

Upbeat music plays in the packed auditorium, where Eric Courtenay's face stares out sternly from huge screens above the words *Face the Future*. Cal has insisted this is the right imagery and messaging from what he's learning in focus groups – the PM looking strong and focused, the message assertive but hopeful. The Conservative Party logo is nowhere to be seen, but the signature bright-blue colour palette beams out across every surface that isn't a photo of Courtenay. The slogan wasn't as easy to land as Cal hoped, though. The PM, perhaps a little carried away with this new presidential image, said, 'Surely you mean "Face *of* the Future"?'

After some back and forth, Cal had to take him aside. 'It's not all about you, okay?'

When Clarissa arrives and is guided to a reserved seat by

Eva, the cameras click madly, before the photographers are corralled back by CCHQ staffers behind the duct-tape lines that are meant to pen them in. Undercover police officers seat themselves strategically around the routes to the stage, keeping a watchful eye on the already security-checked crowd, who wave placards emblazoned with *Face the Future*.

Backstage, Jake faces Bobby, a hand on each of her shoulders. Beneath the hairspray and make-up, she looks absolutely petrified.

'You can do this, okay?' he says softly. 'You're just talking about you. And Tipperton. And how until a year ago, you wouldn't have become a Conservative in a million years. To a room of a few thousand lifelong Conservatives . . .'

Bobby manages a smile. She looks beautiful. Eva helped her choose a 1960s smock dress with brass buttons down the front and a cowl neckline. The low heels and her new haircut, a long, volumised bob, give her a Jackie Kennedy vibe.

'Good luck, sweet girl!'

Bobby turns at the call. It's Percy. He and the rest of the cabinet are lined up, ready to process out to their rows of reserved seats. Madeleine Ford looks admiringly at Bobby's buttons and gives her a little thumbs-up.

Before she can respond, the ministers are led out into the auditorium to loud applause.

'One minute,' the woman running the main stage says quietly, putting an encouraging hand on Bobby's arm. 'There's water and a copy of your speech on the lectern.'

Bobby tries to thank her but has trouble opening her mouth.

'Okay, here we go,' the woman says again, partly to Bobby and partly into her headset. 'Ready? Three, two, one . . . go.'

Bobby feels a firm push in the small of her back and steps out onto the stage to loud applause and thousands of faces, feeling like she's in a dream. She seems to float towards the lectern, almost watching herself from above, and wonders how she'll survive the next three minutes.

But the moment she clears her throat and the auditorium falls quiet, her mind sharpens. Bobby takes a deep breath, looks around at the audience with a huge smile and begins.

Three minutes later, she gets to say the magic words, 'Please welcome to the stage, the prime minister!'

There is rapturous, dazzling applause, the whole crowd on their feet, as 'Right Here, Right Now' by Fatboy Slim booms out of the speakers. The PM emerges onto the stage, looking sleek and confident. He shakes hands with Bobby, shouting, 'Well done – fantastic!' over the din, and walks slowly to the lectern, waving.

Bobby heads backstage into Jake's arms.

'You were *brilliant*!' he shouts over the noise of the still-cheering crowd, into the top of her head. She's still shaking a little, but she smiles up at him. 'Did you enjoy it?'

'I don't know yet.' She laughs. 'Ask me again later.'

The audience has quieted now and sat back in their seats, ready for the prime minister to begin the customary thirty-to-forty-minute set-piece speech.

Bobby, exhausted from her own stint on the stage, sips on a Diet Coke and zones out for most of it. Eva, sitting next to Clarissa in the auditorium and aware of TV cameras panning across towards them from time to time, looks alert and interested, although, privately, she is stewing about Bobby's indisputable star turn on the stage. Pride and jealousy, in equal parts, burn inside her.

It doesn't help that she's nursing what must be in her top five worst hangovers of all time. The champagne in Clarissa's suite yesterday afternoon seems years ago. Later, after dragging Bobby along to the *Spectator* party, Eva continued on with a group to karaoke with a live band. She's fairly certain she performed 'Proud Mary' with her father, but can't be sure. Worst of all, when she went back to her hotel room to get changed between dinner and karaoke, she left the place in disarray, her trusty Rampant Rabbit on the bedside table. When she crawled into bed, her place was already taken by her bright pink friend, tucked up neatly under the sheets with just the tip poking out in a judgemental 'where have you been' sort of way. Clearly the turn-down team having some fun.

Jess, in the media area at the back, listens attentively. Like the rest of the attending journalists, she's clocked the presidential-style, almost Big Brother brand refresh, and the shift in tone in how the PM is communicating. He sounds no-nonsense, committed and strong. And he looks the part. It's very convincing. It's very general election-y.

The speech itself is fairly thin on policy content, but the promised line on age of consent is there. From now on, the oldest age a sixteen-year-old can consent to sex with is nineteen. Ramsey's had been light too (although his proposed ban on cousins marrying dutifully featured, plus a hike-up of the winter fuel allowance and free thermals to try and tempt over traditionally Tory-voting elderly people), both leaders evidently deciding that they want to save up their best announcements for their imminent manifestos, hoping that strident remarks on 'the precious Union', 'the scourge of crime' and 'the nation's pride in the NHS' carries them through. The big, blazing top line carried by every news outlet is the obvious one: there will be a general election on Thursday 2nd December. Parliament will return next week for a final couple of weeks' business – then the gloves are off.

6th October

CCHQ

Now that the Conservative Party machine is gearing up for the election properly, Cal takes the decision to move Don and his team of Americans to a secret location around the corner from headquarters. He's simply not willing to risk the chance of a Labour mole inside the building, or an idiotic staffer blabbing away about what they see on the big whiteboards, littered with numbers and codes.

As a result, Cal splits his time between CCHQ and what he calls 'Tracy Island', named after the secret hideout of the *Thunderbirds*, occasionally popping into Downing Street to update the prime minister on strictly sanitised information. Today is Sunday but the office is so busy, the atmosphere excited, that it could be any working day of the week. This is how it'll be until December. No days off. Hardly any sleep.

Birthdays marked by a massacred Colin the Caterpillar in the communal kitchen. Anniversaries postponed. Only births, deaths and terror attacks will register a ripple on the work ethic of the campaigning machine for the next several weeks.

Still, while these young people work hard, they play hard too. There isn't time for dates or relationships. There is, however, ample opportunity to flirt over late-night policy brainstorms or in the day-to-day banter of sitting in close proximity to dozens of other over-worked and over-sexed twenty-somethings. The mania of a campaign has hit, plunging lows and riveting highs, everyone seeking an outlet in sly one-nights stands, sneaky handjobs in the basement and fumbled, frantic shags in the back alleys of the campaign headquarters.

Cal and Nick sit in a small, sound-proofed glass room in the centre of the ground floor. It's a quiet sanctuary inside the bubbling hubbub of the campaign nerve-centre, and they don't want to be overheard. Cal is taking Nick through Don's latest polling.

'So the big man's conference speech landed well enough, and some of our work from September is paying off, but we're still waaaay,' Cal taps his laptop screen, 'behind. Averaging twenty points. I'm very confident about the model we've built. But this Eckles fella over at Labour seems pretty good. We can't rely on them simply running a shit campaign. We've got to give ourselves an edge.'

'For sure.' Nick yawns, shattered after a sleepover with Miguel. '"Time for Change" is a big old mountain to climb for us. I mean, even I know the answer to "Do you feel better off after ten years of the Tories in charge?". We need to think of something that will distract them from talking about how shit our record is and what their future priorities are.'

'Yup.' Cal strokes his stubbled chin. 'But while we need to divert the Labour campaign off the issues, we also need the

227

media kept well away from what we're really doing. A nice shiny stone to distract two birds.'

Cal taps a key on his laptop to reveal the strange, zigzagging map that Don unveiled at Chequers in August. It has been refined further as the Tracy Island team gets more data and insight into how the public think.

In a straight race, Labour should beat the Conservatives fair and square. Nick's right. 'Ten Years of the Tories' and 'Time for Change', if Labour diligently say this day in, day out, are just too strong to overcome. But what if Cal can persuade them to talk about something else? He needs to find something that Labour and the media won't be able to resist jumping on, something that tears them away from what the race should be. Then, when the time's right, he'll change the tune again.

Cal and Nick are closeted away for another hour before they emerge for a bite to eat and to put their plan into action.

7th October

CON 23% LAB 43%

BBC ACCUSED OF BIAS ON DEBATES/

28° IN OCTOBER

Battersea

Eva is finally able to concentrate fully on getting elected as an MP. Last week she spent her final day on Tracy Island, which is fully up and running, complete with supplementary British pollsters and quants. Eva will miss it. Don and his team have been wonderful to Eva all summer, kindly explaining to her the trickier parts of their work and in return enjoying having a woman around to talk to about 'what British girls want'. She'll miss Cal, too, who seems to be able to think ten steps ahead of everyone else and has helped her understand how he campaigns. But she's got her own race to run now. Every minute she has will be spent in Battersea.

First, though, she agreed to join the chief whip as he accompanied the PM and Anto on a tour of Parliament's undercarriage, the R&R team explaining once again the potential danger that MPs and parliamentary staff were in. The PM nodded along politely but was clearly distracted. Anto was his usual self, confidently recommending the engineer invest in some duct tape for the worst bits of wiring. When a small chunk of plaster hit Anto on the back of the neck as they left, Eva joked with the chief about whether the House of Commons would have any seats intact by the time she's able to take one up.

With all that behind her, Eva enjoys this beautiful morning. She struts through Battersea Park with her sunglasses on, music blasting through her headphones, ready to do battle. She arrives with some shop-bought brownies at her campaign HQ near the station, ready to meet her team. Without them, Eva doesn't stand a chance of getting elected.

David Dalgleish, the outgoing MP, has clearly put in a good word for her. The constituency team of three are friendly, hard-working and very interested in whether Eva's father might be dropping in at some point. They're also damning about the rude young woman from the selection evening, who none of them like. All in all, they're off to a good start.

They spend most of the morning working through the box of brownies and going over the canvassing data they have collected about likely voting intentions over the summer. It's incredibly patchy.

'The problem is, there aren't really enough of us to get every door knocked,' someone pipes up. 'We need to think about how we can get more volunteers. And the real bugger is Labour are making this a target seat. Got quite an impressive guy standing for them.'

'Oh, yeah?' Eva says, trying to sound casual.

'Yeah. Born nearby, a City slicker now and clearly had his eye on the place for a while. Done a lot of local volunteering and charity work. And pretty highly favoured by Vicky

Tennyson, by all accounts. Worked on her economic policy. Perfect package, really.'

You forgot to add 'hung like a horse', Eva thinks glumly.

'Shall we go and have a walk about?' someone says. 'It would be good to get your bearings and we may as well start knocking on doors.'

'Plus we can get some snaps of you buzzing around the place for social media. We can do the library and the leisure centre. Maybe the different stations. Then check out the dog shit in the park.'

'Great.' Eva smiles.

They've been out canvassing for about an hour when, walking into a new street, Eva almost crashes into Joshua Udoka. Without missing a beat, he offers his hand for her to shake.

'Hello, it's my rival.' He smiles widely.

He is, unfortunately, as incredibly attractive as ever.

'Hello, Mr Udoka,' Eva says stiffly, shaking his hand quickly. She's irritated to note that he has close to a dozen people with him.

'Please, call me Joshua. After all, no point us being formal about this. We're both here to do our best for Battersea.'

Eva can hardly look at him. If anything, he looks even hotter than she remembers. Perhaps he's on a special campaigning regime. The brownies churn in her stomach.

'Of course. Well, it's very nice to meet you,' Eva says, trying to step past him onto the road. Perhaps an obliging taxi will swing around the corner and put her out of her misery.

'Yes. Although you're very familiar.' Joshua grins at her sideways. 'Are you sure we haven't met before?'

'Perfectly sure,' Eva fires back. Then she follows up. 'At least, if we have met, I don't remember it being a very remarkable occasion.'

231

Instead of having the wind knocked out of him, Joshua looks delighted. He's having fun.

'Well, I must try harder next time.' He looks meaningfully at her. 'See you around, Eva.'

Once Joshua and his team disappear round the corner, the team let out a collective breath.

'Did you see the size of Udoka's team? We're looking a bit outgunned, aren't we?'

'And he's one hell of a looker . . .'

'First run-in with the enemy. Many more to come. You'll have to do some serious work for the hustings. Proper heavy-weight boxing match, that'll be.'

Eva slumps onto a low wall and, after being offered a ciga-rette, shrugs and accepts. She coughs out her first inhale and thinks. She's already tangled with Joshua once. How much harder can it be fully clothed?

Soon the team are back on their feet, heading down the street to continue canvassing. Over fifty per cent of the houses have got brand-new, bright-red *Vote Labour* signs in the window. Clearly Team Udoka have been busy.

When they break for lunch, Eva checks her phone and sees a direct message on Twitter from @joshudoka.

> How about dinner tonight to kick off a friendly
> campaign on the right foot?

Eva's heart leaps. Christ, how she'd love to accept. But there's no way. He is her enemy now.

Still, she can't help smiling about it for the rest of the after-noon and, not wanting to seem rattled, she replies at 6 p.m.

> That is very kind but I'm afraid I'm busy. Good luck
> with the campaign.

As soon as she gets home, Eva heads to her bedroom, runs a bath and squirms against the shower head, thinking about the dark brown eyes and strong, smooth chest of the ultimate forbidden fruit.

9th October

CON 24% LAB 44%
LAST PMQS BEFORE GE/
BIODIVERSITY IN CRISIS

Tipperton

Bobby's first day in Tipperton is less eventful, which came as a welcome relief after her final weekend in London and the last-minute baby shower that Holly insisted on organising. Holly, a natural with this sort of thing and used to the spectacular baby showers and gender-reveal parties her friends have in the US, filled the Claybourne Terrace garden on a chilly but sunny day with autumnal flower arrangements (pumpkins with cherubs carved into them dominated), alcohol-free warm cider and thick blankets. There were pecan muffins, Babygros to decorate and an enormous red velvet cake, topped with an iced pram. Jess's contribution was the hurried booking of a stripper, abs gleaming beneath a nappy, bonnet and rattle. It's safe to say the gesture didn't land entirely well with Bobby's and Jake's mothers. They cheered up, though, when Percy sashayed down the garden steps to join in, unbuttoning his shirt and pulling the stripper baby onto his knee to smack his bottom.

Bobby's standing now, her hands clasped over her huge belly, feeling the little kicks drumming away inside her and greeting the small group of people drifting into the Tipperton community hall on a chilly evening. Her parents are there, as is Susie Cliveden and the elderly lady from the selection, who has nearly finished knitting the baby cardigan. As well as association members, there are also a few other people from the community that Bobby didn't expect to come, including some nurses from the local mental health unit that Bobby campaigned to save and a few of her father's former colleagues from the police. All of them have come to see how they can help get her elected as their MP.

'Have you had enough to eat? Are you sure you don't want to sit down?' Mrs Cliveden fusses around her daughter. She can't help it. She's been reading a lot recently about the abuse women MPs in particular receive online and she's worried. Some get death and rape threats. How will Bobby cope with these kinds of attacks? There's enough worry about mental health in her family already. And what about preparing for the baby?

Bobby isn't worried, though. There's three weeks between polling day and her due date. People give birth in war zones and igloos. There's no point in panicking just yet.

Claybourne Terrace

Jess is on a high. Literally. She's spent the afternoon lying in bed, smoking a joint, her mind tracing a map in her head, as though she's looking up at a giant spider's web of dates and names on the ceiling. She's finally made a break in the

Ed–Clarissa–Finlayson mystery and regrets not applying herself properly to the problem earlier.

From the StoryCorps HR records, Jess knows that in the early 2000s, Ed Cooper worked as a technology reporter and Clarissa Courtenay worked on the finance desk, writing the daily City gossip email. Like anyone would do, Jess googled Ed when she started working with him the previous year, but it was really just a cursory skim of the internet to see what he looked like, what sort of stories he wrote and what kind of stuff he posted on social media. Once she got a measure of the man, it never occurred to her to go any deeper.

Today, on a whim, she turned to trusty Wikipedia and found that Ed has a page. The first interesting piece of information is about Ed's marriage. In 2000, Ed, a penniless and obscure journalist, married the daughter of a long line of successful perfumiers, and entered a new echelon of society. Mrs Cooper is currently the CFO of the family company – of course Ed never mentions this, unwilling for anyone to know his wife is more successful than he is – and, as Jess reads about her, she feels certain Ed was bluffing about not caring if his wife knew about an affair. The family's lawyers would get to work and Ed's upper-class VIP pass would be taken away for ever.

The second interesting thing Jess learns is that Ed wrote a blog in the early 2000s, presumably to make a name for himself. Using a special platform that reproduces mothballed websites, Jess can see that Ed was blogging about the effects of the dot-com bubble bursting, and he was predicting a second crash was going to follow – this time in shares of big media. But that crash never came. The next seismic shake was famously in 2008. Then, in July 2005, the blog closed down – just in time for Ed's huge promotion.

Jess wonders why Ed, a technology reporter, was blogging

about market crashes. Clarissa was the one with a job on the finance desk, writing the daily email summary. They must have worked together on something. But what could have led to these years of special treatment from Finlayson?

Jess ponders what she knows about Finlayson.

He was announced as the UK's richest man for seven consecutive years from 1991, but there are gossip pieces suggesting he got carried away in the dot-com boom, just in time for the bubble to burst. Shortly after that, he was caught canoodling with an extremely young bikini model on a yacht in St Tropez and Lady Finlayson II began divorce proceedings. Jess can see from stories at the time that Finlayson's lawyers tried to make the case in court that his vast genius made a special case where he shouldn't have to split their assets fifty-fifty with his wife. The court disagreed. The eventual financial settlement has never been disclosed.

After this point, Jess has to guess. What she knows is that divorces are expensive, particularly if you're one of the UK's only billionaires, if you have children with your spouse and if the bulk of your wealth has been made over the course of the marriage. It's pretty common for the better-off half of a couple to try to hide or distort their wealth so they don't have to share everything.

But whenever Jess meets Finlayson for lunch or dinner, he insists on the most ostentatious restaurants. Thousands of pounds' worth of caviar, lobster and champagne. He talks about his many properties in New York, Washington DC, Cape Town, St Tropez, Val d'Isère, Barbados, Scotland, the Cotswolds – and three separate places in London. Private jets, helicopters, Rolls-Royces and Bentleys. Handmade clothes and shoes, monogrammed Dunhill lighters, cigarette cases and hip flasks. Birthday parties and anniversaries attended by A-listers, who are entertained by Elton John and Beyoncé. Hiding his wealth doesn't seem to be a priority.

Jess rolls out of bed and plods down the stairs, wondering what's in the fridge.

When she reaches the kitchen, Holly is chatting to Teddy Hammer.

'Hello, Jess, how's it going?' Teddy tips his chin up from his cup of tea.

'All right. What are you doing here?' Jess looks into the fridge, eventually settling on a Diet Coke and some cheese-stuffed peppers.

'Meeting Percy here, but he's running late.'

'Surprise, surprise.' Holly twinkles. 'If you'll excuse me, I'll just give him a ring to see where he's got to.'

Jess leans against the sideboard and pops a pepper into her mouth.

'You look like you're onto something,' Teddy says.

'Kind of.' She shrugs.

Teddy inclines his head towards the garden. 'Fancy a fag?'

Jess leads the way outside.

It takes a couple of minutes for her to tell Teddy what she knows so far. She hesitates when it comes to the guessing part, though.

'Teddy, you've known Finlayson longer than I have. Do you think . . .' She frowns. 'How important to him do you think it is that everyone knows he's rich?'

Teddy is leaning back in a deckchair.

'Very important, I would think. I see where you're going with this divorce stuff. But what's the big deal with him trying to stop his second wife getting half his dosh? Happens all the time. He's learnt his lesson with a massive prenup for number three, I'm told.'

'Yeah, I know.' Jess nods. 'And what's there for Ed to have on him . . . But then I'm thinking, he cares a lot about people thinking he's rich, right? He was the richest man in Britain for the whole of the nineties. But then he fucked up with the dot-com crash. Maybe he lost even more than we realise. And then he fucks up again with the divorce. What if the settlement to his ex-wife is never disclosed, not because it is such a vast sum, but because it is such a surprisingly small one? Off the rich list, no longer a billionaire ...'

'But he never comes off the rich list.'

'We both know you can say all sorts *on paper*. But what about Ed's blog? A big market crash in media-company shares ... maybe old Finlayson tried to hit again after the dot-com bubble. Double down after his losses, you know? And Ed gets wind of it through Clarissa ... then Finlayson buys them off and manages to pull his shares back from the brink.'

Teddy blows out a long billow of blue smoke.

Jess is getting close. Of course, there's no proof. But Jess doesn't need proof. She just needs to tell Finlayson that she knows what Ed knows – and that she has her own material to blackmail Ed with. But she needs one final nudge in the right direction.

They're interrupted by the sound of loud voices from inside the house. Teddy stubs out his cigarette and gets to his feet.

When he gets to the kitchen door, he grunts something.

'What?' Jess calls after him.

Teddy turns and leans against the door frame. Jess catches it this time.

'Maxwell.'

Jess stares into space for about fifteen seconds, then stands up and marches purposefully upstairs, chucking the Diet Coke can in the bin.

Once she's in her room, she springs onto the bed and snaps open her laptop. Once again, Google and Wikipedia come to her aid. She starts reading about Robert Maxwell, another media mogul and contemporary of Finlayson and

Rupert Murdoch. The man had a colourful life and expensive, flamboyant tastes, much like Finlayson, before his slightly mysterious death. Jess skips through much of it, but she reads and re-reads the section on Maxwell's finances.

After his death, it was revealed that Maxwell's various businesses were in huge trouble, and he had been using his employees' pension-fund money to keep them afloat. Jess keeps reading the same bits over: *pension-fund assets as collateral for loans ... to support the share price of the Mirror Group ...*'

Is it possible that Finlayson did something similar after the dot-com crash? Once again the internet delivers. In the early 2000s, post-dot-com and post-divorce, Finlayson bought a Russian satellite company, having grand plans for an international twenty-four-hour news network, beaming simultaneously from every continent. He made a great song and dance about how he was opening up the media landscape and planning to build the first studio to broadcast from space. But nothing happened. Then, like so many people and businesses, StoryCorps' loans to various banks were called in after the 2008 financial crash and the satellite company was dismantled and sold off. It was clearly a duff idea.

Jess goes back to Ed's old blog. *A bubble in the share price of media companies will burst ...* Ed must have known about Finlayson's acquisition from the business news, after all – which Clarissa would have reported. Fresh from his divorce, his own finances depleted, what if Finlayson 'borrowed' from the StoryCorps pension pot to buy this Russian dud company? And if Ed and Clarissa found out, it would be an obvious thing to blackmail him with. Ed must have had a reason to predict the imminent collapse of media shares. Maybe he knew that one little shock would expose the very precarious financial position of StoryCorps, and he blogged about it to scare Finlayson into promoting him.

Wouldn't the pension fund being raided be clear to those involved? After all, employees retire all the time and draw their pensions from it. Nobody has ever said anything. But so long as Finlayson treats his pilfering as a loan, then perhaps nobody notices – particularly if he's sewn up the trustees. What if, Jess reasons, Ed and Clarissa still have this mysterious grip on Finlayson because he is taking years and years to reimburse the fund? Maybe he's divorcing his third wife in instalments too. A very precarious position to find yourself in, particularly when two of the most ambitious and ruthless people on the planet know about it.

Part Three

Part Three

14th October

United Kingdom

Seven weeks to polling day and the campaigns have kicked off in earnest. Parliament has been dissolved and won't sit again until a fresh set of MPs have been elected. Journalists are now in a strange role reversal. In peacetime, they constantly try to chase stories and get information out of politicians and political parties. Overnight, the flow of information has flipped and they have campaign messages, policies and attack lines about the other side fed to them via an intravenous drip.

Counting on the public taking a keen interest in the election, newspapers anticipate a healthy boost in circulation figures and all reporters are put on a war footing to cover constituencies in every nook and cranny of the country, trying to find a new angle to their competitors. Broadcast news channels are laying on special segments to look at the latest polls and a roster of earnest, mole-like professors of political science blink into the studio lights to analyse the numbers. Foreign journalists have flocked forward for accreditation, the Americans in particular keen to get in some practice before covering their own election next year.

The Conservative Party campaign bus, complete with Eric Courtenay's serious, handsome face and *Face the Future* plastered along the side, launched yesterday in Weston-super-Mare, and things are not off to an auspicious start. Loaded with lobby journalists and young staffers, the bus carried Percy Cross as its resident celebrity to a Somerset orchard and cider farm and, once Percy left, the group tucked into the local nectar. As many hacks were quick to point out, the team did succeed in organising a piss-up in a brewery. But as Callum grumbled on this morning's 5.30 a.m. daily conference call, the first twelve hours of the bus have not exactly encapsulated the professional, statesmanlike persona that the campaign is meant to embody. The winding West Country roads have done little to improve things. George, who is passing the *Sentinel* baton on to Jess tomorrow in Exeter, has warned her to bring sick bags.

The Labour bus was unveiled this morning in Liverpool, a bright-red lozenge with the somewhat predictable, but undoubtedly bang-on, strapline *Time for Change* emblazoned all over it. They've started with Vicky Tennyson, who has spent the morning going to baby banks, nurseries and a library, where she did story time for a group of small children and their parents. The journalists on board understand immediately – Labour are after the votes of families and women. By comparison, the target audience of the Tory first day is harder to assess. Fans of the Wurzels, perhaps.

Meanwhile, the Lib Dem bus, which is fuelled by biodiesel made from chip fat (their key campaign pledge is net zero), has set off rather slowly and is making everyone on board incredibly peckish all the time. As Percy Cross quipped, 'Well, at least they've sewn up the seagull vote.'

At the BBC in London, there is a meeting to discuss the first televised debate of party leaders, and who should moderate it. There's still ten days to go until the big red *On Air* sign lights up, but that doesn't feel like nearly enough time to research the different men in charge – and they are all men, this time – and to memorise their different policies, to think up some tricksy 'gotcha' questions and to ultimately please everybody watching. The BBC bosses want ratings and nifty clips for social media. The different parties want to feel like they've got a fair hearing. And everyone else, left or right, wants to savage the BBC for bias one way or another.

The producer and editor are already exhausted. They've been negotiating with the different parties, all of whom have been threatening to withdraw from the debate if their leaders don't get to make their opening and closing statements when they want, or if they don't get the right kind of lecterns or stools. It's exhausting – and that's before they get on to the actual nuts and bolts of the two-hour programme itself.

In the different campaign camps, there is no time to rest in the evenings after episodes of bricklaying in hard hats and playing dominoes with OAPs. Instead, each team is dedicated to preparing the different leaders for this first debate. Staffers stand at lecterns, pretending to be the enemy, and work out every possible angle their guy can be attacked on, how he can defend himself and where he can lob grenades at everyone else. The strategy is the same for both Courtenay and Ramsey: don't actively fuck up. The TV debates don't make enough of an impact with voters to mean that a star turn will make a difference, but being crap gives the opposing parties the ammo they need to make little clips that will dominate social media for days. For the Lib Dems, the Greens and the SNP, the debates are more of an opportunity. They never get to have so many eyeballs on them at once, so here's a chance to set some fires under the two main party leaders and explain why they're tired, trashed and collectively responsible for the last fifty years' worth of fuck-ups.

The big change in the first week of campaigning is that the polls are shifting. Cal's strategy – using his recently acquired porn intel to target the little cracks in the electoral map, highlighting people concerned by crime and economic insta-bility – is working. The Tories have jumped up five points, closing the gap with Labour to an average of fifteen per cent. But nobody knows this outside of the small group on Tracy Island – until Cal updates the PM one evening after a particu-larly gruelling debate session.

'I don't understand.' The PM sips on his Berocca, his regu-lar tipple now that so much effort is going into keeping him healthy. 'All the big companies say we haven't moved at all. How is your poll so out of sync with everyone else's?'

'Because everyone else is shite,' Cal replies. 'They aren't asking the right people or the right questions. But don't you see? This is good for us. Let Labour and the media be compla-cent . . . for now. Trust me, this'll start filtering through soon.'

Which is true. Within days the national polls catch up, al-though they still see the jump as just three points. What none of the pros can get their heads around is what the Conservative strategy is. Normally it becomes clear who campaigns are going after for support and some silly term like 'Waitrose woman' or 'Workington man' is coined to explain the profile of such a voter. But that doesn't apply this time. The Conservatives seem to be targeting cities and suburbs, towns and villages. Homeowners and renters. Parents, couples and singles. All education levels.

Christian can't make sense of his opponents either. Even the

Tory campaign bus route seems to be random, a full week of zooming around the South West taking different members of the cabinet out for cream teas and rides on beachside donkeys.

Meanwhile the prime minister has confined all of his visits to armed forces barracks, police stations and Border Force checkpoints, where he dons an array of black and navy bomber jackets and strong stares into the distance. As these trips have a national security angle, he's allowed to have Laura Lloyd join him. He's missed her while he's been on the road, his fondness only growing. He's found that, late at night when he's panicking about being one of the shortest-serving prime ministers in history, the best way to fall asleep is to picture himself undoing Laura's brass buttons, one at a time . . . if Clarissa ever knew she would kill him.

There's the odd school and hospital visit, but there are no awkward clips of the PM sitting in tiny chairs, trying to speak to confused children, or shots of him with his tie tucked into his shirt. At all times his sleeves are rolled up and he's having serious conversations with teachers and parents, doctors and nurses. He's also taken to early morning CrossFit sessions in the different cities he's staying in, where a snapper is always nearby. He is a lean, mean campaigning machine.

Ramsey, for his part, can't compete on the alpha-male front, determined as he is to keep his suit jacket buttoned up like a hotel porter. But he is much better at the softer side. The broadcasters are getting reams of film of him playing games with children, mucking about with teenagers at a youth centre and grooming animals at a shelter. Tanya's view is that he comes across as authentic and likeable. But none of these groups have a vote. Christian tries to explain that he wants voters to be able to place themselves in shot with Ramsey, to feel part of the campaign, but Tanya stubbornly refuses to back down.

Still, what is clear is that Christian's ads, which are

everywhere, are working: 'Time for Change – the Tories have been in charge for ten years but do YOU feel better off?' It is a simple question and one that Christian is determined to make the crux of the whole election. Everything else is just noise. He is finding it hard to keep Tanya and the rest of the team disciplined, though.

16th October

Con 28% Lab 41%

Polls tighten in race for No.10/

Record rain in September

Claybourne Terrace

Jess is up early, well ahead of the rest of the household. She's had a fitful night, wondering how Lord Finlayson will respond to her request for a meeting when she calls his secretary at 9 a.m.

She's also down in the dumps because she hasn't heard from Christian since the Labour conference. She chooses instead to speak to Tanya Haines, while Christian, Jess assumes, talks to Ed. Or perhaps the *Sentinel* editor, Philip McKay. If she were to ask Eva or Bobby what they think, they would probably say Christian has just been busy. If she were advising someone else, Jess would say he simply isn't interested. Still, she hopes.

She slumps down to the kitchen to make coffee.

'Fuck's sake,' she says, groaning.

The kitchen is a tip. Percy had Cal, Nick and Teddy over

251

last night and there are empty red wine and whisky bottles, the debris of a takeaway curry and the lingering smell of stale smoke hanging over the table. At least Jess sleeps high up enough in the house to miss the racket they must have been making.

Jess tidies up and is taking the bins out when she sees a brown-paper package by the front door with her name scrawled on it. Wondering vaguely where it has come from, she goes back to the kitchen, pours herself some coffee and tears open the large envelope.

Inside are a few different documents. On one page is an article dating back to May, about a suspected breach at the Electoral Commission, the agency in charge of how elections are run and the regulation of party funding. There wasn't much interest in the story at the time, partly because the local elections passed without incident and with the expected outcome, and also because it was never clear what actually happened in the breach. The Electoral Commission itself has never revealed if any data was taken or tampered with, or even who they were attacked by. It could have been a hostile state, or just some bored but gifted teenagers. Regardless, the media circus moved on and it was forgotten about. At the end of the story, the name of the Electoral Commission's cybersecurity consultants is printed: DataTwerk. And an attached article reveals the founder of DataTwerk to be a very generous Conservative Party donor.

Jess sips her coffee and feels a little jolt of excitement, the kind that only comes when you have a potential scoop on your hands.

First off, the Electoral Commission has dropped a bollock here. No, both bollocks. They've managed to hire a company with a poor track record of stopping hacks to handle the entirety of the UK public's private voting data. Public procurement in a nutshell. And they've not even clocked that this

252

company is a donor to a political party – a donation the EC themselves will have registered. The conflict of interest is huge.

Jess is back in the realms of guesswork, but lets her imagination run on. After everything she's studied about the guy, would she put it past Callum Gallagher to freshen up the electoral roll a little, if he got the chance? After all, who knows if the EC hack was to pilfer information or to muck about with what's already on there. Is this where the mysterious and unaccountable polling gains are coming from? Is he working with a different map to everyone else? The hack happened, after all, just after Gallagher started working for the Conservatives.

It's one hell of a story. And, it suddenly occurs to her, one that will surely interest Christian.

She pulls out her phone and sends him a text, her heart hammering.

Hey. Long time no speak. Are you free later to talk through a couple of things?

He responds immediately.

For sure. Let me know when and where.

Jess pours herself another cup of coffee and practically bounces back upstairs. She's so excited about the possibility of a big story and seeing Christian again that it doesn't occur to her to stop and wonder how – and why – this information has come to her.

Belgravia

Jess rings the doorbell of the enormous townhouse and waits. Passers-by look at her curiously and she has to admit she does look completely out of place in her worn motorbike leathers next to the elderly female residents of the street, dressed in Chanel suits and patent slip-ons. But Lord Finlayson's message said to come immediately, so she has.

At 9 a.m., as planned, Jess called his office and explained that she had an extremely sensitive matter to discuss with him. Finlayson's secretary wasn't particularly interested, but when Jess said, '2005 . . . and satellites,' she knew it wouldn't be long until his diary was rearranged.

A uniformed maid answers the door and asks Jess to wait in the domed hall. Jess tries to seem uninterested in the priceless Louis XV chair she's sitting on. Or the marble black-and-white mosaic floor. Or the Stubbs pictures hanging all around her. She now recalls Lord Finlayson's devotion to racing, despite his famous horse allergy. Anything to get closer to the royals, Jess supposes.

She taps her fingers on the chair's carved gilt arms, feeling nervous. The obvious problem is that Jess doesn't have evidence to back up what she's going to say. But she's counting on this not to matter. After all, the fact that he's responded so quickly to '2005 . . . and satellites' tells her she must be on the right track. The main thing is that she's got other, very specific evidence, that she hopes will hold his attention.

Before she can get too comfy, Jess is shown upstairs by a smartly dressed woman with a tight bun, who regards Jess as though she's climbed out of a skip. Jess catches herself in the landing mirror and sees her hair is plastered to her forehead from her helmet. She quickly runs her fingers through it.

'Ah, Miss Adler. Do come and sit down.'

Jess has been shown into a sumptuous library. The walls are lined with leather-bound books – many of them, she's been told, first editions – and there are gorgeous Persian rugs in deep jewel tones on the floor. The furniture is all mahogany and deep velvets, and a fire blazes in a beautiful marble fireplace with a portrait of his lordship above it.

The real thing is sitting with a glass of whisky in one of the winged leather armchairs near the fire, gesturing for Jess to take the opposite one.

'Drink?' he asks, once she's sitting.

'Thank you. Just some water, please. I came on my bike.'

He looks a little disappointed, as though thinking a drink might have softened her up, but hands Jess a crystal tumbler from the tray beside him and surveys her carefully.

'Well, this is mysterious. I must say, I don't get many of my employees insisting that they see me, and on delicate matters. You're lucky I like you.'

Jess gives a small smile, but gets a little flutter of panic in her chest. She's gone back and forth on what she wants to say to Lord Finlayson, sure in her bones that what she has put together is true. But what if she's wrong and he laughs her out of his massive mansion? Or worse, what if he fires her, both for her impudence and for undermining Ed, his clear favourite?

'I don't want to waste your time, so I'm just going to be straight with you. I know about what was going on for you financially and for StoryCorps in the early 2000s and what I suspect has happened since. Separately, I'm sure you're aware of Ed Cooper's behaviour towards his colleagues. It has cost you enough in legal fees and redundancy packages over the years. The thing that has mystified me, though, is the hold he seems to have on you, Lord Finlayson. I've come to the conclusion that the two things are connected.'

The old gentleman eyes her carefully, almost shamefully. Jess needs to proceed with caution. She mustn't sound too judgemental in case she angers him.

'What I want you to understand is that I haven't been nosing about in your affairs. I have my own reasons for why I've been digging around StoryCorps and they're to do with Cooper. I'm not trying to hurt *you*, sir. So,' Jess continues, when her companion remains motionless, 'I may as well just tell you that I worked out what Ed – and, I suspect, Clarissa Courtenay – knows about you. Some ill-advised investments after the dot-com bubble popped, a bit of Maxwellian rejigging to plug a few financial holes. Your divorce, of course, which must have hurt your bank account—'

'How do you know about the divorce?' Finlayson sits up quickly.

'Well … it is a matter of public record.'

'Cooper never made that link.' The old man scowls, knocking back the last contents of his glass.

'That's because I'm better than Cooper.' She risks a tight smile.

Finlayson grunts.

'Well, what do you want? I assume you've come to blackmail me too. So your price is …?'

Jess can't believe it's this easy. She thought he'd want evidence, or threaten lawyers. Finlayson has shattered on impact with the lightest pressure. What is her price?

'Nothing,' she says quietly. 'I don't have one.'

'Now, Jessica.' Finlayson leans forward, looking panicked. 'Be reasonable. It's admirable to take this story and run it elsewhere. But surely we can come to some arrangement?'

'You misunderstand me,' Jess says firmly. 'I want to do well under my own steam, not because I've screwed a promotion out of you. Literally or figuratively. I've come to help you.'

Finlayson looks at her in utter astonishment.

'Listen, you want Ed off your back. Well, I want him off mine, too. There's no need to go into it, but let's just say that I don't want to work with him any more. But, until I discovered your secret, he had the power to get me fired. Now, I think we can both get what we want.'

'How?' Finlayson refills his glass.

'With a little blackmail of our own. Here.'

Jess pulls out her phone and opens an encrypted folder, which she's saved on various hidden devices and memory sticks, just in case Finlayson turns out to be less co-operative than she hoped. She leans forward and swipes through the photographs of Ed Cooper in varying states of undress, his erect penis and smirking, pouting face in almost all of them. One snap is from his teenage daughter's bedroom, her Harry Styles posters and *Twilight* books clearly visible. In another he has a large dildo hanging out of his bottom.

Lord Finlayson says nothing. He can't even if he wanted to, because he's shaking with uncontrollable, silent laughter, tears rolling down the deep wrinkles in his cheeks.

'I've suggested to him once before that I would show these to his wife, but he insisted she wouldn't care,' Jess says unconcernedly. 'But I think these pictures are something else ... any action he takes risks his wife, his children, his parents and his fellow hacks – many of whom would gleefully take him down – knowing, and seeing, all. His reputation, kaput.'

'Fucking brilliant,' Finlayson says when he can finally speak.

'So you see, I think there's enough here to get Ed off both of our backs. We get him away from the *Sentinel* – perhaps to a new gig or a pay-off. After all, we want to give him a nice, easy choice – with a watertight legal agreement to keep his mouth shut about your little pickle. Otherwise these photos will be released to the world. The only thing is,' Jess looks uncertain for the first time, 'I don't want to be there when it happens. Just get him out quietly, will you? I think after the election. He can just ... not come back from Christmas.'

'Done.' Finlayson raises his glass in a little toast.

'I'm out of ideas on Clarissa, though.'

'Oh, I'm not worried about that. She's got her own problems

at the moment and what's the point of bringing this to her attention? Either the PM wins – unlikely – in which case it's in my interests to keep good relations with her. Or he loses. In which case, they're out in the political desert and out of my hair. There's a small chance, too, that her sucking up to the Duchess of Sussex and Jacinda Ardern will come off, in which case we'll want to stay chummy . . . '

'All right.' Jess drains her glass and gets to her feet. 'I'd better be going. There's an election to cover, after all. And I've got something else cooking.'

'And you definitely want nothing?' Finlayson stares up at her.

'Nothing.' Jess smiles down at him. 'Happy to help.' After all, she knows that he knows what she knows. Surely things will have a funny way of working themselves out . . .

As she turns to go, Finlayson grabs Jess's wrist.

'Thank you,' he croaks, 'and God bless you.'

'No problem. But,' she chances a wink, 'perhaps ease off on the racehorses and private jets until you've got this straightened out, yeah?'

Shoreditch

A couple of hours later, Jess strolls into a small curry house on Brick Lane. As soon as she left Finlayson's house she headed home and jumped in the shower to wash her hair and exfoliate, shave and moisturise every available inch of her body. She's taking no chances in case Christian wants a repeat of the Labour conference. Still, wanting to be clean but not too keen, Jess has dressed in jeans, a T-shirt and biker boots. She's deliberately late, so she can stride in and apologise for her busyness. This is, after all, a last-minute invitation.

Christian bats her apologies away as he gets up to greet her. He looks exhausted but seems pleased to see her, and Jess can't ignore the jolt of pleasure as his hand lingers on the small of her back.

'What are you working on just now?' he asks when they've ordered.

'Nothing really. Dead at the moment ... nothing going on in the news ...'

'All right, it was a stupid question!' Christian chuckles. 'What do you want to talk to me about?'

Jess leans in. 'I have something that I think will interest you. Could spin the whole election.'

'Sold. Go on, then.'

Jess looks over her shoulder.

'Can't here. Too public.'

Jess brings her bottle of beer to her lips and drinks, her eyes not leaving his.

'All right. Can I lure you to my flat to talk about it there?' Christian tries to look away but can't. He promised himself that this evening is just about work. He mustn't sleep with Jess again. If he liked her before, their night in Liverpool has driven him mad with longing. But he needs to keep his head screwed on, at least for the next six or so weeks. For the sake of both their careers, it mustn't happen.

Naturally, they skip dinner and an hour later are naked in Christian's bed, panting.

'Here.' Jess tosses the brown envelope at Christian, then she collapses back into the pillows, wrapping herself in a blanket. 'Knock yourself out.'

Christian opens the envelope and goes through each page in turn. Once he's read everything carefully, he lies back next to Jess.

'How did you get this stuff?'

'Someone sent it to me. But I spent the whole afternoon going through it. It all stacks up.'

'It just feels a bit convenient to me. This is pretty big, if true. Someone just decided to give it to you anonymously?' Christian traces a finger down Jess's ribcage.

'It happens ... Not everyone wants to whistle-blow from the rooftops, you know. The point is, everything written down here is true. And just imagine – "Tories stitching up election" is one helluva headline. I just need to think more about every angle. Either way, leave it with me.'

She leaves the bed to stash the papers in her bag, then turns to face Christian.

'Want to see something cool? Stay perfectly still.'

She shrugs the blanket off her naked body and stands upright for a moment. Then she performs a neat cartwheel and lands with her feet either side of him. She drops into his lap and doesn't get up again for quite some time.

18th October

Con 29% Lab 40%

Tennyson charms business/

Drought in Somalia

Battersea

The event Eva has been dreading most is finally here. She's been chased by dogs and told to fuck off by potential voters. She's canvassed in the pouring rain and posed for embarrassing photoshoots next to potholes and zebra crossings. Yet she would do all of this naked in exchange for skipping the next couple of hours, when she'll be appearing on a platform in a local school for her first hustings with Joshua Udoka.

Eva is petrified. She hasn't been to a hustings before, but understands from her father that they can be anything from 'rambunctious' to 'fucking feral'. Can she debate? She mucked about at the Cambridge Union, but she is way out of her depth now.

For starters, what to wear? She'd like to appear both respectable and approachable to the many faceless people in the room she wants to elect her, but she also wants one specific person there to eat their heart out. What really threw Eva was the mysterious arrival of a huge bunch of roses at the campaign office the day after she bumped into Joshua and his team. The unsigned card read: *Let the games begin*. What the hell is he playing at?

Unusually, good advice is thin on the ground. Jess, stuck on the Labour campaign bus somewhere in the north-west, told her to be extremely rude or to play it cool on the phone earlier, but the signal was so bad that Eva can't be sure. Bobby has her own hustings to think about, while Eva's mother, Jenny, is in Antarctica with her rocker boyfriend and 'the band', dicking about with penguins and lamenting the melting polar ice – despite flying there by private jet. Eva dare not ask her father for advice, as she'd have to reveal the giant bastard of a pickle she's got herself into. Knowing Percy, he'd probably regale the audience with it on his appearance tonight on *Question Time*.

No, it's Clarissa she has turned to – the queen of cool. Calm and mysteriously sexy while simultaneously landing killer jabs as necessary. On a long call from Dubai (Clarissa, tirelessly hacking away at her quest to become a name in her own right, is in conversation to raise money for a possible foundation with Cherie Blair) they discussed how to approach the debate. *Be polite but uninterested. Don't allow yourself to be baited. Do not under any circumstances make eye contact with him. Direct everything you say to the audience. For God's sake, do not mention the roses. They may not even have been from him. And if they were, what's the harm in him wondering if they arrived or whether they were just one bunch of many from chancing admirers.*

It doesn't help that Eva was up late the night before, baking a birthday cake for one of the campaign team. She's hardly got a spare minute these days and is a dreadful cook, but feels obliged to do as many nice things as she can for her staff. At 1 a.m., while scraping the burnt sponge into the bin, she wondered what, if this is what she's doing to get herself elected, she'll be doing as an MP. This isn't quite what she'd had in mind when it came to campaigning. With a pang, she'd wondered what the guys were up to on Tracy Island.

Eva's name is called. She walks onto the stage. All the candidates shake hands. When she gets to Joshua Udoka, she can't resist looking into his face. *Oh dear, fallen at the first hurdle.*

The debate begins, with each candidate making a short statement about why they should be Battersea's next MP. Unsurprisingly, pretty well every one of them singles out Eva as the quintessential evil Tory, whose election signals five more years of decline. When Joshua speaks, Eva attempts to stare into space and tune out his voice, but notices he doesn't name her once, opting instead to talk about the future and what he wants to do for the community. He is brilliant. His pitch and positioning are miles better than hers.

When it's her turn, Eva drops the attack lines a boffin at CCHQ has given her. They insisted that the punches that really landed in the mayoral campaign a couple of years ago against the Labour candidate were veiled race points about 'values' and 'traditions'. Eva wonders for the first time how badly she really wants to win. It just doesn't feel right at all. Now Joshua is in front of her, in flesh and blood and so sporting, she bottles it and talks about housebuilding and travel networks.

A curiosity of the British system is that, on top of the usual Conservative, Labour, Lib Dem and Green candidates, there are half a dozen other independents who turn the debate into a kind of model UN wacky races. Each time an issue like school funding or transport links comes up, 'Mr End All Bicycle Lanes' or 'Mrs There's a Deep State Conspiracy to Control Our Minds with London Tap Water' jumps in with an incoherent ramble. Once or twice, Eva and Joshua catch each other's eye and have to quickly look away in case they laugh.

There is one very sticky point, though, where the whole group is coherent. 'Ms I'm Sick of Career Politicians' gets on a roll, and jabs her finger at Eva, practically screaming, 'And here's our perfect example! No job outside politics, the daughter of a former prime minister and working in the whips' office, learning all the foul tricks of the trade. We have to root out this entitled political class and end parliamentary sleaze!'

Eva grasps around for a response, but the other candidates all dive onto her in agreement. Finally she gets to speak up.

'Look, I'm sorry that I have a background in politics. But on occasion, that can be helpful. Do I agree with how parties govern themselves? No. Do I think the whips' offices are the best way to manage MP behaviour and HR? Absolutely not. Do we need a serious reassessment of how Parliament functions? Of course! But we have to be realistic. The system that we have is the very first of its kind. The mother of all parliaments! Whoever among us gets elected, they'll be honoured to serve everyone in Battersea there – and this brilliant country.'

There's a little smattering of applause. *I didn't realise I could be so hammy*, Eva thinks.

'What about you?' someone shouts to Joshua.

'Yeah, down with the Tories, mate!' yells a voice from the back.

Eva knows it's the perfect moment for him to strike. Joshua's been talking about cleaning up Westminster and fresh starts since the campaign started, as well as lamenting the lack of experience of current MPs in business or charity work or public-service jobs. Eva looks down at her feet, bracing herself for the blow. But it doesn't come.

'I agree with Miss Cross.' Joshua addresses the audience. 'It is a huge honour for any of us to sit in the Commons. And, okay, it's not a perfect system and we do need more people from the real world in there. We live in a cynical time and with some of the goings on in Westminster recently, it's no wonder. But we need to appreciate those who are prepared to put themselves forward to serve us, not tear them down. Who will ever want to step up, otherwise? You wouldn't have an entire stage of candidates to choose from, that's for sure. So let's not lose sight of what this is about.'

There is rapturous applause and Eva can't resist glancing at Joshua, who beams at her. Her toes squirm in her court shoes. He didn't stick the knife in. He actually defended her. And, all right, it painted him as a very good guy, but that's the game.

After the debate, which rumbles on for another thirty minutes or so, Eva takes a seat backstage with a bottle of water, massaging her feet.

'Well done.' Joshua plonks himself down next to her and sighs. 'One down.'

'And only six weeks of this to go ... ' Eva smiles. 'It's exhausting, isn't it.'

'Yup. Pretty cool, though. Apart from the sore feet.'

'You too?'

'New shoes. Massive error. I've got huge blisters under here.' Joshua chuckles. 'So what are you doing now?'

'I guess the same as everyone,' Eva replies. 'Walk thousands of steps a day, much of it in the pissing rain, and scoff junk food. About two hours of sleep, then repeat.'

'No, I mean right now.' Joshua looks intently at her. 'Want to have a drink?'

Eva looks back down at her feet. She can practically hear Clarissa and Jess and her mother and the entire Conservative Party screaming no at her. But she is thirsty. Is there really any harm in just one drink?

'Yeah, okay.' Eva grins, looking up.

Joshua waits for her as she crams her feet back into her shoes and they slip out, unnoticed.

Ten minutes later, they have battled the frosty night and are in a trendy little bar by Clapham Common, sipping on Negronis. Eva intended to be teetotal until the election is over, but she just can't resist joining Joshua's order. The amber liquid, the low house music and the soft, twinkling light feel wonderfully cosy and intimate after the harsh lighting and echoing chatter of the debate hall.

They initially talk about politics, teasing each other about their respective party leaders and MPs, but they move on to films and books. As Eva remembers from his flat, Joshua loves to read. Lots of heavy non-fiction and political biographies, but also sci-fi and romance novels.

'I inherited a load from my mum and sisters. Jilly Cooper, Jackie Collins, Georgette Heyer. I love them.'

'I get all that, but sci-fi?' Eva laughs and wrinkles her nose.

When their third cocktails arrive – margaritas this time – Joshua cocks his head on one side.

'So why did you quit Fawn?'

Eva touches the tip of her tongue to the rim of the glass, getting a little hit of salt.

'It's a bit obvious, isn't it?'

'You thought I was going to shop you? That would have broken the rules. And besides, what an arseholey thing to do.'

'All's fair in love and war and elections, Joshua. Once I saw you'd been selected, I assumed you already knew who I was when we …. met. I felt embarrassed as much as anything. I mean, we have seen each other naked.'

Joshua beams. 'And you'd be voted in by a landslide if you got your kit off for polling day. Well, just for the record, I haven't said anything to anyone.'

'Me neither.' Eva says quickly. Jess, Bobby and Clarissa don't count.

'I say it to myself sometimes, though. Just to say it really happened. It's too hard to believe my luck otherwise.' Joshua slides his hand over to stroke Eva's palm in little circles. Her heart bounces in her chest.

Eva doesn't trust herself to respond right away. Her paranoid little voice has kicked back in. What if this is an elaborate tactic, getting her to crush on him and embarrass herself, an extra little layer of fun on the way to victory? She thinks about the flowers he sent. Is he trying to get in her head?

'What are you trying to do here?' she finally asks, in a tiny voice.

'What do you mean?' Joshua continues his circles.

'Oh, come on.' She feels a bit stronger and pulls her hand away. 'We're opponents! You want to get elected as badly as me. So you must be up to something. You may not believe this, but Labour and Tory candidates up and down the country are not sitting down to cosy cocktails together after their hustings events. They're trying to screw each other!'

'Well, we've already done that,' he jokes, then sees Eva's face. 'Sorry. But, honestly, I understand what you're saying. You don't trust me. I don't really trust you! Who trusts anyone right away that they've met on an app? But I know you'll have been told to go below the belt against me, run some of the tactics like your lot tried against the mayor, and you haven't. And I've been told to paint you as a Tory daddy's girl and I haven't. Okay? All I know is that night in August was mind-blowing.'

Eva thinks hard, puffing out her cheeks. There's no way they can date, that's for sure. But what about something else? *And*, a small voice says, *he thought it was mind-blowing . . .*

'It just feels an insane thing to even discuss.' Eva waves him away, attempting to sound matter-of-fact. 'We. Are. Rivals. Okay? What are we going to do – knock the stuffing out of each other all day and then . . . stuff it back in at night?' Eva starts to laugh. 'Be serious.'

Joshua raises his hands defensively. 'All right ... but I can't wait for this election to be over. The moment it is, I'm taking you out for dinner – stuffing optional.'

When they say goodbye outside the bar, the night is even colder. Through the glow of London's street lighting, a few determined stars prickle above the Common.

Joshua leans in and Eva thinks – hopes – that he's going to kiss her. But it's just a very modest peck on the cheek.

'See you around.'

He's turning to walk off into the night, when Eva grabs his arm. Throwing caution to the wind, she kisses him. And he kisses her back.

They don't make it all the way up the stairs to his flat, or even have their coats off, before they're breathing great sighs of pleasure.

20th October

Tipperton

Two days later, Bobby lowers herself onto a garden wall and lets her head fall between her knees, her massive belly hanging down too. The stretch in her lower back is blissful. Pounding the Tipperton pavements is taking its toll, not least on her feet, which have swollen so much that she's had to buy bigger shoes. However, everything seems to be going well. Her first hustings event was a success and Bobby genuinely enjoyed the debate with her Labour and Lib Dem opposite numbers, who are pleasant, middle-aged men and both out-of-towners. She's done a couple of local press interviews and her small team of volunteers has gradually expanded out into an army. Bobby's father, anxious about knocking on doors but eager to help, has learnt to bake and the Cliveden food mixer and oven are running at all hours of the day as he churns out scones, sponges and tarts to keep everyone going when they're out door-knocking.

Jake and Bobby speak every day but miss each other. She's managed to get down to London once so far for a thirty-two-week scan, which Jake escaped from CCHQ for, and learnt that everything is progressing as normal, although Bobby wasn't being entirely straight about the twenty thousand or so steps she's getting in a day with her leaflets. After the appointment, they went to John Lewis and browsed baby clothes, unable to resist a couple of muslins with rabbits on them and a matching Babygro. What is saving them a fortune is the contents of the Cliveden attic, which has all of Bobby's old kit carefully cleaned and packed away. A buggy, car seat, cot. All the big-ticket items are there, if a little dated. As soon as the election is over, Jake and Bobby will drive it down to London to Jake's flat in Brixton and nest in earnest.

While Bobby keeps Jake updated with her own campaign, he tells her about the national one. The first TV debate will take place on BBC1 on 24th October and Jake is constantly called into prep sessions to school the PM on policy. On the following day, the Conservatives will launch their manifesto, which Jake is responsible for. The job is shattering him, as every single Conservative MP seems to have got hold of his personal mobile number and they're bombarding him day and night with their pet policies. There are a lot of contradictory positions and, as ever, there simply isn't enough money to go around.

Meanwhile, the environment secretary has been caught on secret camera making a few ill-thought-out gags about Terry, the late Longleat lion, and every minister speaking to the media is having to trot out the stale 'well, it's not language I would have used . . . ' line to distance themselves from the remarks, without throwing their colleague under the bus.

Still, though, the polls show the Conservatives closing in on

Labour, with only ten points between them now. The internal CCHQ polling shows closer to six points, but the prime minister isn't convinced.

'I just don't understand why your polls are different from what everyone else is saying. Why are we gaining?' He frowns down at the sheet in front of him when he drops in for another grilling by his team ahead of the BBC debate.

'I keep telling you. It's because we're better than everyone else.' Cal yawns. 'And we're gaining because our plan is working. People are really resonating with you.' Cal realises that flattery will help him here. All he cares about is that the gap narrows between the Conservatives and Labour, and that everyone assumes it's a mistake and Labour stay complacent.

'What I want to know is why the bus seems to be going about in circles around the bottom half of the country. Why aren't we campaigning everywhere?' Anto tucks his thumbs into the armholes of a natty new orange gilet.

'Because we're not welcome everywhere.' Cal is tired of explaining this. 'A scattergun approach of talking to everyone won't work. A lot of the country fucking hate us, okay? We don't want to antagonise them more. There's different ways of speaking to different people and for some that is total silence. Some we don't even want to know there's an election on . . .'

Meanwhile, Christian's internal polling is showing Labour's lead as about eight points. Jess told him last night, after she turned up on his doorstep wearing nothing beneath a trench coat, that she's preparing to publish the story about DataTwerk and the Electoral Commission. He wishes she'd hurry up.

Jess is on the Lib Dem bus today, which has stopped stinking of chip fat but is smelling very strongly of spilled rum. She squelches on board, her feet sticking to the floor, and settles in for a trip to a Norfolk solar farm.

'What happened here?' she asks a friend from the lobby.

'Absolute carnage. One of the staffers' birthdays last night. We all went to the pub and for some reason thought it would be good to have an after-party on here. The driver's not very happy. I just hope there isn't CCTV, mate. Proper bacchanalian, it was.'

Jess accepts a cup of coffee from a green-faced Lib Dem campaign team member and shakes her head in disbelief at the reporters' stories of last night's strip poker and truth or dare, which mainly involved running laps of the bus naked in the cold. It happens surprisingly often on the campaign buses. The same group of people on the same bus – Jess is unusual to just be joining for the day – barrelling around the country for six weeks. It blurs the lines between the sensible and the insane. And it sounds like there were some major lapses in judgement last night.

'I'm pretty sure those two had sex over there.' Her friend points at two shifty-looking staffers in their twenties, who are carefully avoiding eye contact with anyone, then she points at a seat by the kitchen area. 'At least, it smells very suspicious today ... still, nothing to what I'm hearing about the other buses. There was a threesome on the Tory tour! And Labour are in an exhausting dispute with their bus company, after someone hung a string of anal beads from the rear-view mirror. Driver nearly crashed at a roundabout when he saw them ...'

Jess offers paracetamol to the various sore heads, then opens her notebook to prepare for the interview she's been assigned. When she gets a text from Christian, her heart leaps, but it just reads:

Got any idea when you're going to publish?

Jess wants to sit on the story just a little longer. It will likely be the scoop of the year and possibly decide the outcome of the election. Once she sits down with Philip McKay and begins to write, she can't row back on it. Jess's two best friends are standing as Conservative MPs and she only has a roof over her head because of a Conservative minister. This doesn't mean she won't do it, of course, but she just wants to linger a little longer, before the floodgates open and Bobby and Eva spot her name on the byline of a piece accusing the Conservative Party of tampering with the UK's democracy. She's had big stories before but this is potential history in the making – and she can't shake off a mysterious bad feeling about it.

Jess's fingers are just hovering on the screen, wondering how to reply, when she sees Christian is typing again.

p.s. Are you free tomorrow night? Bring a tooth-brush . . . x

She grins and switches on her Dictaphone, ready to interview the leader of the Liberal Democrats at the back of the bus, wishing she could wear a face mask to escape his notoriously foul breath.

25th October

White City, London

Five days on and it's an average Friday afternoon across the UK. People race home from work or school, often via a supermarket or corner shop, glad the weekend has arrived. Teenagers smoke sly cigarettes or puff on blue cherry-flavoured vapes by leisure centres and skate parks and betting shops. Kids have a kickabout in the park and retirees watch on, play bingo or help with nursery pick-up. Fish-and-chip shops and curry houses prepare for a busy evening. Secret affairs, stag and hen dos and birthday parties get underway. Families and friends congregate and observe religious festivals or their own clannish traditions. The nation is blissfully unaware of the hand-wringing and cold sweating going on behind the scenes at the BBC studios in west London.

Most members of the public will see only the highlights of this evening's leadership debate. The faithful of SW1 and die-hard politicos and journalists are on hand, though, to lead the way on commentary and analysis – and to confidently inform everyone of the 'winner'. Up and down the country, candidates and activists are primed at their phones and computers to do everything from Tweeting to Snapchatting their support for their party leader. The evening feels intensely significant to a surprisingly small number of people. For everyone else, the whole event will either pass them by or piss them off.

The studio is ready to go. The stage, with its lecterns and the huge desk that Victoria Derbyshire will use, is all set up, wired with everything from a clock and stopwatch to a teleprompter. Victoria herself is in a dressing room, having her hair lacquered with hairspray to keep it in place and her face painted and powdered against the blazing studio lights. Outside in the corridor, she can hear the different leaders' teams arriving. They have each done a rather awkward catwalk, leaving their shiny blacked-out cars and heading into the studio, via a mass of TV cameras and photographers. Every one of them looks nervous and tight-lipped, no matter how hard they try to wave in a carefree sort of way.

Heading down the corridor before her soundcheck, Victoria drops into the green room, which has been curtained off into sections so that each candidate has a bit of privacy with their teams. She greets each in turn, wishes them luck and heads down to the studio.

A few rooms over, Percy Cross and Madeleine Ford are preparing to watch the debate so that they can spin to journalists afterwards about the prime minister's superior performance. A few years ago, they were good friends – Percy gave Madeleine her first cabinet post – and their shared political rebirths have brought them back together again. Both are cheerful and relaxed this evening, deeply relieved to not be doing the debate themselves.

They chat to Vicky Tennyson, who is spinning for John Ramsey and who seems similarly unconcerned by how the next couple of hours will go. She loved doing the debates in the Labour leadership contest last year. Her husband is also having a nice time with Holly Mayhew and Michael Ford, who have both come to support their partners and soak up a little atmosphere. There's great excitement when the US ambassador to the UK arrives to meet them all before heading to join the audience, eager to get a taste of the best of British political debate. Percy is quick to disabuse him of this notion.

In Tipperton, Bobby's parents are hosting a small viewing party. Bobby's father has outdone himself and built his own small brick pizza oven in the garden and made fresh dough. In the fridge is an enormous rectangular chocolate cake, iced in black with a white *10* on it. A number of Bobby's volunteer army sit on sofas and the arms of chairs in the living room, ready to cheer and boo accordingly.

In Battersea, Eva has joined her team in the constituency office to watch. She's ordered an enormous takeaway curry and some beer and the group is enjoying some well-earned bonding time. They've covered a lot of ground this week. Still, campaigning to become an MP is not easy. Or cheap. She won't earn a penny over the course of the election and is constantly shelling out for food and drinks for the team, as well as charity boxes and donations. And she doesn't even pay rent or travel expenses, or have to think about childcare or taking time off work. For the first time it's occurring to her that becoming an MP is out of the grasp of most people, simply on the grounds of practicality and resources.

Deep down, she knows she isn't really in this. Eva's constantly drawn to what her father is telling her about the national campaign, about the internal polling and 'bloody smart stuff' the 'data chappies' are up to. Has she made a mistake in agreeing to – being flattered into – a seat rather than learning everything she can from Cal? She doesn't have the same interest in this rosette-wearing campaigning as she did in what was happening at Tracy Island. Additionally, Eva finds everything Joshua Udoka is saying really quite compelling. She doesn't want to admit it, but it is clear when they've talked about politics – generally in his bed, which they secretly sneak off to a few times a week – that he is far more passionate about public service than Eva is. He's dreamt of it for a long time, thought carefully about how to get elected and is simply better at media performances and policy thinking. Joshua is genuine, while Eva is just ambitious.

Over at CCHQ, Cal has allowed the TV debate to be played on big screens, but on the strict condition that anyone with little to do goes home or to the pub – this is not a chance for people to get boozed up in the office and lose focus. The Americans remain on Tracy Island, oblivious to the excitement in the main office, while two desks are flat out: Jake's team, preparing the policy final lines ahead of the manifesto launch tomorrow, and Nick's team, who will spin, Tweet and clip their way to TV-debate victory. Nick himself is in White City, pumping the PM up.

Cal is closeted in the glass-walled centre room, looking at Don's latest poll on Vicky Tennyson. She did a stump speech this morning and has been making the case to the affluent Tory heartlands about wealth distribution with a surprising amount of success – 'Do you want higher taxes? No. Do you want more money to be spent on public services like healthcare, schools, parks and infrastructure? Yes. Well, then – we want the same things' – which even the *Telegraph* is struggling to undermine. Tennyson also shouts the 'So the Tories have been in charge for ten years but do you feel better off?' question the loudest on the campaign trail. Cal thinks she's the complete package, a once-in-a-generation politician with brains, charisma and integrity, and, judging by Don's polling, the public agree.

Over at Labour HQ, Christian is looking at the attack lines for the Conservative manifesto launch. A few policies have leaked out and it can be hard to tell what is a malicious leak, what is 'pitch rolling' from the campaign to test how an idea lands and what is just nonsense fed to Labour to trick them, because ideas like changing the drinking age to twenty-one or forced sterilisation for sex offenders seem both bonkers and yet quite likely at the same time.

As for the TV debate, he knows Ramsey will do a fine job, but any media lines out of it will undoubtedly be knocked off the agenda once the story he's most interested in breaks. His eyes keep darting over to his phone, wondering how Jess is getting on.

Jess is at the *Sentinel* offices, closeted away with Philip McKay, combing over the story once more.

'And you really want this going out under Ed's byline, even when you've done all the work?' Philip pushes his horn-rimmed glasses up his nose.

'Yes. And it wasn't that much work ...' Jess doesn't quite meet his eye. She's thought about it long and hard and, after her friendship with Eva and Bobby was nearly destroyed last year when a story Jess was connected to came too close to Claybourne Terrace, she can live without bylines. Besides, she still can't shrug off this lingering feeling of doubt about the story that has crept in.

Philip doesn't argue with her, but he is astonished that one of his most ambitious writers wants to gift what is perhaps the story of the election to her superior – let alone a superior she is constantly complaining about.

Jess, though, has made up her mind. The way she sees it, she wins both ways. If the story is a success, Philip and Finlayson know who found it. If not, Ed takes the fall.

Philip McKay shrugs and pulls out his phone to summon Ed into the office. Jess glances at the documents one last time, then heads off to meet the rest of the team to catch the last of the TV debate, arriving in time to see Percy Cross in the spin room, Madeline Ford struggling to keep a straight face next to him as a photo of John Ramsey looms on a screen behind them.

'Yes, you're right. We *have* been at the helm for ten years. The question for viewers at home is, "Is it safer to carry on with the devil you know, or should you jump to the devil pretending to be something new?" From tonight's performance, you can see John Ramsey is just the same old devil, but in a far uglier suit . . .'

It's not exactly the party line.

25th October

Hull Maritime Museum

A casual, unbiased observer could only describe the Conservative Party's manifesto launch as complete pandemonium. The policies themselves, falling into Cal's instruction to be strong and clear, are fine. Aside from raising the drinking age and sterilising sex offenders (which has turned out to be a sincere and surprisingly popular pledge), the punchier stuff on skills, defence and civil service reform, as per Cal's agreement with the PM on joining the campaign, have been included. But at the press conference, every single journalist asks a question following up on the *Sentinel*'s sensational splash, all essentially asking, 'Are you trying to rig this election?'

'If we were, don't you think we'd be doing a bit better than trailing nearly ten points behind?' Nick shouts into his phone afterwards, zooming in the prime-ministerial convoy to the nearest airfield, ready to catch a flight back to London.

Still, the prime minister handled the questions remarkably well, seeing as it was essentially an exercise in ritual humiliation. Eric Courtenay can take a beating, so long as he's told what to say. He was able to issue denial after denial, without hesitation or deviation (alas, avoiding repetition is beyond his communications skills), standing upright and serious, never once blushing or stuttering. But as Nick and Cal insisted, the moment the story broke late the night before, this will blow over soon. They just need to get to the bottom of it. It can surely be easily explained away.

The trouble is, that's proving difficult. The Conservatives can deny all they like, but because nobody seems to know one way or another what happened in the Electoral Commission data breach, their donor association with DataTwerk looks dodgy. After all, the Conservatives must be desperate to win – and is cheating really beneath them, when you factor in all the other sleaze from that last couple of years?

When they get back to CCHQ, the PM is irritated by Cal's lack of interest in the debacle.

'It's not that I'm not interested, it's that I don't want us derailed by it. We must stay focused. We've put the Americans onto working out exactly what's gone on, but otherwise there's no point in us talking about this all the time, kowtowing to the chatterati and generally making this situation even worse.'

The PM is somewhat pacified. It's like following through on a military objective, ignoring distractions. He's been fired on before now. If he can cope under a rain of bullets, he can manage this. Besides, Laura Lloyd sent him a congratulatory text after the press conference. He could feel a lot worse.

'All right, well, there's something else I want to discuss with you.' The PM lowers his voice conspiratorially. 'Anto took me aside earlier. It seems that, well, he says he has been made aware that we are advertising on a website called ... BBBs?'

The PM knows exactly what the website is called, seeing as he's a frequent user of it himself. But he does his best to look and sound ignorant.

'BBBs?' Cal looks nonplussed.

'Uh.' The PM blushes furiously and murmurs, 'B-Blue Balls and Bazookas. Apparently it's some sort of porno site ...?'

To his surprise, Cal and Nick start laughing.

'Is that so.' Cal grins. 'And may I ask how Anto came across this advertisement?'

'Well.' The PM frowns. 'He didn't disclose that ...'

Cal raises an eyebrow.

'Firstly, yes, we are advertising on there.' Cal raises a hand to hold the PM's protestations. He needs to explain this carefully, without producing more questions that could lead to revelations of their much wider porn piggy-backing. 'It's a good place to test if our tech is working and we tend to get very strong responses to surveys and so forth. It's completely legit, boss.'

'A bit uncouth, isn't it?'

'A matter of taste, I think.' He needs to get the PM off this. 'I wouldn't worry about it. And perhaps just check that Anto isn't stumbling across our ads on any of his work devices ...'

Christian is cock-a-hoop. Unusually for a manifesto launch, where they would typically criticise various policies, the Labour attack team hardly had to do anything. The lobby have been far too busy getting thoroughly excited about the apparent stitch-up the Conservatives are daring to try under their very noses. Every newspaper is asking the 'big and serious questions, which must be asked' in the interests of the UK as a functioning democratic system. Privately, Christian is happy not to be taking shots at the Tory manifesto. After all, some of it – the stuff on civil service reform and skills in particular – he is quite interested in.

It also helps that he's got Jess's legs wrapped around him in the bath. In fact, the only question mark is why Ed's byline appeared on the *Sentinel* story. Jess insisted she had her reasons, but Christian is mystified. Perhaps it is so nobody can accuse her of helping Labour.

For her part, Jess is just relieved it's over. Or her role in it, anyway. The story may run for weeks, but she can focus on the rest of the election and forget about the gnawing sensation she's had for the last few days. True to form, Ed has been bothering her.

On a high from his latest and largest scoop – evidently Philip McKay has kept his word and not told Ed who got the story first – he has been texting non-stop with messages ranging from the suggestive to the genuinely revolting. Knowing she only has to put up with this for a couple more weeks, Jess has simply stopped replying. She hasn't felt this carefree in ages.

Breathing in the smell of Christian's hair, she wishes they could be grafted together permanently. The sex is fantastic, but these moments afterwards, where they bathe or lie down in bed, talking and laughing, are becoming her favourite bits. She's never experienced anything like it before, being one for getting hers then making off into the night. Jess stays over until the morning now, and she and Christian even have a routine of coffee and eggs. It's nice. But she doesn't know what it all means. Are they dating? Or is this just the courteous way that men with a bit of Scandi blood treat their fuck buddies? Jess hasn't been in a relationship before, so this limbo makes her incredibly uneasy.

To escape these needy, pleady thoughts – honestly, who is she, Eva? – she slips into her natural defence. Keep him interested with sex.

She begins to kiss and nibble at Christian's ears, letting her fingers massage in circles on his chest. He leans his head back so she can kiss his throat and neck, while one hand slides down beneath the water. Once he's hard, Christian pulls Jess around so that she's sitting on his lap, her back to him, her hands reaching up to run her fingers through his hair. He pulls the shower head from its holster and pushes the jet below the surface, between Jess's thighs, while his spare hand traces softly over her breasts. When she's moaning, he slides into her from behind, water lapping over the sides of the tub.

4th November

South London

After two weeks of solid working hard, playing hard and screwing hard, Christian and Jess are in bed. They've been asleep for about three hours when Jess wakes to realise Christian is writhing in pain next to her. The sheets are soaked and, when she takes his temperature, he's burning up.

Could it be flu? He has been working himself to the bone recently, and Jess isn't exactly helping him rest. Maybe it's all catching up with him. But his abdomen is hurting him, far worse than any gastric flu could do.

'You don't think you strained yourself earlier, do you? You know, thrusted yourself a hernia?' Jess attempts to tease him.

But Christian can't speak; he just stays rolled on his side in a ball, breathing through his teeth.

Jess starts to worry now. She tries to move him, to see if he can stand and get some clothes on to go to hospital, but when he uncurls by more than an inch he immediately bunches up in agony again. Then he vomits. Jess calls 999 and realises in a surreal, vague state that this is the first time she's spoken to a call handler. It's hard to keep the note of panic out of her voice.

While they wait for the paramedics, Jess dresses herself and manages to get tracksuit bottoms on Christian. She dithers about putting a blanket over him – should he be kept warm if he has a temperature? – and wets a flannel under the bathroom tap to dab at his forehead. He manages to soften the corners of his mouth in response but still can't speak, focusing all his energy on breathing, his eyes scrunched up tight. The minutes crawl by, the fear in Jess's chest pushing the air out of her.

When the ambulance arrives, Jess lets the team in and explains what has happened in the last thirty or so minutes. One of them, a young man, attends to Christian, taking his vitals and speaking to him in a clear, reassuring voice, while the other, an older woman, asks Jess questions. No, he's not eaten anything odd – or nothing that Jess hasn't also consumed – and he has seemed fine recently, if rather run down with fatigue.

'Looks like his appendix.' The young man turns his head over his shoulder as he works. 'Might have ruptured.'

The older woman nods, then asks Jess about any underlying conditions or medication, but Jess can't help at all.

'Sorry, what's your relationship to him?'

The woman says it without any kind of edge, just asks. But Jess has no idea what to say. Can you reply 'professional-acquaintance-slash-regular-fuck-but-I'm-hoping-for-more'? She stands there with her mouth open, struggling for something to say when there is a rasp from the bed.

'She's my girlfriend,' Christian gasps.

Then he passes out, like the effort of his words have knocked the final bit of life out of him.

The paramedics leap into action, establishing that his heart is still beating and that he's breathing normally. Within a minute, Christian is on a trolley and Jess is bustling out with the group to a waiting ambulance, only stopping to grab her and Christian's phones, his keys and her wallet.

As the ambulance tears to St Thomas', Jess sits next to Christian and holds his hand. *My girlfriend.* The words ring in her head as she oscillates between terror at Christian's condition – a ruptured appendix ... is that life-threatening? – and a little glowing ember of joy. Clearly there would have been better ways to hear these words, but the point is he said them. And when he couldn't say anything, really. The message that took priority in his mind was about her.

A few hours later, Jess is woken from the doze she's fallen into on a plastic chair by a consultant. Christian is stable but the problem is indeed his appendix. Jess struggles to focus as the doctor explains that, although the operation has been successful, Christian will need to be in hospital a couple of weeks to clear his entire abdomen of infection.

'Thank you so much, Doctor.' Jess pats his arm. 'Really ... thank you.'

Jess is allowed to go and see Christian, who smiles dopily at her from the bed. She sinks into a chair.

'How are you, girlfriend?' he asks weakly.

'Thank fuck for that,' Jess says, relieved. 'I thought perhaps you were just talking gibberish in your fevered state.'

Christian takes her hand.

'No, I just thought I should press my advantage. You were hardly going to contradict a dying man ...'

Jess, laughing, leans in to kiss him.

They talk for a while about what being hospitalised will mean for Christian's ability to run the Labour campaign.

'You can work remotely, you know. I'll get your laptop and

all that. You can do conference calls from here,' Jess says, trying to reassure him.

'No, it won't work. You have to physically be there. I'll do what I can from hospital,' he winces as he sits up on his pillows, 'but someone will have to take over while I'm rocking this gown. Hand me my phone, will you?'

Christian sends messages to John Ramsey, the core campaigning team and his family. It's only 5.30 a.m. but Ramsey calls him immediately.

Wanting to give them privacy, Jess kisses Christian's forehead and mouths that she'll be back soon. Then she shuffles back to Christian's flat to have the quickest of naps, to shower, change and to pack him – *her boyfriend* – a bag of essentials.

12th November

CON 32% LAB 39%

QUESTIONS DOG TORIES/

IS ACID RAIN BACK?

St Thomas' Hospital

Christian has been in hospital for over a week. While he tries to do what he can from his sick bed, he is out of sight and therefore out of mind in much of the day-to-day running of the Labour campaign. This means that, try as he might, he can't stop his team, under the new stewardship of Tanya Haines, from focusing all their efforts on the 'Tories are stitching up this election and are undermining our democracy' story. He calls, he texts, he pleads with Tanya and Ramsey to not lose focus on the real issues and the 'Time for Change' mantra, but they have the bit firmly between their teeth, intoxicated by righteous rage that power could be stolen from them. The only person to ignore the new Labour campaign edict to lean into the story is Vicky Tennyson, who is steadfastly talking about the ideas she has for governing – from the Treasury, of course – and repeating the 'Tories have been in charge for ten years' message.

The trouble is, as Christian can see from the internal polling he's getting, Tanya's plan isn't working where it matters. In smart metropolitan areas like parts of London, Oxford and Cambridge, people are incredibly excited about the story, writing letters to newspapers and venting on social media. People who tend to pay for more than one subscription or supplement fall into this camp, as do the well-educated and well-off. They have loud voices and Tanya and co. lap up their anger, but most of them were never going to vote Tory. Across the rest of the country, people aren't nearly so bothered.

For starters, with only two parties really in the race anyway, elections always feel stitched up. Additionally, it's quite a complicated story to explain, as most people haven't heard of the Electoral Commission or take much interest in cybersecurity or party donors. The SW1 circuit is obsessed, however, with journalists and commentators joyfully dogging the airwaves and newspapers with what a huge problem it is for Eric Courtenay's electoral prospects and egging Labour HQ into increasingly crazed and remote statements about democracy and conspiracy. No matter how hard journalists try, though, CCHQ won't be drawn into it. Christian watches the prime minister's interview with Andrew Neil on his little hospital TV. The exchange says it all.

'Prime Minister, this story about potential election tampering has now been running for nearly three weeks and your party has been unable to shrug it off. Some of your own MPs are now begging you publicly to come forward with an explanation so a line can be drawn under it for the remainder of the campaign. Do you worry that this story will cost you the election? And how do you still not have a proper answer?'

'Well, Andrew, I don't deal in conspiracy theories. We

haven't said anything because there's nothing to say. What we're finding is that the public are far more interested in how we can help them buy homes, raise their families and care for their elderly parents than the weird conspiracies of metropolitan types. They want to know how we are working to help them get careers that they feel proud of, and how we'll give them peace of mind over their finances and household budgets. And they want to know how we'll keep them safe from terrorists, criminals and foreign threats. I'm sorry that John Ramsey and the Labour party have got their tinfoil hats on, but as you can see from the polls – there's no need for us to rig the election. We're catching them up, only a few points in it, because we're listening and leading. Not crying foul play because we're being chipped away at.'

Christian clutches his head in his hands. It's absolutely true. Less than three weeks until the election and the polls show that the Conservatives are catching Labour up, well into single digits. Unable to scream with frustration, Christian fires a message to the core team WhatsApp group.

Just looking at latest polls. We MUST get back onto the real issues – NHS, schools, economy etc. I know this EC story is interesting but our babbling about it isn't working!

Tanya: *You should see the response we're getting to it out and about. Just been to Brighton with JR and people were cheering him from the rooftops.*

Christian: *That's because it's Brighton! What are they saying in Workington and Bradford??*

Ramsey: *Tanya's right. I think the polls will shift towards us once more people understand it. We just need to double down and talk about it more. I feel really strongly about this, Christian. The election is being RIGGED!*

Christian bangs the back of his head against the wall in frustration. This is a nightmare.

CCHQ

Cal sits in his usual glass-walled room, watching John Ramsey's interview with Robert Peston. The leader of the Labour Party sounds half mad and he looks it too. His eyes seem to be bulging slightly. Try as he might, Peston is struggling to get the Labour leader off the Electoral Commission story.

'All right, well, I have a policy question for you,' Peston says exasperatedly, getting tired of Ramsey's ranting. He asks a long and complex question about windfall taxes on large profits for British companies.

Ramsey looks at his interviewer blankly for a moment.

'Well, Robert, what I think people really want to know is why this election has been stitched up—'

'Maybe. But that remains to be seen. I'm here now and I want to know the answer to this question. The shadow chancellor had an interesting take on it when I asked her about it yesterday, but there is no mention of it in your manifesto. So I'm asking you.'

Ramsey looks horrified. It's perfectly clear that he has been so focused on doubling down on a stitch-up message that he has no idea what Tennyson said to Peston yesterday. Pro-business? Or anti-fat cats? He decides to guess.

'Well ... of course, we have to tax fairly. We believe in fair wealth distribution and therefore large profits on all companies should be taxed, so the less well-off can benefit.'

'All companies?' Peston lets the question sink in, seeing blind panic in Ramsey's eyes as his lack of preparation hits him. 'That's interesting, as that isn't what Vicky Tennyson said—'

'We're absolutely in lockstep,' Ramsey gabbles quickly. 'But our chief concern is that the election has been rigged and we won't get the opportunity to—'

'All right, well, we have a studio audience this evening. Let's ask someone at random what their question is ...'

'Yeah, hi. Less of a question, more of a comment,' says a balding man from Milton Keynes. 'I'm tired of John Ramsey saying he's had the election stolen before we've even voted. All politicians are cheats, so just tell me why I should vote for you, John!'

Meanwhile, the porn data model is working a charm. The Conservatives' internal polling suggests interesting splinter groups and regions, previously turned off by the Tories or at least very shy about supporting them, are coming round, tired of Labour's inability to offer a decent alternative and receptive to carefully targeted messaging that's come out of their porn searches. For example, the team tried and tested all sorts of theories about why car-related searches – dogging, sex overlooking busy roads and fantasies about liaisons in taxis and Ubers – are popular in the south of England. Finally, they've cracked it: people are anxious about fuel prices, ULEZ charges and a new Labour car-pooling policy from their manifesto.

Cal sniggers and turns the TV off as Peston's audience continue to quiz Ramsey. Then he calls Nick in.

'You know, we've got twenty days to go until D-Day. I reckon we let the rigging thing run to the weekend then knock it on the head. Too many "don't know"s in surveys about it. We're asking people to go out and vote in the cold and dark. And probably wet. We need them to feel sure we're the way to go.'

'All right.' Nick nods. 'And I'm actually starting to feel sorry for Ramsey. Time to set him straight.'

18th November

Con 33% Lab 38%

Two weeks to new PM/

Ski season cancelled in Alps

Central London

After a full two weeks in hospital, Christian and Jess are packing up his belongings. He's finally been given a clean bill of health and discharged.

'Want to get some breakfast before you go into the office?' Jess asks, winding his laptop cable into a neat bundle.

But before Christian can answer, the BBC News channel, which has been playing a story about the future of Alpine skiing in the corner, pipes up with a Breaking News alert. Christian watches in horror, wondering if his appendix has exploded again.

A clip of Laura Kuenssberg sitting opposite the prime minister, Eric Courtenay, in an elegantly lit room plays.

'Prime Minister, there have been grave concerns raised about the Conservative Party's connection to the recent data breach at the Electoral Commission, as one of your donors is responsible for their cybersecurity. You have repeatedly dodged giving a straight answer on the situation and we are now two weeks out from polling day. Can you now tell us, yes or no, whether there is any link between your party and this breach?'

'Well, Laura, I think it's important that—'

'Yes or no, Prime Minister,' Kuenssberg replies, her eyes narrowed.

'All right then . . . no, there's no link. And we can prove it.'

'How?' Kuenssberg asks. She was clearly ready for the usual fobbing off and the 'now let me be absolutely clear'-isms.

DataTwerk have been able to establish that nothing was stolen in the recent Electoral Commission breach, but in the interests of propriety and transparency, the Conservative Party will be cutting all links with the firm and returning their donations. Additionally, Courtenay explains, the Conservatives will provide the full version of the electoral roll that they have, so the Electoral Commission – and, indeed, officials from other political parties – can compare the data and satisfy themselves that they all have the same thing.

'But if it is as easy as providing your data to show it matches, why take nearly a month to do so?' Kuenssberg asks.

For the first time in the interview, the prime minister looks irritated. This is exactly what he demanded to know from Cal.

'Because this is a huge and complex data set. We're talking about millions of people's details and we wanted to be absolutely sure we were not inadvertently misleading anyone. And we wanted to give DataTwerk and the Electoral Commission – which are independent organisations – space and time to confirm that no data was stolen or tampered with during this recent hack. We hope this news gives the public confidence that nothing murky has happened here, contrary to Labour conspiracy theories. Now, what this episode does mean is we must review how information is stored and protected in the

UK. We cannot have our precious democracy or indeed any of our institutions at the mercy of terrorists, rogue actors or foreign interference . . . '

'*Fuck*.' Christian slaps his hand down on the hospital bed. 'Fuck, fuck, fuck.'

Exactly what he has been worried about has happened. Against all his advice, Labour have thrown every resource into 'this election is being rigged' rather than 'Time for Change' and their core policies on health and education. Now the Conservatives are off the hook, Labour have less than two weeks to try to get back on track – and to change their image from mad conspiracy theorists to statesmanlike grown-ups, ready to lead the country into the future.

Without another word, he winces as he swings his laptop bag over his shoulder, kisses Jess and stomps out.

Back at the office, Christian is practically frothing at the mouth with rage.

'I told you,' he says before the meeting room door closes. 'I told you to pivot away from this conspiracy-theory shit. And now it's too fucking late. How can we get back on track and talk about our priorities with only two weeks to go?'

'We're doing okay on the economy,' an ashen-faced Tanya Haines says defensively.

'Yeah, well, that's only because Vicky Tennyson has had the good sense to ignore the calls from you lot to talk like a nutter about stolen elections and cracked on with her actual fucking brief. WHAT?' Christian storms at a knock on the door.

'Sorry, I just wanted to let you know that I've tried to hold up the leaflet printing as you asked,' a young woman addresses Tanya, 'but I'm afraid it's too late. The order's done and all our candidates – everywhere – have already distributed most of them over the weekend.'

'Show me,' Christian hisses, taking a leaflet. The front is dedicated to the message *Fight for Your Future and Your Freedom* and carries a photo of Eric Courtenay with red, demon-like eyes. Christian's mantra of *Time for Change – the Tories have been in charge for ten years but do YOU feel better off?* has been squeezed onto the back.

The young woman leaves and the rest of the group look like they wish they could follow her. Everyone knows these leaflets are useless now. In fact, they're probably libellous. Christian balls it up and throws it in the bin.

'What if we—' Tanya begins tentatively.

'Just shut up for one fucking minute. I need to think. Please.' Christian cups his palms over his eyes, like a horse wearing blinkers.

But nothing comes to him. He's out of ideas. Ramsey pats Christian gingerly on the shoulder.

'I told you,' Christian says with a groan. 'I fucking told you . . .'

'I know, mate, but we've got to look forward now. We can still do this. We can't let these scumbags win. If you ask me, it has taken a suspiciously long time for them to provide their version of the electoral roll. Maybe they've bought off the Electoral Commission. Or . . . how can we be sure they haven't spent a month cleaning it up to look legit and kept the original version for them—'

'*Stop*,' Tanya almost whispers, looking at Christian, who appears on the brink of tears. 'We have to stop this, okay? The story's a dud. We've got to get back to the real issues. We've got one final TV debate on ITV tomorrow night. We've got to focus on everything Christian's been saying and show people we should be in charge of the country, not Area 51.'

CCHQ

The prime minister arrives early for the ITV debate prep to see his team. Anto, of course, barges in to join them. For some reason, he is vibrating with silent rage.

'So what do you reckon?' the PM says, pacing nervously.

'We've got focus groups starting shortly, so I'll be able to tell you how it has all landed later on. But I think we're looking good.'

'Good?' Anto snorts and folds his arms. His feet move even further apart in a wide stance. 'Good that for two thirds of the campaign we've been on the ropes about this bloody data hack, that we didn't even do?'

'Yet, all the time, improving in the polls.' Cal can't resist countering. 'Fancy that.'

'*We are dealing in pornography,*' Anto thunders out of no-where, his face contorted with rage.

'Someone alert the village elders!' Nick murmurs, smirking at Percy.

'You're not still on about that are you, Anto?' Cal says. 'Nobody here cares if you like a good cum shot. Who among us, eh?'

'I'm not talking about me,' Anto storms back, his face flushing. 'Do you know how many of our MPs have been in touch to say they've seen our ads on those sites? We're just lucky they're so discreet.'

'Oh, sure ... very discreet about noodling around on porn sites—'

'That's not all!' Anto hisses. 'I've also been informed that, well ...' He turns apologetically to Percy. 'I'm afraid, CDL, I'm reliably informed that there is footage of you with a ... *star* of one of these sites circulating.'

'Is there?' Percy asks vaguely.

'I mean that there is a video going round of you having . . . relations . . . with a young, blonde, full-figured—'

'Perce, you and the missus haven't been making some amateur stuff, have you?' Cal manages to keep his face straight.

'No, we bloody haven't.' Percy looks sulky. 'She won't even consider it. Anyway, how do you know it's me? Show me this damn thing.'

Anto hands his phone over to Percy. The others can't see the screen but have to listen in agonised silence to the audio, which is a mixture of a woman sounding like she's being eaten by a shark, bite by bite, and the unmistakable voice of Percy Cross 'ooh'-ing, 'aah'-ing and 'oh my word'-ing.

'That isn't Holly,' Percy says firmly, once the clip ends. 'In fact, I don't think that's even me. But Christ knows it does look very like me. And I've been to some pretty fruity parties . . . can't rule out that this happened at some point or other.'

Cal leans over and takes a look. 'Probably an AI deep fake. Easy to get footage of your face and voice from anywhere. Knocked out in minutes. We'll just issue a statement saying it isn't you, if anyone bothers us about it.'

'A shame, really.' Percy glances proudly at Anto's phone screen again. 'She looks like she's having a terrific time.'

'Keep him away from the hacks.' Cal addresses Nick, jabbing his thumb at Percy.

'But what about my media round tomorrow? Percy's meant to be doing it all, starting with the *Today* programme,' Nick says.

'No way. We need someone credible . . . Madeleine Ford. She's just the person to reassure the public that all this DataTwerk stuff is sorted. Not our former Prime Sinister . . .'

'Okay, okay,' the PM interjects. 'Can we get on with this debate prep? I want to know the minute those focus-group results are through. And, for the love of God, can we get these porno adverts down? If this gets out we'll be a laughing stock.'

'Why? It's a legitimate place to advertise. News flash, Prime Minister: people actually use these sites,' Cal insists.

The PM blushes for a moment. He's been shutting himself away with his laptop a lot lately, picturing Laura Lloyd's face on the strong women he's been viewing.

'I don't care.' He smacks his knuckles smartly on the table. 'I don't want any more of it. In fact, I want your solemn promise that there'll be no more mention of the Conservatives and pornography from this point on.'

The PM's confidence has grown over the course of the campaign and he's starting to get assertive. Nobody seems to register this as a problem except Cal, who eyes the PM's fist warily.

Cal, Don and Nick exchange glances. They're too far in to make that kind of commitment. Cal, though, continues to smile.

'We can try, Prime Minister,' he says silkily. 'But MPs will be boys. As, it seems, will chiefs of staff. BBBs, was it, Anto?'

Anto glowers at Cal as he trails out behind the PM.

Tipperton

Bobby flops down on the sofa. It's been another long day of pounding the pavement, door-knocking and talking as enthusiastically and energetically as possible. Her feet, back and head all ache. Even her stomach muscles hurt, presumably from waddling her enormous belly round the town all day. Her eyes are watering from the cold and her fingers are numb, despite the thick gloves her mother got her from the garden centre.

'Here you are, love,' Mrs Cliveden says, carrying in a tray with three plates piled high with mashed potato, sausages and onion gravy.

'Mum, you're a lifesaver.' Bobby props herself up on some cushions and breathes in the gravy smell.

Her father nods in fervent agreement. The three of them sit together on the sofa like old times, although now, instead of the 6 p.m. headlines and a quiz show, they watch the different news channels, getting their national and local coverage fix.

The big news is that the Conservatives have been exonerated in the Electoral Commission breach. Although, as Bobby points out, she hasn't had a single question from people in Tipperton about it.

'I feel sorry for the Labour candidate up here, to be honest,' she says with a sigh. 'They've tried their best to talk about transport and hospitals and so forth, but all the material they've had from their HQ is about this stuff.' She points with her fork at the TV screen, where the PM and Laura Kuenssberg are having their back and forth.

Next there is a Sky News clip of a John Ramsey interview, where he is asked by Adam Boulton if he will apologise to Eric Courtenay for accusing him of rigging the election.

'I'll never apologise for defending our democracy,' Ramsey replies stoutly. 'But what we must now do is focus on the real issue at stake. The Conservatives have been in power for over ten years. I am sure that most people, if asked, will say they feel worse off than when the Conservatives first came into government ...'

Almost in answer to Ramsey's slicker messaging, Bobby's abdomen gives an unpleasant lurch of pain. She cries out, but quickly reassures her parents.

'It's totally normal. I asked the midwife. Just my uterus and organs and so on making room ...'

The reassurance falters when, for the first time in Cliveden family memory, Bobby refuses a slice of the steaming treacle tart that Mrs Cliveden brings out during the sports bulletins.

'I'm sorry, Mum. I'm done for tonight.'

'I knew you were overdoing it! You need to rest, okay? You've got a few weeks to go now and you'll not be getting any sleep soon. You're not invincible, all right? Now, time for a bath, young lady.'

'Thanks, Mum.' Bobby cranks herself up from the sofa. 'And hold on to that. I'll probably have it for breakfast . . .'

25th November

CON 34% LAB 37%

FINAL SPRINT TO NO. 10/

RARE SANDSTORM IN ESSEX

Battersea

With one week until polling day, Eva has agreed to join a slightly different hustings event at Battersea Dogs and Cats Home, where the four-legged residents will decide who they think their MP should be. She lines up with Joshua Udoka and the rest of the candidates and kneels on the grass, trying to coax some puppies towards her. She can't help but laugh when one little dog cocks its leg against the Green candidate.

'Probably thinks you're a tree,' calls Joshua, who is surrounded by squirming, warm, furry bodies. He reveals to Eva afterwards that he had the foresight to stuff his pockets with dog biscuits that morning. His suit had to be dry-cleaned, but the sacrifice was worth it.

'He'd be better with a Staffie,' murmurs Eva's campaign

manager, still cross that Eva didn't launch into Joshua at the first debate. 'Gang dog would be a nice touch.'

'Literal dog-whistle campaigning. Nice,' Eva hisses back, shrugging him away from her.

Only one dog approaches her. A very fat, dumpy basset hound, who trips over her ears as she ambles over and curls up in Eva's lap.

'Mabel came to us recently,' one of the kindly staff explains. 'She's only two but has had dozens of pups already. She was impregnated again and again at a horrible puppy farm.'

Eva rubs Mabel's ears, watching her yawn deliciously and burrow herself deeper between Eva's thighs. She looks across at Joshua, who is happily trying to protect his face from the rough tongues and sharp little teeth of the excited puppies who are clambering all over him. Nobody would have a clue that they woke up together this morning. Sneaking around is so exciting. But what happens in a week's time? Regardless of which of them wins the seat, might they be able to develop this affair into something else? Maybe they can defy expectations and make something work. It occurs to Eva that 2nd December is looming larger for her about her future with Joshua than it is for her political career.

She continues to stroke Mabel, feeling her warm belly and soft snout. Her doleful eyes blink pitifully up at Eva, looking desperately sad.

Eva messages her WhatsApp group with Bobby and Jess:

I did something.

Then she sends a picture of Mabel stretched out on the living room sofa, her face a picture of floppy ecstasy. Just in shot is Percy, his feet apart and hands on his head. Like *The Scream* by Edvard Munch, it's hard to tell if he's looking ecstatic or horrified.

Jess and Bobby immediately reply, demanding further photos and, of course, how the new Claybourne Terrace resident came to be. Eva scrolls up the chat and sees it has been over a week since they've posted on there, the longest stint ever. She misses her friends as, between her sly nights at Joshua's, Bobby's stint in the north of England and Jess's obsession with her mysterious new boyfriend, they're hardly in touch. Jess is yet to reveal Christian's identity to Eva and Bobby, partly because they are all so busy, and partly because fraternising with the enemy feels best left until the election is over. What will they make of Eva's own secret romance? Will everyone come round when it turns out to be the real, star-crossed thing?

Jess, meanwhile, is also in limbo until the election ends. Christian is down in the deepest of dumps, morose that all of his work to win John Ramsey the keys to Number Ten has possibly been for nothing. A couple of bitchy pieces, presumably orchestrated by Tanya Haines, finger him as the reason the Labour campaign has fallen flat, completely ignoring his stint in hospital. Nobody in the lobby knows about Jess and Christian's relationship so when idle chatter turns to him, she can't even defend him as she'd like – ideally with her fists. The only good thing to have come out of the last couple of weeks is that she was right to gift Ed Cooper the Electoral Commission story.

Ed seems to have sensed a change in the winds and, very late in the day, is suddenly toadying up to all of his *Sentinel* colleagues, women included, offering advice and help. Jess is coming in for her fair share of flattery too, but is being careful to be polite and friendly and ultimately out of his way. She's had a stint on each of the campaign buses now, each a deeper pit of depravity than the last – she learnt that a few days before she arrived on the Tory bus, a group of young Conservative canvassers in Dorset were caught playing a game of soggy biscuit – and has had a set-piece interview with each party leader. Then she's belted back to London to look after Christian, who is still recovering, as much as she can. The only problem is that she's so used to cooking for five, the meals for two that she whips up are proving mountainous.

Meanwhile, Bobby's giant dinner days are behind her. Her stomach is under so much pressure from her huge belly that she's developed horrible acid reflux. She potters from doorstep to doorstep, bottles of Gaviscon clinking together in her huge coat pockets, trying to squeeze out the last bit of support that she possibly can before polling day. Whatever happens, despite the hardship of campaigning when pregnant, she's had a wonderful time. She's learnt more about Tipperton and its residents than she could have imagined and made new friends in every neighbourhood. Her parents have loved feeling purposeful and busy, especially her father, who is working on an enormous election-night feast.

Despite the amazing experience, though, she misses her friends and she misses darling Jake, who visits her more often now that the manifesto is out of the way, and who is dedicating his spare time to reading all the baby books that Bobby hasn't had time to look at. He's even squeezed in a couple of solo NCT classes. Bobby, meanwhile, says she's focused on getting one stint of pushing and crying out of the way on 2nd December before she tackles the real thing.

2nd December

CON 35% LAB 36%

DECISION TIME/

RECORD RAINFALL DUE ACROSS UK

United Kingdom

It's still dark and wet when polling stations, located in schools, leisure centres and village halls across the country, open. Over the course of the day, busy office workers slip in before or after their commutes, parents go around school drop-off and pick-up, pensioners wait for a break in the rain and students huddle in clumps with energy drinks and hangovers.

Press photographers are sent all over the place to find unusual polling station scenes, from people arriving on horseback in the Cotswolds to pulling up by boat on remote Scottish islands. There are, of course, the obligatory vanity shots of party leaders voting with their wives, all of them doing their best to look as smug as possible.

The entire country is enveloped in the worst weather for a general election that anyone can remember. Pundits urgently speculate on whether this is good news for parties or bad. Surely only the most ardent supporters will bother venturing out in this.

The lobby journalists catch up on a little bit of sleep with a lie-in, as they have a long night ahead of tracking the results when the polls close at 10 p.m. In most elections, editors have a pretty good idea of who they think will win, so they can start planning their front pages accordingly. This time, though, it's neck and neck. Labour have seen their generous lead quietly hacked away by the Conservatives in every poll, but the Conservatives haven't pulled ahead. Rumours of a hung Parliament – where there's no party with a big enough majority to lead a government, so they either need to find a coalition partner or hold another election – are snowballing.

Over at the different TV studios, the teams are tuning up for a blockbuster night for ratings. The BBC executives, confident in the abilities of David Dimbleby, Laura Kuenssberg and Professor John Curtice to draw in the largest number of viewers, are busy checking on the champagne, canapés and guest list for their results party. And they aren't the only ones.

At the different campaign headquarters, desk drawers have been surreptitiously filling with plonk throughout the week, staffers clear that they will either be toasting their win or refusing to work through a night of misery while sober. Plush parties have been planned for donors and party bigwigs, many of whom have made sizeable bets on the outcome of the election – not all in favour of their own party – and are feeling sweaty at the thought of the agonising night ahead. For a betting man, it's like watching the Grand National in painfully slow motion.

For activists, though, this is the final push. Most have been up since 5 a.m., in what's known as a 'dawn raid' to GOTV: Get Out The Vote. This means they've been up with torches and clipboards to knock on front doors and push reminder leaflets through the letterboxes of people they feel certain will vote for them today. The weather requires strong persuasion. Labour prod students out of bed and Tories help load old people into minibuses to get to the polling stations, both parties looking after their most faithful followers.

Eva is up in Battersea with the team, shivering under an enormous waterproof duvet of a coat in the dark. At least she has the thought of seeing Joshua at the count later. She should try to get a blow-dry, seeing as there'll be photographers and TV cameras everywhere – win or lose. And when the result comes in, what should she say to Joshua? Maybe she could simply embrace her inner romantic comedy – it's almost Christmas, after all – and just kiss him in front of everyone.

Bobby wakes up before her dawn-raid alarm, her body flooded with adrenaline.

'Only one more day to go, little one.' She strokes her belly and tries to breathe herself calm, four counts in and six counts out, until her alarm goes off.

Bobby's dropped off to meet her team by her parents, who return after an hour with bacon butties, homemade currant buns and flasks of tea in the boot of their car for the team. Everyone is bleary-eyed but excited, wondering if they've done enough to make sure Tipperton is blue.

Jess wakes up considerably later than her friends to an empty house. Percy is doing a media round and Holly has a personal-training session. She stretches and realises it's the first time in ages that she's woken up in her own bed, alone. She immediately texts Christian, Bobby and Eva masses of luck and turns on the radio, to hear Percy on BBC Radio 2. Jess laughs as the host, who has allowed Percy to choose the music for his time slot, reluctantly plays 'We're going to Ibiza!' by the Vengaboys. She jigs about in the bed, then runs a bath. She needs to think how to fill her day before the Battersea count and her tour of the different TV studios to give her reaction to the results as they come in.

BBC Broadcasting House

Five minutes until 10 p.m. and the closing of the ballot boxes. It's also the announcement of the all-important exit poll, a survey of people leaving polling stations around the country on how they've voted, which may well predict the overall outcome of the election before the specific seats come in. All over the country, from City boardrooms to local constituency counts, MI5 offices to family living rooms, people gather around televisions to learn what government they can likely expect by morning. In Parliament, the duty staff make their regular rounds to check for any fire or flooding hazards. After the torrential rain, it's due to be the coldest night of the year and the building's old pipes aren't above bursting. Happily everything seems to be in order.

Big Ben gongs ten o'clock and David Dimbleby stands before a vast screen.

'Our exit poll is suggesting . . .' The screen changes from the famous clock face to Eric Courtenay and John Ramsey's faces. 'Goodness me. Almost a dead heat! The Conservatives on 291, Labour on 283. We'll have to see how the night unfolds but it looks like we are headed for a hung Parliament. I'm going to turn now to Laura and John, to see what this means.'

'Well, David.' Laura smiles serenely. 'It means there's a long night of negotiations as Labour and the Conservatives race to court the smaller parties, to see who can get enough seats together to form a government . . .'

*

310

'Trust me on this one,' Cal says calmly to the PM, his arms folded. 'You don't need to pick up the phone to anyone. They've got it wrong. Hold your nerve, okay? Now, you'd better fuck off to your count. None of this is relevant if you haven't held your own seat.'

Eric Courtenay leaves CCHQ in a flap, wondering what Clarissa will say if they really are finished.

'Strap in for a long night,' Cal grunts to Nick. 'I'm heading over to Tracy Island.'

Nick stays sitting at his desk for a while, panicking for the first time about their massive gamble.

At Labour HQ, there is much excitement.

'I knew things would hold steady!' Ramsey crows. 'And the Tories have no chance of persuading someone into bed with them. Not after last time. Now, we just need to think very strategically about who we want to do business with ...'

Christian sits alone in silence, frowning at his laptop screen. He's not confident in these exit-poll figures. He looks around the room, hoping to see someone else with his doubts etched on their face. But he's alone in a mass of chatting, shining faces. Vicky Tennyson is nowhere to be seen.

At Claybourne Terrace, the mood is subdued.

'You don't think Cal's fucked it, do you, Dad?' Eva asks. She's so shattered from the past few weeks that she feels on the cusp of hysterics. All that stupid trickery with porn and they'll end up with a hung Parliament anyway. Has she been completely taken in by the idea of a campaigning genius?

'I dunno,' Percy says, staring at the TV. Eva's never seen him so uncertain before. She had been counting on him to bluster through and tell her everything is fine.

Holly and Jess sit in silence, wondering what to do next.

311

They can't have a drink, because Eva will be on television when the result is called and she oughtn't to sway on camera. Eventually, Holly decides to pass the time by meditating and Jess motors out to her first TV-studio appearance.

The only person who seems happy about the exit poll on the Tory side is Natasha Weaver. If the polls are wrong and the Tories have won an outright majority then she still has a job. If they're right and the Tories have lost (a coalition will be out of the question) then she has a chance to run as party leader and take over the helm in opposition. As far as Weaver's concerned, she can't lose.

To celebrate, she's gone to her favourite Mayfair members' club for an election-night party on the very top floor, reserved for the most exclusive guests. By midnight, she's braced with her arms against a sink in the bathroom, being slapped really very hard on the bottom by a hereditary peer. Having slightly overdone it on the champers, he misjudges a particularly snappy thwack and lands his palm on her rather more sensitive area. Her knees buckle at the surprising sensation that shoots up her spine. Fired up, she shoves him onto the lavatory and goes to town. Five minutes and one broken loo seat later, they emerge to a very grumpy queue of young members, gagging to dip their noses into their little baggies.

3rd December

Downing Street

It's 1 a.m. and the prime minister – as he is, for now – has assembled his top team in the study, just as he did for the local elections in May.

The results have started to come in and Labour and the Conservatives remain neck and neck. The PM paces around the room, fretting. Nobody speaks. Even Cal is worried. Only the safest possible seats for both parties have come in so far – the ones where inflatable dolls wearing the right colour rosette would win – which means they can't tell whether their strategy targeting those marginal places has worked yet.

'Ah, shit,' Percy mutters. Every head snaps round to look at him, assuming he's seen a bad result come in on his phone. 'Got to go to Battersea for Eva's count. I'll be back.'

He stumps out, glad to leave the heavy atmosphere. The rest of the group return to staring at their phones or into space, or watching the PM wear a bald patch into the carpet with his pacing.

Courtenay shoves his hands in his pockets, wishing Laura Lloyd were there. Not that it's her place to be – but all the same.

Then something happens.

The Conservatives win an unexpected inner-city seat. Then a couple of Northern towns. They even get a few student hotspots. The group in the study watches the blue column on the screen creep up.

The PM stops pacing. Nick starts to breathe more easily. A small smile creeps onto Cal's face.

Labour HQ

John Ramsey is screaming his head off.

'What the fuck, guys?' He jabs his finger at the TV screen.

Christian remains expressionless. He knew days ago that they were in trouble, but he dared to hope that perhaps the exit poll was wrong. Well, it was wrong. Spectacularly so. The Conservatives are making surprise gains all over the place.

'We've still got a load of metropolitan seats to go, boss,' Tanya says reassuringly, coaxing Ramsey into a chair and offering him a KitKat. 'Look, they're about to announce Battersea.'

They all watch the TV screen, which is showing a small stage in south London. The camera pans to Percy Cross, who looks absolutely delighted with the turn the night is taking. He shakes hands and takes selfies with members of the assembled crowd, his plain-clothes officers standing nervously by.

'Good luck, pork chop!' he shouts, cupping his hands to his mouth.

On stage, Eva feels nervous and excited. Cal and the Americans have done it. The plan she helped with all summer has worked after all. Now the whole country seems to be swinging towards the Conservatives, Eva can feel all the hard work and the sleepless nights building into euphoria at what's to come here, too. She can see her dog, Mabel, who has happily got her chin on Holly's shoulder in a cuddle, gazing out of the crowd at her. Jess gives her a little thumbs-up from the side of the room.

'Good luck,' Joshua whispers, as the candidates jostle on the platform together, blinking under the bright lights. Her heart hammering too hard to speak, Eva smiles back at him.

This is really it. She's going to do it.

Except she isn't.

'The Conservative candidate, 20,791 votes. The Labour candidate, 24,203 votes . . . '

There is a roar from the people in the crowd wearing red. Eva stands there, numb, hardly moving when Joshua Udoka shakes her hand before stepping forward to the lectern. She can see he's speaking but all she can hear is a strange buzzing. She tries and fails to pull herself fully together, and settles on looking alert and slightly wistful. She can see Joshua's supporters clapping and cheering, while her father and Holly, standing quietly to one side, hold Mabel tightly as though transferring their hugs to Eva through the dog.

When the candidates file off the stage, Eva goes straight to her team to thank them for all their hard work.

Then she waits for Joshua, who is high-fiving his campaign team and chatting delightedly to journalists. Jess fights her way over and gives Eva a big hug. She's surprised to find Eva isn't crying.

'Do you know, I'm just relieved it's all over,' Eva says, starting to adjust to the shock. She really thought she might have done it. 'Anyway, at least I can tell you what's been going on.'

Jess raises a questioning eyebrow.,

Eva gestures towards Joshua. 'We've been sleeping together.

For the whole campaign. And now I'm not going to be the MP, I wonder whether we can be more . . .'

Perhaps aware of their eyes on him, Joshua turns and heads over. Jess feels a jolt of horror. She's been so focused on Eva's night, she completely forgot that 'J' would be at the count.

'Congratulations.' Eva smiles, patting his arm. But Joshua is looking at Jess.

'I didn't expect to see you here, Amy.'

Silently praising her foresight for using her middle name on Fawn, Jess replies, 'Sorry, you must mean someone else. I'm Jess. Adler. From the *Sentinel.*'

Joshua looks quizzically at her. Luckily Eva seems to assume an honest mistake and presses Joshua's arm again so that he turns to face her.

'So what are you doing later?' she leans in and murmurs in his eye. 'Want to celebrate your victory?'

Joshua looks guilty and pulls her to one side.

'Eva . . . I need to apologise to you. I know I said I wanted to take you out for dinner after the contest was over. That I didn't care about you being a Conservative and stuff . . .'

Eva's throat tightens.

'But I don't have to do any of that any more,' Eva says quickly. 'I . . . I'll leave the party. Or . . . or . . .'

She tries to keep the note of desperation out of her voice, but it's hard.

'There isn't anything you can do, Eva. I don't want to mess this up. Everything else comes second. I'm really sorry if it feels like I've led you on.'

As fat tears begin to roll down Eva's cheeks, Joshua looks around, aware of the packed room of cameras and activists. He glances at Jess, pats Eva's shoulder and says, as gently as he can, 'Take care of yourself.'

Tipperton

In an echoing sports hall, Bobby checks her watch. It's 2.30 a.m. All around her she can hear the rustle of paper as individual voting slips are checked and put in piles. Surely they'll know the result soon?

Susie Coleman comes to stand with her and explains that the Conservatives' number of seats is shooting up, which Bobby holds on to, hoping that she might just make it too.

'Oh dear, have you seen Eva lost in Battersea?' Susie says, holding up her phone screen.

Bobby thought Eva was a dead cert. As a former prime minister's daughter, surely she had the best chance of anyone. If Eva can't do it, then what chance does Bobby have? She feels a painful, nauseous jolt in her belly.

'I just need to sit down for a second.' She winces at Susie and limps off to the edge of the hall to a folding seat. She takes a few deep breaths and feels better.

Claybourne Terrace

At 3 a.m, Jess wonders what to do. She has whisked Eva away from the count on her motorbike and roared back to Claybourne Terrace, swerving past groups of cheerful young Tories revelling in election excitement.

When they get home, Eva slumps into Mabel's dog basket.

'Joshua's so wonderful,' she wails, her face buried in Mabel's neck. 'I can't believe I've been so stupid to think that he might want to have something proper with me after all this . . . and he was so kind with his break-up . . .'

Jess gingerly pats Eva's back and considers what to do.

'He's not that great,' she says. 'After all, don't you think

he's treated you pretty badly these last few weeks? Maybe . . .
maybe this was his plan all along. After all, Fawn is designed
for just hookups. Once he saw you on Fawn, he sort of – led
you astray?'

Eva looks up mournfully. 'Not everyone's a shit, Jess. I just
know he's one of the good ones. It's all so sad! If only bloody
politics didn't get in the way. Think how it could have been
otherwise. Fawn might be for hookups, but what are the
chances of us both meeting on that app as first-timers?'

Jess takes a deep breath. This is not going to be pleasant, but
it's the only way to get Eva out of her rose-tinted melodrama.

'It wasn't his first time,' Jess says flatly.

'How do you know?' Eva frowns.

'Because . . .' Jess sucks her teeth, bracing for fireworks.
'Because I connected with him months ago.'

There is a long silence.

'Did you . . . ?' Eva whispers.

Jess shrugs apologetically.

'Listen,' she says quickly. 'I haven't said anything because I
thought your thing in August was a one-off and I didn't want
to upset you going into the election. He was Public Enemy
Number One! And I just didn't think it would come up
again . . . or that you actually liked him. I'm so sorry, Eva.'

'It's fine.' Eva climbs out of the dog bed.

'But—'

'I said it's fine.' Eva marches into the hallway and starts
pulling on her coat and scarf. 'It's not your fault that you got
there for the first fuck. I just can't believe you didn't tell me
when we realised he was the Labour candidate. Do you think
I would have carried on with him in secret if I'd known about
you and him?' She bends down and attaches Mabel's lead to
her collar.

'Eva, I—'

'Just fuck off, will you?' Eva snaps, turning for the door. Without another word, she heads out into the night with Mabel.

Jess sits on the sofa in the living room and stares into space. Surely Eva will cool down after a walk and come home soon. Still, this doesn't feel good. All this hassle for one okay-ish shag.

She's roused from her reverie by the sound of keys in the door. Jess jerks her head around, ready to apologise to Eva again, but Holly steps over the threshold. She doesn't seem surprised to see Jess looking glum. As Eva's best friend, Jess would of course be sad about her losing out to Labour in Battersea.

'Percy's gone back to Downing Street for the rest of the results.' Holly plonks herself down next to Jess. 'So I thought I'd come home and get some sleep.'

Holly yawns and stretches back on the sofa. Jess follows her left hand as it reaches into the air.

'Holly . . . what's that?' She points at an enormous emerald-and-diamond ring, her mind momentarily distracted from her guilt.

Holly giggles and wriggles her fingers.

'Percy popped the question.'

'Wh . . .when?'

'This evening. Before we headed out to Battersea for Eva's count. He got home from Downing Street and was so morose with the way things were heading. He said the only thing that could possibly cheer him up was if I agreed to marry him. Apparently he'd been saving this for the big win, but said he didn't need it in the end.'

'Oh, Holly, that's wonderful!' Jess hugs her tightly. Then she pulls back. 'Does Eva know?'

Jess pictures Eva trudging aimlessly around Pimlico, her dreams in tatters and her father on to another marriage, this time to someone near enough her own age.

'Uh, no.' Holly hesitates. 'We thought perhaps she should just have one bit of news at a time ...'

No shit, Jess thinks, heading out to another TV studio.

Eva and Mabel walk slowly, Mabel stopping to sniff a lamppost or postbox every few metres, the crisp night making every scent sharper after the rain. They don't see a soul, enjoying the quiet. Once they've circled a couple of Georgian squares, they amble down to the Thames, to the twinkling lights of Albert Bridge, which looks spun from the palest pink icing sugar against the smooth, black surface of the river.

Occasionally they meet a group of revellers, who, despite the hour, stop and admire Mabel, who pants winningly, her wagging tail making her body snake back and forth.

When they reach the middle of the bridge, Eva stops and stares out over the river, watching the lights dance on the surface of the water. She feels so foolish, unable to believe that just hours ago she was daydreaming about her and Joshua Udoka being some kind of modern political Romeo and Juliet, their love reaching across the divide ... What an idiot. Still, she can't help but feel furious with Jess. The thought of Jess and Joshua entwined together makes her feel sick.

Mabel gets bored and starts to whimper.

'Come on ...' Eva mumbles. They continue south over the bridge, then turn to follow the river east, where the city is just starting to wake up in the distance.

Tipperton

In Tipperton, Bobby is uncomfortable. Ahead of joining her fellow candidates on the makeshift platform, she locks herself in the sports hall's disabled loo and allows herself to slide down the wall to the floor. She's starting to feel hot and sweaty, and her belly continues to ache. Is it possible that, having fought off colds and flu for the last six weeks, her body has finally succumbed to a bug? She notices a huge ladder in her tights. Cursing, she peels them off, reasoning that bare legs are better than laddered ones on the national news.

Just breathe, she tells herself as she washes her hands. *It's over in a few minutes.*

Bobby walks onto the stage and wishes each of her fellow candidates luck, doing her best to keep her face neutral, despite the grinding pain in her abdomen.

'And Labour, 14,107 votes. The Conservatives, 23,796 votes . . .'

Roberta Cliveden is the MP for Tipperton.

The thought hardly registers before another wave of pain hits and she just stops herself doubling over in time. Gritting her teeth, Bobby congratulates the other candidates in turn and steps forward to the microphone to make her victory speech. She can see her mother's face, shining with pride. Her father is openly weeping. Susie and the other team members are hugging each other. Bobby clears her throat.

But before she can open her mouth, something gushes down her bare legs and splats onto the floor. At 4.30 a.m. on 3rd December, almost three weeks ahead of schedule, Bobby's waters have broken.

South London

After an hour of walking, Eva and Mabel reach Vauxhall and join a queue of clientele from the nearby gay clubs and saunas at a small café under the railway arches. Mabel revels in all the attention she gets from the young clubbers, flopping over to get her tummy rubbed and her ears caressed.

By the time they leave, she has a decent dusting of glitter all over her.

Eva's thinking about her future. Now that they've likely secured a majority, she could have her pick of government jobs. But she doesn't want one. Is she destined to follow Jamie's original plan for her after all, fanny around the Conservative Party until it's time for her to squeeze out a few children? She trudges on along the river.

As they near Lambeth Bridge, the sky gradually begins to glow.

Eva looks down at Mabel, who has stopped and is sniffing the air. She casts her eyes up to the sky. It's getting lighter by the minute. But it's too early for the sun. Her watch says 5.30 a.m.

Eva begins to walk faster, pulling a reluctant Mabel along behind her. She almost runs through the Lambeth Bridge underpass, but stops abruptly and stares in fixed disbelief on the other side.

Across the river, the Houses of Parliament are on fire.

Stunned, Eva moves towards St Thomas' Hospital, her eyes on the burning building. Flames lick the Gothic windows and parts of the roof have already caved in, sparks bursting out into the early morning sky. Emergency sirens wail in the distance, screaming closer and jolting her from her horrified reverie.

It's too late, though. Eva, appalled, holds Mabel on a bench, as fire engines, helicopters and river boats frantically try to spray water and flame-retardant material on the old building.

Within minutes, a crowd, mainly of NHS staff and visitors from the hospital, has gathered around them, everyone dumbstruck by what they're seeing. A few film on their camera phones but most just stand in shellshocked silence.

Tears drip down Eva's cheeks as the clock face of Big Ben comes away and crumples into its tower, disappearing within, the clang of the falling bell just audible over the roar of the inferno. The group of watchers gasp in horror.

Eva realises that her phone is ringing. It's Jess. She doesn't pick up, but Jess calls a second time.

'What do you want?' Eva sniffs.

'Have you heard?' Jess cries.

'I'm here. Watching it.' Eva is sobbing.

'What? In Tipperton?'

'Wh . . . what are you talking about? I'm on the Southbank. Parliament . . . it's burning down.'

Jess gasps. 'Shitting fuck! I was calling to tell you that Bobby's gone into labour. I'm taking Jake to the station now . . . I . . . Jesus. Let's meet at home, okay?'

'Okay,' Eva croaks, all thoughts of betrayal and spite gone. All her problems seem pathetic now. Mabel begins to howl.

The devastation is absolute – the Houses of Parliament are gone. Nobody seems sure how the fire started, but detectives seem confident that there was no foul play. As parliamentarians were aware, any number of wiring, flooding or vermin problems could have triggered the inferno. Thankfully nobody was killed, although some parliamentary staff and firefighters were treated for smoke inhalation.

The footage from helicopter news crews of a charred, smoking black chasm looks as though a bomb has been dropped on Central London. Great crowds of people swarm as close as they can get, many bringing flowers, most of them crying. Parliament has been a place for derision and rage, but that's because of the people in it. The building itself was an icon, a reassuring figure on the banks of the Thames for hundreds of years, recognisable to every Briton.

Eric Courtenay has won his fresh majority, but the situation is unprecedented. It feels wrong to call a press conference on the steps of Downing Street or to have a victory rally. It only feels right to join the public in sheer, funereal shock.

The prime minister heads straight from his meeting with the king at Buckingham Palace to Parliament, to view the damage and to thank emergency-service staff for their efforts. He is seen consoling the Speaker, whose home has now been destroyed too.

As he walks among the wreckage, Courtenay thinks a flurried combination of 'we should have listened to the warnings' and 'what happens next?' and, inevitably, 'am I in trouble?'

A well-placed microphone picks up the only utterance he makes, at the melted remains of the Big Ben bell. 'Fuck.'

4th December

Notre-Dame experts offer help to British
authorities to restore Parliament/
Plans for new eco-Chamber mooted

Millbank

At 10 a.m., Vicky Tennyson stands at a lectern before a packed audience in front of the charred remains of the Houses of Parliament. Once the results of the election were clear, John Ramsey resigned as leader of the Labour Party. His phone traffic fell off a cliff and he disappeared into obscurity. Journalists were so consumed with what will happen next for the freshly elected parliamentarians now that their institution is gone, that they hardly acknowledged Ramsey's end.

They have, however, all turned up for this – Tennyson's event to announce her candidacy for the Labour leadership. She looks energetic and hungry, and she's ready for the job. Such is the shortness of political memory, nobody notices that a number of the special guests in the front row are the summer's infamous leaders of the refuse-workers' and baggage-handlers' unions.

Her speech goes down a storm and her answers to journalists' questions are clear and frank. Afterwards, Tennyson heads to her blacked-out car, where her new chief of staff – Christian Eckles – is waiting for her. It was his idea to launch her candidacy in front of where Parliament once stood. Now the whole thing has burned to the ground, there's a chance to rebuild something entirely new, a clean, transparent gathering place, where the dirt can't be swept away. No more dark corners for sleazy deeds. No more vermin and leaks. And if they can rebuild Parliament, brick by brick, then why not the rest of the country?

Jess leaves Tennyson's speech and heads to her meeting with Philip McKay. This morning she was named the *Sentinel*'s new political editor, the youngest person in the lobby to reach such seniority. The real stir, though, has been caused by her relationship with Christian Eckles. With her old ally Teddy Hammer the new Downing Street director of communications and Christian the likely new leader of the opposition's right-hand man, Jess's address book has never looked better. Her lobby pals are furious.

The lift doors are just closing to take her up to Philip's office when Ed Cooper hops inside to join her.

Shit, Jess thinks. *The last person I want to see.*

Before she can say anything, Ed pats her on the shoulder.

'Well played,' he says ruefully. The man is no fool. Jess has beaten him fair and square and, frankly, he's fortunate to have struck a deal with Finlayson where he can make decent money in a minor executive role and keep his marriage intact. In many ways, it is a relief to take some stress out of his work. Perhaps a book is in order.

The lift pings and the doors open. Ed turns to Jess.

'I ... Congratulations. And good luck.'

Jess thanks him, then the doors close. She never thought she'd say it, but that was an unexpectedly tasteful move from Ed Cooper, noble in defeat.

Eva's just about to put her phone into a cubby by the Number Ten front door when she spots a text.

> Just thought I should let you know, I got engaged last night to an amazing girl called Lucinda. Wanted to tell you before you found out another way. Bad luck about Battersea. Hope all well, Jamie

Bloody fantastic. As though her mood could get much worse.

When she arrives at the PM's study, Eva glances around at the serious faces. Only Jake is missing, up in Tipperton helping Bobby look after their baby girl, Rose, who arrived safely – if rather dramatically.

The PM sits at the round table, Anto to one side of him and Percy on the other.

'Well, I must say,' the PM says to Cal, 'you did what you promised. But this new situation with the Houses of Parliament is unprecedented. There's going to be an inquiry . . .'

The PM and the chief whip exchange uneasy looks. Neither wants to admit in public how often they refused to face up to how vulnerable Parliament was to a major accident. Once the shock of the fire wears off, awkward questions will be asked and they don't have any good answers.

'Maybe so, Prime Minister,' Cal says softly, his eyes fixed on the PM. 'But we agreed that I would help you on the condition that we seriously restructure how the state is run. Now's the time.'

Cal gestures towards a pile of newspapers on the table. One headline screams: *The wrath of the gods – time for rebirth.*

Pictures of the PM, looking the part as usual, touring the devastation, are on every front page. Every letters page expresses the need for serious reform, now that so much of Westminster will have to be rebuilt.

The PM knows that he and Cal had a deal, but now the election is won, the prime minister doesn't want to be pushed about any more. He, Eric, did the impossible and turned the polls around. He, Eric, had his face plastered all over the bus and the billboards and posters. When he took office last year, everyone told him he didn't have a proper mandate because he wasn't elected by the people. Well, look at him now.

He's really not sure he can be arsed with the fuss of fiddling with the big levers of state. Besides, he hardly thinks the burned-out shell of Parliament is an opportunity.

'Sorry?' the PM says, playing for time.

Cal pulls out the piece of paper Courtenay signed months ago. 'I've got it all here, as I thought you might have forgotten.'

'I ... I've changed my mind. It ... It's a no-go on the state change, Gallagher.'

'I see.' Cal raises an eyebrow. 'Well, I see I'm no longer needed here then.'

There is a long and uncomfortable silence.

'Well, if you're not having Cal, you're not having me.' Percy speaks up stoutly. 'You wouldn't even be here if it weren't for him.'

'But, Percy, I was going to make you Chancellor ... Foreign Secretary ... Ambassador to Washington?' The PM pleads with him, but Percy remains unmoved. He was willing to lose Gallagher, the blunt tool to win a campaign but not what he wants for governing. He never thought he'd lose Percy.

'B-but,' the PM stammers, as they stand up and head for the door. 'What about the inquiry? What should I do?'

He sits back in his chair, looking dumbstruck. Clarissa will kill him when he gets upstairs. He's meant to be leading the nation in mourning the mother of all parliaments, and have plans to rebuild the place. And what the fuck will he say to the inquiry? He hasn't a clue where to start, with Vicky Tennyson barking at the shiny black door.

Epilogue

24th December

A WHITE CHRISTMAS

Central London

At a small chapel, Percy and Holly's select group of family and friends have gathered.

Percy stands nervously at the altar with his best man, Eva, and his ushers, Teddy and Cal. Eva has managed to find a beautiful morning coat that fits her, complete with a teal cummerbund and high-waisted silk trousers. Her hair, in a smooth, shining chignon, sits under a brushed top hat. Mabel sits at Eva's feet, a big bow around her neck.

Eva can see Jess, in a silver sheath dress and scarlet veiled hat, holding hands and quietly laughing with Christian. Next to them, Bobby, a navy velvet cape around her shoulders to match her thick hair band, quietly rocks her baby girl, Rose, and smiles at Jake. Despite willing herself not to care, Eva still feels a little prickle of jealousy and wishes once again that things were different with Joshua Udoka. Her friends have found their person. Someone to exchange secret signals and in-jokes with. Someone who's there for her more than anyone else. It isn't that she wants to be with him, but Jamie is engaged and that at least hurts her pride. Eva is up on this stone platform in full view of everyone. It would be quite nice to have a particular person's eye to catch and to have as a base camp to frequently return to at the reception afterwards.

A few rows behind Bobby and Jess sit the Clivedens and Susie Coleman, excitedly nudging each other at Jenny Cross's rock star beau, who is wearing scuffed cowboy boots beneath his beautiful vintage suit. Jenny leads him over to sit with Lord and Lady Finlayson, who are behind Don and his team of Americans. Miguel and Nick O'Hara are holding hands.

In a pew near the back, Madeleine Ford, sporting a dark-green Victoria Beckham trouser suit, chats happily to Vicky Tennyson, resplendent in deep-orange satin. Their husbands lean behind them to compare notes on history books. The women are laughing about the latest development. It seems it never occurred to the prime minister that Callum Gallagher wouldn't slink off with his tail between his legs. A few nights ago, in an hour-long BBC interview, Cal explained in painful detail how the Conservatives went from electoral oblivion to resounding victory by tapping into the nation's porn habits. It has caused quite a stir. Cal even recalled Anto finding the ads on Blue Balls and Bazookas. Anto has headed home for Christmas to 'spend more time with his family' and is unlikely to return in the New Year. Natasha Weaver has been quick to capitalise on the story, submitting a letter of no confidence in the prime minister – the mechanism to get Conservative leaders replaced – and explaining to party members that, say what you like about her sexual proclivities, she is at least firmly analogue in how she goes about pursuing them.

331

There's not been a lot to improve the prime minister's Christmas spirit. A few days ago, fresh off a bollocking from Clarissa for yet another cock-up, the PM told her where to go and sought out Captain Laura Lloyd. He finally, tearfully declared his love for her and that he would leave Clarissa for her. He reasoned that, now he has won a new term for the Conservatives and with Clarissa so unpopular with the public, he could weather the scandal of taking up with his MA, seeing as she's his true love. Time to allow himself to be happy at last. Laura looked at him in complete astonishment.

'Prime Minister,' she said, in her sing-song way. 'I'm very flattered, but I'm afraid I'm not at all interested. I thought we were, well, mates. I'm very fond of you but ... I'm gay, you see.'

Courtenay had no choice but to stick his head under a cold tap and crawl back up to the flat to grovel to his wife. Clarissa – who has finally started work on a foundation with Melinda Gates – briefed the whole sorry tale to an ecstatic Tim Shipman.

The *Sentinel*'s new political editor, meanwhile, broke the story that Madeleine Ford has also left government, but under slightly different circumstances to Percy: in January, she'll be starting her own campaign, this time to become UN Secretary General.

Itching to meet Ford is Holly's father, Cooper Mayhew III, who is helping his daughter and ex-wife out of a Rolls Royce onto the glittering pavement. Ford could be a very useful friend when he shoots for the presidency next year.

Mayhew's ex-wife goes to join his current wife on the front pew, both battling it out to be the all-time heavyweight-champion diamond-wearer of the world. Then the music starts and everyone stands and cranes round at Holly, who glides down the aisle on her father's arm in a pure white Emilia Wickstead dress, a huge Philip Treacy hat perched on the side of her head.

'Here we go, Dad,' Eva whispers to her father.

'Wish me luck, pork chop,' Percy murmurs back.

Eva listens to the vicar recite his standard passages on matrimony and glances around the church. Jake and Bobby coo quietly over Rose, Bobby's parents ready to drive them to Tipperton for Christmas later. Jess smiles up at Christian, her hand folded in his. He is whisking her off to his family Christmas in Hastings, where she'll meet the Eckles clan and brave billowing walks on the beach between fireside Scrabble games.

Eva will be staying at Claybourne Terrace with Holly and Percy, who have arranged for a sumptuous Christmas lunch with Holly's family at Claridge's tomorrow. Even Mabel's invited. She's not sure what next year will bring, now that she's left government like her father. Cal has mentioned something about another campaign, but nothing's set in stone. As she stands on the step and watches Jess and Bobby beaming up at her from their pews, Eva knows that life will never really be the same again. It's the end of an era.

Author's Note

As of November 2023, website traffic tracking results on *semrush.com* showed that three of the world's top 15 most visited websites were adult ones. *Netflix* was ranked 24th. The *BBC* was 89th. In short, as a nation we're watching a lot of pornography. *Pornhub,* which is one of these three adult sites, publishes an annual 'Year in Review' complete with a map of the UK featuring the most searched for categories in a region compared to their neighbours. On studying the 2022 map, I had to look up what quite a few of the terms meant, although 'glory hole' (the South West), 'pegging' (Scotland) and 'chubby' (North West) seemed clear enough. In a previous life I worked in campaigns and would most often examine a map of the UK to think about constituency boundaries or spots to allocate campaign resources, the data for which often relies on participants in polls and focus groups being 'honest' with their answers.

Shortly after discovering the Pornhub map, I read some articles indicating that Southern Conservative states in the USA – those with the highest number of anti-LGBT laws and Republican voters – had the highest number of Google searches for Trans-related pornography.* Are people searching for 'femboy' out of fear and hatred or out of secret desire for the taboo where they live? Is it possible that the voters of the South West tell us more about their politics by their interest in glory holes than by answering surveys on how satisfied they are by energy policy? After all, what could be more honest than our most secret desires, fears and fetishes?

This book is the result of a weird marriage between these two maps. As such, it is dedicated to all those truly filthy British minds out there – as what could be more honest than our most secret desires, fears and fetishes? Speaking of filthy minds, this book is the product of the author's imagination, so the characters and events in it are fictitious and any similarity with real people or events is coincidental. Honest.

---

* https://lawsuit.org/general-law/republicans-have-an-obsession-with-transgender-pornography/

Acknowledgements

Most sincere thanks have to go to my husband, Tom, who makes everything so incredibly fun and funny. Thank you also to my family, who still live in hope that I'll get myself a pen name.

To some very clever minds, who helped me work out the mechanics of data modelling and who no doubt would prefer to remain anonymous.

I didn't know a thing about publishing until my first novel, *Whips*, came out. Any author will tell you that flogging books is hard, but my experience was made far easier by the constant support of two brilliant young women at Corsair, who masterminded all of the media and marketing. So special thanks to Niamh Anderson and Celeste Ward-Best, who not only did a fantastic job but who also made the whole thing so enjoyable.

She must be tired of being thanked in the back of books the whole time, but a huge thank you to Caroline Michel, my peerless literary agent, and her absolutely wonderful team at PFD (particularly Rosie, Tris, Sam, Bea, Fran and Kieron), who make everything possible.

Last but not least, thank you to James Gurbutt, who is not only a brilliant editor but is now a wonderful friend. His fantastic team, not least the dedicated Alice Watkin, are the best in the business.